What was that noise?

It penetrated her sleep and she sat up. Will stood at the open door, silhouetted in the morning light.

Whomp-whomp-whomp.

Realization dawned. A helicopter. Someone to rescue them.

Newfound energy surged through Sylvie, and she ran to Will on her injured ankle. "Why aren't you out there signaling them?" She pushed by, prepared to limp outside. "If you won't, then I will."

"Sylvie, no." He gripped her shoulders, his eyes imploring her to listen. "The help I radioed for won't be here for hours." He nodded toward the helicopter. "That's not our help."

She froze. "What are you saying?"

"I'm saying that could be the men after you."

She backed away from him. "No, that can't be. How—"

A spray of bullets ricocheted through the woods. Will slammed the door and pressed his back against it. Determination was carved into his features. "We have to get out of here."

A chunk of fear lodged in her throat. When would this end? She knew the answer...and that's what scared her.

ALASKAN MOUNTAIN PURSUIT

ELIZABETH GODDARD
&
SARAH VARLAND

Previously published as *Tailspin* and *Mountain Refuge*

LOVE INSPIRED
INSPIRATIONAL ROMANCE

LOVE INSPIRED®

INSPIRATIONAL ROMANCE

Recycling programs for this product may not exist in your area.

ISBN-13: 978-1-335-91232-9

Alaskan Mountain Pursuit

Copyright © 2021 by Harlequin Books S.A.

Tailspin
First published in 2016. This edition published in 2021.
Copyright © 2016 by Elizabeth Goddard

Mountain Refuge
First published in 2018. This edition published in 2021.
Copyright © 2018 by Sarah Varland

This edition published by arrangement with Harlequin Books S.A.

For questions and comments about the quality of this book, please contact us at CustomerService@Harlequin.com.

Love Inspired
22 Adelaide St. West, 40th Floor
Toronto, Ontario M5H 4E3, Canada
www.Harlequin.com

Printed in U.S.A.

CONTENTS

Elizabeth Goddard is the award-winning author of more than thirty novels and novellas. A 2011 Carol Award winner, she was a double finalist in the 2016 Daphne du Maurier Award for Excellence in Mystery/Suspense, and a 2016 Carol Award finalist. Elizabeth graduated with a computer science degree and worked in high-level software sales before retiring to write full-time.

Visit the Author Profile page
at Harlequin.com for more titles.

TAILSPIN

Elizabeth Goddard

But they that wait upon the Lord shall renew their strength; they shall mount up with wings as eagles; they shall run, and not be weary; and they shall walk, and not faint.

—Isaiah 40:31

To my Lord and Savior, Jesus Christ,
who truly does renew my strength.

Acknowledgments

When it comes time to write acknowledgments,
there are so many people I want to thank.
Too many to name in a short paragraph, but all my
heartfelt gratitude goes to my family—my parents
and grandparents who encouraged me, always
telling me that I could be whatever I wanted to be.
They taught me the sky was the limit. To dream
as big as I wanted to dream and accomplish
even more. The journey to this place of living my
dream of writing novels has taken years, and it's
a journey I would never have made without God,
who continued to nudge and direct me to answer
His call. Along the way I've made many deep and
lasting friendships—my partners in writing and in
life. You know who you are. Thank you. I want to
thank my wonderful editor Elizabeth Mazer, for
your encouragement and suggestions that
make my books the best they can be. I could
never forget my amazing agent, Steve Laube.
Thank you for believing in me.

ONE

The scuba-diving dry suit, along with the warm layers beneath, protected Sylvie Masters from the biting cold waters of the channel that carved its way through the Alaska Panhandle.

Breathe too fast, you could die. Hold your breath, you could die. Stay too long, you could die. Ascend too fast, tiny little bubbles of nitrogen on a death mission enter your bloodstream.

Her mother's words, an effort to dissuade her from her love of scuba diving, gripped her mind as she searched for the missing plane in the depths. Her mother had worried about Sylvie's diving, but in turn, Sylvie had reminded her that famous undersea explorer Jacques Cousteau had lived to be eighty-seven, his death unrelated to his underwater endeavors, and his sons were still alive except the one who died in a plane crash—a seaplane, no less!

Sylvie never imagined her words would be so prophetic. Never imagined that horrible phone call two months earlier, telling her that a seaplane with her mother on board had disappeared without a trace, and that her mother was missing and presumed dead.

A sea lion glided past, much too close for comfort, and Sylvie exhaled sharply, her pulse accelerating. The enormity of the creature this close left her in awe. The large mammal, intent on a search of his own, swam away, putting a comfortable distance between them.

Slowing her breathing, she flutter-kicked and moved on. The glint of painted metal, something completely unnatural to the environment, caught her attention. A wing thrusting from the sandy bottom? The final resting place for a plane and passengers?

Her heart jumped, taking her breathing with it. Not good. At two atmospheres, or forty feet, this was a simple recreational dive. But she still needed to maintain slow, steady breaths. Two cardinal rules: never overbreathe and never hold your breath.

Inhale...

Exhale...

Her body was like a carbonated drink. The deeper the dive, the harder the shake. She only had to remember to open the bottle slowly, ascend at the proper rate with the right stops and then, upon surfacing, her body wouldn't explode with nitrogen bubbles like a shaken can of soda opened too quickly. She wouldn't get decompression sickness.

The bends.

As an instructor for a diving school in Seattle, and a volunteer member of a local dive rescue organization, Sylvie had ample experience and was trained to solo dive. Good thing, too. Chelsey, a friend at the school, had planned to come with her, but Chelsey's sister was seriously injured in a car wreck the day before they were to leave, and she needed to be at her sister's side. Sylvie didn't blame her for that, but neither would she wait until Chelsey could join her for yet another search for her mother's missing plane.

She'd already taken the vacation time. It was late September, and the water would soon get colder with winter. It was now or never. Besides, she wasn't sure she wanted to drag anyone else with her on what could be a morbid discovery.

Six weeks ago the powers-that-be had given up on ever finding the plane, but Sylvie would never stop.

She pushed her thoughts back to the present and her task. More fish darted past, drawing her gaze from the metal for only a moment. She loved the water and all its inhabitants. Her mother had always told her she should have been born a dolphin or a whale, some sort of sea mammal. Just give Sylvie the ocean any day as long as she didn't have to fly.

Because the cold water was clearer, she could see much farther than on a warm-water dive. She spotted the remnants of an old shipwreck, which had created an artificial reef for cold-water sea creatures. Brightly colored starfish and anemones in every shade of pink and green mesmerized her, reminding her of everything she loved about diving.

Except she wasn't here to enjoy the scenery this time.

She was on a mission and had been for the past several days. And she'd found nothing, seen nothing, until now. In the distance, she could still see the glint of metal, and needed to keep her focus on that or she might lose it.

Excitement and dread swirled together and gurgled up in her stomach, much like the bubbles escaping from her regulator and swirling around her head on their way to the water's surface. She kicked her fins furiously, hoping to find what she was looking for. When a shadow moved over her from above, she noted another boat on the water coming or going, crossing over her despite her diver down flag, but she kept going.

Something grabbed her fin and tugged.

Sylvie turned around and faced another diver, who wielded a glinting diver's knife and lunged. Her mind seized up. Survival instincts kicked in. He could fatally wound her, or go for her hose, hold her down and drown her. Kill her a million different ways. She turned and tried to swim away.

But he caught her fin again.

Sylvie faced her attacker. Murderous dark eyes stared back at her from behind a diver's mask. She couldn't swim her way out of this. She'd have to fight her way free. She struggled but he was physically stronger.

She'd have to be smarter. She could hold her breath longer than most, though holding her breath could kill her, too.

Help me, Lord!

His knife glinted in the water. Sylvie kicked and thrashed to get away, bumping up against sharp coral that ripped a hole in her dry suit and a gash in her back. Frigid water rushed through the hole in the suit. She ignored the shock of cold biting her skin and the salty sting of her wound.

The crazed diver whipped the knife around and sliced through her regulator hose.

Sylvie flailed and swam for the surface, but he dragged her back.

This couldn't be happening.

Who was this man? What did he want? The next few moments could be her last. Sylvie fought, but fisted against water, flailed and then…relaxed.

Dead.

The man released his hold on her.

Now.

Sylvie yanked the hose from his tanks. While he struggled with his own breathing apparatus, she ditched her weight belt and thrust her way to the surface. She released air from her lungs with a scream and tried to ascend at a controlled pace, which would also expand the air in her lungs as she released it instead of having them pop like balloons. If this worked, she wouldn't be unconscious by the time she reached the surface.

He wouldn't be fooled twice.

When Sylvie breached the water, she dragged in a long breath. A boat rested a few hundred yards from her, but it wasn't her boat. Treading water, she searched the area. Her boat was gone. Panic rose like a fury in her throat, and she stifled the frustrated scream that would surely alert whoever was left on the boat, waiting for the diver who'd come to kill her.

She had to hurry. He'd be up and after her soon enough. She'd only delayed him long enough to make a temporary escape.

But where should she hide? In this part of Alaska, she was surrounded by islands and trees, and trees and islands, and oh yeah, rain. A slow drizzle started up—of course—pock-marking the water around her. With no other choice, she headed to the scrap of land that barely passed for an island.

Could she make it there before the boat ran her down or the diver caught up to her?

Will Pierson couldn't imagine living any other way. He was an eagle soaring over the awe-inspiring landscape of southeast Alaska. Okay, so he wasn't an eagle. He was a simple bush pilot sitting in a tin can, bouncing and twisting and riding the rough air to deliver packages or people to the Alaskan bush.

And today, while he did his job, he searched for his mother's plane like he'd done every day since she'd crashed.

He flew low, swooping over a forgotten part of God's green earth, waters of the channel shimmering in the cold morning sun, what there was of it. His Champ 7GC glided over green and misty islands and jaw-dropping fjords. He often looked down to see the wildlife, maybe a few off-grid pioneer-types, sometimes bear or elk.

As he soared over the wide-open spaces, he admitted the joy he found in the view was overshadowed by loss and grief.

His mother, the packages and one additional passenger had disappeared, and no one knew exactly where or even why. It wasn't as if their bush pilot planes were big enough to warrant cockpit voice recorders or flight data recorders or the "black boxes" carried by commercial planes. And out here in the Alaska bush, they flew without radar coverage for the most part. Investigators had suggested that she'd been flying below clouds in poor visibility and slammed into the ground or the side of a mountain. He refused to believe it. As a bush pilot flying southeast Alaska for the past two decades, she knew the area too well.

Since that day two months ago, Will had flown a thousand times over the area where her plane should have gone down. He tried to trust God to give him the peace he longed for, but his need to know what had happened drove him crazy. Surely he owed her that much—

a decent burial and a clear understanding of what had caused her death.

She'd taught him to survive. Alaska was about survival of the fittest. She'd taught him to spread his wings and fly above the storms of life like an eagle. In this way, they had survived his father's brutal scuba-diving death and built a solid life for the two of them that had lasted until the day she'd gone to pick up a surprise package she'd said was going to shake things up. Well, things had been shaken all right, and his mother was dead and gone.

She was a skilled pilot. Something must have gone wrong with the plane. Equipment failure? Or worse. Had one of the packages been a bomb?

The thought made Will edgy with every trip he took. Every package he picked up or delivered. He didn't want any surprise packages. He just wanted answers.

His Champ hit a rough spot, a pothole in the air as he liked to call it.

And that was when he saw someone running.

She was not out for a jog wearing a diving suit. That much he could tell. She looked as if she was running for her life. Will flew in close, sweeping the area, and searched. Was she running from a bear? The woods were thick around the meadow where she ran. Where was she heading? She was too focused on her escape to glance at his plane swooping low. He didn't have to get any closer to see she had terror written all over her face.

And then Will saw him.

A man with a rifle. Will took a dive, letting the guy know he should back off. Between the trees, the man appeared to gaze through his scope at Will. He backed away, lifted higher and out of range. But not fast enough. He heard the ping of a bullet against the fuselage.

Will tried to radio for help, but to no avail, which was just as he'd expect out in this part of southeast Alaska. No one on the other end of his radio call answered to help this woman, so that meant he would have to do. Even if he had reached someone for help, what were the chances they would arrive in time? Zero.

He was on his own.

But how could he help her? He swung around the small island to come back and find the best place to land on the water, hoping she would see him. Hoping the rifleman wouldn't.

Right. That was going to work.

Will sucked in a breath and veered wide and plunged low, coming around to find the woman. He'd seen a boat anchored nearby. Was that hers? Or the rifleman's? Somehow he had to intervene and get her out before the man got to her. Flying low over the thick trees, he couldn't see either one of them.

But he needed to keep his distance, too. Bad enough the man was shooting at someone—and Will wouldn't stand idly by and let that happen without a fight—but if his plane was badly damaged then both Will and the woman would have nowhere to turn, no way to escape.

How could he let her know he was friendly and not with the hunter? And how could he find her at all? She'd dropped completely out of sight. Had she found a place to hide in the woods? Or…was she headed for the water? She wore a diving suit, after all.

He prayed this would all end well as he made for the water somewhere near the direction she'd been headed. Then he could offer her a ride home.

Will maneuvered his floatplane onto the water. This was cutting things close.

The pontoons touching down, he proceeded forward, watching the rough edges and sandy beaches where the land met water and the rocky outcroppings, searching for the woman and the rifleman. Both of them could be heading away from him for all he knew. Or they could be moving straight for him through the island rainforest of the Tongass National Forest. As he steered closer, Will found his weapon and placed it on the passenger seat.

Closing in on the island, he slowed the plane. A slow burn worked its way up his gut as he took the plane right up to a small section of sand, remaining wary of the thick forest hidden with danger. Which one of them would he see first?

The woman, running for her life?

Or the man with his rifle, aiming to kill?

TWO

Fear drove her past the pain of her injuries, through the shock of it all. Sylvie pushed her body because her life depended on it. Grateful for the diving boots she'd worn under her fins to protect her feet, she ran from another madman, this one holding a high-powered rifle instead of a diver's knife.

If she could just make it to the water.

Again.

Hard to believe she'd escaped the crazy diver beneath the surface only to face off with another dangerous man. This wasn't some random meeting, but an elaborate plan to assure her death.

She could almost laugh at their efforts—how hard had they believed she would be to kill?

Her legs screamed, and she stopped to lean against a Sitka spruce, catching her breath. The dry suit hadn't been designed for running.

At first she'd thought the plane was just another part of the plan. A diver. A man with a rifle. Why not a float-plane to attack her in some other, horrible way? But then the man who'd been there to give her an unfriendly welcome as she dragged her body from the water onto the rocky shore had taken a few shots at it.

Providence had sent someone to save her in the most inappropriate manner. God had a sense of humor. Why couldn't it be another boat? Why not the Coast Guard? She would never fly unless she had no choice.

But then Sylvie had never needed saving before.

And now that floatplane that had flown low and deep to find her running, and had made waves for her would-be killers, meant everything to her. She assumed the plane waited just beyond the trees. She'd seen that much—but unfortunately that meant the rifleman had seen it, as well.

Breathing hard and fast, Sylvie pushed through the wildness of this uninhabited land, brushing past thick and lush sword ferns and alongside a thorny undergrowth that shredded her dry suit. Through the trees she could make out the water.

She continued on to the water's edge and searched for the plane. Down from her a few hundred yards, the plane waited. The whir of the props echoed across the water. Her stomach lurched. Would he leave before she could get there? How could she signal him to wait? Draw his attention without giving away her position?

God, please let him wait for me! Help me!

It was too far for her to quickly traverse the thick brush and rocky shore, but there was another way. Sylvie rushed into the water and dove beneath the surface, quickly reminded of the brush against the coral during her struggle with the mad diver. Her dry suit no longer protected her from the cold water that seeped in, icing across her skin and into her bones, it seemed, slowly stealing her body heat away.

Hypothermia would set in soon. Never mind her aching joints that brought to her attention another problem. Sylvie was too experienced to ignore the symptoms or write them off as the shock of nearly being brutally murdered.

No. She had to face the truth.

She had the bends. Decompression sickness.

But she had to keep it together until she made it to the plane. Holding her breath, she swam just under the water's surface to keep out of sight. Without her mask, her eyes burned in the salty water as she remained vigilant in watching for the boat and the man with the rifle. She prayed the other diver wasn't right behind her.

The flash of an image rushed at her—the diver's knife, glinting in the water as he cut her hose. Shivering, she tossed a quick look into the depths behind and beneath her. She had to be sure the diver wasn't closing in. At least she was safe for the moment. Head bobbing to the surface for a quick breath, she continued to swim, her limbs growing sluggish.

She drew near to the plane.

Almost there.

The pilot scrambled from the plane and onto the beach, brandishing a weapon. Her pulse quickened. Could that be for her? *God, please let him be friendly. Please let him be someone here to help me.* She didn't know what she would do otherwise.

Dizziness swept over her, swirling through her core with the shock of the last few minutes.

But Sylvie was strong. She couldn't have excelled in her career as a diving instructor if she wasn't.

Then she heard it.

The echoing fire from a rifle. Sylvie ducked under

the water. Had the rifleman seen her? Was he firing at her now in the water? Or at the pilot?

She was cold and numb and drained. Wasn't sure she could breach the surface again. She heard the rumble of the floatplane before she found the energy to bob above the water's surface and see it moving.

Disappointment weighed her down into the depths.

The rifleman was shooting at her rescuer. If he'd come to help, he'd been scared away. Sylvie fought the desire to give up, to sink and keep on sinking. Anger burned in her chest along with the need for air.

No, God! Her life couldn't end like this.

Like her mother, Sylvie was a fighter, and she'd find a way to survive this. There were a million reasons to live, not the least of which was that she had to discover what had happened to her mother's plane.

She had to be strong.

She'd always believed it was her faith in God that would see her through. But with nitrogen bubbles coursing through her blood, hypothermia threatening to sink and drown her, and men who were trying to kill her, Sylvie struggled to trust God to see her through. How much could she trust Him? How much did she do on her own?

Right now she had never felt more alone. Had never had to draw on her own strength, or even on her faith in God, in this way before.

Like her dry suit, her faith and strength failed her.

Will couldn't leave without the woman. Neither could he stay with a man taking shots at him and his plane. He'd landed here because she'd been running in this direction. Now where was she?

In his Champ, he skipped across the water's surface,

searching and praying. If he saw nothing, he would circle
the island and come back to this spot, but he needed to
draw the rifleman away from her. She could be hiding
in the woods and afraid to run for the plane.

There!

The woman breached the water and waved, not
twenty-five yards from him. If he hadn't been looking
in the right direction at that exact moment, he might
have missed her. Now to get her out of here without getting either of them killed. He slowed the plane, guided
it close…closer…until he was as close as he could get
without risking harm to her.

"You'll have to swim the rest of the way," he called.
"Can you do that?"

The way she dipped below the water, that desperate
look on her face, he wasn't sure she had any reserves
left enough to swim all the way. But she was already
swimming toward him even as the words left his mouth.

He stood on the pontoon and leaned out, encourag-
ing her and at the same time glancing intermittently to
the shore, watching for the shooter. They had to hurry.

"Come on, you can make it."

Determination flooded her features as she inched
forward. Will reached for her at the same moment she
grabbed on to the pontoon. She rested her head against
it, catching her breath. Intelligent hazel eyes stared up,
measuring him, her bluish lips quivering.

He thrust his hand out. "We need to get out of here."

She grabbed his hand and held his gaze. "Thank you."

Rifle fire exploded in the distance. They both in-
stinctively ducked, but other than the plane itself, there
was no cover.

"Hurry." He assisted her up and into the plane, not

missing that she was bleeding from a gash in her suit. She needed help in more ways than one.

When she was secured in the seat, he found a blanket and threw it over her, then quickly secured himself and headed away from land. Another chink let him know his plane had taken another hit.

A wonder the rifleman hadn't succeeded in killing them already. But depending on the damage to the plane, the outcome remained to be seen. If he felt any trouble he could land them quickly enough, but he had to get them away from this place. He lifted off the water and glanced at her, noticing she visibly paled.

"You're not going to get sick on me, are you?"

Shivering, she shook her head. "I don't know. Maybe."

Well, which was it? But he wouldn't give her a hard time.

"I need to get my diving gear."

"You've got to be kidding me."

She stared at him, the gold flecks in her hazel eyes blazing. "Please. I appreciate your help, the risk to your life, everything you've done, but I might need to treat myself for decompression sickness."

"You're with me now. I'll get you to Juneau where they can treat you." Treating oneself was never a good idea.

"Can we just do a flyby to see if it's safe or not?"

It didn't sound as if she believed he would get her to Juneau. Will held back anything derogatory he might have said. "All right. Where is it?"

"I stashed it on the north side of the island where I'd been diving. There was a boat there last I saw, so that might mean trouble for us."

"I don't suppose now would be a good time for you to tell me what's going on."

"I would if I could. I don't know exactly. I was scuba diving when another diver appeared and tried to kill me. I escaped and swam to the surface, but my boat was missing. I swam to the island and barely made it out of the water and stowed my gear when I saw the man with the rifle. I'd been running from him, well, until you came along."

"And you believed you could trust me?" Now that almost had him grinning.

"When he shot at you, I knew you were here to help."

Will banked to the right, flying around the island to the north, hoping the boat she'd mentioned would be long gone. He looked her over. She'd tugged the hood of her dry suit off and worked the blanket over her medium-length hair to dry it. He wouldn't say she was pretty, in so many words, but she definitely had a presence about her that he might find compelling if he was looking to be compelled.

"There's the boat. We might have a chance." Will kept his disappointment in check. "But we need to make this quick. Where's your gear?"

She pointed. "Over there along the shoreline in the trees. See that big, funny-looking boulder?"

"And you're sure this is a good idea?"

"No."

Just what he wanted to hear. "I like an honest woman."

Will brought the plane down on the water and eased up against a sandbar. He pulled out his weapon. "You stay put. Tell me where exactly, and I'll find it."

Her eyes grew wide. "No, you don't have to risk your life for me."

A little late for that, but he didn't say as much. Without another word he hopped from his plane. "Where?"

She pointed. "Just there, by that larger boulder."

The rifleman was well on the other side of the island, but Will didn't know who else he might have to contend with. Wary of his surroundings, weapon at the ready, he crept forward until he spotted her diving gear—double tanks. He hated the sight of them. Diving had killed his father. He grabbed the tanks but couldn't get a grip on the fins as well as hold his weapon in case he needed to use it.

She appeared next to him and snatched up the rest. Regulator, mask, snorkel, fins and buoyancy vest. "It's all important."

Carrying her dive equipment, they hurried back to the plane. Will noticed the boat heading their way. "We're out of time."

He lugged the tanks into the back as she tossed in the rest of her gear. Then he started the plane, speeding away on the water as he waited for her to secure herself in the seat.

Once they were airborne again and flying safely away from the boat and the island, Will glanced over at her.

Eyes closed, she pressed her head against the seat. "You said you're taking me to Juneau, right?"

"Unless you have a better idea."

"As long as they have a hyperbaric chamber." She opened her eyes, but squeezed the armrest.

"I'm flying low enough, the pressure shouldn't cause you more DCS problems." She didn't seem to find that comforting.

The plane hit turbulence. Will had long ago learned to ride the waves in the air—better to flow with them than to fight them. But his passenger's face went a shade whiter. These flights were rough on most others who weren't accustomed.

He had to get her mind off it. "What's your name?"

"Sylvie… Sylvie Masters." She gripped the armrest so hard, he thought she might break it.

She didn't ask for his name in return, but it was that moment when he should give it. Billy Pierson was the name everyone called him. Will had never much liked the name Billy as a kid, and wasn't sure why he continued to put up with it as an adult. With his father gone, changing it seemed almost disrespectful. But now his mother, who had called him Will, was gone, too. Maybe it was time he changed things out of respect for her.

Even though Sylvie didn't ask, Will told her anyway. "You can call me Will. I'm Will Pierson."

And with the pronouncement he felt the slightest hitch in his plane, a very unfamiliar sensation that had nothing at all to do with turbulence.

THREE

"Will. I like that name." She squeezed her eyes shut again, forcing her mind on anything but the bouncing plane. She was powerless against the jarring movement that barraged her with images of a rodeo cowboy riding a disgruntled bull. Her stomach roiling, she prayed she'd last more than the required eight seconds before being thrown.

Tossing a quick glance at Will, she hoped he hadn't noticed her distress, though it was not likely he would have missed it. His black hair was neatly trimmed beneath his Mountain Cove Air ball cap. It looked as if he was trying to grow a beard, or he hadn't shaved in a few days. Though he looked barely thirty—late twenties even—he had an edge to him, an aura of experience about him that made him seem older. Despite his jacket, she could tell he was strong and fit.

"If you hadn't shown up when you did, I don't know what I would have done. My options had run out. But in helping me, you might have gotten yourself wrapped up in my troubles."

"And what are your troubles?"

"You know as much as I do. I don't know why someone would want to kill me." Sylvie wished she hadn't said the words out loud. They disturbed her. She quickly changed the subject. Riding in the death trap of a plane was enough to handle at the moment. "Where're you from, Will?"

"Mountain Cove."

Sylvie couldn't help the shiver that ran across her shoulders. Her mother would have snarled at the mention of Mountain Cove. From all she'd told Sylvie, Mountain Cove was nothing but a bunch of backwater, back-stabbing gossipers. Her mother had reason enough to feel that way, Sylvie supposed, considering she'd had a secret affair with an already married pillar of the community and the man had ended his relationship with her. Pregnant, Sylvie's mother had been ashamed and fled Mountain Cove.

Sylvie kept to herself the fact that her father was from Mountain Cove. She'd never met him, though that would be impossible now that he was deceased. But her half siblings lived there, too. A surreal desperation flooded her—she wanted to meet the Warren siblings—her half siblings. See what they were made of. Come to her own conclusions about them, and what her real father was like and the people of Mountain Cove.

Despite all Sylvie's mother's negative talk about the town, she'd been on her way back to Mountain Cove for reasons unknown to Sylvie when she'd taken that last, fatal flight. But Sylvie didn't want to share any of this with Will. She didn't know a thing about him except that he'd saved her today.

The plane lurched to the right and Sylvie's stomach went with it. She released a telling groan.

"It gets rough through here. Sorry."

"So far it's been a walk in the meadow." Sylvie regretted her sarcasm. Will didn't deserve it.

But he laughed. He had a sense of humor, which was more than Sylvie could say for herself. Somehow the thick timbre of his mirth relaxed her.

"You never did say where you're from, by the way."

No, she hadn't. He hadn't asked, but normal conversation would have required she reciprocate when he'd told her he was from Mountain Cove.

"The Seattle area. I teach scuba diving for commercial divers and I volunteer for search-and-rescue dive operations."

The man next to her shifted in his seat and seemed uneasy. "My dad died in a diving accident. I haven't gone diving since."

"I'm sorry to hear that. My mother died in a plane crash." She regretted her tone. She hadn't meant it to sound as though she was in a competition.

The plane jerked with his reaction, subtle though it was. "Well, we have something in common, after all. My mother died in a plane crash, too."

Oh, why had she revealed so much? She wasn't sure what more she should tell him, if anything. He didn't deserve to get mixed up in her problems. But what if he already was? Had the men who tried to kill her today paid attention to Will and his plane? Would they track him down and exact some sort of killing revenge?

She should have realized this from the beginning. The attack on her today must have to do with her mother's plane crash. She was close to finding the crash and someone didn't want her there. What else could it be? Or was she exhibiting the crazy imagination of someone suffering through mild hypothermia and the bends all at the same time?

A snippet of her mother's voice mail raced across her mind.

I'm flying to Mountain Cove on a bush plane. I know what you're thinking, but I'll tell you more when I get there. It's Damon... Oh... I've gotta go...

A rattling din—something entirely new—rose above the whir of the propellers, and a tremor joined the rattle. Was this normal? She squeezed the armrests again because there wasn't anything else to grab. Sylvie's warnings to her mother about flying came rushing back, swirling with images of her mother. Her relationship with Sylvie's stepfather, Damon Masters, and the endless arguments.

Secrets.

Was her life flashing before her eyes like she'd so often heard would happen in the last few moments of life?

"What's happening?"

When Will didn't answer, she risked opening her eyes. His features were tight.

Okay, well, that doesn't look good. "If I survive this, I'm never flying again. I wouldn't be on this plane now if I had any other choice. No offense."

"None taken." His voice had an edge to it. "You miss out on a lot if you don't fly. You'll never see the world like this, see the wonders of Alaska, if you don't get in the air and soar with the eagles."

"Are you saying this is normal?" Her teeth clattered along with the plane.

"You just have to roll with it if you can. But if it makes you feel any better, I know what I'm doing."

Then the plane lurched to the left, and a sound like the crack of thunder rocked the plane, vibrated through her core. "Will, I can't die today. I have to find my mother's plane!"

Her words held some kind of meaning for him personally, but he couldn't figure it out when their survival was on the line, so he tucked them inside his mind to pick apart later. He'd just reassured her he was a good pilot. He needed to live up to his word.

"You've been honest with me to a point, so I'll be honest with you. I think the rifleman might have done some damage to the plane. It's taken time to work its way through, and now we're feeling the pain of it."

"What are you saying?"

"I'm saying I'm a good pilot—a great pilot—but it never hurts to say your prayers. Get your affairs in order with God."

"Are you kidding me?"

"I wouldn't kid you about something so serious." He hated to scare her, but neither could he hide the gravity of the situation.

As he struggled to bring the vibrating plane in, to find a body of water on which to land, he thought back to his mother. Was this how she'd felt when her plane was going down? She'd been a great pilot, too. The best. And yet his mother's plane was missing. It had to have crashed somewhere. What had Sylvie said about needing to find her mother's plane? He couldn't think about that now—he had to focus on keeping them alive.

A friend lived within hiking distance of the strip of water he aimed for. Even if they landed safely, Sylvie wouldn't survive without some place warm to wait until help arrived.

The plane kicked, a rumble spilling through the fuselage. His gut tensed.

Though he struggled to grip the vibrating yoke, he reached over and pressed his hand over Sylvie's white knuckles that squeezed the armrest. Surprising him, she released her grip and held his hand, strong and tight. Maybe it had nothing at all to do with reality but more to do with looking death straight in the eyes, but Will had a sense of connection with Sylvie Masters—a complete stranger—which made no sense.

God, please let me save Sylvie. Save the day. Like her, I want to find my mother's plane. Find the answers. Then he understood what his mind could not comprehend earlier.

God had to have brought them together for this same purpose. They couldn't die today.

"We're going to be okay, Sylvie. Just keep praying."

Her reply came out in an indistinguishable murmur. Indistinguishable but understandable, all the same. She fought to hold herself together. He couldn't blame her. He didn't want to release her hand, finding a comfort in her grip that he hadn't known he needed, but he pulled away and gripped the yoke.

"There, see the water? That's all I need for a smooth landing." He thought of his mother again. That was all she would have needed, too. He'd long begun to suspect her plane hadn't crashed where they could find debris, but had gone down and sunk to the bottom of the ocean, a channel somewhere, just waiting to be discovered like a shipwreck full of treasure.

The thought sickened him. His stomach pitched with

the plane. Sylvie hunched over her knees, covered her head as if she was prepared to crash. As if her efforts would save her.

Will couldn't be sure they would land on the water or that he could keep his word. Rain pelted the windshield, and as comfortable with flying as any bush pilot could be, he had to admit—but only to himself—this had been the ride of his life.

He piloted the plane forward and tried again to radio for help, but they were still in no-man's-land.

"Sylvie?"

She mumbled. Groaned. Kept her head down.

"Promise me something."

Another groan.

"Promise me you *will* fly again."

"Are you crazy?"

At least he'd gotten a coherent response from her. "Promise me."

"You mean if we survive?"

"Yes. I mean if I land this broken hull of a plane and we climb out of it in one piece."

"If I say yes will you try harder to land?"

The crack in her desperate voice sent him tumbling.

"Sylvie, I couldn't try any harder, but I thought I'd take the opportunity to extract a promise from you. I wouldn't want you to miss out on seeing the world the way I see it."

Sylvie stared at him, wide-eyed. "Why would you care how I see the world?"

Will couldn't say why it was important to him, but in that instant, facing a one-of-a-kind death, he knew it was. He opened his mouth to reply but the plane shuddered and plummeted. Water swallowed them, then everything went black.

FOUR

Water rushed into the plane that had hit too hard. Sylvie fought the panic. Sucked in air hard and fast. Must. Slow. Breathing. Hyperventilating would do her no good. Passing out wasn't an option. One of them had to get the two of them out.

With Will unconscious that would leave Sylvie.

Forget what she'd already been through. Survive. She had to survive—to reach down and find strength she didn't know she had.

Water poured in.

The plane was sinking.

Sinking?

Sylvie had always thought floatplanes were, well, supposed to float. But then she remembered Jacques Cousteau's son, also a diver, who died in a floatplane that crashed and sank.

Surely the pontoons would prevent it from completely submerging. Wasn't that the whole purpose of pontoons on a floatplane? But that didn't mean that Will wouldn't drown in the meantime.

A small gash in his forehead bled. She unbuckled the

strap, bracing herself for the rush forward into water that had quickly covered the controls.

Sylvie pressed a finger against Will's neck, confirming he was still alive. She couldn't accept anything less. Then she worked to unbuckle him from the shoulder harness, but it wouldn't budge.

"Come on!" she yelled at the buckle.

What she wouldn't give for her diver's knife. It had to be in here somewhere. They were both fortunate her tanks hadn't flown forward and cracked their heads during the impact.

"Will, come on, you need to wake up."

The plane creaked and groaned. It would pitch completely over and upside down soon, and then Will's head would be fully under water. They would both be. Sylvie searched his pockets.

There.

She found a pocketknife.

But before she set him free, she opened his door, left it hanging forward before the water pressure could seal it shut. More water rushed in at the bottom.

She was running out of time.

Quickly she sawed through his shoulder strap. Though she prepared to catch Will, his dead weight fell forward on her and smashed her against the dashboard, the yoke gouging into her back. The blow knocked the air from her lungs. She worked to push his head above the waterline.

Now to get him out. They were going to make it. She could do this. Sylvie slipped by him in the small space then tugged him out into the water. She'd swim him to shore, keeping his head high. This was lifeguard 101, and was actually much easier to do with an unconscious victim than one who was awake and struggling.

With regret, she left her diving equipment in the plane to save Will. She wouldn't think ahead, wouldn't concern herself with what to do, until she made it to shore. She positioned him on his back and hooked her arms under his armpits. On her back, she swam them to shore. She tried to keep her thoughts from what she might face— the immediate danger of exposure to the elements— and instead focused on what she could do. After all, two men had tried to kill her, and this seemed small in comparison.

She could swim.

Had been born with a natural affinity for water.

You're in your element, Sylvie.

Just breathe. Swim. Save Will.

Regardless of her attempts at self-assurance, feeble though they were, fear twisted inside, corded in the sinews of her muscles. She hadn't expected things to turn this way. Hadn't expected to face death twice in one day.

Bad enough someone had tried to kill her. Worse, she'd almost died in a plane crash like her mother. Though she'd admit that Will's plane—and Will himself—had saved her the first part of the day. And Will would be sick about the loss once he woke up.

He *would* wake up.

He had to wake up.

Her back scraped across pebbles and sand and rocks. Ignoring the pain, she dragged Will the rest of the way onto a small strip of sand. Sylvie examined his head then the rest of him. She could see no other injury besides the gash in his head that was no longer bleeding so profusely. Hopefully, it would stop soon. She had nothing with which to staunch the flow.

She could swim back and get a first-aid kit from the plane before it sank. Or her scuba equipment! But her body was too cold. It wouldn't be safe. She might not make it back.

She held his face in her hands. "Will, can you hear me?"

He'd lost his ball cap in the melee, and his hair was thicker than she'd initially thought. He had a jutting chin on a nice strong jaw. She felt strange holding his face, touching him like this. It seemed entirely too intimate with someone who was practically a stranger, but this was a matter of life and death. She didn't think he would care. She wished he would open his eyes—those warm brown eyes. Though she hadn't appreciated his questions or his humor at first, the warmth in his tone had comforted her when she'd needed it.

"Will," she whispered. "If you'll wake up, I might just agree to fly again."

But Will didn't respond. The cold water hadn't shocked him awake like she would have expected. It had shocked her system, though, and she was shivering even now. She released his face, hating that his color wasn't good. Looking at the thick temperate rain forest behind her and across the water on the other side, she studied the mountains peaking above the treetops in the distance.

She knew enough about the geography to believe they were somewhere south, way south of Juneau. Far enough that it might as well have been a thousand miles. Sylvie dropped to where the water lapped and pressed her head into her knees.

Just what was she supposed to do now?

* * *

Cold prickles stung his face. Shivering, Will opened his eyes to raindrops bombarding him, along with what felt like an anvil pounding his temples.

Where am I?

His mind raced, competing with his pulse as he pushed up and caught sight of the woman sitting next to him, face pressed against her knees. Guilt tackled him. Though his mind was fuzzy, he somehow knew he'd failed her.

"Sylvie." He reached over and pressed his hand against her arm. "Are you okay?"

Lifting her head, she turned to face him, her hazel eyes drawing him in. "Will, I'm so glad… I thought you were…"

Will couldn't understand why she was still here. She was going to die if she didn't get someplace warm. He would, too, for that matter. They'd both been soaked to the bone, and right now the temperature wasn't much different on the ground than in the water. It was his fault she was here now. Somehow it was his fault. But his mind still struggled to understand.

Think, Will, think.

Then the all-too-fresh memories rolled over him. "How long have I been out?"

She lifted her shoulders as if called to action. "Not that long. The plane…" Sylvie looked out to the water.

Will followed her gaze. He stood, taking it all in. He'd nearly gotten them both killed. Something had gone wrong—something partly out of his hands, out of his control. But he should have improvised or adjusted. Why was that part still such a blur? He raked his arm across his eyes and forehead. It came away smeared with blood.

"You're okay," she said. "The bleeding stopped."

He drew her to her feet while he stared at his plane, completely flipped nose down and sinking. "I've never personally seen that happen."

Nor had he experienced anything like it. That he'd lost a plane today, to add to the loss of his mother's plane, pressed against nerve centers he hadn't known he possessed. But that was nothing compared to losing his mother.

Still, none of these thoughts would help Sylvie. Getting her someplace warm and safe was his priority. And knowing he had a mission, someone to help, would keep his head in the game, despite his losses.

"How did I get here?" He looked back at her, grateful the rain had eased up. "You pulled me out and swam me to safety?"

She nodded, rubbed her arms.

"Thank you."

"I didn't know where to go after that, what to do. Seemed like I was back where I started, only with an injured man this time. But at least no one is trying to find and kill me at the moment."

As far as you know. But he didn't voice his thoughts.

Will hoped that would remain the case for a long while. Forever would be nice. He grabbed her hand and squeezed. "It's going to be okay, Sylvie. We're going to be okay."

Those words reminded him of something else, but he couldn't quite remember what. Something hovered at the edge of his mind. Something about today that connected him to Sylvie. He hoped he'd remember while it still mattered.

A smile softened her grim features. He hadn't thought

her pretty at first, but now he changed his mind. Her smile brightened her eyes and emphasized appealing dimples against soft, smooth skin. Something else thrived behind her determined gaze that drew him to her.

Her shiver snapped his focus back to where it should be.

"I have a friend who lives not too far. I'm sure he saw us go down—I'm surprised he hasn't already shown up." That was only partially true. He'd said the man was a friend, but in fact, he was only a client and a recluse who liked his privacy. Will had no idea what reaction they would get when they showed up. Will had never actually been invited to the cabin, but knew from flying over where it was relative to the beach.

"Are you okay to walk?"

"Yes, lead the way." She hugged herself.

"Good. Shouldn't take long." He trudged ahead of her.

Will wished he could hold her close to share some body heat, but that would be awkward. He didn't think they were that desperate yet. Yes, Sylvie had taken a beating today. With her ripped suit, circles under her eyes, bluish skin and lips, anyone could look at her and see how badly she'd been hurt. But in her eyes, those hazel eyes, Will saw her unbridled determination and knew she wouldn't accept his help.

What man could help but admire her?

They neared the tree line and he followed the brook that would eventually lead them to the off-grid cabin where John Snake lived. Snake—he liked the nickname to keep out the riffraff—usually met Will near the beach for his packages, but that was when he knew to expect Will.

He turned to check on Sylvie, but she was farther

behind than he'd thought. Frowning, he made his way back. She was strong, but she'd been through a lot both before and after he'd come on the scene in his floatplane.

"Hey, you doing okay?"

Seeing her purse her lips, he got the sense she wanted to smile, but couldn't. "How much farther?"

Will hated to tell her it was still a couple more miles, and the terrain wasn't getting any easier. Add to that, the rain was icy cold and coming down harder.

He didn't like the glazed look in her eyes. "A mile, maybe."

She dropped to a log and hung her head. "Okay. I can do that. I just… I think I might have sprained my ankle. These diving boots are no good in this type of terrain."

He frowned. "No kidding."

"Give me a minute to rest."

Was she serious? Will wouldn't expect her to walk if she was injured. In fact, he shouldn't have let her walk to the cabin even before finding out about her ankle. What with hypothermia setting in and she hinting at having decompression sickness, she was in a world of hurt, but he didn't want to step on her strong and capable toes, so he hadn't offered any help.

Until now. There wasn't time to rest. They had to get out of the weather.

He scraped his arms under her knees and around her back and lifted her.

"What are you doing?" Alarm jumped from her gaze and her voice.

Will settled her against him until she felt right. She was lean and solid, as divers tended to be, but light enough he could manage the distance. "Don't take offense, Sylvie. I need to get you out of this weather."

Her gaze softened. "Thank you. I didn't mean for you to have to do this."

"I figure I owe you. After all, you pulled me from a sinking plane and swam me to shore. Saved my life. So it's my turn to carry you." There. Hopefully, he hadn't offended her strong and capable woman sensibilities.

Sylvie didn't argue and instead rested her head against his shoulder. That ignited familiar feelings inside. Protective feelings. He'd forgotten he could feel that way and instantly remembered why he hadn't wanted to. A year ago he'd given it all to Michelle and she'd made a fool of him, practically leading him around town by the proverbial ring in his nose until she'd dumped him. In the end she couldn't take the fact Will was a bush pilot. He was gone all the time and he wasn't there to do her bidding or entertain her. She'd claimed she was afraid he would die out there in the bush and she'd be left alone. It was her or flying. He'd had a choice to make.

So he'd come back early, canceled a job and was almost ready to give it all up for her—against his mother's strong advice, of course—when he found Michelle with someone else.

Everyone had seen the fool that Will had been except for Will until it was too late.

He wouldn't allow that to happen again. But this situation had nothing to do with that one.

Two different women.

Two different scenarios.

If Sylvie had any hint of his thoughts she'd be out of his arms in a second, and that would do neither of them any good. Will had to get his mind off Sylvie's proximity. He tried to focus on the steps he took rather than the warmth of Sylvie's body against his.

If he could get her talking about what happened today, maybe it would distract him and they could find some answers to boot.

"Tell me about those men, Sylvie. Why did they try to kill you?"

"I already told you I don't know anything."

Was she telling the truth? "So this was just random, then? Two men were there, and you were at the wrong place at the wrong time? What could you have stumbled on? I can't imagine they were out there minding their own business and decided to kill whoever showed up for no reason."

Had she stumbled on something and was hiding that fact? There had to be much more to this story. That something gnawed at his mind again, just out of his reach. A cup of warm coffee and some rest might ease the ache in his head and set him thinking clearly again.

She released a sigh that tickled his neck. "Obviously I have a lot to figure out, but I can't think a straight thought."

"Right. You need food and warmth and sleep." Just like he did. If only he could find that cabin. He hoped he didn't run into those men after Sylvie. But they couldn't have followed him. He'd take comfort in that. Then again, letting down his guard could be a mistake neither of them could afford.

Too many unknowns made him edgier by the second.

As the cold rain came down harder, tumbling through the canopy of spruce and hemlock, Will focused on stepping his way over slick boulders and freezing ground, careful to avoid slipping, especially with his burden. Though Sylvie was small, carrying her the distance began to weigh on him. His arms ached, challenging his confidence. He should have come across Snake's cabin by now. If he wasn't going to find the cabin, then they needed to make shelter while there was still enough light.

The rain eased to a fine mist, blunted by the forest canopy.

He stopped, thinking about putting her down so he could build a fire.

"Will." Her warm breath caressed his cheek. "Through the woods…"

Will's pulse jumped. The cabin? He peered through the trees, eyes following where she gestured. An elk. Disappointment jabbed through him that it wasn't the cabin. How could he tell her the disheartening news that he didn't know where he was going, after all? He set her down, steadying her to sit on a fallen log, and drew in a breath to tell her the bad news. Before he could say the words, the fog in his mind lifted, and he saw clearly what he couldn't understand before.

Sylvie had been looking for her mother's missing plane—the same as him.

His next words took a different tack altogether.

"Tell me about the plane you were looking for." Ever since she mentioned her mother's plane, Will suspected they were both on the same search. His mother's plane was the only one that had gone missing in the area in more than a year, and there had been one passenger. A woman. Sylvie's mother—he was sure of it. And from the look on her face, she was making the connection, too.

"You're a bush pilot. Mountain Cove Air. That's your company?"

He nodded. "My mother was flying a surprise package back to Mountain Cove two months ago when her plane went missing. I've been searching for her ever since. I think we've both been looking for the same plane." How could it have flown so far off the intended path that search parties—Alaska Air National Guard, Alaska State Troopers, Alaska Fire Service, Coast Guard, Fish and Wildlife Guard, the list went on—hadn't found them? Then again, they had thousands of square miles of islands, water and mountains to search even on the flight path she should have taken. Not counting where she might have detoured.

That was it, then. She'd taken a detour and Will suddenly knew. Why hadn't he thought of that before? She'd kept a postcard his father had sent her years before of a beautiful waterfall. What if his mother had been showing Sylvie's mother the sights, including her favorite?

Will remembered the postcard because of the scripture quote written on it. "But they that wait upon the Lord shall renew their strength; they shall mount up with wings as eagles; they shall run, and not be weary; and they shall walk, and not faint." Isaiah 40:31

From the moment he'd seen the postcard and read the verse, Will had always pictured himself as an eagle when he flew. Seeing life from above, the big picture of things, must be how God saw things.

Could the plane be there?

Sylvie rubbed her arms. "Oh, Will."

"Do you know anything about a surprise package?" he asked. "I keep wondering if…" He couldn't bring himself to say the worst. He didn't want to believe his mother had delivered a surprise that turned out to be an actual explosive device. The idea was too far-fetched.

"I think the surprise was my mother. She lived in Mountain Cove years ago. She left after she had an affair with a married man. It was a bad breakup. And then she found out she was pregnant. She had to leave."

Will hated where this was going. Hated it for Sylvie. "Was she pregnant with you?"

"Yes." She hesitated then added, "My mother's name was Regina Hemphill. My father was Scott Warren. I have half brothers and one half sister. Maybe you know them."

"I do." He released a heavy sigh. "That is *one* surprise package. But you're an even bigger surprise."

"Yeah, a surprise nobody wants to hear about. Or at least, that's what my mother told me as gently as she could when she explained why I shouldn't try to contact my father or half siblings. I guess she didn't want to see me get my expectations up and get hurt. I can't be sure she even told him about me. When I finally worked up the nerve to face him on my own, I couldn't because he had died." She shivered, either from the memory or from the chill in the air.

Will was reminded that he needed to find shelter. They could search for a cave, but what if they didn't find one in time? He needed to build at least a rudimentary cover. A debris hut would be quick and easy and keep them warm. He'd prefer a bough structure to reflect the warmth of a fire. The problem was a rainforest was much too wet, and the chances he could start a fire were close to zero.

God, please, we need Snake's cabin.

"It's not fair," she whispered. "And I have half siblings who may not even know I'm alive. I can't tell you how often I've thought of them, wanted to meet them."

Strange to think her mother, given the circumstances of her having to leave Mountain Cove, would have told

Sylvie about her half siblings. Or had she done her own research? But she wasn't finished talking and he wouldn't interrupt. Instead, he began creating a mound from the forest floor.

"On the other side of that, they could resent me for the reminder that their father betrayed his marriage vows with my mother. They could hate me. So it's almost better if I never meet them. Then I can stick with believing they'd want to meet me, but don't know if I exist or how to find me if I did." Sylvie groaned. "I can't believe I'm telling you all this. You didn't exactly ask for the whole shebang."

"I know the Warren siblings would love to meet you." He knew the siblings were aware of their father's affair, and knew they'd tried to find out if they had a brother or sister out there. These were conversations he couldn't help but overhear when piloting the Warrens to Juneau or sometimes even delivering them to a SAR—search and rescue—command center. They trusted Will. But in all of this, what he'd really like to know was if his mother had known where Regina had gone all along, but said nothing. "I'll help you make that happen."

"No, please, no. I'm not sure I'm ready to face them. I'm torn about it. I need time to think it through. I want it to be on my terms. Please don't ever tell them. I'll be the one if it happens."

"Okay, then." If Will's mother had kept Regina's secret, he thought he could feel some of what she might have felt when someone extracted a promise like that.

Still, it would be a hard promise to keep, depending on how all of this unfolded. From what had happened so far, this seemed to be shaping up into quite an adventure that Will could tell his grandchildren about one day. But he couldn't think of it as an adventure until it was over and they survived. Grandchildren? He'd never get married so children were out of the question.

Will needed to excavate a hole in the debris, and then he and Sylvie would have to crawl into the pile, supported by loose branches, and hope to keep warm. Tomorrow he could build something better, if it came to that.

She tilted her head. "I thought you were making a fire."

"A fire? It's too wet."

"Oh, I guess you're right. I should be helping you." Sylvie stood then fell back to the log.

"You're injured. No need to help." Will took a short break and sat next to Sylvie on the log, hoping his body heat would warm her, wishing his headache would subside.

"I know it's hard to understand how I can ask you to keep my secret. Mom made it sound like the whole town of Mountain Cove gossiped about her. Practically ran her out of town. That's why I need to work up my nerve before approaching the Warrens."

"You? You've got nerves of steel." Will inserted some humor into this too-serious conversation to cover his own growing anxiety about their chances of survival.

"Nerves of steel don't matter. Under the right circumstances even something as benign as salt can turn corrosive and erode steel." Sylvie shifted next to him. "Despite her feelings about the town, she was on her way back to Mountain Cove. I guess I'll never understand why, but I wanted to find her plane. I want to know what happened."

"You and me both, Sylvie. You and me both." Will

waited for Sylvie to go on, one question burning in his mind. When she didn't continue, he asked, "Did you find what you were looking for? Did you find the plane?"

Sylvie opened her mouth to speak.

A twig snapped from the shadows. Will sprang from the log to face the threat. He stood in front of Sylvie to protect her and reached for his weapon, but came up empty-handed. He'd forgotten that he didn't have it. It was submerged with his plane.

Wearing a hood, a man emerged from the trees. Friend or foe?

"Snake?" Will squinted, studying the intruder.

The man stepped forward and tugged back his hood. "What are you doing here?"

FIVE

What kind of name is that?

Will glanced over his shoulder at Sylvie. She stood from the log, easing onto her good foot and using Will's back for support. She wanted to be standing in case they needed to make a run for it.

"Sorry for the unannounced visit, Snake. You know I'd never intrude if it wasn't an emergency. But I had some plane trouble. A hard landing and Sylvie and I... we've had a brush with death or two today."

The man's expression darkened as he studied both Sylvie and Will. It seemed that he had issues with trust. Clearly he lived a reclusive life away from civilization. Away from the prying eyes of the law. She wouldn't second-guess his reasons. This wasn't her world.

"Come on, then." He turned and disappeared into the trees.

Will lifted her back in his arms and followed. "Only a little longer, Sylvie. You hanging in there? Doing okay?"

"I'm good, thanks to you."

"You'll be thanking Snake before too long. He's the one with the cabin and a warm fire. I bet he'll have a big pot of game stewing, too. That's what I'd do in this weather if I were him."

Sylvie's mouth watered at the mention of food. She could already imagine the warm fire and wanted nothing more than to sleep in a soft bed, covers piled high. Safe, sound and secure. She sighed at the thought. Was that asking too much?

But she had to remain vigilant. This wasn't over yet. She couldn't rest until it was. And Will deserved an answer to his question. "No. I didn't find the plane. I thought I saw something, though. The glint of what could have been part of a plane. That's when I was attacked."

Lines pressed between his brows.

"There's something else," she whispered. "I'm grateful for your help and for Snake's, but you know I need to get out of here. I need a decompression chamber. And I don't want to put anyone else in danger."

There, she'd said the words that had been crawling over her ever since Will had made an appearance today and put himself between her and the men trying to kill her.

"One thing at a time," he said. "Snake has a radio. While I was in the air trying to figure out how to rescue you, I tried to radio for help a few times, but no one connected on the other end." He glanced at her, his strong, scruffy jaw and warm brows much too close. "I'll make the call for help first thing. Only Snake isn't going to like it."

"Why not?" But she thought she already knew.

"He lives off-grid. Doesn't want anyone to know he's here. Doesn't want to draw attention to his castle in the glen. Once people know about his castle, he might be overrun with marauders."

"Out here? Nah, I doubt it." Sylvie couldn't help but grin at his medieval references. He was definitely chivalrous, a real knight in shining armor, now that she thought about it. With his strong arms holding her, carrying her over and through the terrain—not an easy task in places—and keeping her pressed against his warm, muscular form, she couldn't think straight.

She had to get her mind on something else. She was strong and independent, and didn't like that being near him turned her soft and compliant. Made her needy. She couldn't afford to be like her mother when it came to men, and get hurt in the worst of ways. With all that had happened today, she feared her suspicions that her mother had been murdered were confirmed, and she'd almost blurted it all out to Will. She wasn't ready to tell him her darkest of secrets yet. Not until she was absolutely certain of it. She didn't want to think about it now, didn't want to face the truth of what that would mean. So she turned her thoughts back to Will and Snake.

"But *you* know where he lives."

"That, I do. He needs someone he can trust to bring him supplies *and* keep his existence a secret."

"Are you telling me the Alaska State Troopers or the Coast Guard or some other entity doesn't know he's here?"

"Maybe they do, maybe they don't. The point is that he is off the grid and off the radar. Or at least, he was."

"And now you've blown his trust."

"He invited us to follow him, didn't he?"

"Doesn't mean he'll let you use his radio."

"That remains to be seen."

Sylvie wasn't sure she liked Will's answer. Was he going to use the radio or not? And if not, how did they get out of here? The need to get them out of his sanctuary should be reason enough for Snake to let them call for help.

Sylvie could barely make out the man's silhouette ahead of them since he made better time, crept stealthily through the forest much faster than Will, who carried Sylvie. Once again, she found the need to distract herself from Will's sturdy body, and the great care and attention he took to making the ride as smooth as possible despite the slick, sodden boulders and fallen trunks and debris he had to step over and around.

Finally, Will stood at the open door of Snake's log cabin and then carried Sylvie over the threshold.

"You can set her down over there." Snake referred to her as if she were a box of supplies and gestured to a long sofa near the woodstove.

Will was right. The man had something going on the stove, and the aroma stirred her hunger. After Will gently settled her on the sofa—worn out but more plush than she would have expected—Snake appeared by Will's side with a first-aid kit.

"Thanks." Will took the kit. "She needs dry clothes, too. Got any extras? I'll make sure to reimburse you."

"No need for that." Snake nodded and disappeared through a door off the main room.

"I agree," she said. "There's no need for you to reimburse Snake for any dry clothes he offers me. I'm perfectly capable of doing that myself."

At Will's surprised glance, she added, "And I'm perfectly capable of being grateful." She offered a smile of her own. "Thank you, Will, for your thoughtfulness. For carrying me through the woods. I'm sorry you had to do that. Besides, you need them, too."

"What do I need?" Will crouched near her ankle and examined it.

"Dry clothes."

"I'll manage. And you're welcome, by the way. All in a day's work."

Yeah, right. When he touched her ankle, she winced.

"It's not so bad," he said, "And probably the least of your worries. Am I right?"

"You know you are."

He shot her a grin that tugged at her insides. She was losing it. Cold and hungry and injured and…well…that made her vulnerable. Sylvie wouldn't read anything into his grin. She couldn't afford to get sidetracked.

"I'll wrap this after you change out of the dry suit." Will stood when Snake appeared and held out a couple of large flannel shirts and some jeans.

"These do?"

Will cocked a brow at Sylvie, humor flickering in his gaze.

"It'll have to. Thank you, Snake." Saying his name felt awkward on her lips.

Will slung the extra clothes over his shoulder. "Thanks, Snake."

Sylvie hated to ask, hated to need help, but worse than that, she hated to limp across the floor. No, falling on her face would be worse. She had some vertigo. Not good. She hoped she only had a mild case of DCS. She'd never before gotten the bends. The dive hadn't been that deep, and she'd descended at the appropriate rate. But her ascending straight to the surface without any stops had been all it took to throw her body chemistry into turmoil. The cold water and exertion from fighting off a killer hadn't done her any favors.

The next few hours would be telling, especially if she didn't get help. But first things first. Right now she simply needed to make it to that room for some privacy. "Will, can you assist me to the room so I can change?"

"Sure thing. Um… Sylvie… I need to doctor that gash across your shoulder and back, too."

"You don't think that can wait?"

His grin from moments ago quickly faded. "No."

"I need to doctor your head," she said. Fair play.

"Snake has a mirror. I can take care of it."

But Sylvie couldn't reach her shoulder and back, even with a mirror, so that was that. She let the compassion and concern in Will's warm brown eyes calm her nerves. He was good in that way, even addicting if she wasn't careful.

"While you guys take care of business," Snake said, "I'll dish up the stew. Got strong coffee going, too. When you're ready, we'll eat."

"Sounds good." Will assisted Sylvie into what was obviously Snake's bedroom and set her on the bed. He frowned down at her.

All she wanted to do was lie down and sleep forever. This close to a bed, the warmth of the cabin and the aroma of the stew, she could sense the adrenaline crash coming.

Hold it together. Just a little longer.

"You okay to get out of that suit without any help?" His tone and the look in his eyes said his only concern was for her. He wasn't going to take advantage of her. She didn't trust easily, but he'd brought her this far. She wanted to trust him.

"Thanks, Will, but I can handle it."

"Good. Call me when you're ready."

"Okay." His words held tenderness that pricked her heart. She was definitely vulnerable. Somehow she had to get her guard back up. She'd been through too much already.

Her stepfather had been a wonderful father during her childhood. Someone she could trust, someone she had been proud to call *Dad*, until she'd become older and wiser. When she was a teenager, she discovered he was having an affair. The betrayal devastated Sylvie. She didn't know where to turn. She didn't want to hurt her mother, but finally shared his duplicity, only to learn that her mother already knew. How could her mother let him treat her like that? At first Sylvie thought her mother hadn't left because she loved him—which just proved how dangerous love could be. Sylvie built a wall around her heart that day. She could never trust anyone again. And from that moment on, she called him Damon.

But then, behind closed doors, she heard the arguments. Raised voices. Her mother crying. And then Sylvie began to suspect that her mother hadn't left Damon because she was afraid of him. Afraid to leave. Damon was a powerful man.

None of that mattered now, except to remind her to keep her guard up around Will. She needed to keep herself together until she was back home. Or at least in that decompression chamber.

Sitting on the edge of the bed, her ankle throbbing, every joint in her body aching badly enough to make her completely forget the open gash in her back, she drew in a breath and prepared to peel out of the dry suit and layers of clothing beneath. All she wanted was a hot shower, but she supposed the best she could get at an off-grid cabin was a sponge bath. She looked down to see the ripped, practically shredded suit. She hadn't wanted to look too closely. Seeing it now, a replay of the last few hours flashed through her mind, reel after reel.

All the way to her soul, Sylvie was torn and ripped like the dry suit she wore.

She pressed her face into her hands and let everything she'd held back come flooding out.

Will had changed quickly so he'd be ready to dress Sylvie's wound. Behind the door he could hear her quiet sobs. She'd been strong, held it together in front of him. He wasn't sure why the sound rocked through him, knocking against the hidden parts of his heart. He pressed a hand on the door as though he could comfort her. He didn't know this woman at all, but he didn't have to know her to feel the pain with her.

He let his hand drop. He wouldn't go rushing in. He wasn't a knight and she didn't want to be saved. If he knew anything at all about the woman shut away in the room, it was that she didn't want him to see her vulnerable. Sucking in a breath, he glanced up and caught Snake watching him from where he hovered over the fire, dishing up the stew that he cooked in a cast-iron pot hanging over the flames, old school.

Will had another situation he'd been avoiding. He needed to face off with Snake about using the radio to call for help. He knew the other man wouldn't be pleased. The harsh environment along with fifty-plus years had made the man hard and lean. He kept his long silver hair in a ponytail hanging down his back, and time spent away from civilization kept his expression harsh, especially when faced with having to make conversation.

But he'd still saved them. Will would give him that. He hadn't been anything but helpful—so far.

Snake's bushy eyebrows creased together as he stood from the fire and held out a bowl. "You hungry?"

Will took the bowl, but set it on the table. "Thanks, but I'll wait for Sylvie."

"Suit yourself." Snake remained standing and wolfed up a few spoonfuls of his stew then paused, the spoon halfway to his mouth. "Something on your mind?"

Here comes the moment of truth. "I told you we had some trouble. That trouble includes men who tried to kill her, kill us. They shot at my plane. Caused some damage and we went down. I hope I haven't brought the trouble to your door."

Snake's eyes narrowed. He set his bowl on the home-crafted table and crossed his arms. "What do you need?"

"I need to use your comm to call for help."

Snake shook his head. "You're not bringing them here."

"You can see she's injured."

"Call them and make arrangements to meet them elsewhere. I'll help you get there."

Will scraped a hand over his face, exhaustion creeping into his bones. "She has the bends, and with her other injuries she needs treatment right away."

Snake's eyes lit up, surprising Will. "Why didn't you say something before?"

"Would it have made a difference?"

"I'm a diver. Got the equipment. Worst case, she could recompress in the water."

Will shook his head. "That *is* the worst case. It's too risky. Better to wait for a hyperbaric chamber, which is why I need to use your radio."

"Well, you know the option is available. Why don't you tell her and let her make the decision? She isn't afraid of diving."

Had Will been that readable?

Snake disappeared through a door, reappearing a minute later to set his scuba equipment out in full view. Was that because he didn't trust Will to bring it up?

Will frowned.

"Make your call. Pick a meeting time and place. Early morning's best. Give us time to rest up and gather the gear we'll need."

"I can't ask for more than that."

Will hated to put it off that long, considering Sylvie needed assistance sooner rather than later, but Snake was right. If they were forced to travel to make contact, they couldn't do it in inclement weather in the middle of the night. He had to persuade Snake to shorten the distance they needed to travel.

"Just how far do you want us to go?"

"I don't want anyone coming within five miles of my cabin. That might sound harsh, Will, but let me remind you that if it was someone else I'd seen tromping through the woods, I wouldn't have shown my face. I wouldn't have offered an invitation into my home. I wouldn't even have opened my door."

"I know." Will was grateful to Snake. The man had chosen this lifestyle for reasons unknown to Will. He wouldn't pry.

"About those men who tried to kill you? You sure they didn't follow you here?"

"I don't see how they could have, but neither can I be sure. I don't know who they are or why they tried to kill her." He had his suspicions. Some things were trying to fall into place, but mostly it was still a mystery.

"What do you know about her?"

"Nothing. I just happened to be flying overhead in time to see her running for her life." Will struggled with whether or not to share the full of it with Snake, considering he didn't particularly seem the kind of person who would want to know the details about others' lives, nor would he reciprocate. Best to keep things simple and not share that Will and Sylvie had both lost their mothers on the same MIA airplane. For now.

From Snake's expression, Will knew that Sylvie was behind him.

He turned. She leaned against the doorjamb, clinging to it, more like. Will had meant to be there before she put any pressure on that ankle.

He rushed to her side. "I didn't mean for you to have to walk on your ankle. I should have waited by the door."

She shrugged away from him. "You don't need to take care of me. I'm perfectly capable of taking care of myself. My ankle will be fine."

Will sensed she needed to convince herself more than him.

"Sure it will." He backed off. "But I still insist on doctoring your back. Why don't you sit down at the table." Will assisted her there, ignoring her attempt to limp on her own.

"Thanks." She turned her back to him and adjusted her shirt over her shoulder to expose the gash that ran from her shoulder to mid-back.

He winced. This was going to hurt.

Add to that, she was shaking all over. She'd had time to warm up, so it couldn't be from the cold. It must be a symptom of decompression sickness. She needed that hyperbaric chamber. And he was about to inflict more pain on her when he doctored this gash. He sent up a prayer, feeling helpless in all this.

Lord, when we are weak, You are strong. I need You to be strong for the both of us.

His prayer gave him a measure of peace. Sylvie could use some comfort and reassurance about now, too. But how did he give it?

Will grabbed the first-aid kit. He didn't like the look of the cut. It needed stitches. But he would do what he could and keep her talking so she wouldn't focus on the pain.

"I'm sorry for snapping at you," she said. "You don't deserve that. I'm just tired."

And injured. "No need to apologize. This has been a hard day for you."

"For you, too. You helped me, someone you didn't even know. Not too many would have done the same. Snake included."

Ah, so she'd been listening in longer than he thought. He was glad Snake had ventured outside for the moment.

"I'm nothing special so don't make me out to be."

"I can't say that I agree. Nor can I thank you enough for what you did today. What you're still doing."

"You're welcome."

"I heard you talking to Snake. He sounded upset with you for bringing me here. And what was he saying about five miles?"

She'd definitely heard more than he thought. No matter. He hadn't said anything he was ashamed of saying. "Don't worry about that for now." Will was glad he'd finished with her wound. "There, that should do it."

He made to stand, hoping to escape from her rush of questions. He didn't blame her, but he wasn't prepared to answer them fully until he figured things out. He needed to talk Snake out of the five-mile hike. And he needed to use the radio.

Will scooted the bowl of stew toward her. Sylvie grabbed him before he could get away. Heat danced up his arm from where she touched him. "I don't know how I'll ever repay you, but I'll find a way."

He already knew her well enough to expect that from her. She couldn't receive a kindness without needing to repay it. She thought she owed him. He eased his arm from her grip. "Don't worry about that. It's more important that you focus on staying alive."

More important that they find out who wanted to kill her. The same person who had already killed their mothers?

SIX

With warm stew in her stomach and a mesmerizing fire, Sylvie had never been more exhausted. The sofa was comfortable and broken in, and cocooned her, inviting her to sleep. She didn't want to close her eyes. After all, she was in an out-of-the-way cabin with two strangers. Two men she'd only known a few hours, never mind they had both been an intricate part of her survival so far.

When they figured out she was too exhausted to offer coherent conversation, they left her alone to rest—though she could still hear their hushed tones from the far side of the cabin where they practiced knife-throwing against a chunk of wood. Besides the shelf of old books against the wall, that could be Snake's only entertainment out here, and a necessary skill. Will's apparent expertise surprised her. She wouldn't want to face off with him. She remembered she'd lost his knife when she'd had to cut him out of the harness and swim him to shore.

Her gaze drifted to the diving equipment sitting out. It must belong to Snake. *Her* equipment was still in Will's plane. Had the doomed craft already sunk, never to be seen again—a reminder of the plane she'd come to find? At what point could they come back to retrieve her diving equipment? What did it matter? She couldn't get it in time to do her any good and might use Snake's gear to recompress herself. That was a seriously risky scenario that could kill her. She was counting on getting out of here at first light. Better to wait for the hyperbaric chamber in Juneau.

Will called her name out, jarring Sylvie awake. Somewhere behind his words, she heard a vibrating noise over the crackle of the fire in the otherwise quiet morning. That noise penetrated her catatonic state—and she forced herself to sit up, listen. Will stood at the open door, looking out, the gray of morning illuminating that portion of the cabin.

Whomp-whomp-whomp.

Realization dawned. A helicopter. Someone to rescue them.

Newfound energy surged through Sylvie. She eased from the sofa and limped over to where Will stood, hanging through the opening and letting the warm air out while the cold Alaska morning whipped inside and swirled around her feet.

Intent on listening, he didn't acknowledge her. She lifted her hand to touch his arm then dropped it when he tensed, as if he'd expected the touch. As if he hadn't wanted it.

"Why aren't you running out there to signal them?" Panic engulfed her. Sylvie pushed by, prepared to limp outside to wave at the helicopter. Will and Snake couldn't keep her here. "If you won't, then I will!"

"Sylvie, no." Will snatched her back.

Pain shot through her ankle. She screamed, hoping someone would hear her.

Will gripped her shoulders, his brown eyes imploring her to listen. "Last night I radioed Chief Winters with the Mountain Cove Police. He's someone I know and trust. Chief Winters is sending a SAR team to meet us at ten. That's not for another three hours. I figured it would take us that long to hike the terrain to the meet-up point, especially with your injured ankle. That helicopter isn't our help."

"How can you know that?"

"This isn't where I told them we'd be. And it doesn't sound like the type of chopper medevac uses. This is a single-engine. Small, maybe a two-seater."

She froze. "What are you saying?"

"I'm saying that I don't know who is flying the helicopter. Chief Winters didn't send this one."

"It could be someone who could help us. Someone willing to fly us to Juneau."

He pursed his lips. "Or it could be the men after you."

Sylvie backed away from him. "No, that can't be. How could they find us?"

"They could have spotted the plane sitting halfway out of the water if it hasn't already sunk. Then on foot they could have tracked us. Or the helicopter might be simply looking for smoke from the nearest cabin, knowing that would be our only shelter for miles."

"But how could they have found your plane? Covered that much ground without knowing where you were going?"

Will's eyes penetrated, stabbing at her core. "Easy enough. They could guess we were headed to Juneau and follow our general flight path. And if it's the men after you, you have to consider they're tracking you somehow. Maybe they put a tracker on your boat, or they're tracking your phone."

"I'm no longer on my boat and don't have my phone with me."

"Your diving gear, then. They found you in the channel and then could have followed you here. Your diving gear is on my plane. Maybe they figured I had landed, even if they didn't realize I crashed. But they've had enough time to get a helicopter and track you. So I don't want to risk it if it's them. Not when I know help that I trust is coming."

A tracking device on her diving gear? That was a frightening thought. And worse, it would mean that it was her fault if their attackers tracked her here, since she was the one who'd insisted on going back for her diving gear and loading it onto Will's plane. She didn't have time to think through the implications, not with Will's suspicious gaze on her. She'd told him she didn't know who was after her or why. And she didn't. Not really. But if they were together much longer, she'd need to share everything with him—what had driven her to search for the plane to begin with.

Will waited and listened, staring out the door, the porch both covering and hiding him from the searchers.

"Where's Snake?"

"He went out."

"You need to warn him."

"Don't worry. He won't be waving at the helicopter. If anything, he's angry that someone is looking for us and will inadvertently discover him."

A spray of bullets ricocheted through the woods. Will slammed the door and pressed his back against it. Determination carved his features. "We have to get out of here."

Scrambling around the cabin, he grabbed coats and

packs that must have been prepared while Sylvie had slept. He tossed Sylvie a pair of Snake's boots. "Try those. They might be too big, but you need something to protect your feet besides the diving boots."

Sylvie understood the urgency and worked to put the boots on. There wasn't time to look for socks. It didn't matter if the boots didn't fit. But how could she run with her injured ankle?

The sound of the rotor blades drifted away.

"Do you think they'll come back?"

"They're not really gone. They're just looking for a place to land. They're onto us, Sylvie. They know we've taken refuge in this cabin."

"I'm surprised they didn't use a more stealth approach. They would have caught us off guard."

"It also would have taken longer, and they wouldn't want to give us a chance to get away." He pulled on his coat. "They're determined to find you. What haven't you told me, Sylvie?"

In the distance more automatic gunfire resounded outside, saving her from a reply. A big chunk of fear lodged in Sylvie's stomach. When would this end? She couldn't imagine it would end well.

Will went to the door and opened it.

"Wait! What are you doing? You can't go out there. You're going to get yourself killed."

"I have to find Snake. Make sure he's okay." Will grabbed a weapon off the table and chambered a round. He handed it to Sylvie. "You know how to use this?"

"Well enough." She didn't want it, but these were dire circumstances.

Once it was in her grip, she stared at it, a vise of fear

squeezing her chest. Finally, she looked up at Will. All this she'd brought on him. On Snake. "Be careful."

Understanding passed between them. They were in this together. "Stay here and be ready to run when I get back."

Sylvie set the weapon on the table and sat in a chair to slip on Snake's boots. They rose above her midcalf and, if she tightened them enough, they just might be adequate support for her ankle so she could run.

She heard him outside on the porch. He hadn't left yet. Good. The too-big boots secured as much as possible. Sylvie shoved from the chair, pulled on the coat and opened the door to say words she'd never thought she'd say to anyone.

"Don't leave me!"

But Will had already disappeared through the woods to find Snake. She feared he would come face-to-face with the gunmen.

There was nothing he hated more than leaving Sylvie, but it couldn't be helped. He'd keep one eye on the cabin as he searched the nearby woods for Snake, who'd gone to one of the outbuildings. He should have returned by now.

When Will had first heard the helicopter, he'd tucked his borrowed weapon in his shoulder holster and prepared for what the next few moments would hold. And now he was in the thick of this fight for survival.

Hiding behind trees as he searched, he moved with stealth through the woods, watching the cabin as he went. "Snake," he whispered loudly. "Where are you?"

The man could have taken off and left Will and Sylvie there to fend for themselves for all Will knew. But

Will didn't want to believe it. The helicopter still hovered in the distance, confirming Will's belief the pilot was searching for a place to land or release someone who would soon come for them on foot. He couldn't be sure that someone wasn't already on the ground.

A glance back at the cabin told him no one had approached, but that could change at any moment. He had to get Sylvie out of there. Using the trees for cover, he searched for the missing man.

"Snake."

An ominous dark color surrounded a mound by the woodpile. Will's gut tightened. After another glance at the cabin and through the woods, he ran forward, dropped to his knees and searched for a pulse. But the wound in Snake's head and the blood-stained ground told him enough.

"No…" Will cried. Acid burned his throat. "No, God, why?"

Snake's death was his fault. He shouldn't have brought Sylvie here, but he hadn't known it would end like this.

He said a quick prayer over Snake then, "I'm sorry, Snake. Real sorry."

Will pushed to his feet and scraped the raw emotion from his face, letting anger and determination push up and drive him forward. He hefted Snake in a fireman's carry and trudged to the cabin. He'd have to get to Juneau before he could organize a funeral for the man, but until then, he wouldn't leave his body to the wolves.

Wolves came in many different forms.

When he made it to the cabin, the door opened and Sylvie stood there wide-eyed and waiting.

"What happened?"

"They got Snake. We have to leave now. I heard them landing."

"I'm so sorry." Sylvie looked as if she would cry, but ran her hand across her eyes and swiped the emotions away.

"No time for regrets. If we want to live we have to go." Will looked her over. "Looks like you're ready. The temperature is dropping. We have at least three hours to hike and evade capture while we wait for a rescue. Grab the packs. I'm going to use the radio one last time." He went to the small room where Snake kept his Ham radio. Again, old school, but Chief Winters kept one, as well.

Will made the call and warned Chief Winters what had happened so he could bring backup and understand the urgency and danger they would face. Will wasn't sure how long he and Sylvie could last, but knowing that others were on their way to help bolstered his confidence. He had a smidgen of hope they would survive.

It didn't last long. Not when he heard what the chief had to say next.

He finished on the radio and hung his head.

"What's wrong?" Sylvie asked from behind.

"Their helicopter was diverted to another emergency and delayed. Chief Winters promises to find other resources for us and send them as soon as possible. For obvious reasons, I can't hang out at the radio and call someone else for help."

He left the room and grabbed one of the packs that Sylvie had set next to the sofa. Snake had prepared food and supplies for them. Will scrambled to put it on as Sylvie did hers. Wait. Will had to carry Sylvie instead of the pack. Snake was supposed to carry one of them and now he was gone.

Sylvie leaned against the sofa and watched him. "What are we going to do?"

"We're going to survive." He refused to let her see the fear that gripped him. Only his determination to stay alive.

"You ready?"

She nodded.

"Let's go."

He tried to assist her, let her lean against him to walk across the cabin, but she shrugged out of his reach. "I can do this."

He'd let her think that until they had to run. For now it was awfully quiet out there. Will peeked through the door, weapon at the ready. They would be most vulnerable leaving the cabin, but he'd stay close to the trees. Snake had done well in using the canopy to hide this place, though the smoke from the chimney had most decidedly given them away to anyone bent on finding them. But all they had to do was stay alive just long enough to make their rendezvous—and hope that help would actually arrive, as planned.

Before he opened the door wide, he looked at Sylvie. "We're going to make a run for it. And you might not like this."

Her eyes grew wary. "What?"

"I'm going to carry you piggyback style. It's the best way for me to run and make good time and get us out of danger."

Sylvie opened her mouth to argue then shut it. She blew out a breath. "Okay."

"All we have to do is stay alive long enough. Help is on the way. They're coming for us." Just not as fast as Will had hoped.

He'd never had to run for his life. Never had to protect someone or help them this way. He never wanted anyone to depend on him like Sylvie depended on him, though she'd never admit to that. But he could see the uncertainty and apprehension in her eyes—beautiful hazel eyes that he wanted to look at again under much different circumstances.

Knock it off.

Will opened the door and positioned her on his back. "Are you okay? Am I hurting you?"

"No. I'm fine."

But he heard the discomfort in her voice. She wouldn't tell him she was in pain.

A bullet slammed into the log next to his head.

They were out of time.

SEVEN

Sylvie fought the scream that exploded in her throat.

Will slammed the door shut. Ignoring her ankle, Sylvie slipped down to let him catch his breath. He pressed his back against the door.

"God, we could use some help here," he said between gasps. "They're a good distance away so we have this one chance to escape the cabin."

After gesturing her out of the way, he motioned for her to duck down. "Be ready to run."

Then he opened the door again to deliver a round of bullets. He slammed the door and picked her up and ran to the back of the cabin. He set her gently against the wall as if she were porcelain.

"We have seconds before they make the cabin."

She gulped a breath. "How many... How many are there?"

"I don't know." Will struggled with the window. "Two maybe."

She hoped he didn't make too much noise so they'd focus on the front door. "Before, there were only two men. Diverman and Rifleman." That she knew about. Had there been someone equally murderous driving the boat? And obviously, someone had stolen *her* boat, moving it out of her reach. Destroying the evidence she'd even been there.

Will finally got the window open then quietly slipped through, watching the woods as he assisted her out. The trees made good cover here, if nothing else. But then there was an open patch they had to cross. Sylvie followed him through the window, ignoring her pain, bruises and scratches from yesterday. What did any of her injuries matter if someone shot her in the head like Snake?

Once she climbed through the window, Will let her scramble onto his back again and then he sprinted as though she weighed nothing, which she knew wasn't true. She might be small, but her solid frame made her weigh more than other women her size.

By the time he made it across the small clearing between the cabin and outbuildings and into the thick cover of woods, Will was breathing hard. He stopped behind a big tree for cover and panted. Sylvie wanted her freedom from the position on his back but knew to keep quiet. They weren't out of trouble yet and she wasn't sure they would ever be until help came.

He crept forward between the trees, putting distance between them and Snake's cabin. She'd brought danger to Snake that had killed him—a man who'd chosen to live away from civilization. Her stomach soured. It never should have happened.

She couldn't let it happen to Will. She tried to watch the woods to help him, but twisting her neck around while she jostled on his back made her dizzy. Neither did she want a bullet in the back. Maybe the pack she wore would provide protection enough. Will stepped into a brook and waded upstream, getting his boots wet. She wasn't sure how far they'd gone when he stepped out of the brook and paused in the crack of a bluff between large boulders. When he set her down, she collapsed onto soft, mossy ground and shrugged out of the backpack.

He plopped down next to her, his face drawn tight. "Are you okay?" he whispered.

She nodded.

To her surprise, he ran a finger down her cheek, picking something off. A leaf, dirt, she wasn't sure, but something in his gesture made it feel as though he cherished Sylvie. That couldn't be true. Nor did she want that from him or anyone. Unfortunately, her heart jumped at his touch no matter her personal resolve.

"What are we going to do?" she asked.

"We can hike to town if we have to."

Right. She blew out a breath. Like she would believe that. Time to face the truth. "Even if that were true, it won't take them long to track us. We're too slow and we can't outrun them. We can't make it to town before they find us."

"Then we'll just stay alive until help arrives." Will leaned in closer until his face was inches from hers. So he could lower his voice? "Do you trust me?"

His brown eyes seemed to caress her. His masculine scent—a woodsy mixture of loam and pure, wild adrenaline—grew heady and wrapped around her until she couldn't breathe. She struggled to speak. "I don't know."

She couldn't rely on anyone but herself. Still, she wanted to trust Will. Just how far, she wasn't sure.

His brows knit together.

"I trust you to do your best, but don't lie to me about

our chances. I'm grateful for all you've done, but I don't see how we're going to make it."

Hurt spilled from his gaze. He eased back, pulled his weapon out. "Have a little faith, will you?"

"I've never had anyone shoot at me before, have you?"

"No." He angled his head to listen. Through the opening between the boulders he watched the woods.

She didn't like this position. They were trapped. Someone could ambush them. What was he thinking by stopping here?

When he turned back, the warmth had returned to his eyes, but under it was a cold resolve that hadn't been there before. It scared her. This wasn't the Will she'd come to know in a few short hours. Was this experience changing him, like it changed her? And yet, how could it not?

"What are you thinking?" she asked, not at all sure she wanted to hear his answer.

Drawing a breath, he worked his jaw. She was close enough she could feel the muscles in his shoulders tense. "I've never had anyone shoot at me. Nor have I ever shot at someone until today. And I've never—" he exhaled long and hard "—killed another human being."

He hung his head, and once again Sylvie held her breath even with her heart pounding wildly. "Will." Her whisper was a mere croak.

He lifted his eyes to hers. The way he held her gaze, searched for something inside her, Sylvie almost thought he was trying to decide if she was worth the cost, but then she knew he'd already found that answer. He'd claimed that he was just doing what anyone else would have by rescuing her yesterday, but he was going far beyond what she ever could have expected from a stranger.

And Sylvie had the strangest sensation that this moment in time bonded them together forever. Gave them a connection like no other. She didn't want to be that close to anyone or dependent on them. She saw where that had gotten her mother. But at that moment her connection to Will was her lifeline, and it went far deeper than she cared to admit.

Whatever the bond, he broke it with his next words. "My father taught me everything I know about weapons. Told me if you're going to learn how to shoot a gun, you'd better be prepared to use it."

Sylvie wasn't sure she liked where this conversation was going. Her insides quaked, but at the same time she resigned herself to the fact that they might have to kill to survive. "Meaning?"

"I will protect you, Sylvie. Whatever it takes. Whatever that means. If it comes to that, I'll kill for you."

His words elicited dread in her eyes. He wanted her to believe in him, believe they could survive this. The words were meant for him as much as for her. He had to speak out his resolve, let it sink in. When he'd fired his weapon from the cabin, he hadn't been aiming at anything or anyone in particular. The shots had been meant to deter their pursuers. He wasn't in a position to make a kill shot then anyway.

But if they were on their own, if help wouldn't come soon enough, Will would cover ground, as much as possible. Then he'd lie in wait and make the kill if it came to that.

"We need to keep moving." He hoped they hadn't rested too long. "You ready?"

"No, I'm not. How long do we keep running?"

"Until it's over." His tone had turned brusque. He didn't recognize himself at the moment. But he didn't like the feeling that death was swooping down on them like a raptor just waiting for the right moment to stick its claws in.

He peered from behind the boulder. Watched and listened. Patches of light dappled the woods. At least it wasn't raining at the moment. The thick greenery was tranquil except for birdsong and skittering small animals through brush. A red squirrel darted into Will and Sylvie's hiding place between the boulders then back out. They probably stood too near where the creature had stashed acorns. They'd leave soon enough and the squirrel could get to his stash.

If the woods could be trusted, there didn't seem to be any sign of their assailants.

In the distance a twig snapped, and a hush fell over the forest. Even the breeze dropped. Another snap and it almost sounded as if the man had taken a wrong turn. Was going in the wrong direction. That would give Will and Sylvie a chance.

After he positioned Sylvie so they could make good time, he crept quietly, slowly, from behind the boulder. Relief washed through him. No answering gunfire was there to meet them. And yet he couldn't afford to let down his guard for even a second.

They were still a few minutes away from making their original meeting place. He could have asked help to come to the cabin, but he and Sylvie couldn't outlast a gun battle there and would be long dead by the time help arrived. So he'd kept to his original plan, hoping he could evade their pursuers and arrive around the same time as their rescuers.

He'd asked that they come as soon as possible.

Now he wished he would have begged.

Come on, Chief Winters, where's the helicopter? Where's our rescue? Didn't I make it clear we were on the run from killers?

Not clear enough, apparently. Will's back and legs ached, but he kept moving toward the rendezvous point and in the opposite direction of the men after Sylvie. At least he hoped.

Finally, Will was spent. The muscles in his arms had been cramping for an hour. Still, even carrying a woman on his back, over rough and difficult terrain, they had made good time.

He let Sylvie off his back and nestled her against the thick trunk of a Hemlock. Moss grew at its base along with the vast greenery found in the temperate rainforest. He wished for the bluff with the boulders. That had been good, quiet and safe cover. But they could hide here, too, melt into the forest and wait it out until their rescue helicopter came.

Will leaned against the tree and hung his head to catch his breath. Gather his composure before she looked too long and hard at his face and saw the truth. Sylvie reached up and squeezed his arm. Reassurance?

"Thank you," she whispered.

He peered at her. Those hazel eyes would get to him every time. "Don't thank me yet."

"Are we going to keep moving? What's the plan?"

"No. We stay here. This is our rendezvous point—or near enough. But we need good cover until help comes. When we hear *our* helicopter, we'll make a run for the meadow up a ways where it can land. From here, though, if we must, we hold our ground."

She held up Snake's weapon, a grin contrasting the somber expression in her eyes. "Like in an old shoot-'em-up movie."

"Something like that, but let's hope we don't have to get into a shoot-out." He hoped all that was left to do was wait and watch. Wait for the rescue helicopter. Watch for their assailants. He perused the woods. Heard nothing. Saw nothing.

"Right, because I'm no marksman."

"I don't know how many there are but I suspect two. Three at the most, but I'm hoping for one. I should be able to pick them off if I see them in time."

Admiration filled her eyes, surprising him. Something warm tugged at him, fighting to get inside, but Will wouldn't let it. He didn't like that he cared what she thought about him. Until that moment, he hadn't realized her opinion of him mattered. He wouldn't let himself give in to the draw of her beauty, both inside and out. No, Sylvie wasn't a manipulator like Michelle had been. Far from it. But that didn't mean Will would allow himself to be vulnerable again.

"You're full of surprises, Will Pierson."

"There's more where that came from." He didn't just say that.

"What do you mean?" She angled her head.

He paused before he answered, listening to their surroundings and watching the forest for signs of the men after them. Prickles crawled over him.

A bullet pinged against the tree above Will's head. "Get down!"

Then another cracked the bark.

Will peered around the tree.

Aimed.

Fired twice.

The man ducked out of sight.

Again, Will watched and waited. He prayed they could get out of here without facing off with the men, but that was not to be. How many men were out there? Just the one he'd spotted, or were there more? He couldn't be sure. After too much time had gone by without any more sound or movement, he thought he should check and see if he'd injured the man. He hadn't shot to kill, would only take that step if there was no other choice. Instead, he was holding on to that one last hope their help would arrive and capture the men. He and Sylvie could get their answers that way.

But he'd protect her at all costs.

"Sylvie," he whispered.

She didn't answer.

"Sylvie?"

Will held his weapon steady but glanced behind him. She was slumped over. Will dropped his weapon and grabbed her, spotting a hole in her coat. He tugged it off her shoulder and down her arm.

There, red spread across her shirt. A lightning bolt of pain struck Will's heart.

"Oh, no, please, no…"

He tugged the shirt open and found the gunshot wound through her shoulder, blood gushing out. His whole body shook at the sight. Ignoring the cold, he tugged off his coat and then shirt, pressing it against Sylvie's wound. He prayed the bullet hadn't nicked an artery, but this heavy bleeding told him otherwise.

I have to stop the bleeding.

"Sylvie, please don't die on me, please don't die." Bile erupted in Will's throat.

God, where is the rescue helicopter? Please, don't let me down.

But *Will* had let *Sylvie* down. He told her that he'd protect her and keep her safe but his shots had been too little and too late. Her life poured from her, the shirt he'd used saturated with it. His hands were covered in her blood. Emotion burning behind his eyes, his heart tripped up, tumbled over.

She wasn't going to make it.

EIGHT

The world spun around him—the trees and sky swirled, the brook trickled too loudly from a distance—then time seemed to slow along with the whop of rotor blades from the helicopter hovering above him.

Panic crawled over Will.

Was it their help arriving at last? Or the enemy helicopter? Will grappled with the sound, trying to recognize the kind of bird, but his focus was shot. His hands slicked with Sylvie's blood, he grabbed his weapon, ready to protect her, defend her. But his head told his heart he was too late. He'd already failed.

Two men lowered from the helicopter. Faces he recognized. Cade Warren and a paramedic whose name failed him. He couldn't comprehend their words as they pushed him back and away from Sylvie.

"No, stay away from her!" He yanked Cade away. But what was he doing?

Cade gripped Will's shoulders, pinned him against the tree and removed the weapon from Will's grasp. "We're here to help. Get a grip, man. You're in shock."

Compassion eased into Cade's expression. "Are you good?"

Stunned at the words, the truth of them, Will squeezed his eyes. "Yeah, yeah. I'm good. Just save her. Save her..."

He prayed that the world would quit tilting on him. "God, save Sylvie."

I thought I could save her. That I could protect her. She was right next to me, behind me, practically. Behind the tree. And still, I let her get shot, and now she's fighting for her life. How...how did this happen?

The next thing Will knew, they hoisted a basket holding Sylvie to the helicopter. Cade remained behind. Another man—a police officer—stood nearby, his gun drawn. How or when had he gotten there?

"Is she going to make it?" Will hung his head, seeing the blood-stained moss at the tree's base. Would he ever forget that image? When Cade didn't answer, Will lifted his gaze.

His expression grim, Cade said, "I don't know."

"When gunfire erupted, I returned fire. I wasn't aiming to kill. Not yet. Just trying to hold out until you guys arrived. But the man never fired back. There was no movement. I need to know if I killed him. Or...if he's injured." Will should have thought of that and already informed Cade. He was failing miserably. "There was another helicopter that fired on us earlier—that killed John Snake, the man who gave us shelter last night. That's why I pulled my gun on you. There could be more men. I can't be sure."

"We don't have much time." Cade signaled the Mountain Cove officer. "Chief Winters sent one of his men in lieu of the troopers. He was afraid we wouldn't get here in time if we had to wait."

And they almost hadn't anyway. Will pushed away

from the tree and hurried to the place where the man had been shooting from, Cade and the officer on his heels. There was nothing, no one, next to the tree. Will hadn't seen anyone coming or going. What use was he in protecting Sylvie? None. He let his gaze roam the area. The rescue helicopter must have sent the man running.

"And Snake. His body is in the cabin. We need to get it."

Cade shook his head. "Don't worry, we'll come back for Snake. This woman's life is on the line. We need to go and now!"

Cade led the way back to where the helicopter still hovered, and the three of them were each lifted into the craft. As the helicopter flew over the forest, Will looked outside, searching the woods for their attackers. He looked anywhere but at Sylvie, where two medics worked on her. Isaiah Callahan, Cade's brother-in-law, flew the helicopter. Will almost wished he would have stayed to find who had done this. Or that the police officer would have stayed to search for evidence. They could have done Sylvie more good on the ground.

But it was too late now. There was nothing left to do except pray. Will squeezed his eyes and hung his head, trying to shove aside his own guilt in what happened, and his concern and worry over Sylvie.

Just have a little faith.

Hadn't he told her the same?

Cade nudged him. "Sorry it took us so long, man."

Will didn't want to hear excuses. Angry with them, angry with himself, he couldn't respond. Time stretched on and took far too long to get to the nearest hospital where Sylvie could get the blood she needed to survive and a hyperbaric chamber to resolve the decompression sickness.

"Who is she?" Cade asked.

"Sylvie Masters." It hit him then. He sucked in a breath, pulled his gaze from the terrain below and stared at Cade.

He doesn't know that she's his half sister.

Cade didn't realize. *Oh, Lord, help me...* Will didn't want to betray her trust—the promise she'd extracted from him—but Cade needed to know.

"What is it?"

God, what do I do? Do I tell him? Will Sylvie speak to me again?

Will pressed the heels of his palms in his eyes. "Okay, this isn't for me to share, but maybe she'll understand."

"Tell me."

"You have to keep this to yourself. Can you do that?"

"Depends, Will, you know that."

"Yeah, well, try to keep this under wraps for her sake. Sylvie Masters is Regina Hemphill's daughter. The child she conceived with your father before she left Mountain Cove."

Will stared at Cade, watching as his pupils dilated, as realization knocked him back into his seat, pinned him against it. The man's expression morphed, pain etching his features when he glanced over at the woman fighting for her life.

Finally, an exhale burst from his lips along with, "She's my half sister."

Light filtered into her dreams, stirring her awake. Sylvie wanted to open her eyes but her lids were heavy. Nor could she move or lift her arms. Was something pressed on top of her, holding her down? No, it was more that she had no strength. She wondered how she could have survived the freight train that had obviously barreled over her.

"Sylvie." A familiar male voice wrapped around her. "You're going to be okay. You're going to wake up soon and everything is going to be fine."

Where was she? Sylvie frowned. At least she could do that much.

"Sylvie, please, wake up."

An image came into her mind. The face that belonged to the voice. Who was he?

"Will?" her voice croaked out, sounding as if it had come from down a long, dark tunnel. As if it had come from someone else.

A large hand with a strong grip squeezed hers. She squeezed back.

"Can you hear me?" he asked.

Sylvie's eyelids fluttered and she found the strength to open them—though she could already tell that keeping them open would be a problem. She looked at Will now, the details of his handsome face coming into sharp focus. Only he looked beaten up, haggard in a way she hadn't remembered. What had happened to him?

"You're awake." His grin thrilled her, but concern, as well as delight, poured from his gaze.

Now she started to remember. His brown eyes taking her in when she climbed into his plane. The wariness in them the first time she'd seen him. There was a tug at her heart that he was there with her now. She was glad to see him, but wasn't sure why. Who was he to her? What was wrong with her that she couldn't remember?

She drew in a ragged breath, unsure how much energy she had left to keep her eyes open much less speak. "Where am I?"

His grin quickly faded, but he squeezed her hand again. "You're in the hospital. They're taking good care of you."

"What happened?" She had to know. Had to remember before she lost her strength.

"You lost a lot of blood." He inched closer. "Sylvie, I'm so sorry."

"How long... How long have I been here?"

"Two days. You're going to be fine. They say it will take you some time to regain your strength. You had a mild case of DCS, and with the gunshot wound it was complicated."

"Oh, right." She'd needed the hyperbaric chamber, but...gunshot wound?

And why was Will here instead of her stepfather? Sylvie tensed, hoping they hadn't known to contact him, or hadn't been able to reach him since he was out of the country.

Sylvie felt herself drifting in and out, and Will's voice, his face, did the same.

"You should rest."

Will said nothing more, and Sylvie's sluggish mind took time to process the words. Soak up his presence. Something about him sitting next to her gave her a sense of security, though she struggled to understand why she needed it. Then the horror came rushing back and she wished it hadn't. Wished she could feel safe with Will without the harsh memories of the attacks against her.

A nurse entered the room and insisted Sylvie needed to rest, confirming Will's suggestion. She didn't want to release Will's hand, let go of the strength there, but he pulled away from her. Sylvie wanted to look in his eyes, let the warmth there wash away the disquiet in her heart, but her lids betrayed her. Then darkness replaced light.

When Sylvie awoke again, she found two men in her room. Fear jumped down her throat, then Will stepped forward. She hoped he would reach for her hand again, but he didn't.

His grin, revealing a couple of dimples, could make her feel better, but his eyes weren't convincing.

What was wrong?

"How are you feeling?" he asked.

I'd be better if you'd sit close to me and hold my hand. But she couldn't say that. She hated how vulnerable and needy she'd become.

A nurse came in and repositioned her pillow and bed so she could sit up. She brought her a tray of hospital food. Sylvie had no appetite. She felt uncomfortable with the stranger and waited for Will's explanation. When the nurse left them alone, he stepped closer. He looked as though he hadn't slept in days. How long had she been here? She got the sense that he hadn't left her side, but she was certain she was just fooling herself. She couldn't be that important to him.

"The police are going to question you soon," he said.

She turned her hand over, hoping he'd take it. It hadn't required a conscious thought, simply reflexive need. And Will, apparently attuned to her subtle needs, took her hand. She wasn't sure what she felt about her desires or his response to them.

"I don't think I'm coherent enough to answer questions."

"Do you remember that you were shot?"

She shook her head. "I'm not sure. I remember clinging to the tree as gunfire erupted. Everything is blurry after that."

"I tried to protect you but he shot you."

"Who, Will? Who shot me?"

"I don't know. I fired back, but he got away. We think the rescue helicopter sent him running."

"The police are hoping you can give some answers about who might be trying to kill you." The man standing in the shadowed corner of the room finally spoke.

Was he with the police? Sylvie let her gaze travel to him.

Will chose that moment to sit on the edge of the bed. It seemed like such an intimate gesture for a man she hardly knew, but they'd been through something together. She had a bond with him and struggled to remember what it was. He'd stayed with her through this; she believed that. Why couldn't she remember more?

"I'm sorry, but I couldn't keep it from him."

"What are you talking about?"

"When our helicopter came and the rescuers hoisted us up, I had to share your secret with him because...well, I thought you were..." Will hung his head. "I thought you were dying."

Dying...

She had almost died?

"What secret, Will? You're scaring me."

"Please forgive me for telling him, but I believed the circumstances warranted full disclosure."

The man stepped closer. With the deep set of his woodsy-green eyes, thick head of dark-roasted-coffee hair and his good, strong features, the face was somehow familiar, and yet she was sure she had never met this man.

"Sylvie." His grin was big and welcoming to an extent that seemed inappropriate coming from a stranger. "I'm glad to finally meet you. My name is Cade Warren."

Ah, now she understood the grin. And the sense of familiarity. Her heart beat wildly. She wasn't ready for this. What did she say to him? This wasn't how she'd wanted to meet him, if she'd ever been ready to make that leap. And Will, it seemed, couldn't be trusted with secrets. She thought to glare at him, but she couldn't take her eyes from her half sibling in the flesh. A weight pressed against her chest. She was bungling this first meeting, and badly, with her reaction. Or rather, trying to hide her reaction to him.

Pain flickered in his eyes but compassion quickly took its place. "I'm your half brother."

"I know who you are." She hesitated. "I just don't know what to say. How to feel."

Despite her clumsy words, he tossed her another easy smile and she finally relaxed.

"I know this is a shock for you. It's a lot to happen at once." He grabbed Will's shoulder and squeezed. "And please don't blame Will, but I was there on the scene to get you guys, and well...we weren't sure if you would make it. Will didn't think it was right for him to keep your identity from me."

"I understand. I... I just wasn't ready for this. For any of it." For someone trying to kill her. For meeting Cade Warren. "I had dreamed of meeting you under different circumstances."

Now Sylvie could finally offer her own smile, begging for some grace. By his demeanor and the look in his gaze, she believed he gave her the understanding she needed and much more.

involved, she needed to tell him everything. But how? She wasn't sure she could trust him with everything. "Thanks again for coming back for me on the island."

"I'm not sorry I'm involved," he said. "I'm just glad I was there when you needed someone. Even knowing the danger, I would do it over again, Sylvie."

Sylvie didn't have time to ponder his meaning. Two Alaska State Troopers stepped into her room and sent Will on his way.

NINE

While in Snake's cabin, Will had contacted those he trusted, and the North Face Search and Rescue team—including Cade Warren—had responded along with someone from the Mountain Cove PD. But they weren't the ones investigating the crimes now. The Alaska State Troopers were the law-enforcement entity to ask the questions. The crimes had happened outside Mountain Cove and even the large area encompassing Juneau's jurisdiction, but there were no county sheriffs in Alaska.

Even though the Alaska State Troopers were officially in charge, Will would also share everything that had happened with Mountain Cove Police Chief Winters. What happened to Sylvie and Will, this investigation, somehow involved Will's mother. If he followed through with this line of thinking, she had been murdered right alongside Sylvie's mother. But what Will couldn't be sure about was which one of the mothers was the target and which one was the accidental victim. Or had they both been caught up in something together that had gotten them killed? His mother, Margaret Pierson, had been a citizen of Mountain Cove since she and his father had moved there from Montana three decades ago. Chief Winters should be kept informed on everything about her murder so he could do his own investigation if warranted.

After Will sipped the last of the vending-machine coffee, he crushed the paper cup and tossed it, growing impatient with the troopers to finish taking down Sylvie's statement. He had a burning question of his own. Would Sylvie share anything more with the police than she'd shared with Will?

If Will went with his gut on this, then he thought Sylvie had suspected her mother had been murdered long before men had come onto the scene and tried to kill her. The attack just confirmed her suspicions. It was those initial suspicions that had sent her looking for the plane.

What did she know? What or whom did she suspect was responsible?

Or maybe Will was wrong and Sylvie knew more but didn't realize it. But that didn't seem likely, either. Sylvie was smart. No. She knew something about that plane and was holding it close. Was she protecting someone?

He didn't like being played or manipulated, but to be fair, Sylvie hardly knew him. Why should she trust him? Except they had this one strange connection, this one thing in common.

Their mothers had both died together in that crash.

That gave Will a reason to see her again. He'd already told her that he'd help her find out what had happened to their mothers. Still, his reasons for wanting to see her again went beyond the precarious situation they found themselves in together. The thought took him by surprise.

But Will couldn't follow through. He'd already suffered with the deep pain that came from experiencing a shattered heart. If remembering the pain from his past wasn't enough to keep his heart safe, he'd simply remind himself that Sylvie hated to fly. He got up every morning eager to meet the sky. Nothing inspired him more than drifting or soaring in the air through wide-open spaces, over the lofty snow-covered peaks of Alaska, or dipping deep into the valleys and seeing the fjords and waterfalls.

Nothing better than soaring with the eagles where the sky had no limits.

Nothing inspired him more. He would never give that up. No sense in falling for another woman who disdained his greatest joy. Will didn't have time to ponder more when the two Alaska State Troopers exited Sylvie's room.

Will kept his distance. He didn't want to be dragged into more questions for which he had no answers. Plus, he figured she would need a few minutes to compose herself. He had needed that himself. They had to have drained her with their interrogation, as they had him, and he hadn't been recovering from a gunshot wound or decompression sickness. He hadn't lost so much blood that he'd almost died.

The thought sent his mind back to their narrow escape through the woods behind Snake's cabin, and then to the tree behind which they'd taken cover. To the gunshots fired and to Sylvie nearly bleeding to death. Shaking the morbid thoughts away, Will thanked the Lord for Sylvie's life. In the waiting area, he stayed in the shadowed corner a little longer and sent up another prayer for the Lord's protection. They were going to need it. Until these men were caught, they were both in danger.

Will opened his eyes in time to see a male nurse

enter her room. The man's scrubs pulled tight across his chest and over large biceps as he glanced both ways down the hall before he closed the door. Will frowned. Something didn't feel right. He might be too paranoid after everything they'd been through, but he always listened to his instincts.

He shoved from the wall and headed to her room, wondering why the Alaska State Troopers hadn't thought to post an officer by her door. Asking them would be Will's next order of business after he checked on her. Will opened the door and stepped inside the room.

Sylvie slept, looking exhausted and fragile. The nurse prepared a syringe presumably to stick in Sylvie's IV, adding medication to the drip. His gaze flicked to Will—and something in the man's eyes sent warnings through Will's head. Yeah, it was always in the eyes.

Will edged close to the man, getting in his space, preparing for a negative reaction. "What's that you're giving her? She's already asleep."

The nurse threw a fist at Will but he ducked in time. Adrenaline surging, Will launched at the brawny man, pulling him away from Sylvie as he tried to insert the needle into Sylvie's arm instead of the drip. Will had him in a choke hold but still the syringe edged dangerously close to Sylvie's arm.

"Help!" Will yelled. "Sylvie, wake up."

She needed to help him fight for her life.

With every ounce of strength he could muster, Will pulled the man back away from the hospital bed, and he fell on top of Will, knocking the air from him. But at least the syringe slid across the floor and out of reach. Will would crush it. Destroy what had to be a deadly poison.

Except the man posing as a nurse climbed off Will and pulled out a gun.

He aimed at Sylvie. She was awake now, her eyes wide with terror as she screamed. Will scrambled to his feet and shoved the weapon's trajectory away from Sylvie, aware that if the gun went off, it could very well go through a wall and injure another patient or hospital staff. He didn't want that, but neither would he let this man kill Sylvie.

Will wrestled to gain control of the thick-necked bouncer man again, trying to force him to release the gun by twisting the man's arm back and over the corner of the nightstand. The weapon fired.

Once.

Twice.

Three times.

A cacophony of screams erupted, echoing through his ringing ears.

God, help me! Protect Sylvie. Protect us all.

Muscles straining, sweat beaded his forehead. But he wouldn't let the man shoot Sylvie. "Get out of here, Sylvie. If you can, get out."

She tried to move from the bed to escape, but in her weakened condition she collapsed to the floor. Releasing a grunt, Will shoved the man against the wall, slamming his arm and pinning him, crushing his wrist until the man cried out and the weapon fell. Strong though he was, the man wasn't as motivated to kill Sylvie as Will was to save her life.

Will kicked the weapon across the floor against the wall.

The man growled and twisted out of Will's grip then shoved Will out of the way before running out the door.

Breathing hard, Will glanced at Sylvie, who'd crawled to the corner of the room. "I'm all right," she said.

A nurse rushed in as Will exited. "Take care of her and call security, call the police if you haven't already."

"Will!" Sylvie called. "Don't go!"

Her words knifed through him. He didn't want to leave her, but neither could he let this man get away. Instead, he rushed into the hallway, quickly spotting the man who was shoving doctors, nurses and hospital staff along with their carts, out of his way, leaving screams and clattering trays in his wake. Security guards appeared at the opposite end of the hallway. Of course. They would never catch up. Will gave chase and followed him down the hall. He pushed through the doors into the stairwell a mere ten seconds behind the man.

Hastening footsteps echoed through the stairwell below. Will continued his pursuit, wishing he had a weapon, or that he had grabbed the man's gun even though he knew that same weapon could get Will killed when the security officers or police caught up. Still, why was he the one giving chase? Where were the police when you needed them? Frustration churned in his gut, propelling him forward.

He had to catch this guy. Couldn't let him get away, or he might try to hurt Sylvie again. Lungs burning, he flew down the steps, taking more at a time than was safe. Another door opened and slammed shut. Will peered over the banister and saw nothing. But there was only one exit. He reached the last floor and shoved through into another hallway where it was obvious the man had torn a reckless path through hospital staff and bewildered patients.

"Where did he go?"

Visitors and nursing staff stared at him, their eyes wide and mouths hanging open.

Will kept running, following the trail of destruction, and peered through every door that would open as he went. Nothing. "Please, somebody help me. Did you see which way he went? I need to catch him."

A brunette staffer pointed. "Out the door."

He nodded his thanks as he passed. *God, please don't let me lose him.*

When he ran out into an alley he found a garbage receptacle and a delivery truck. Will carefully searched as he ran down the alley and into a hospital driveway, the visitor parking lot across the road. Catching his breath, he turned, searching the area for the man running from him. Cars came and went along the street that encircled the hospital. Could the man be driving one of them, making his escape?

Will sagged in defeat. He'd been so close. *How could I have lost him?*

Someone shoved through the door behind Will. A security guard. He looked at Will ready to pounce.

Will had to deflect those thoughts immediately. "He got away," Will said. "Drove off. Disguised himself. Melted into the walls. I don't know."

He could still be in the hospital for all Will knew. Sylvie needed 24/7 protection. Someone was willing to go to great lengths to kill her, and there could be no doubt that they would be back.

They would keep trying until they succeeded.

Sylvie sat on the edge of the bed in her hospital room, anxious to be free of this prison. She was grateful for the clothes Heidi Callahan—her half sister—had purchased for her. Only a few years older than Sylvie, Heidi sat across from her in the only chair in the room. Her rich and thick chocolate hair splayed across and down her shoulders. Both the hair and the deep warmth in her smile reminded Sylvie of Cade. She was so beautiful. Sylvie wondered why she hadn't inherited some of those looks, but that was the least of her concerns.

Still, she could see some resemblance between them.

Sylvie had mixed emotions about this whole thing. "I wish we could have met under different circumstances."

"Whatever the circumstances, at least we've met, and at least you are alive." Heidi pushed from the chair, her five-month pregnancy barely showing. She was pregnant with the niece that Cade had mentioned. "I'm looking forward to spending some time together when this is all over."

"Yes, when this is all over." Sylvie knew her own smile was tenuous, at best.

"I have an appointment with my OB soon but I'm going to use the little girl's room before I leave. Not like I didn't just go. Just wait until you get pregnant." Heidi gave a bashful grin then disappeared.

At her words, Sylvie could hardly hold back her tears, and let them fall when Heidi was gone.

The fact that Heidi was pregnant drove home Sylvie's misgivings about the trouble she was facing—she hadn't known her search for answers would put others in danger. Nor had she known she would meet her half siblings like this—and had been completely unprepared in that respect. They'd all stopped in the day after Cade's appearance. He'd given her a day and not one minute more to prepare for meeting the rest of the family. That meeting had all but overwhelmed her on top of another attempt on her life.

They'd all crowded into the room to see her. First, Heidi and her husband, Isaiah, then Cade's wife, Leah, who had presented her and Cade's son, little Scottie. Then firefighter David and his wife, Tracy, who had newborn twin boys; and Adam and Cobie, who'd recently gotten married. What a wonderful, beautiful family, and if Sylvie had any regrets, it was that she had missed out on knowing them all this time, and on knowing her real father.

Would that have been so bad? Having time to know him? To know them all? She couldn't help but think he would have wanted to know her, too. But she'd been informed he hadn't been aware of her existence. And what about her grandfather? Had Regina even told *him* about her? Tears burned her eyes, mingling with the anger of it.

Mom, why? Why didn't you tell him? Why did you keep me a secret until it was too late?

She wiped away the tears. She couldn't complain about her childhood. She'd had a good one. The man she'd known as her father, the man her mother had married, had been good to her. Had loved her, though he'd never adopted Sylvie. She'd grown up using his last name, regardless, and had taken it as her own.

Maybe her mother had wanted to keep a legal tie back to Scott Warren, Sylvie's real father. But she had a feeling her mother had prevented Damon from legally adopting Sylvie because even though he'd been a good father, he'd been an awful husband. Yet she'd stayed with him.

Sylvie didn't know the reasons.

All she knew was that she was torn between trusting the man she'd loved as a child, and nursing her bitterness over the betrayal she'd learned about as a teen. And the fear she'd heard in her mother's voice. How could he treat her mother one way and Sylvie another?

She was relieved he didn't know she was in the hospital and wasn't here. How sad was that?

But she couldn't trust Damon Masters, the man who'd been a father to her. He manipulated people for his own purposes. She'd trusted her mother, although the woman had kept secrets. Secrets like what she planned to do in Mountain Cove that would "shake things up." Secrets that Sylvie believed led to her death.

The search for answers had now turned treacherous.

There was only one good thing to come of it and that was meeting her family—the whole bunch of them. Was this the only way she ever would have met them? Forced into it by circumstances?

Didn't matter anymore. She was in a situation that required her full attention.

Sylvie fiddled with the splash caddy that had protected her driver's license and bank card, secured against her body while in the water. The troopers said her boat hadn't been recovered, and she'd reported it stolen to the insurance company. Other than the rotating officers guarding her room, the police hadn't been back since their initial questioning. She had no idea if they would search the area where she'd found what might have been part of the missing aircraft, but they were definitely searching for the man who'd tried to kill her twice now. Once in the water and then in the hospital. Regardless, Sylvie believed she was on her own in finding out the truth.

Heidi returned from the little girl's room, as she called

it. "Billy should be here soon. Do you want me to wait with you?"

"Billy? You mean Will?"

Heidi angled her head, a curious smile playing on her lips. "I guess so."

Sylvie shook her head. "No, no. Please, go to your appointment. I'll be fine."

"Okay, then, I'll head out—but there's something I want to say first. Growing up with three brothers, I always prayed for a sister. Then I got three sisters-in-law, Leah, Tracy and Cobie, and now you, a half sibling. I just wish we could have known each other growing up." Heidi's face colored.

Now that would have been awkward. She suspected Heidi thought the same thing. Sylvie was still baffled at how graciously the family had received her—the child their father had created while cheating on their mother. Learning of his betrayal, even as adults, had to leave them confused and bitter. Would they have been able to handle it as children? She wasn't sure. But she did know that her life would have been richer and fuller for all these years if her siblings had been part of it all along.

"Yeah, me, too." Sylvie had been on the outside of the family looking in until this week, when she'd entered the hospital fighting for her life.

Will stepped into the room and relief whooshed through Sylvie. She wasn't exactly sure why.

"Well," Heidi said, "I should get going. I want to head Isaiah off at the entrance. He's being so wonderful—overprotective, but wonderful. See you guys later." Heidi waved and stepped out.

Will turned his attention to Sylvie, his brown eyes cocooning her in warmth and safety. She tried to shake it off. The effect he had on her scared her. She needed distance. Especially since being near her had put him directly in harm's way too many times already.

How did she remedy that?

Will was all she had in this. The only person she could trust. She'd never needed anyone before. Didn't want to need him now. Was it really necessary to depend on him? Surely now that law enforcement was involved, she'd be able to get through this on her own.

He sat in the chair. "I'm sorry I'm late. Have you signed the release papers yet?"

"Yes, I'm waiting on the nurse to bring the wheel-chair, which is so stupid."

"Hospital policy."

"Yeah, I get that." Sylvie needed to say goodbye. She needed time to regroup and figure this out alone. Not put him in danger anymore.

He'd argue, of course. They were on the same search, after all. But Sylvie wasn't at all sure that she wanted him to find the answers. She was afraid of what that truth was, and she couldn't trust Will with secrets.

He'd already shown her that.

Sylvie shifted, uncomfortable with her thoughts. Her need to get away had as much to do with the warmth she felt—the increase in her pulse at his intense gaze—as it did the need to keep him out of danger, and perhaps to keep him from learning things she'd rather keep hidden.

What was he thinking, just now?

He'd quickly flown right over the barriers she'd erected to protect her heart. How could that happen when Sylvie knew better than to let her guard down? Her mother's life had practically self-destructed over two different men she'd loved.

She let thoughts of the way her real father had hurt her mother wash over her. Images of how Damon had treated her mother accosted her. Those thoughts should do the trick. Help her cut Will loose.

"What's wrong?" His brows twisted. "Sylvie, tell me."

"I don't know what you're doing here. You didn't have to come."

He stood, startling her. "What do you mean? Of course you know why I'm here. Have you forgotten we're in this together? Someone is trying to kill you, tried to kill both of us, and our mothers died together. Sylvie, this involves us both."

She averted her gaze, hating the pain she was causing him.

"Sylvie, look at me."

She didn't want to. "Will, I'm going home. I'll take a cab to the airport and be back in Seattle in a few hours."

"Are you forgetting that someone found you scuba diving in the middle of nowhere? That someone followed us both to Snake's cabin and shot down the man who rescued us? And someone came into this hospital and tried to kill you here. Are you forgetting that?"

Sylvie hated how weak she still felt, but she sprung to her feet to meet Will's challenge. "No, Will, I haven't forgotten. But I cannot be responsible for anyone else getting killed in the crossfire. No one has tried to kill you, except as a way to get to me. Even yesterday, the man with the gun—he only aimed it at me. Your life was at risk merely from your proximity to me. Now, argue with me on that point."

The nurse came in with the wheelchair and cocked a

brow. "Keep it down in here." She gave Sylvie a cursory glance. "You ready?"

Nodding, Sylvie sat in the wheelchair.

The nurse pushed her forward, and she felt all the more an idiot—getting scolded for yelling like she was a misbehaving child. Stupid hospital policy. She wanted to tell Will to go home, but she wouldn't make more of a scene in the hospital. Wouldn't embarrass him.

"You hate flying, Sylvie." He walked next to her as the nurse pushed the wheelchair.

"What?"

"You're not going to fly back to Seattle because you hate flying, remember?"

Sylvie refused to continue this conversation until they had privacy. Thankfully, Will didn't press her for an immediate answer. The nurse pushed the wheelchair onto the elevator. They rode the box down to the next floor. The wheelchair rolled forward until Sylvie was finally wheeled through the hospital exit. She stood and bid the nurse to take the wheelchair and go. Sylvie wished she had called for her own cab, but Heidi had interrupted her with the clothes for which she was grateful. And then Will turned up to escort her.

So she couldn't escape right away. But at least now she could reply to Will. "I remember."

His eyes were devoid of their usual warmth. "Then you'll remember that my mother also died on that plane. I'm in up to my neck. I can't keep you here. I can't even force you to work with me on this, but I'll ask you to do me one favor."

"What's that?"

"Tell Chief Winters everything you know, so that we can work on things from Mountain Cove."

Mountain Cove.

Sylvie blew out a breath. She hadn't exactly told them everything. She hadn't mentioned her suspicions about Damon because she had nothing to go on, no specific proof to inplicate him, nor had they asked. But Sylvie'd heard the fear in her mother's voice, and she was still trying to figure out why her mother was running to Mountain Cove, of all places.

Once again, Will waited for her reply. Sylvie watched patients being wheeled from the hospital and greeted by loved ones. Others entering the facility. She thought again of her mother's last words. The voice mail she'd left.

Sylvie, it's Mom. I can't say much over the phone but please be careful. Hesitation, then a whisper, *Watch your back, baby. Be aware of your surroundings. I'll explain why tomorrow. I'm flying to Mountain Cove on a bush plane. I know what you're thinking, but I'll tell you more when I get there. It's Damon... Oh... I've gotta go now, but I wanted you to know just in case... well, that I love you...*

Just in case what? That her plane crashed? At first, she actually thought Mom had been reminding Sylvie to be careful while scuba diving.

But to Mountain Cove? That meant all kinds of trouble.

The way she'd said *I love you* like it might be her last time, and the fearful tone in her voice, and Sylvie knew her message had layers of meaning. That she was scared. She'd brought up Damon. What had she been going to say? Was she finally trying to leave him?

And now she was dead.

Sylvie decided she should try to contact Ashley Wilson as soon as she made it back to Seattle. Her mother and Ashley, Damon's assistant, were friends. Sylvie had joined them for lunch on occasion. Ashley might know something that Regina had failed to share with Sylvie.

But whatever Ashley might say, Sylvie could only think of one reason her mother would return to Mountain Cove.

She was running from Damon.

He would never believe she had gone there, since he knew about her bad memories of the town. It was the only place she could escape him.

Sylvie couldn't forget that Damon was not only her stepfather, but he was also a powerful man. And apparently more dangerous than she could have imagined. Nausea roiled at the thought.

A chill ran over Sylvie. She glanced at Will, who still waited for her reply. She had to admit the man was patient.

"I've already talked to the Alaska State Troopers. I don't have time to go to Mountain Cove. My vacation time is up in a week."

"No need to go to Mountain Cove to talk to Chief Winters." Will gestured behind Sylvie.

She turned and a man stepped forward from where he leaned against a column. Though he wasn't dressed in uniform, she glanced back at Will. "Chief Winters?"

TEN

Will ushered Sylvie into the taxi that he'd called, and Chief Winters flanked her on the other side.

Inside the cab Sylvie's wide, questioning eyes trapped him. "What was that about?"

"I was afraid the attackers might not let you walk away from the hospital without trying something else. I asked Chief Winters to come today as a favor, to make sure you were able to leave safely."

Will wished they could have had a big security detail of Juneau Police or Alaska State Troopers, but Sylvie's troubles didn't rank, and all he could get was Chief Winters. This wasn't even the man's jurisdiction. The Alaska State Troopers were looking into Snake's murder and investigating Sylvie's story. They worked off facts, and Will and Sylvie didn't have many to offer. Add to that Alaska was one-fifth the size of the lower forty-eight. The geography and remoteness presented barriers.

"Thanks, but..." She lifted fiery eyes to him, defiance burning in them. "I can't live in hiding. I'm not going to hire a bodyguard to go with me everywhere."

Now, there's an idea. Something Will could have grinned about if this wasn't serious.

Sure, he had a business to run, but he'd put it on hold until he resolved this. He had two planes to recoup and needed to discover the truth about what happened to his mother before he'd open up for business again. In the meantime, he referred his business to other bush pilot friends and hoped his regulars would come back when this was over.

"First things first." Chief Winters rubbed his ear. "Let's get some coffee. Grab some lunch. I'm starved. And you can tell me your story while we eat."

Sylvie gave Will a look. She didn't want to repeat herself. He understood, but he kept silent until they made it to their destination.

They entered the coffee shop a few streets over from the hospital. Chief Winters chose a booth in the far corner, his back to the wall. Of course. Following his lead, Will sat next to him, regretting his move when Sylvie slid in across from them. He hoped she didn't feel as if she was under interrogation, with them ganged up against her. She eyed their surroundings, and Will did, too. A couple of older men at a table. A young mother coddling an infant and toddler with Cheerios while she waited for someone. The door chimed when another man entered and searched for a seat.

Was he someone following them? Someone bent on silencing Sylvie? Will continued to watch the man, while the waitress approached their booth and took their orders.

Will waited until she'd returned with their beverages then said to the chief, "Thanks again for agreeing to meet us."

"Your mother was a friend, you know that." Chief

Winters sugared up his coffee. "I want to keep my finger on the pulse of this investigation."

He glanced at Sylvie, who sipped iced tea and looked like a caged animal watching for an escape. So far, she hadn't said a word since they'd left the cab. He'd hoped she would feel more comfortable with Chief Winters than with the Alaska State Troopers who had interrogated them both.

"I'm glad you're out of the hospital," Will said. "I can't think of a less safe environment for you, confined to a bed like that, even with the security detail stationed at your door. I noticed he was conveniently gone today."

"They're spread too thin, Will, just as we all are." The police chief shifted his gaze to Sylvie. "So, tell me about yourself."

Will leaned against the seat back. With his easy ways, Chief Winters was good at getting people to talk, and Will was counting on that. But after half an hour, Will knew nothing more about things than he had before. At least Chief Winters heard her story, and Will could trust the man to stay in touch with his Alaska State Troopers counterparts regarding the investigation, if it went anywhere.

Sylvie pushed her emptied plate forward. "Thanks for the meal. Much better than hospital food. And, Will—" appreciation poured from her hazel eyes, but it was mingled with regret "—I know you want answers to what happened to your mother as much as I want them for myself, but there's nothing else I can do here. I need to get home and regroup. Figure things out from there, if I can."

"This is about more than getting answers." Will couldn't say why he did it, but he reached across the table and grabbed her hand, which put a different meaning on his words than he'd intended. "This is about keeping you safe. Someone's trying to kill you, Sylvie."

Her lips curved into a soft smile. "You're my hero, Will. But…"

"I'm not looking to be a hero. I wasn't waiting to hear you tell me that. I want to know how you're going to stay alive. What's your plan?"

"I think… I hope all this was just a warning. If I go back home then it should stop."

Will removed his hand from hers. She was too smart to believe that. What was she trying to pull? Will wouldn't let her try to fool him. "Don't do this. Don't treat me like an idiot."

"Excuse me?"

"You're too smart to believe it was only a warning. I know that. *You* know that."

Sylvie looked to Chief Winters for help. Will kind of wanted his help, too, in convincing her she couldn't do this alone. Wisely, Chief Winters chose to say nothing at all.

"Okay, so you got me." She fidgeted with her paper napkin. "But it doesn't matter. I'm leaving today. I have to go home. Look what happened to your plane because of me. Look what happened to Snake! I won't be the reason something even worse happens to you, Will. Now, gentlemen, if you'll excuse me, I'm leaving."

Sylvie slid from the booth and started for the door. Will moved to follow her but Chief Winters grabbed him, held him captive. "Let her go for now."

"But…"

"It's clear she needs space. We can't force her to stay."

"You agreed to be here when she left the hospital in

case these men tried something else, and now we're just going to let her go? Shouldn't we watch out for her?"

"We can't follow her to Seattle."

They watched through the window as Sylvie climbed into a taxi, vulnerable, defenseless.

"Maybe you can't follow her, but I can."

Amusement flashed in Chief Winters's gaze. "I'm getting the sense that this is about a lot more than a murder investigation for you. More than just keeping her safe."

The man's words hit him in the gut. "I'm not interested in her, if that's what you mean. I'm only interested in protecting her and finding out who had the motivation and ability to knock a plane out of the sky. Who is trying to kill her."

"A noble cause, to be sure." Chief Winters stretched his legs beneath the booth. "But looks like Sylvie isn't the only one who hasn't realized the truth."

Will hoped Chief Winters wasn't reading too much into his reaction. He didn't want to accept that he was growing more attached to Sylvie every day. But the police chief, trained to read people, hadn't been fooled. Will had been the only fool. He had some kind of thing for Sylvie Masters. How did he cut off those feelings and protect her at the same time?

Will stood and dropped a few small bills on the table. Enough to pay for their meals and a tip.

"Better hurry if you're going to catch her," Chief Winters said. "Don't worry about me, I can find my own way home. Let me know what you learn, if anything. I'll do the same. And Will, be careful. Don't let your attraction to her cloud your judgment. These people play for keeps."

* * *

Sylvie stood on the ferry that would deliver her to Bellingham, Washington. If she'd flown, it would have taken a few hours. By boat, it would take two and a half days to get there.

Nausea roiled inside. What was she doing here on this ferry filled with strangers? The boat was packed with fishermen, those seeking work or adventure, retired couples and a few that looked like they were up to no good.

The ferry from Bellingham to southeast Alaska was commonly termed "the poor man's cruise." She'd been fortunate to book passage, but she'd been too late to get a cabin. Nor had she had the foresight to bring a small tent like so many others who would sleep out on the deck and under the solarium.

She'd have to join the ranks of those sleeping on the chairs. At least she could rent a pillow and blanket. If only she'd gotten over her ridiculous fear of flying, but her experience with Will had only served to deepen her fears. That, and the fact her mother had died in a plane crash.

So she couldn't bring herself to book a flight from Juneau to Seattle.

Supposedly, flying was the safest way to travel. But Sylvie had never been one to count the stats. Standing outside, the wind blew cold and continuously with the movement of the ship. She tugged her hood over her head. Drew in a breath of fresh Alaskan air. Took in the view. Gray clouds hung low, sometimes hiding the peaks of snow-capped mountains. Tree-laden islands, some surprisingly small and others massive by contrast, dotted the channel of the Inside Passage. The scenery brought a measure of peace.

And at least for the time being, Sylvie felt safe from killers. After all, how could the men looking for her have known she'd choose this route to get home? If they were looking for her, surely they'd be looking at airports.

This hadn't been such a bad idea, after all. She needed time to think about everything that had happened without nurses hovering or interrupting her thoughts every couple of hours, and without Will's hospital visits. Now that she had been released, she was free. She could put distance between them and keep him from harm's way.

Why had he come to see her so often and stayed so long every time he came to the hospital? He said it was because they were in this together because of their mothers. But the tenderness in his touch and the care pouring from his eyes told her it was more than that. He was there because he believed there was something more personal between him and Sylvie.

Was he right? She wasn't sure. His presence scrambled her thoughts. She liked him, and she didn't want to like him. She owed him her life, and she didn't want to owe anyone. Sylvie couldn't lead him on like that. Couldn't hurt him, couldn't hurt herself, letting something develop between them that could go nowhere.

But despite her persuasive arguments to leave Will behind, she knew she could use someone's help right now, which had her wishing she hadn't pushed him away. Make that run away. And that was what Sylvie had done. She'd run away from Will.

Leaning over the banister, she watched the ferry's wake. As a diving trainer, she understood the importance of being smart and planning out her actions down to the minute. Anything else could get her killed. And yet she'd almost lost her life due to her gross miscalculations. How could she protect herself now? Backing off seemed the most obvious answer, but it was one she wouldn't accept.

Regardless of her mistakes, she would keep searching for the truth that someone didn't want her to find.

A shiver crawled over her. She turned her back to the beauty of southeast Alaska to watch other passengers, wondering if she might actually be in danger from any of them.

Were her attackers still after her? Would they follow her back to Washington or wait for her there?

And the biggest question of all. Who was *they*?

A gust whipped across her face, raking her eyes. Sylvie blinked to moisten them.

Was Damon involved? Had he killed her mother? Her heart ached at the thought. She couldn't accept that he might be the reason her mother was dead. Couldn't be behind those who had tried to kill her. Even though their relationship had been strained these past few years, and even though he was an adulterer, Sylvie found it hard to believe Damon could be capable of murder. Could she trust him? No. And he certainly had the means.

She wished she could think of someone else who might be responsible, but she couldn't.

Across the channel, she watched a cruise ship make its way north. Sylvie blinked up in time to see a man standing on the other side of the ferry. His gaze flicked away from her. Had he been watching her? He disappeared around a corner.

Dread coiled around her spine.

She was definitely in over her head. If someone had followed her, intending to kill her or push her over the side, how could she protect herself? How did she stay alive long enough to solve this—something her mother hadn't been able to do? If only Will was here. If she'd asked him, he would have come.

Stop it! Stop thinking about him. What was done, was done. Sylvie was on her own now, as it should be.

Thinking back on their last conversation, she decided that a bodyguard wasn't such a bad idea, at least until this was over. Normally this would be something for which she would ask for her stepfather's assistance. He had his own security detail. But she couldn't trust them now—not while she suspected he might be involved. Sylvie hated the tumultuous thoughts coursing through her. He'd given her a good home, everything she'd wanted except for two parents who loved each other. What had her mother running to Mountain Cove if not her husband? She was always on a witch hunt; what had she discovered? Whatever it was had gotten her killed.

Suddenly, the wide open space, the waters of the channel and the forest, closed in on Sylvie. The air smothered her. When she glanced around, she realized that she was alone on this portion of the deck. Where had everyone gone? The cafeteria for a hot meal?

She had to get out of here, but she was stuck on this ferry for three days.

Three days.

Her pulse shot up as Sylvie pushed from the rail to run, to flee. To where, she had no idea.

She hurried around a corner and ran into a wall of a man. A yelp escaped as the man gripped her. Her heart jumped to her throat and she tried to free herself, except his grip tightened as he pulled her close.

Familiar brown eyes stared back. "Sylvie."

"Will?" Relief rippled through her.

"Yes, I'm here. What's wrong?" He slowly released his grip, his concerned gaze roaming her face then scrutinizing their surroundings.

"What…what are you doing here?" She hadn't meant to sound so harsh, but anger battled with her sheer joy at seeing him.

"You don't seem glad to see me." His brow quirked.

Her jumbled emotions kept her from a coherent response, then finally, "Why are you just now letting me know you were here? I…" Yeah, she was glad to see him, but she wouldn't let him know how much. She was more than angry he'd been following her against her wishes.

"I wanted to make sure you were safe. But I wasn't sure about your reaction when you found out." He glanced off in the distance. "I was working up my nerve to approach you, but then you disappeared."

"Will…" She managed a shallow gasp of his name. Pressed her forehead against his chest like an idiot. He would see right through her if she didn't pull herself together. "I had a feeling I was being followed. If only I had known it was you."

"I could have misjudged the situation. Are you saying I shouldn't have come?"

Oh, now he was teasing her. Of course he could tell that she was glad to see him. Her reaction said everything, more than she wanted to reveal. But she wouldn't say the words to him. Tell him that she liked that he'd come after her, that he'd followed. That he wanted to protect her.

"Will, I'll ask again, why are you here?" She wanted to hear all those things from him.

"I wanted to protect you. I was scared for you when you left, so I followed. I would think that was obvious, after everything we've been through. After I already told you that we're in this together. And after…" Will's attention snagged on something behind her. "Looks like someone besides me followed you, and he's coming this way."

ELEVEN

Will shoved Sylvie behind him and faced the man who strode toward them. This part of the deck was empty of others who might interfere at the moment. Could be the man had nothing to do with Sylvie, and Will was acting the fool—but he wasn't going to take that chance.

The man, wearing a dark navy jacket, had the broad chest and thick neck of a marine. The stride of someone who never lost a battle. He watched the mountains beyond them as though interested in the scenery, except his eyes flicked to Sylvie. One time. That was all it took to telegraph his intentions. A tall, skinny woman strolled along the railing with a video camera, heading their way. If the man was going to strike, it would be now, before anyone else approached and got in the way.

Sylvie tugged at him, tried coming around from behind him. He knew she didn't want him to get hurt, but Will stood his ground, protecting her if the man was bent on harm. As he closed in on them, strolling along as if he was simply riding the ferry back to Washington, Will braced himself for what was to come. The truth was always there in the eyes, just like it was in this man's eyes now. This wasn't the guy from the hospital, but he

read the man's intentions all the same—his sheer determination to kill Sylvie.

This scene had become all too familiar.

"Will." Sylvie fought him now, making his task more
difficult. "This is why I wanted to leave you!"

The man approached quickly, lifting his arm from
beneath his jacket, leaving Will only a millisecond to
respond. He lunged, forcing the man's weapon-wield-
ing hand down. A bullet fired off, hitting the water to
the left. Screams erupted from elsewhere on the ferry.
The woman with the camera began shouting for others
to come and assist, while she filmed the whole thing.

Who was Sylvie that someone would risk killing her
on a ferry in the middle of the water, leaving the attacker
no escape, nowhere to run? Her killers were becoming
more desperate.

Will's muscles strained as he held the man off. He
grunted with the effort. "Who. *Are.* You? What do you
want?"

If Will could hold the man in this position long
enough, the ferry security guard would arrive and de-
tain him. They could get to the bottom of this, but the
man broke free. Will landed a punch square to his jaw.
The weapon dropped to the water.

To Will's astonishment, the attacker climbed over the
rail and jumped into the cold waters of the channel, a
good drop from the deck of the ferry.

Will wanted to follow him. Sylvie grabbed him.
"Will, no! Are you crazy?"

Adrenaline coursed through him as he started over,
determined to swim after the man and beat the truth
from him. End this for Sylvie. Men flanked him and
pulled him back. One of them was a security guard.

They all watched in silence as the guilty party swam away. In the distance, a boat appeared. Was that the same boat that had been waiting where Sylvie had been attacked beneath the water?

"Aren't you going to do something?" Will asked the guard. "Follow him?" Will leaned over his thighs to catch his breath, his ribs throbbing. He hadn't remembered being jabbed there.

"We'll call the Coast Guard."

"I taped the whole thing," the woman with the camera said. "You can see if you can identify him."

The security guard thanked her.

Will pushed himself upright and looked into Sylvie's tormented eyes. "Are you okay?"

"Me? I'm fine. You're the one who's hurt. Why do you keep doing this? Showing up and standing between me and the bad guys?"

He would have expected gratitude, but all he saw in her eyes was anger. "And what if I hadn't been here? What if I hadn't come this time? Where would you be? Could you have fought that guy?"

"I don't want anyone else to get hurt because of me, but you're right, Will. I can't do this alone."

The security guard escorted Will and Sylvie to a room where a nurse saw to Will's injuries—a bruised rib, she determined—and the security officer, a retired police officer out of Sitka, questioned them. Sylvie explained that the Alaska State Troopers were investigating, and would need to be informed of the latest incident. At least the woman had documented what happened for them.

When they were left alone in the sparse and economical office, Will watched Sylvie stare out the window and hug herself. Her hazel eyes had lost their shimmer. That cut him to the bone.

"Did you recognize that guy?" he asked.

"No. Like I told the police, and you and Chief Winters, the guy in the hospital, he was the diver who came at me. I only saw his eyes behind his mask, but I could never forget them. But this guy, nope. If I had recognized him, I would have gone for help immediately once I saw him."

"So Diverman was at the hospital, and maybe this guy was Rifleman, the man who was on the island and shot at you and my plane. We need to see if the police will put you in a safe house until they resolve this."

She gave a scoffing laugh. "Which police, Will? The jurisdiction is all over the place. Besides, I think this originated outside Alaska, and I'm heading back to Seattle. I can talk to someone there."

"I've always had the feeling you knew more than you were saying, Sylvie. Now would be a good time to tell me what you do know. Tell me everything."

Sylvie flinched but didn't answer. She liked to think before she responded. He'd give her a few moments. Ignoring the pain in his ribs, Will shoved to his feet and approached. From behind her, he watched out the window, as well. Everything looked so gray and hopeless. He fought the urge to wrap his arms around her, hold her, chase the darkness away. He wouldn't get the answers he wanted, couldn't hang around long enough to protect her, if he scared her away by trying to force her to comply. Force her to answer.

Will couldn't help himself and lifted his hand. Indecision kept it hovering above her shoulder, then finally, he let it drop on the soft threads of her navy fleece hoodie. She tensed then relaxed. He thought she might even lean into him as she'd done on the deck when he'd first revealed himself.

She exhaled and slowly turned. Facing him, she was much too close. He let his gaze take in the face he had once thought not quite pretty, but he'd changed his mind so quickly. Once he got to know her and saw her inner strength—that light shining from within that poured from her eyes and her smile—she became the most beautiful woman he'd ever seen.

He'd let his hand drop from her shoulder, but now both hands rubbed her arms. More reassurance? He wasn't sure, but his hands had a mind of their own, and he let them. He was rewarded when he coaxed the smallest of smiles into her drawn face.

"I'll tell you everything I know, Will. I'm sorry. I should have trusted you completely. It seemed too private, too personal, and I wasn't sure about any of it. Wasn't sure I wanted to share my family secrets. But now I know what I want to do, and where I want to go."

"I'm listening."

"I want to go home. To my mother's home where she lived with Damon, my stepfather. The house where I grew up. In my last conversation with her, she was running scared. She called to warn me to *watch my back*, and said she would tell me more when she got to Mountain Cove. Then she told me that she loved me. Something in her tone made it sound like she was telling me in case she never got the chance to say it again."

"Do you have any idea who might have scared her that badly?" Will asked gently.

"My stepfather. Damon cheated on my mother," she replied. "A lot. I don't understand why she didn't just leave, but he had power over her to keep her. I think she was scared of him, too. She brought up his name in her voice mail but didn't finish what she was going to say. Regardless, it seems she finally freed herself or got the courage to leave. But that's why she went to Mountain Cove. He would never think to follow her there in a million years. And she would never go there except to get away from him."

Sylvie pressed her face into her hands.

Will gave her time to compose herself.

She dropped her hands and moved to sit in the chair. "As soon as I heard that she had died in a plane crash, I listened to her message again. Then I heard it for what it was. She was running scared. Tried to warn me. I knew I had to find that plane so that I could know if someone had murdered her."

"Then men showed up to silence you."

"And I knew then. I mean, you and I were running scared and it took me some time to come to grips with it, but deep down, I knew."

"How did you find out about the plane crash, her death, if your mother was able to keep her whereabouts a secret from your stepfather? Who knew she'd gotten on that plane? Even I didn't know. She was the surprise package. My mother made her living delivering unscheduled passengers and surprises to the bush."

Sylvie stared at him, unblinking. "Damon, my stepfather. He called to tell me the news. He knew where she was, after all." She contemplated the words. "Will…he's a powerful man. He could afford to pay someone to sabotage the plane. He could afford to send people after me."

"But you don't want to believe it."

"No, even after everything, I don't want to believe

it. And that's why I have to go home. I need to find the truth. She had to have left something. Maybe I can prove that Damon wasn't involved."

"Let me get this straight. You're saying you suspect your stepfather could have something to do with the plane crash. That he killed your mother and now you want to go see him. You want to go right into the lion's den?" Will couldn't help his incredulous tone. "Sylvie, why haven't you told this to the police, if you suspect the man?"

"I have nothing concrete. I don't want it to be true. I don't want all the ugliness that happened between them to have resulted in her murder. I want to prove my suspicions wrong. But I think I could find some answers if I look through Mom's things. After the memorial service I couldn't face going through them as if she was gone, never to return. I think that's another reason why I wanted to find the plane first—because that was the only thing that could make it real."

He understood that all too well, and it was what had thrown their lives together. "I don't think you should go see him."

"I'm not going to see him. He won't even be there."

"I don't understand why you didn't share this information. If he's guilty, the police could have resolved this by now."

She shook her head. "No, he's powerful. They wouldn't investigate him without a reason."

Who was this man? What did he do for a living? What was Will missing here? Questions stumbled around in the back of Will's mind, but he wouldn't interrupt.

"He loved my mother in his own way, but like I told you he cheated on her." She glanced at Will. "Don't say anything, okay? Believe me, my mother tortured herself with the guilt over what she'd done in Mountain Cove and felt like it had all come back on her. She'd committed adultery with a married man, now it was her turn."

"I'm not judging anyone, Sylvie."

"On the surface he was good to the both of us. A wonderful father to me. There wasn't anything I wanted that he didn't give except for more time with him. But there was another side to him, which made him seem cruel and manipulative. He hid that from me as much as he could, but I still caught flashes of it—and I think my mother saw more. He knows how to be very persuasive and has kept my mother by his side even with his ongoing affairs. On the one hand I love him, and on the other I hate him for how he treated her. The betrayal. I heard the arguments down the hall, or my mother's tears after phone calls. I cried myself to sleep at night. And between my two fathers, and how they treated my mother, I never wanted to be in a relationship myself." She'd rushed the last words, as if she hadn't meant to say them. "But that's beside the point."

Will heard her loud and clear. She'd dropped that little hint to make sure he understood there could be nothing between them. Fine with him—he had his own reasons for avoiding relationships. "I don't think it's safe to go to his home even if he won't be there. He sounds like a dangerous man."

"You don't understand. He doted on me. Made me feel like a little princess. That's why I'm so torn. I can't imagine that he would ever harm me. In fact, he taught me to be strong and independent, and to find my own way, which is exactly what I did. I pursued a career in the thing I loved most—scuba diving. So I can't—I won't—point the finger at him if I don't have to. I need to find proof that he isn't involved. In finding that truth, I'll find out what happened to my mother. Who killed her and who is trying to kill me."

"And you can't think of anyone else who would want to harm your mother?" Or his. Will didn't put much stock in someone trying to kill his mother when all the focus seemed to be on Sylvie and her almost discovering the plane.

"I wish… I wish I could. Can you imagine if I accused him to the police, what that would do to him if it wasn't true? And that's if I could even get the police to take the idea seriously. No, I need to find out for myself." Sylvie dropped her face into her hands. "I've never been in so much pain."

He didn't like seeing her hurting. Nor did he like her plan. Sylvie could be right that the evidence they'd find would exonerate her stepfather. Or she could be so completely blinded by her need for a loving father figure—considering she had two fails on that point—that she wasn't willing to face the truth.

He couldn't stop himself this time and reached for her, tugged her close and wrapped his arms around her. He was surprised she came into them so quickly and molded against him willingly. It felt right. He wanted to hold her for the sake of holding her, in spite of their mutual determination to avoid relationships.

"You need to realize that your safety is more important than finding out the truth."

Sylvie was becoming more important to him personally than anything else.

And that thought scared him to death. That truth was more dangerous than anything he'd faced so far. But he had the feeling that she'd started something that would never stop, even if she quit searching. It wouldn't end well for Sylvie, for either of them, unless they uncovered the truth and exposed the killers.

God, please don't let it be her stepfather. That would crush her. But what other possibilities were there? He'd see this through with her until it was over. Then, in order to protect his heart, in order to survive, Will Pierson would say goodbye to Sylvie.

It was all about survival of the fittest.

TWELVE

The ferry to Washington had been the longest three days of her life, and though Will had tried to convince her to get off in Ketchikan where he could get them a seaplane ride into Washington and shorten their trip, she had refused. So they slept under the solarium in the deck chairs with the rest of the ferry crowd who hadn't brought tents or rented cabins.

She'd never met anyone like him. Somehow through all this she had to keep her distance emotionally. And given that she'd just spent almost three days with him putting aside thoughts of the danger chasing them, and instead enjoying the sites of southeast Alaska—even getting a chance to watch the whales—like it was some sort of vacation, keeping her distance emotionally was becoming harder every day. Still, she wouldn't have had it any other way. He'd kept her company and he'd kept her alive.

So far.

But it would all come to an end soon.

She and Will expected her pursuers to be watching and awaiting their arrival in Washington.

Once the ferry docked at the terminal in Bellingham,

Will rented a car for them at the Avis counter while she hung back against the wall, watching the crowd for any familiar faces. Her car was still parked at the marina from which she'd taken her boat up through the Inside Passage on her own. Had it really been more than a week ago? Will insisted she leave her car sitting and let him do the renting so they wouldn't leave any unnecessary trails, credit card or otherwise.

When he finished at the counter he had a big dimpled grin when he found her, and then he led her out the door and to the parking lot of rental cars. They passed by every one of the midsized sedans. Practical and economical. Then stopped at a cherry-red Chevrolet Camaro SS.

"Seriously, Will?"

"This has a V8. We need something with a powerful engine. I don't want to be stuck in a Prius if I need to lose someone. Besides, they were all out of BMWs." He opened the door for her, his smile fading as his gaze took in the parking lot and others climbing into the more practical midsized cars. She scanned the crowd, as well, and saw no sign of the man who'd attacked her at the hospital or the one from the ferry.

So far, so good.

When he looked down at her sitting in the sports car, the grin came back again as he shut the door. He dropped into the seat on the driver's side.

"Are you sure this isn't just your way of living out some unrealized juvenile dream?" She hoped he caught her teasing tone.

"I live my dream every time I climb into a bush plane." He started the ignition and paused to listen to the engine purr. "But if I can't fly, this will do in a pinch."

Looking out the window, watching for their pursuers, Sylvie smiled as Will steered them from the parking lot. This guy might be a lot of fun in a world where she wasn't being pursued by killers. But Sylvie shoved those thoughts out of her mind.

They stopped at a strip mall where she and Will bought a few additional items of clothing and grabbed some lunch. Better to buy new clothes and avoid going back to her apartment where dangerous men could be waiting to kill her, until this was over.

She had one destination in mind, and that was her stepfather's mansion, where she'd grown up. The last place her mother had been before her tragic death. Although the killers had found Sylvie in the waters of the channel, in Snake's cabin, in the hospital and on the ferry, she could hope they wouldn't follow her to her stepfather's home. If the worst-case scenario was true, and he was involved, he would never allow anything to happen at the refurbished historical mansion he'd purchased for her mother as a wedding gift.

A morbid way of believing she would be safe there. All things considered, though, it was as safe a place as any.

At least he wouldn't be there this week, and Sylvie could search Mom's things without having to face him. He was the head of an international corporation and traveled often, and Sylvie knew he was in Asia for a month. He hated the house, and she figured he would move out and into another monstrosity as soon as was socially acceptable given the loss of his wife. With all the doubt and suspicion coursing through her, she didn't think she could look him in the eyes. If she saw him now, in her current frame of mind, she might accuse him to his face just to see his reaction. But he could be convincing,

even if he was guilty, which meant she had to find solid
evidence—something only she could get her hands on.

Would she be strong enough to see through him if it
came to that?

God, please don't let him be involved in her death…

She didn't think anything could hurt worse than his
betrayal of their loving, happy family, but a murder
would certainly slice her heart in two.

Her thoughts were jumbled as each passing mile put
her closer to home. She thought about what she would
say to the housekeeping staff when she arrived. Though
the house had been Sylvie's home, too—her bedroom
was still the same and she was always welcome—she
wouldn't give her usual courtesy call to let the staff
know, to give them or her stepfather any prior warning,
in case there was anything to hide.

How she hated these ludicrous, suspicious thoughts.

She'd forgotten about getting in touch with Ashley, Damon's assistant, but that could wait until she'd
searched the house.

The home was located southeast of Bellingham, toward the national forests. Damon had preferred his home
near a seaport or an airport, but agreed to move inland to
the mansion sitting on the side of a mountain for Regina.
Sylvie directed Will, who was clearly enjoying driving
the Camaro. If she tried, she could almost imagine they
were out for an afternoon joyride to take in the scenery
of thick forests. They had been on the road for almost
an hour when they hit Marblemount.

"Better stop and get gas here. Not many stops after
this. We can grab some snacks, too."

Will filled the tank while Sylvie grabbed sodas and
junk food. She exited the gas station and let herself ad-

mire Will as he topped off the gas. She had to admit he looked good standing next to that car. But then she caught the expression on his face.

Something was wrong.

The realization made her trip up as she approached. "What's the matter?"

"Someone's following us," he stated grimly.

"What?" She started to turn—

"Don't look." He leaned in as if he would kiss her, obviously trying to make it look as though they hadn't noticed their tail.

Her breath hitched at his nearness, at how much she wanted him to kiss her. She stepped back and handed off his snacks, gathering her composure. That had been a close call. He was a huge distraction in her efforts to figure this out. Sylvie tried to look nonchalantly across the street as she made her way around the car and climbed in. Once inside she flipped the visor down to look through the mirror but couldn't see anything.

Will pulled out of the gas station and continued onto the state highway.

"Don't turn around, Sylvie. Don't give us away. Let them think we don't know they're back there."

"How long have you known?"

"I've had my suspicions from the start, but the gas station stop more than persuaded me."

She sank down in the seat. "I don't want to lead them to the house and cause problems for my stepfather or anyone there."

"On the contrary, maybe they're letting your step-father know that you're on the way and to be prepared for you. Don't let your guard down around that man or anyone who works for him. I know you want to believe he's innocent, but at the same time you've more than convinced me he's not."

"He's not even there. But I hear what you're saying. Let's lose the tail anyway."

"Tell me about the road ahead. What am I going to see?"

"A lot of twists and turns as we climb into the mountains. Motorcycle enthusiasts love this road."

Will blew out a breath and grinned. "I think I'm going to love it, too."

"Don't get us killed, Will."

"I'm not going to get us killed. I'm trying to keep you alive. Don't you trust me by now?"

Her throat tightened. That was a loaded question. "You haven't let me down yet."

"They're closing the gap. Before we lose them, can you see their faces? See who it is? Is it Diverman and Rifleman?"

She flipped the visor again. "I can't tell."

"All right, then. Hang on."

Sylvie pressed back into the seat as Will floored the accelerator. "If I punch it enough, I should be able to lose them around this next curve. Turn off on a side road or drive."

They whipped around the mountain curve, and Sylvie got a better look of the rocky ravine below than she wanted. She squeezed her eyes shut, willing the centrifugal force to release her. Will turned off onto a private drive and followed it up.

"I saw them drive by. We'll wait here and see if they backtrack." He found a place to turn the car around and waited.

"Do you think we lost them?"

"I have a feeling they already know where we're going so it probably doesn't matter."

Sylvie didn't like his answer, but she didn't know what else to say. She sat back and waited with Will. Finally, he shifted into gear and eased out of their hiding spot back onto the road. They didn't see the vehicle that had tailed them.

She let him enjoy the twists and turns, squeezed her eyes shut when the road hedged the river gorge. A few miles more and they came to the gated drive to Damon's house, and Sylvie punched in the code to open the gates. "We're going to wait on the other side and make sure nobody comes inside the grounds after us, okay?"

"Works for me." Will drove through and waited for the gate to close behind him.

The men that had followed them earlier drove by slowly on the road. The two men peered out at them but acted casually, as if they were out for a Sunday drive.

"At least it's not Diverman and Rifleman."

Will frowned. "No, it's two more people we need to watch out for. Told you they already knew where we were headed. They look like Feds to me."

"How do you know?"

"I've delivered a few Feds to parts unknown now and then."

Sylvie blew out a breath. She couldn't worry about more men following her now—especially if they might just be law enforcement. She had a bigger problem to face head-on and up ahead. Going through Mom's things in search of incriminating evidence against Damon or proof of his innocence was not going to be easy.

A sour taste rose in her mouth.

Sylvie wasn't sure what she hoped to unearth but anything at all that would give her a clue, a look into what happened, was worth this trip. She remained quiet while Will maneuvered the curves of the two-mile paved and winding driveway to the mansion. She thought about Will's warning that she was taking them into the lion's den, right into the mouth of the lion.

The mansion loomed ahead, resting on the side of a mountain and overlooking the river. To the right was a great steel-enforced deck and helipad. The house was all brick and stone stacked in horizontal and vertical planes and overhangs. Sylvie waited for Will's reaction.

"It looks like something from an Alfred Hitchcock movie." Will chuckled. "I'm sorry if that didn't come out right. I think it's magnificent."

"I think the architect was a Frank Lloyd Wright student. As for Alfred Hitchcock, you're thinking of that movie *North by Northwest*. This is similar to that, yes. Though it's modern-looking, futuristic in some ways, it's a decades-old historical mansion that's been refurbished."

"I had pictured something else altogether." Will shifted in his seat. "You never actually said who your stepfather is. I have the feeling he's someone important."

"Damon Masters is the CEO of Masters Marine Corporation. The great-grandson of the founder."

"Um…wow. Just. Wow. Regina did well for herself when she married."

Sylvie frowned at the comment, but didn't say anything. She knew Will hadn't meant any harm.

"So what exactly does the corporation do? Obviously it has to do with the ocean and seafaring vessels, and I sound like a real idiot."

"It's a marine solutions company. Transportation. Logistics. International and domestic. A holding company for other marine businesses, as well. And don't ask me more than that because then I'll sound like an idiot. Not saying you did, but then you'll find out how little I really know."

Sylvie's mother had started out as her stepfather's assistant, then eventually married him. Sylvie had wanted no part of the business in that capacity. Sitting in an office all day turned her into a puddle.

Had Will sunk down into his seat?

"And you're the princess." He'd said it matter-of-factly, as though there was no question in his mind.

She bristled at his words but was unsure how to respond. After all, there was truth in them and she'd said as much herself. And that left her torn. Yes, her childhood had been privileged. But that wasn't always a good thing. Money could cover up a lot of ugliness, but it didn't make the pain go away. How could this beautiful old mansion, refurbished and loved, shelter a family that had loved and hated and perhaps even killed? Just what secrets did it harbor?

He slowed the Camaro and parked in the circular drive. The helicopter was parked on the helipad, which overhung a steep cleft in the mountain and had drawn his attention. He shut off the ignition.

"Look at me."

He slowly turned, an entirely unfamiliar expression on his face.

"Don't be intimidated."

He stiffened. "Who said I was?"

"That's why I never tell anyone who my stepfather is."

"Why aren't you involved in his business?"

She'd already told him she was a diving instructor, but

not the details of how and why she ended up getting that job. "The Masters Diving School is one of the subsidiaries. I guess the name gave that away." She shrugged and studied the immaculate grounds. "I guess my biological father's blood runs through me. I'm more interested in getting my hands dirty. Doing hands-on work, like he did with the avalanche center, and as a search and rescue volunteer. I love diving, and teaching others. Volunteering on the search and rescue dives. The rest of it, the business side of a large international corporation, just isn't for me."

Will scraped a hand over his face and around his neck.

"It's okay," she said. "You're going to be fine. Other than the staff, no one is even here. So what are you worried about?"

"This brings everything to a whole new level, Sylvie. Why didn't you tell me?"

"I mentioned he's a powerful man. That he could afford to pay someone to sabotage the plane and send people after me. You didn't believe me?" She watched him. "Don't tell me you're backing out already."

"No. Never. I'm in this until it's over. If I had known it could have helped me to prepare myself. We're in over our heads. What if this is more than murder or a crime of passion that someone wants to keep hidden? Maybe it's corporate espionage stuff. If so, this case is something more for the FBI than local law enforcement, don't you think?"

"Not yet. No, I don't think. I was in Alaska when someone tried to kill me. That doesn't link anything back to my stepfather's corporation." Per se. Could her mother have found something out that was bigger than

Sylvie had imagined? Something that could have huge repercussions for her stepfather's company? Two men who Will thought were Feds had followed them.

"And yet you're here, at the house, believing you'll find answers to where it all started."

Sylvie couldn't argue with that. She rubbed her eyes then blinked over at Will. "I brought my bodyguard with me."

She'd hoped to elicit a smile, but Will had anything but a smile on his face.

"Men have tried to kill you. This isn't a game."

"I know that. Just… I know that. Consider this a covert operation. Nobody has to even know what I'm looking for. We pretend we're here for a quick getaway…" How else would she explain Will's presence?

She saw the same question in his eyes.

"We'll get in and get out quickly." She hadn't wanted Marguerite, who oversaw the housekeeping and meals, to make a big fuss over her. Though her stepfather's meager security detail would know of her arrival as soon as she'd entered through the gate, she'd try to keep this as low-key as possible.

She opened the door to exit the car, but leaned closer to Will. "We can't sit here all day."

Sylvie climbed out of the car, quietly shut the door then waited for Will. Together they marched up the steps. She feared he might turn around and hightail it back to the car, but she resisted the urge to grab his hand and drag him forward with her. He'd wanted to act as her bodyguard, after all.

Before she reached the massive front door, it swung open and a familiar form stepped into view.

Damon Masters, Sylvie's stepfather.

THIRTEEN

Will grabbed the hand Damon Masters offered after Sylvie performed the introductions. The grip strong and sure, the man measuring Will, just as Will measured him. In his midfifties, Masters exuded the power that one would expect from someone who ran an international corporation. He was also a handsome sort, looking like the type of man that could have any woman he wanted—if not with money and power, then with looks. His dark eyes continued to study Will as he greeted them in a friendly manner. But suspicion and questions lurked behind his gaze aimed at Will.

On the other hand, the man was clearly pleased to see Sylvie. "I didn't realize you'd be here." Her tenuous smile could give them away.

Masters chuckled. "You sound like you're not happy that I'm here."

"Just surprised, that's all. I thought you were supposed to be in Asia."

His eyebrows edged together. "I had to come back for some unexpected business. But there's always a silver lining, isn't there? And you're it. I'm grateful for the serendipitous meeting. Two ships passing in the night.

Unfortunately, I'm tied up with a conference call this evening and then leaving quickly after that, but I'd love to spend a few minutes with you." Behind Masters, a woman entered and smiled at Sylvie, stepping over to give her a hug.

Sylvie's face brightened. "Ashley, it's good to see you."

The young woman, in her early thirties, if that, was stunning. "And you, as well. I just arrived an hour ago, myself. Damon and I needed to prepare for a meeting."

"Would you please have Marguerite bring refreshments?" Masters said.

Ashley's face clouded but she recovered with a quick smile, then disappeared around a corner. Following her with his eyes, Will caught sight of the walls of windows displaying a breathtaking mountainous view.

Will had never seen anything like it, except, well, from his bird's-eye view in the sky when he flew. Sylvie dragged Will through the house after her stepfather, leaning in to whisper, "Ashley's Damon's assistant. She was close to my mother. I can talk to her while she's here."

"There's no need for refreshments," she said next, turning her attention to Masters. "Don't treat me like a guest." Sylvie moved away from Will and stepped down into a sunken, spacious living area with sleek sofas and chairs. She trailed her finger over the spines of books lining the wall.

"I see you so rarely."

"I still have a room here."

Now what? Would Masters block her efforts to go through her mother's things? Or would Sylvie's life be in more danger now? Will wanted to be prepared for anything, but he was pretty sure he wasn't. After everything she'd told him about her stepfather, he'd not been prepared for the man he saw now, nor Sylvie's reaction to him.

"Of course you're not a guest, but your friend is. And either way, I'd like a few minutes with you before I have to leave."

The man headed to the wet bar and poured himself a glass of amber liquid. He glanced over his shoulder. "Something for you, Mr. Pierson?"

"No, thanks."

A woman who Will guessed to be Marguerite entered, holding a tray with two pitchers and fancy snacks that would pass for hors d'oeuvres. "It's a while until dinner, Sylvie. I hadn't expected guests, but I'll be sure to cook something nice for you and your friend."

"Thanks, Marguerite. This will do for now." Sylvie took the glass of lemonade the woman had poured.

She glanced at Will over the rim of her glass as she drank, determination, and not just a little fear, in her eyes. What was she planning? Will preferred the iced tea and drank up, not realizing how thirsty he'd been.

When Marguerite left the room, Masters turned to face them, swirling the liquid in his glass. "Why are you here, Sylvie?"

She set the glass on the tray. "I want to finally go through Mom's things."

"I'm afraid you're too late. I've had Ashley box them up and put them in storage."

Will imagined he felt Sylvie's pain. The man had sounded so cold with his pronouncement. Why hadn't he gone through her things himself? Treasuring each item, remembering his wife with each touch? And for that matter, what was the rush? The plane crash had been only two months before. Something definitely seemed off here. Except Will had yet to do that with his mother's things. He'd left everything in her home just as it was. He'd needed closure first. Needed to find the plane. Find his mother.

"How could you? You knew I wanted to go through them."

"It's been two months."

"Where are the boxes, then?"

"What's really going on, Sylvie? You can't expect me to believe you brought a stranger here to go through your mother's belongings with you." He eyed the two of them.

Will bristled.

"I think someone murdered her. I want to look through her stuff to see if I can find any clues to find who might have wanted to hurt her."

Will set his glass on the tray and moved to stand by Sylvie. Apparently, she wasn't all that great at the covert operations she'd mentioned. No matter, he'd stand by her regardless.

Masters set his glass down, too, his gaze slowly darkening. Then, in an instant, concern replaced anger. He moved to Sylvie and took one of her hands in both of his. "You're still grieving, Sylvie. Of course you are. It's only been a couple of months. I'm struggling to accept her death, as well. Please, sit down."

Sylvie surprised Will by doing as her stepfather instructed. Did the man still have so much sway over her?

When Masters sat next to Sylvie on the sofa, Will felt like the proverbial awkward third wheel and might have left the room, leaving them to have their private conversation. Except Will believed Sylvie was in danger, even from her stepfather. Especially from her stepfather. It was easy enough for him to be wary of the man, but he understood how torn Sylvie must be.

"I can arrange for you to see a therapist," Masters said. "The best in the country. I'm so sorry I didn't realize how hard this has been on you. But I know you. You keep it all inside. You wouldn't have shared it with me before this moment, even if there'd been an opportunity."

"I've been afraid that you were involved."

Masters flinched as though he'd been slapped.

Will wondered if he should intervene, but had no clue how to do it. Better to let things play out. He wished he had a weapon with him, if Sylvie's stepfather was the threat she believed.

The man glanced at Will. "Could you give us some privacy, Mr. Pierson?"

Um…no. "I need to stay."

Masters gave a slight nod, letting Will know he wouldn't be underestimated. Then Masters turned his attention back to Sylvie, as if she were a stepdaughter he clearly loved as his own. "That's ridiculous. Shocking. I'm not sure how to respond, except I wish I could cancel my meeting and stay here with you. Of course… *of course* I didn't kill Regina. How could you think it for one second? She was my wife and yes, we argued, had our problems, but I loved her. I could never murder anyone, especially my wife. Someone I loved. She died in a plane crash, Sylvie. It's tragic, but it happens to people every day. There was no murder. What has gotten into you?"

The man sounded sincere. But didn't crimes of passion—murder of a spouse—make up for a big percentage of the world's murders every year? Even if he truly had loved his wife, that didn't mean he hadn't killed her.

"I have enough problems with everything going on at…" Masters didn't finish. Instead, he inched away from Sylvie and leaned against the sofa back. With a haggard expression Will imagined not many had seen the powerful man show, he swiped his hands down his face and stared at the carpet.

Tears slid down Sylvie's cheeks. Will wanted to be the one sitting there next to her so he could comfort her. Was she being manipulated and influenced by Masters? Was he putting on an act?

"Your mother wasn't murdered, Sylvie. I'm going to call someone who can help you realize that." Masters stood and reached for his cell.

What was happening here? Their plans were crumbling before Will's eyes. Did he even have a clue what he'd walked into with Sylvie? He took a step forward, dark thoughts pushing him into dangerous territory. Did her stepfather have the power to whisk Sylvie away and have her institutionalized? He'd heard stories about how people were locked up by their families and never got out.

Sylvie grabbed the cell away from him. "You're not listening. Someone's trying to kill me."

Masters glanced at Will for confirmation. He was in it now. No going back. He nodded. "It's true. She didn't dream this up. I intervened when I saw someone attacking her. One of my friends was killed in the crossfire." Will left out that Sylvie had been shot, too. He'd let Sylvie tell the man if she wanted him to know.

"Then you need protection." Frowning at Will, Masters took his cell back. "Real protection."

Cell to his ear, he spoke to Sylvie. "And the police should be involved."

"They already are," she said. "The Alaskan State Troopers are handling the case."

"You'll need a bodyguard. I'll hire an investigator if the police can't get to the bottom of this." He turned his back on them to speak into his cell.

Sylvie stood and rushed to Will. Things were taking a completely different turn than they'd expected. By the expression on Sylvie's face, she didn't like it, either.

"What's happening?" Will whispered. The question was stupid, but he didn't know how to react. Was this a good thing or a bad thing? Did she believe her stepfather was innocent now?

Sylvie leaned in as though she would give Will a peck on the cheek and whispered, "Just go with it, Will."

Masters ended his call and turned his attention to them. "I've got people on it. Stay at the house, Sylvie. There's no reason for you to leave until your life is no longer at risk. You're more than welcome to stay as well, Mr. Pierson, though I imagine you have a job you need to return to."

Will grinned. He was self-employed, which meant he had to work harder, but it also meant that he decided when he worked. And right now he wouldn't let Masters get rid of him so easily. "I'm with Sylvie until I know she's safe."

The man ignored Will and gave Sylvie a hug, then grabbed her shoulders and looked her in the eyes. "I don't want you hurt, do you hear me? I need you to promise you won't leave the house until I've resolved this."

"I have a job, too."

"In a roundabout way, you work for me, remember?"

"I don't want you to intervene. I don't want your favors there. Officially, I'm on vacation right now. This will be over before I have to go back."

"You'll stay?"

"Yes, I'll stay."

"Good. I'll take care of things. I know you don't like to hear that. You've always been so independent, but we're talking about your life." He stepped back, tucked his chin. "Please tell me that you don't think I murdered your mother. That you don't think I would try to kill you."

The man appeared genuinely crestfallen.

"I know you didn't. You're right. I've been upset about her death. I've not been thinking clearly these past couple of months. And now I'm scared for my life." Sylvie pressed her hand over her mouth a moment then dropped it. "Thank you for your help."

"I hope you'll never hesitate to come to me in the future. And… Sylvie—" he stood taller, like a man who'd taken control back "—don't bother looking for your mother's things. That would only upset you more. Fortunately, they've been packed away and I doubt you could easily find them. Don't bother enlisting Marguerite's help. I'm leaving her with strict instructions about that. I suggest waiting until you feel better. I'll make them available to you then. Please, try to get some rest while you're here." His gaze found Will. "I'm trusting you to keep her occupied if you stay. There's plenty to do here. A heated pool. Trails to hike. Just stay close to the house and take the bodyguard even if you're staying on the grounds. I've already made the arrangements. Protection is on the way."

He headed for the door then turned back to them.

"If I didn't have this mess on my hands, I'd stay here with you."

"What mess?" Sylvie asked.

"I'll explain everything when it's over. There's too much at stake and I have to go. I'll be back as soon as I can."

And with that, the man was gone, leaving Will alone with Sylvie, his head spinning with the power the man wielded. Too much at stake. Something bigger than Sylvie's life? "Why did you agree to stay?"

She shook her head. "I don't know. What was I supposed to do?"

"You manipulated him."

"Same as he worked me. If he thinks I'm tucked away safely here and that I believe he's innocent, then we'll have more opportunity to search for my mother's things."

"What do you believe, Sylvie? Is he involved or not? He could be trying to hold us prisoner here while he cleans up this mess. For all we know, we're part of the mess he wants to clean up, and that's why he's pushing for us to stay where he can get to us."

"You could be right. Or we could wait here where we'll be protected by the bodyguard he called and a private investigator searches for the truth for us."

"You're talking weeks. Months. And that's only if we actually trust the investigator and bodyguard to do their jobs."

"I'm talking tonight. We're not waiting around for anybody. We're going through my mother's things tonight, after my stepfather is gone, and then we'll get out."

In her old room she sank onto the bed. Seeing Damon had shaken her, but his preoccupation with business troubles would give her the chance she needed to search. She and Will enjoyed a quick and simple pasta meal Marguerite had prepared, eating alone while her stepfather and Ashley took their conference call and then prepared to leave. This was a lot of work for after-hours. But with an international corporation, it was always business hours somewhere in the world.

Although there wasn't anyone to watch her, she made a show of unpacking and then putting away the few items she'd brought, as though she had every intention of staying in her old room like she'd told her stepfather. Like she was a little girl again—a princess—as Will had put it.

Sylvie wasn't a princess. She was a woman on a mission who'd dragged an unintentional hero along with her. In keeping with their ruse, Will was in one of the guest rooms at the far end of the hallway. Not too far. And yet, entirely too close.

Part of her wished she hadn't needed his presence to chase away her fears. Regardless, they were both in it deep now, if they hadn't been before. There wasn't a moment to lose or any time to let her guard down, especially now that she'd revealed so much to Damon.

With his reaction, he'd made her doubt every conclusion she'd reached. When she'd seen him in the doorway, she hadn't known what to do or expect. Had no idea why she'd blurted out the truth, but she'd desperately wanted to know if he was involved, had been willing to risk hers and Will's lives to know the truth about the man who had raised her.

A chill ran over her.

She hadn't liked what she'd seen behind his gaze. He was hiding something. Something was terribly wrong but Sylvie couldn't tell if it was related to company woes, as he'd mentioned, or her accusations. But Ashley, his assistant and her mother's friend, was here, too. Despite the fact Sylvie hadn't wanted to see Damon, she'd been glad to see Ashley. If only she would get the chance to speak to her privately before she left.

The thrum of a helicopter drew Sylvie to the window. Darkness had taken hold, but lights kept the helipad well lit. Ashley at his side, Damon hurried toward the helicopter that would deliver them to their meeting. But then they paused, appearing deep in conversation.

There was a soft knock on the door. Probably Marguerite, coming to ask if she needed anything more before retiring to her own room. Sylvie had grown accustomed to living on her own. No maids or staff hovering, watching her every move. It had been surprisingly easy to get used to. Sylvie craved freedom and privacy. She swung the door open. Will stood on the other side.

"Sylvie—"

She yanked him into the room and closed the door. "Keep your voice down."

"Why all the cloak and dagger?"

"Because I'm supposed to be in bed already. I'm tired, remember? You, too."

"You told me you'd come get me in a few minutes. It's been half an hour. I got worried."

"Honestly, I needed a few minutes to myself. Being here is hard. Seeing him drained me."

"Since we're being honest, I've been in the hallway outside your door, standing guard. I got tired of waiting."

Watching him lean against the door now, anxiety in his eyes mixed with concern for her, warmth tingled through her belly. A feeling she couldn't ignore. A feeling she couldn't afford.

She turned her back rather than risking that he'd see her face and read the thoughts rushing through her silly-girl head. Rubbing her temples as if thinking things through, she said, "We have to get to work before the bodyguard shows up in case Damon has instructed him to spy on us or stop us. I've been waiting for the helicopter to leave with him. I don't want Marguerite to know what we're up to, either."

"What's your plan, then?" Will's voice was close behind her.

Without looking at him, she moved to the window again, watching for any sign of a vehicle arriving with a bodyguard.

"We head for the basement."

"The basement?"

"That's my first stop to find the boxes with Mom's stuff." Sylvie turned, ready to escape the room and the memories that rushed at her. "That's one of the big differences in a regular house and a Frank Lloyd Wright house. His houses had no basements or attics."

Will stood in her way, grabbed her shoulders. "I don't care about Frank what's-his-name. I care about you and this situation. I have a bad feeling about this. We're risking too much by just being here. Your stepfather was right about one thing. This can't be easy on you. It must be hard to think he could murder your mother."

"Hard enough hearing the arguments they had over the years. Knowing that he cheated on her."

Sylvie couldn't look at him anymore and rushed to the door. What he must be thinking—that her mother deserved to be cheated on, considering Sylvie was the product of an adulterous relationship. All of it serving as a reminder to Sylvie that she couldn't go through that kind of pain, loving a man and getting married. Couldn't expose herself to that kind of hurt. The reminder was good timing, helping her keep her heart distanced from the man standing just behind her, his concern for her resounding in his panicked breaths.

Placing her hand against the knob, she spoke softly, "Let's get this over with."

The sooner she discovered the truth and exposed it, the sooner she could put safe distance between her and Will Pierson.

FOURTEEN

What would a basement inside a place like this look like? Will wasn't sure he wanted to find out. Didn't want to go down in the dark and be trapped if someone tried to attack them again.

As far as Will was concerned, the longer they stayed, the greater the danger, now that Damon Masters himself knew they were here.

Trailing Sylvie down the hallway, Will fought the urge to creep around like a couple of criminals. Just like Sylvie, he wanted to find out what really happened to his mother. But since their arrival here, he was beginning to think that Sylvie was leading them on a wild goose chase. Surely Masters would have destroyed any evidence against him rather than packing it away in the basement. Still, he couldn't bring himself to tell Sylvie that. Instead, he followed her around like a puppy. Hadn't he been here before? Following Michelle around? Whoa…what was he doing, comparing the two women? He'd been in love with Michelle. He and Sylvie were trying to solve a murder together and stay alive while they were at it.

He should ask the obvious question. Should have

asked a long time ago. "Why would your stepfather leave anything incriminating in your mother's things if he thought she had something to hide and had killed her for it? I'm thinking that's the main reason he had the stuff boxed up and put away before you got to it—so he could go through it and get rid of anything problematic."

She cast him a glare. "I don't want to believe my stepfather is a murderer, and that's why I'm here to find out who is responsible. But you're right, if he is involved he would… Wait… He had Ashley do it."

"So he says."

"Look, it's the best place to start."

"But you were looking for the plane first—you thought that was the right place to start."

"I went looking for the plane so I could find out what happened. If I found it then I could let the authorities know and they could see if it looked like foul play. I was only working on the slightest suspicion. Now that I have a strong reason to believe that it wasn't an accident, I need to see her things. Make sense?" Sylvie paused and turned to face him. "Why are you asking me this now? If you didn't want to come along, you could have said so earlier. I told you I didn't need your help."

Disappointment flickered in her eyes. Will wanted to kick himself. "I'm here, aren't I? I told you I'd see this through with you. I'm just thinking out loud, is all. The basement doesn't seem like a good idea to me. What could you hope to find?"

Turning her back on him, she started down again. "I can't tell you what I'm looking for. Only that I'll know it when I see it."

At the end of the hallway, Will followed her down a spiraling wrought-iron staircase that seemed as at odds with the stark lines of the home's architecture as he was with Sylvie at the moment.

With each step drawing them closer to the basement, Will's concern for her increased. "Your stepfather told you not to look for your mother's things. It might be too upsetting. Are you sure about this, Sylvie?"

At the bottom, she turned on him. "He wouldn't be the man he is today if he wasn't skilled in the power of persuasion. He's very convincing. I've listened to him persuade my mother that he loved her and only her and would never cheat on her." Her voice cracked.

Her pain was palpable, and he wanted to take her hand and squeeze it. Reassure her. Instead, he whispered, "Sylvie…" And with that one breath he conveyed all the turmoil and emotions he felt about their situation. About Sylvie. But he didn't know how to comfort her, or if that was even something she wanted from him.

She had a smudge on her cheek and for some reason Will couldn't fathom, he reached up and pressed his thumb against the silk of her skin and wiped it away. An innocent-enough motion, but it somehow had his breaths coming faster. And sent his heart into his throat.

Sylvie inched back, wiping the moment away. "Okay, the basement is just down another flight of stairs."

Will followed her, descending a slim and dank staircase. Everything beyond the spiral staircase looked as if it belonged to a different house entirely. A different century, even. Sylvie slowed as she approached. A single bulb flickered from the ceiling. She took the last three steps to stand in front of the door and tried the knob.

"It's locked. I should have known."

"There's a chair here, too. Would he have a guard on the door to keep you out?"

"I don't know what to think."

"Well, if there was a guard here, he might be back soon. We need to hurry."

Pulling out his pocketknife, Will tried to work the lock free, but the dead bolt was obviously engaged. "Why not ask for a key?"

"You heard him. He didn't want me in her things. I can't ask for a key. All the more reason for me to look."

Sylvie's stepfather had told her to stay away, so she would do the opposite. "I'm not sure what's worse. That what you just said makes some kind of sense to me or that the door is locked and our whole reason for coming is shot."

Sylvie scraped her hands through her hair. "Being in this house drains me. I can't think straight. That's why I moved out and went to work doing what I love. But down here in the dark and dank, I feel like the walls are closing in on me."

Will could relate. "What now?"

She cocked her head. "Do you hear footsteps?" she whispered. "Someone is coming down the stairs."

"If it's the same someone who is guarding the door we can ask for a key." He grinned, but only to bring levity to the moment. He didn't like this one bit.

Someone was definitely creeping down the steps, their footfalls soft.

Panic swirled in Sylvie's eyes. "There's no place to hide."

"We're not going to hide anymore. We're going to walk up the stairs like we have every right to be here." Will would go first in case this house harbored the villains after Sylvie.

On the next corner, he came face-to-face with Marguerite, who stood two steps above him. She gasped, covered her mouth and let out a stream of words in French.

Sylvie pushed by Will and hugged Marguerite to her. "You scared us to death. Marguerite, we need to get in the basement."

"I thought I might find you down here when you didn't answer your door. You cannot be here, Sylvie. I don't have the key, and even if I did, I would be afraid to help you."

Sylvie released Marguerite, a woman she'd known almost her entire life. "Why do you say that, Marguerite? Please tell me. I need to know everything. Do you know what happened to my mother?"

The woman shook her head vehemently. She pressed a finger to her lips. "The house has ears, too many ears," she whispered.

"I'm not leaving until I get into the basement."

Marguerite's eyes grew wide. "Of course! Do you not remember you grew up in this house? Back then, you had your own secret passages."

Sylvie's face scrunched up.

"Of course I knew about them. You think I wouldn't know?"

"Thank you for reminding me." Sylvie kissed Marguerite on the cheek then looked at Will. "I used to get into the basement all the time. I had my own secret way in. Why didn't I think of that before?"

Sounded like the house really was closing in on her and choking her thoughts.

"Probably because you weren't thinking you'd need a secret passage as an adult." He was glad they hadn't faced some new threat on the stairwell. "Lead on."

"Wait." Marguerite stood in Sylvie's path. "Be careful. There have been strangers here. More than that, I cannot tell you. Make your search quick and then please leave. Promise me."

"Of course," Sylvie whispered. "I promise. And thank you, Marguerite, for your help. Now promise me you'll go back to your room. I don't want you involved."

"Don't worry about me. Unless they need something from me, I'm only the help and invisible to the strangers. Even to your stepfather."

Sylvie and Will waited until Marguerite had disappeared before they continued on. Once it was quiet again, Sylvie led him to the top of the stairwell where they ducked into a dark closet that smelled of pine-based cleaning supplies. She turned on the light and bent over. Started removing the boxes beneath a shelf.

"See? An old laundry chute. The laundry wasn't done down there anymore, even when I was a child, and this was closed off and forgotten. I'm so glad I ran into Marguerite."

If she expected Will to climb down that, she might need to think again. It would be a close fit, if he could do it at all. The thought of crawling through that tight space made him shudder. "Isn't that kind of far for a child to slide?"

Sylvie rummaged around, looking for something in old boxes. He had a hard time seeing her as the kind of child to play in a basement, given her love of the water and diving—a wide-open space she could explore. Just like the skies were for him. His only use for big bodies of water came in landing his plane.

"Found it. I can hardly believe it's still here, but I guess looking at all the rest of this junk, it makes sense."

She held up a fire escape ladder. "My mom made sure I had a ladder I could hang from my window in case of a fire."

"That's good emergency protocol."

"I found another use for the ladder."

Sylvie unfolded the ladder to its full length, let it drop down into the laundry chute, and hooked it in place. Will felt silly. But if there was no other way into the basement without that key, then...

"I'll go down first," he said.

"I don't need a hero, Will."

"Sure you do." He grinned then made sure the thing was secure.

At Sylvie's wide-eyed stare, he almost laughed. He had an innate urge to plant a kiss on her lips that had formed into a half frown, half smile. He could tell she didn't know what to make of him. "We're in this together, remember?"

Before she could argue he disappeared down the ladder, hoping a big load of trouble wasn't waiting for him at the bottom. Will climbed down as far as he could but then the ladder ended. How much farther was the drop? Sylvie said she'd done this as a child. He should be okay to let go and fall then, but it was dark down there. He had no idea what he was dropping onto or into.

He squeezed his eyes shut. *Lord, help me out here?*

"Will?" Sylvie whispered.

"Yes?"

"Are you okay? What are you doing? I need to come down, too."

"I'm working up the courage to drop into the unknown."

"The ladder doesn't go all the way?"

"No. Maybe you don't remember exactly how this worked."

"I remember that ladder went all the way. But if you want me to go first, I'll go. I told you I didn't need a hero."

"Especially if he's dead," he mumbled.

"What's that?"

"Nothing." Will let go and slowed his progress with his feet and hands as he slid the rest of the way. As he neared the bottom, he could finally see his surroundings. Someone had left a dim light on. Will didn't care why, only that it lit his way enough.

Beneath him boxes were stacked high. He could drop and hopefully stand on them, or fall and get hurt. He slowly lowered himself onto the first box. Held on to the rim of the laundry chute then grabbed on to a beam while he got his bearings, put more weight on the box. He bounced a little to get the feel of it.

Then he heard Sylvie making her way down. Oh, no. He wasn't prepared for that yet.

"Wait up," he said into the laundry chute.

Will climbed down, removed the boxes from beneath the chute and found the sturdiest-looking old chair. He stood on that to catch Sylvie. "Okay, careful coming down."

Sylvie slid down the chute rather than crawling out, which surprised him. She would land hard. Then she appeared, popping out, and Will caught her in his arms, surprising them both.

"Will!" she gasped his name.

And he laughed.

The chair collapsed beneath them.

* * *

Will kept his balance and her in his arms. "Are you okay?" she asked.

The chair lay splintered on the floor. He was entirely too close, the masculine scent of him wrapping around her and making her dizzy. Making her feel things she didn't want to feel.

"Yeah, but I think we might have woken the dead."

"We don't need to worry about them. It's the living we should worry about. The guard, if there is one, outside the door."

"Which brings me to a question I should have asked before we made this leap of faith down the laundry chute," Will replied.

Sylvie studied the mess in the basement. What looked like old IKEA furniture was piled high, along with the wooden chair Will had just broken. Her spirits sank. She couldn't imagine someone actually storing her mother's things in the basement. "So what's your question?"

"You climbed down here as a child. How did you get out? Because there's no way we are climbing back up."

"Oops. I hadn't thought of that." At Will's grimace she laughed. "We go out the door. It's locked from the outside to keep people from getting in. But it can be unlocked from the inside to prevent someone from accidentally being locked down here."

Sheer relief registered on Will's face, along with a day's worth of stubble. His beard would grow thick and fast, by the looks of it, if he didn't shave every day. Why was she thinking about that? She pulled her gaze from Will's features in the dim lighting and glanced around the basement. Where to start?

"I remember it being much brighter down here when

I used to play." Now it was dark and gloomy. Cobwebs hung in every possible place. Where were the spiders that had left all these? Still alive and well? Her skin crawled. "There's another light somewhere. You can be a hero now, Will, and find it. Knock down some of those webs, too."

Something unseen skittered away in the corner. Sylvie froze. Locked gazes with Will. Humor shimmered in his warm eyes, but understanding gleamed there also. "I don't like cold, dark spaces with spiderwebs, either, especially when other vermin can be heard vying for front-row seats."

"Very funny." She had no plans to entertain the rats.

"Why do you think I love to fly? You never see a web in the sky. Or spiders, for that matter."

"No cobwebs in the water when I go diving." But the thought reminded her of her mother's plane and what it might look like with the passing years if no one discovered it. They had to get busy.

Sylvie had never been afraid of the dark, but she couldn't shake the images of creepy creatures with any number of legs lurking in the shadowed corners. To his credit, Will grabbed a broom and scraped a few silken, dusty webs down. Since there was a small lamp on in the corner, Sylvie wondered who had been down here and why hadn't they disturbed the webs. The lamp might mean that someone had, in fact, brought her mother's things down.

Together they searched the basement, which seemed to go on forever. Someone needed to take this old rubbish to the Dumpster, and the decent furniture to the Salvation Army. Finally, she found some newer-looking plastic bins stacked among old cardboard boxes stained with rat droppings.

Her skin crawled again, and she sneezed. If Ashley had actually put all her mother's things down here… Sylvie would be furious. Sylvie switched on an over-head light and started looking at the bins, hoping they were labeled. Will searched on the fringe with a flash-light he'd found.

The way dirt and dust had been disturbed, someone else had been here recently doing something more than turning on a lamp.

"I found something," Will said.

Sylvie left the bin she was examining and made her way to him, bumping into the corner of an old desk. "What'd you find?"

He held up an old pocketknife.

The breath whooshed from her. "Can you be serious and help me?"

"You never know when one of these is going to come in handy. I lost the one I carried."

The knob jiggled; keys jingled.

Sylvie stared at Will. Panic gripped her stomach. "What do we do?"

"Just tell them what we're doing?"

"We can't do that. You heard Marguerite. There are strangers in the house. We can't trust them." Sylvie grabbed Will's hand and dragged him deeper, behind stacks of boxes. She yanked the chain, switching off the light in that part of the basement. The only light on now was the lamp near the door that had been on when they'd arrived. Backed into a dark corner, something tickled in her hair and she pushed down the scream threatening to erupt. Shoving away the webs she'd backed into and the possible spider that went with them, her skin crawled at the thought of the little creepers.

She'd give anything if she could run out of the basement screaming and shaking her hair free of creeping things. Sylvie dragged in the breaths before it was too late. In, out. In, out.

I can do this.

Spiders are just tiny animals. They don't want to hurt me.

Will wrapped his arm around her and leaned in close. His warm breath fanned her hair. What? The webs didn't bother him? Apparently not. She let his presence calm her nerves. Together they waited and watched. The door opened and heavy footsteps clomped around while larger-than-life shadows fell across the walls from the dim light of the lamp. The beam from a flashlight danced along the rafters and ceiling.

The laundry chute door hung open.

Sylvie almost gasped.

Would the man notice? Become suspicious?

Will was right. This was just plain stupid to hide like children who'd been caught. They should face this man head-on and get their answers. Sylvie would rather face him than stay in the spiderwebs. She started to move from Will's grasp, but he held her in place. She glanced at him. He pressed a finger against his lips and motioned for her to look through a space between the boxes.

From there, she could see the man—he was the one who'd pretended to be a nurse at the hospital in order to kill her. She would never forget his dark, sinister eyes. It was Diverman.

FIFTEEN

Will stiffened when Sylvie sucked in a breath. That had been much too loud. He held his breath. Stood perfectly still.

Had the man heard?

Seconds ticked by.

Carefully, Will peeked through the boxes again. The man stood stock-still. Listening. He'd heard something, all right. Will wished the rodents would make their presence known. Maybe that would distract the man.

Will wanted to rush from where they were hiding and tackle the man while he had the element of surprise. Secure him and call the police. Get the answers they needed. But he spotted the man's weapon tucked in his pants and he didn't want to put Sylvie at more risk than she already was. She'd been shot once before, and Will couldn't let that happen again.

But if Diverman decided to search, the two of them would be discovered. Jumping the man might be his only choice. He just wasn't sure how to achieve that. Will would have to wait until the man drew closer and they could push the stacks of boxes over on him. Gain the upper hand. Will couldn't risk communicating his plans to Sylvie and hoped she understood. From where he stood, he scanned the boxes, looking for the best angle. Wishing the guy would come closer and yet hoping he would simply leave.

Shining the flashlight in the corners, the man crept forward, frowning at the cobwebs, too. Will swallowed, sent up a silent prayer and prepared to storm the boxes, toppling them over.

Then someone called the man from the doorway. Was it Marguerite? She'd just saved them. The man switched off the lights, closed the door behind him, leaving them in utter darkness. Will and Sylvie expelled a collective breath.

"That was too close," she whispered.

"I was about to tackle him." His pulse still sky high from the close encounter, Will reached for Sylvie and pulled her to him. Reflex. Pure reflex.

Her heart pounded against the crush of his chest, and he held her until she calmed. Until they both did. "Diverman is here, and probably Rifleman, too. Now we know who the strangers are and that this is the worst-case scenario. We have to leave."

There could be no doubt her stepfather was involved in the attacks against them. Will couldn't imagine what that knowledge, that confirmation, did to Sylvie, who'd been hoping to prove otherwise. But what way the man was involved, Will couldn't be sure. He still couldn't fathom the man who'd been so concerned for his stepdaughter would want her dead. Send men to kill her. Was Diverman the bodyguard that he'd called?

"But I haven't gone through the boxes yet. I'm not leaving until I find something I can use to..." Her voice shook as she trailed off.

Neither of them wanted to say the words. Too harsh. Too cruel.

Sylvie felt around and found the chain and yanked the light on.

"I don't think your stepfather would have left anything of value in the boxes."

"But why did Diverman come down here, then? Maybe...maybe now that my stepfather knows I want to look in the boxes, he must have sent this man to remove them."

Will gripped her shoulders. "The man is here at this house to kill you, Sylvie. He could be back down here at any moment, as soon as he learns you are not in your room."

And Will had let her come here, into the lion's den. Like he could have stopped her.

"Don't you see?" he added, hoping she'd understand the urgency. "There's no time to search."

"You're right. Now that Diverman is here, we know something we hadn't known for certain before. But I don't get it. Why hasn't he already tried to kill me? He has to know I'm here."

"Maybe he planned his attack for tonight when you'd be sleeping. Could be he was in your room looking for you already."

Sylvie pressed her hand to her forehead. "Of course. That's it. My death needs to look like an accident, *and* needs to happen far away from the mansion. Killing me here would raise too many questions and a possible investigation that my stepfather doesn't need. But if I had died in a diving accident like I was supposed to, then that would have been the end of it. Even in the hospital, you said he tried to inject me with something first. Using his gun was his last resort."

"Come on, then. Let's get out of here." Will grabbed her hand and headed to the door.

"If I had left well enough alone, just let my mother's death and plane rest at the bottom of that channel, then this wouldn't be happening. You wouldn't be in danger, either." She sighed. "We need to call the police."

"I don't plan on hanging around long enough to make that call until we're at a safe distance."

"Agreed. Let's turn this light off so they won't know we've been down here. Maybe I'll get another chance to look sometime later."

Sylvie yanked the chain, throwing them back into complete darkness.

"I think I remember the layout of the basement," he said.

"Let me lead." Sylvie tugged him to follow. "I could find my way out of here in a blindfold."

Following Sylvie, he only stumbled once as they made their way to the door. When they got there, Will pressed his hand over Sylvie's on the dead bolt. "What if he's on the other side of the door, sitting in the chair we found?"

"He didn't strike me as the sort of guy to sit and guard a basement."

Nevertheless, Will felt along the wall for something hard—a brick. Just in case the small pocketknife wasn't enough.

"Ready?" she whispered.

"Yes."

She gently turned the dead bolt. They both stood in silence. Waiting and listening to any reaction on the other side. Will stepped in front of Sylvie and opened the door, prepared to use the brick, but no one was there.

"Come on." He led the way as they hurried up the steps with as much stealth as possible until they made it to the wrought-iron spiral staircase. This house was a veritable maze. When they made it to the main floor, Will headed for the front door, but Sylvie held him back.

"Wait," she whispered. "Where are you going?"

"Out."

"I need my purse, my wallet, bank card, and don't forget the keys from your room. We aren't going anywhere without those."

"Hurry, then." Will kept close to Sylvie as they crept up another set of steps, and felt like the eyes from the old Masters family portraits were watching. He held tight to the brick. What he wouldn't give to have a real weapon.

Together they walked by the room Will would have slept in if they were staying. He opened the door and flipped on the lights, prepared to face off with Diverman. He snatched his keys from the dresser and the small pack he'd brought and together they headed to Sylvie's room.

Reaching for the door she paused and looked at Will, caution in her gaze. Would Diverman be inside, waiting for her? If so, Will would be there to stop him this time, just as he had twice before. He urged her out of the way and shoved through the door, prepared to protect her.

Cautiously, they entered the room. When it appeared empty, Sylvie slipped by Will and went for the bed to grab her purse.

A woman stood at the window, with her back to them.

Ashley turned from the window.

"What are you doing here?" Sylvie glanced at Will.

They had believed the room empty. "I thought you left with Damon."

Come to think of it, she hadn't actually seen Ashley leave. Should Sylvie tell Ashley about Diverman? None of them were safe here. But something in the subtle shake of Will's head let her know he was advocating caution. They didn't know whom they could trust.

Not yet.

Ashley rushed to Sylvie's side, her smile tenuous. "I was supposed to go. But we both agreed that I should stay and make sure you're okay until the bodyguard arrives. And when I found your room empty I was more than worried. Where have you been?"

Her gaze leaped from Sylvie to Will as she rubbed her forefinger over the edge of an envelope she held.

"Just showing Will around the house. What's going on, Ashley?" Sylvie eyed the envelope.

Ashley hesitated, studying Will.

"It's okay. You can talk in front of him."

The woman nodded. "The company is in trouble, or else Damon…your stepfather would have stayed here with you himself. But this gave me the opportunity I needed to speak with you."

Sylvie released a sigh. "Oh, good. I had wanted to talk to you, too. But you start—what did you want to tell me?"

"Since we were friends, your stepfather had me box your mother's things away a few weeks ago. I was here working with him, along with the others, on a specific project for a weekend work retreat, if you can imagine that. He was too heartbroken to face it. You can blame me, if you want. I'm the one who persuaded him to let me. I worked on the bedroom first and those things are in boxes in the basement. I hadn't started on her office until last week, and that's when I found this letter addressed to you."

Sylvie's heart jumped. "A letter?" *Why not an email? Or a phone call?* But then her mother *had* called her before she left and given her a vague warning.

Ashley handed the envelope over. "I'm sorry I hadn't gotten it to you sooner. It has a stamp. Obviously, your mother intended to mail it. Maybe she changed her mind. I probably should have mailed it as soon as I found it, but given the circumstances I thought I should deliver it personally. And here you are."

Sylvie held the envelope, wanting to tear into it. "And you haven't opened it?"

"No. Of course not. But Sylvie, I know that she was…"

"What? Tell me."

"Scared." Ashley moved back to the window and stood against the wall, looking out as though she feared someone watched them.

"Scared of what or who? Did you tell the police?" Will asked.

"Yes. I told a detective that she was scared. Left in a hurry and then died in a plane crash."

Sylvie understood the frustration in Ashley's voice and found a measure of reassurance that she and Will weren't alone in their suspicions that there was something sinister about her mother's death. But Sylvie also knew that, in the end, the authorities did not seem to suspect foul play. They were treating the attack on Sylvie as an unrelated incident. Without a plane or bodies, nothing was being done to satisfy Sylvie regarding her and Will's mothers' deaths.

She ripped open the envelope and reached for the letter inside.

"I'm just going to wait out here in the hall," Ashley said.

"There's no need. You can stay."

"No, I think you should have privacy. I'll be right out here. Who knows, maybe that bodyguard will arrive."

She glanced at Will as she moved to the door.

"I'm staying," he said.

Nodding, she slipped outside into the hall. Will rushed to Sylvie, who turned her back to him. She wanted to read the letter alone.

"Sylvie, what are you doing? Let's take the letter with us. We can read it once we're somewhere safe."

"Somewhere safe? Where would that be?" She hated the defensiveness in her voice. "I can't wait one second longer. This could be the key to everything."

"Or the key to nothing. A ploy to keep you here."

She unfolded the letter to see that it had been neatly printed out instead of in her mother's flowing handwriting. "We're safe at the moment with Ashley here, at least until the bodyguard arrives. Diverman won't act with witnesses."

"Really? Remember what happened on the ferry?" Will paced the room.

"Nothing can happen here, at my stepfather's house, that would bring him into question." At least that's what she was counting on at the moment.

Rotor blades resounded outside, the helicopter returning to the mansion after dropping her father at the airport. She tried to push the distractions away so she could focus on her mother's letter to her. Will thrust his hand through his hair and blew out a breath. His pacing would drive her nuts, but Sylvie focused on the letter.

Sylvie,

I've tried so many times to share this with you, but I didn't know how. Despite my troubles with Damon, he's been a good father to you. I haven't wanted to destroy that relationship. But now I fear for my life and I must warn you, as well. I've written this out to mail to you instead of sending an email that could be too easily discovered, recovered on the hard drive. I've found incriminating evidence against my husband, Damon, your stepfather, on an international scale.

I have the information saved on a thumb drive and have kept it with me. It is worth millions of dollars, far more than my life to some. I don't know who I can trust, who to turn to with the information. I cannot trust the police here—Damon has too much influence for me to believe they'd seriously investigate him. I'm being followed and I need to get somewhere safe. I have a friend from Mountain Cove whom I've stayed in touch with all these years. The same friend who helped me to leave over twenty years ago—a bush pilot, Margaret Pierson. I've resented the people of Mountain Cove for too long. Have hated the place and at the same time I've longed to return. From there I'll contact the authorities. I know I'll be safe in Mountain Cove. No one would ever guess I would return there.

And once I'm done with this—once we're through with this—I could rebuild my life on my

*father's property. But in the meantime, I wanted to
warn you to keep safe. Warn you in case the worst
happened to me so that you would know.*
Love,
Mom

Sylvie pressed the letter to her heart, tears burning
her eyes as fear swirled through her mind. She didn't
know when or how, but she found herself in Will's arms.
He held her and she could have stayed in his arms forever…but she couldn't let herself be that weak. Sylvie
never wanted to be so fragile. Still, she couldn't find the
strength to step from the comfort he offered at every
turn.

Someone knocked.

"Sylvie?" Ashley's muffled voice came through the
door.

Sylvie shrugged away from Will and crossed the
room. She opened the door and let Ashley back in. "You
have to get out of here, Ashley. It's not safe. Someone
tried to kill me and he's here in the house. He was in the
basement. We have to warn Marguerite, too."

Ashley's eyes widened. "How's that possible? There
are security measures in place here. The bodyguard was
just an added layer of protection."

"Because it's Damon who hired him." Sylvie struggled to say the words. "He's part of it."

"You can't mean that, Sylvie." Ashley appeared
stricken. "I can't believe it."

"My mother says as much in her letter. And you said
she was scared. Who else would she have to fear?"

Hands trembling, Ashley held her cell at her ear. "I'll
get Jeffers up here. He's in charge of security at the

house. And we'll call the police. But your stepfather has a bodyguard on the way for you. Oh." She shook her head as realization struck. "Why would you trust a bodyguard if you think your stepfather is trying to kill you? For that matter, can we trust Jeffers?"

Ashley spoke to someone on the cell, explaining there was an intruder in the house. Then she turned her attention back to them. "I know how much he loves you, and I don't believe it's true that he'd try to hurt you. There must be some mistake. Someone else must be behind these attacks. But Sylvie, get out of the house now and call the police. I'll wait for Jeffers and we'll look at the security cameras." Ashley shooed at them. "Go on…"

"But you're not safe, either, if you stay here and work for a murderer."

"Don't worry. I've taken a position with another company. This is my last week to work for Damon, if that will ease your mind."

Will stepped close to Sylvie. "We're leaving *now*."

"Go, Sylvie. Get out of here." Ashley opened the door for them, urging them to hurry. "I'm calling the police, too."

"In her letter, my mother said she couldn't trust the police here, so neither should you."

Sylvie should let her read the letter, but she held it close.

Ashley pursed her lips. She took Sylvie's hand. "Go and be safe. I'll do what I can from here. I know you resent him for the struggle he and your mother had, but Damon is a good man. Trust your heart. He loves you. He wouldn't try to kill you."

An emotion flashed behind Ashley's eyes. What was it? Love? Hate? Was Ashley in love with Damon Masters? Was she his most recent lover? Sylvie didn't have time to ask her, or to consider it further when Will pulled her through the door.

SIXTEEN

Pulse pounding, Will led her down the hallway, watching every corner, every angle, knowing that the man after her could jump out and kill her at any moment. They bounded down the steps, and after a cautious peek through the front door into the waning light of day, Will ushered Sylvie through.

"We should have waited for Jeffers to see us out, Will." Sylvie rushed with him down the steps and to the circular drive.

Except...

"Where's the car?" Hands on his hips, Will glanced around, searching the property. "Where's the Camaro?"

Dread twisted his insides. How would he get her out of here?

"Who would have moved it?" Sylvie asked.

"I think we both know the answer to that. Diverman, of course. And he left us without an escape. Now we're trapped, unless we want to hike out on foot."

"Just relax. We can use one of Damon's cars. Let's head to the garage."

Of course. Why hadn't Will thought of that? Damon Masters would have more than a helicopter for his transportation. Will kept the sarcasm to himself. *And where was that Camaro? In the garage?*

There was no telling what—or who—else they'd find in the garage. Will fingered the knife, pulled it from his pocket. It wasn't much, but it was something.

Sylvie led him around to the side of the house with its innumerable overhangs, and wait…a waterfall? Really? Water trickled over stones, pouring from a peaceful pond, and the brook journeyed to meet the river, he assumed.

Will wasn't sure this was the answer. "Where's the garage, Sylvie? Maybe we should hike out, after all. Get to the nearest town and get help."

What he wouldn't give to have a small plane sitting on an airstrip right over there to the left of that helipad.

The helicopter!

A man—Diverman—stepped from behind a dark corner and grabbed Sylvie. She screamed. Will started to lunge but the man instantly pressed his gun at her temple. "You've caused me more trouble than this ever should have been."

"Let her go." Adrenaline pumped through Will, blurring his vision with rage.

Diverman laughed. "I don't think so. You're not slipping out of my hands this time."

"Who…who hired you?" Sylvie tried to sound strong and unafraid, but her words crackled with fear. "Damon?"

"Wouldn't you like to know?"

"You're not going to kill me. You can't kill me here."

"You're wrong about that. I *can* kill you here. Right here and now and nobody would *ever* find you. Same as they haven't found your mother. I'll make sure you join her since I have to go back there anyway, to search for that thumb drive. All because you couldn't just let her rest in peace."

Will couldn't lunge at Diverman or he would make good on his word. By the look in his eyes as they took Will in, the man was ready to kill, and he would start with Will. Get him out of the way. While he shot Will, that might be Sylvie's chance to escape, but Will needed to harm him, to maim him so she'd have a fighting chance of getting away.

He'd dropped the brick long ago, but he couldn't have thrown it and made a difference. But the knife…the knife was made for moments like these.

In an instant, the man turned the weapon on Will, who flicked the knife in a straight throw, piercing Diverman's gun hand. Screams erupted from both Sylvie and Diverman, as pain burned Will's shoulder. The man grappled for his weapon with his other hand, and Sylvie rushed to Will. He wasn't in a position to fight Diverman, who still had a gun, but at least his aim would be off, his left hand obviously unwieldy at best.

"Come on!" Will grabbed Sylvie and they sprinted away from the house and garage and across the lawn.

"Are you okay, Will? He shot you!"

"No time to worry about that now. Just a scratch."

"But the garage is back that way."

"Right, and so is Diverman. I have a better idea." Breathing hard now, he dragged her to the helipad.

"You've got to be kidding me."

Will wouldn't stop running until he made it to the helicopter. But Sylvie dug in her feet, and that brought Will to a halt. He turned. "What are you doing? We have to get out of here."

"We can't steal the helicopter. What if he needs it?"

Had she lost her mind? "We're not stealing it, we're borrowing it. It belongs to your stepfather, remember? We were already planning to take one of his cars—this isn't that much worse. Desperate times call for desperate measures."

"What about the pilot? We could ask him to fly us out?" Her shoulders drooped. "You're right. He could be involved."

"Diverman is coming, Sylvie. No time."

She didn't trust Will to fly with his injury. That was understandable. Will climbed in but noticed Sylvie hadn't followed suit. He jumped out and ran around to her side. "What are you waiting for? Let's get out of here before we miss our chance. You hate to fly. I haven't forgotten, but we have no choice." Will rubbed her shoulders. "Come on, Sylvie. You promised me you would fly again. This is the time to do it."

She squinted at him. "You sure you can fly this thing?"

"As good of a bush pilot as I am, I'm even better in a helicopter." An exaggeration, but desperate times…

Will spotted a figure in the shadows running toward them from the house. "I think our time is up. Get in."

After he made sure Sylvie was in the helicopter, Will ran around and climbed inside. Glanced at the console, taking it in quickly. He didn't have time to go through a flight checklist. It was now or never, and he'd rather take his chance that the helicopter was already prepped. At least the engine was still warm.

Once they were in the air, Will glanced down to see the man running after them, clenching his hand beneath his arm, and firing his weapon off—way off. Will could almost smile at that, but he needed to focus on getting them out of range. He didn't want to risk a random bullet catching them. He and Sylvie had theorized that her death was supposed to look like an accident, especially if it were to happen at her stepfather's house. So much for theories. Diverman had become desperate to fulfill his deadly contract or else.

Will had been through this twice now—someone shooting at him while he was airborne. Shooting at Sylvie, rather, and that was two times too many. He was ready to resolve this, but how? Where to go next?

"Are you okay? He shot you."

"The bullet grazed me, that's all."

"I'm sorry that I hesitated. I know that could have cost our lives. It's just that… I never told you why I hate to fly. You never asked. You probably assumed it was just a phobia, but there's more to it."

"I'm listening."

"I attended a private school in Seattle, growing up. Living secluded as we were here, that meant a daily ride in the helicopter to and from school. That drew too much attention to me. Even though most of the students came from wealthy families, I was embarrassed. But then, one day while on the way to pick me up, for reasons unknown, the helicopter crashed and killed the pilot. A man I had come to love and trust. Not to mention I, too, could have been on the helicopter. I guess the whole incident traumatized me. But after that, I had a tutor at the house. She was a Christian. Faith had never really been part of my life before that. Mom started taking me to a tiny church in town just up the road. Then I went off to college and followed my dreams. I haven't flown since then…except with you that day when you saved my life."

Will cleared the thick emotion from his throat. "I'm sorry to hear that happened, Sylvie. Real sorry." And now, of course, she could add her mother's death to the list of reasons to be afraid of flying. He had his own morbid story but they had other issues to discuss. Will flew low and radioed the flight tower in Bellingham, hoping to land there. *And where was that Camaro?* His stomach tightened as he thought about what they'd been through. What they must still face.

"Tell me about the letter now."

Sylvie pulled it from her purse, and using a small map light, read the letter to him, her voice shaking. The letter revealed much and yet remained cryptic. They needed a plan and quick.

"So what's next, then, Sylvie? Since your mother didn't feel safe going to the police, should we follow her intended path and head to Mountain Cove? Nobody would expect us to go there, would they? We could show Chief Winters the letter, or get back in touch with the state troopers."

When she didn't answer, he found her staring out the window. She always liked to think before she spoke. He had learned that much about her. She must be more than confused, as was he, about whether Damon Masters was involved or not, considering Ashley had tried to convince them otherwise. The woman sounded emotionally attached to her boss, though—in a way that might color her opinion. Had Sylvie caught on to that? What was Ashley's role in this, if any, other than as assistant? Will had a lot of questions, but he needed time to think. To clear his head.

This was moving too fast.

"No."

"What?"

"We can't talk to anyone until we have that thumb drive in hand." She shifted in her seat, turning to look at him. "Don't you see? Nothing can be proved, even if we go to the police, without the solid evidence on that drive. That's why they wanted to kill me, so that I wouldn't find it. They knew I was getting too close. If they'd succeeded, who knows if anyone would have found me for months or even years, if ever?"

Just like their mothers in the downed plane. Will frowned, watching the airport lights grow near. "If they wanted the thumb drive they would have made the dive and searched for it already."

"No. They haven't found the plane. Only knew that I was diving in the general vicinity where they expected it would have gone down. I haven't found it yet, either, but I spotted something suspicious—something that looked like it could have been part of the plane, just before Diverman attacked. Think about it, Will. Diverman is the same one we've seen everywhere, trying to kill me. He and Rifleman. He hasn't been diving after the thumb drive or else he wouldn't have had time to follow us. And it's doubtful he, or whoever is calling the shots, wants to bring in yet another person just to dive for that plane. The fewer who know about the thumb drive and information worth millions, the better. Diverman's only mission, at the time, was to kill me there. Make it look like an accident, but he failed. He told us he doesn't have the drive yet—that means we still have a chance to get there first. We have to go back. We know what we're looking for this time, and it's about much more than finding my mother."

Will thought he heard tears wrapped around desperation in her voice.

"We have to get justice for them, Will. And we might just be running out of time to do that. We have to go back and get the thumb drive before someone beats us to it. I have a feeling Diverman knows that, too. We have to beat him there. We have to find that plane so we can end this once and for all. Our lives are on the line here. I'm not going to trust anyone else with them."

Will didn't respond while he landed the helicopter. He grabbed the first aid kit. They jumped out and he grabbed her hand and they ran. Seemed like they were always running. Sylvie was always behind him. What would life feel like once it returned to normal and he and Sylvie were no longer running for their lives?

He led her into the airport terminal. Will took care of his wound in the restroom. Fortunately, it wasn't more than a graze, just as he thought. That could have been so much worse. He'd never discount what his knife-throwing skills could accomplish. Finished with dressing the wound, Will hurried out and found Sylvie waiting for him, then pulled her into a secluded corner. She stared up at him in surprise, her mouth half open as if she wanted to say something, then she shut it.

Now. Will was ready to respond to her pronouncement. "Let me get this straight. You want to go back to where this all started. Where a diver tried to kill you. And look for the plane?"

She shook her head. "You heard me right."

"You're asking me to dive?" Didn't she remember the part where he told her he hadn't been diving since the diving accident that killed his father?

His throat tightened up at the thought. He always panicked anyway, breathing too hard and fast. The wide-open sky was more to his liking. Why did their mothers' plane have to sink?

"You don't have to, but I was sort of hoping you would. You mentioned diving with your father before, so I assumed you're certified. You've come this far with me, even though I didn't think I needed your help. But I know now that I was wrong. This time I'm *asking* for your help. I can't trust anyone else. And like you keep telling me, we're in this together."

Her lips puckered a little. She couldn't know what she was doing to him. Even he didn't understand the power she had over him. He wanted to wrap her in his arms, protect her from the world. Whisk her away if he could.

And he wanted to kiss her. The deep ache of it nearly overcame him. Will steeled himself against the crazy feelings stirring inside. He couldn't do this to himself. But he was big enough to shove his fear of getting entangled with her out of the way to help her.

Despite his warning thoughts, he leaned closer. Another centimeter or two and their lips could meet. Sylvie closed her eyes, like she expected, even wanted, him to kiss her.

He drew in the essence of her. He could live on that for months. The thought shocked him back to his senses and he took a step back. Her eyes popped open. Flashed with emotion. What? Disappointment?

Will should take another step back. Put more distance between them. He stood close to her as though this was an intimate conversation. True, he didn't want anyone overhearing their discussion. Deep down, though, he knew it was more than that. His heart betrayed him.

Hand pressed against the wall, he barricaded Sylvie from the prying eyes in the terminal.

Just to be clear, he leaned close again and spoke in hushed, but deliberate tones.

"I'll dive with you, Sylvie. I wouldn't let you go alone. You have to know that by now. But we're doing this because time is of the essence. And if I'm going to dive that means you're going to fly. We don't have time for the ferry. You're going to get on a plane with me. I have contacts here, so I can probably get us a deal on a plane rental. It'll be faster than flying commercial since I doubt we can get a flight out until early morning anyway." Will got on his cell to begin his search. Since it was night, he'd have to file a flight plan to fly IFR, using Instrument Flight Rules instead of visual, which is how he usually flew in the bush. No scud running tonight. "We can be in Mountain Cove in a few hours. Get the diving gear we need and I know where we can get a boat. Do we have a deal?"

She paled slightly, but stood taller. Her chest rose with her intake of breath. "Deal."

That was the Sylvie he knew and had come to care deeply about. Wait. Care deeply about?

"So by this time tomorrow it could be over." But it was going to be a long night getting there.

Will's cheeks ballooned then he blew out a breath. By tomorrow his credit card could be maxed out, and they would either have succeeded in finding the plane and the thumb drive or they would have failed. He'd know if he had survived diving, but he doubted his heart would survive Sylvie.

So much for being a survivor.

* * *

Here she was, flying with Will again, and in a bush plane, no less. Prop planes were the worst, if you asked her. The little plane rocked and rolled. Puddle-jumpers, they called them, and for good reason. She wished she had it to do over again and try to renegotiate with Will. Her stomach lurched.

Oh, Lord, what was I thinking? Please let us live. Let us survive this.

Hadn't that been her prayer for days now? But at least it seemed to be working so far.

The whir of the props droned on, and the flashing strobe on the wings competed with the flicker of lights below. Eventually, the small plane drifted over a completely dark abyss. They were over water.

"At least they predicted good weather," she said.

"I always plan it being worse than the forecast."

"Is that experience talking?"

"Sure is," Will said. "You might as well get some sleep. It'll be a few hours, and with what we have planned, you need your rest."

"I don't think I can sleep. This ride isn't exactly smooth."

"All you have to do is let go. Just let go and trust me. I know that might be hard to do considering our last trip, but those were extenuating circumstances, and I *did* land the plane. I *did* get us to our destination."

Sylvie wasn't sure that reminder eased her fears. But she certainly couldn't change the outcome by worrying the whole flight. Maybe she should trust Will. Maybe she should let go and trust God. It was time she gave up trying to control the outcome and believe that she really could trust this entire situation—not just flying, but the search for the truth—to God.

"Will you need to stop to fuel up?"

"Yep. But I know my way around, remember? Leave this to me."

"I trust you, Will. I know you'll get us there." It felt good and right to say the words to someone. To say those words to Will. She could sense it pleased him, too. She wanted to pull her gaze from the window. Wanted to look at him, but was afraid of what that would do to her at that moment. Afraid of just how much trust she'd put in one person. The emotions he stirred in her battled against her resolve never to trust anyone, especially men, when it came to matters of the heart.

But who was she kidding? She had nothing to worry about. Once this was over and the killers were imprisoned, they would each go their separate ways.

Will would go back to his bush-piloting business.

Sylvie back to her scuba diving.

Even if she trusted him with her heart, could trust him to be true to a committed relationship, they were just too different to make it work. She closed her eyes, willing herself to drift to sleep amid tumultuous emotions the letter had stirred, confirming the very thing she'd wanted to disprove—that her stepfather had killed her mother. That he was not only guilty of orchestrating her murder, but also of trying to kill Sylvie to prevent her from discovering the truth.

She thought she was going to be sick. How could she sleep with so much riding on her finding the thumb drive? With so much twisting around her throat and choking off her air.

And at that moment she struggled to breathe. She

was strapped in the seat belt and couldn't free herself as Will's plane sank deeper and deeper. Bubbles escaped her nose and she looked to her left. Will was in his seat, his eyes closed.

"Will!" She shook him but he wouldn't wake up.

She couldn't save him if she couldn't free herself first. Finally, she unlatched the seat belt—only her stepfather was on the other side of Will pulling him out of the plane. Then her mother was in the water. Alive and in the water, fighting Damon.

Sylvie's lungs screamed. She had to get air or she would drown. She fought her way to the surface, but Diverman was always there pulling her back down. She fought him but she'd already been beneath the water's surface far too long.

She would die. They would all die.

Releasing her last breath, she yelled into the water.

Sylvie fought the arms that gripped her. Shook her until her eyes opened. Will's face filled her vision as she sucked in a breath. But she was back in her seat, strapped in. Sylvie fought to disentangle herself from the straps.

"Sylvie, calm down." Will tightened his grip. "It's all right. You were dreaming."

Her brain finally caught up with her panic and she slowed her breathing. "I thought I was drowning. We crashed again, in the water like before. Only this time we sank."

"Well, then, you'll be glad to know that we have safely landed in Mountain Cove."

She relaxed back in the seat. "I don't want to fly again, Will. Don't make me."

"Your dream was about drowning not flying." He tucked in his chin. "Maybe we shouldn't dive tomorrow."

"Tomorrow?" Oh, that's right. It was the middle of the night. "I forgot we have to wait until morning to get the equipment we need."

Sylvie feared she wouldn't make it to the downed plane first. She had the keen sense she was on a race to the thumb drive, if she already wasn't too late. She was on a mad rush to save her own life by destroying her stepfather's.

"Relax, Sylvie. There's virtually no way Diverman can beat us there. I've made a lot of friends in this business. I do favors for them. They do favors for me. A few phone calls should get us into the local dive shop to get the gear we need."

"But I don't want to involve anyone else in this. I don't want anyone else to get hurt. No one can know what we're doing. That is, until it's over."

"Don't worry. If people want me to keep their secrets, as in some of the outrageous packages I've picked up or delivered, then they'll have to keep mine. I think we should let your half siblings know what we're doing, though. Let Chief Winters know, too."

"Only if you think he won't try to stop me, or tell me not to go." By the look on Will's face, he couldn't promise her that. "Will, you understand everything is at stake here. Our *lives* are at stake if we don't find the one thing that can put these men away. We can't let them get to the evidence first. They won't wait for Chief Winters or the AST to act."

Will frowned and exited the plane.

Exhaustion and guilt weighed heavily on Sylvie and she almost succumbed to the paralyzing effects, remaining in the seat until Will opened the door on her side and assisted her out. The dream—more of a nightmare—had zapped her reserves.

Will steadied her on her feet. Would she be stronger if Will wasn't here to help her? Was she leaning on him too much, something she never wanted to do? She wasn't sure, but she decided to simply be grateful. What kind of person went to the lengths he'd gone to help her? But it was about his mother, too. She couldn't forget that. And he wasn't helping just her. He was helping himself, as well.

Would they even survive?

SEVENTEEN

The sunrise eclipsed the fears that had driven him mad during the night and finally awakened him. He steered the cruiser over the water to the remote part of southeast Alaska where he'd first come across Sylvie, running for her life.

He almost turned the boat around a thousand times. Finding the information that would answer their questions and set them both free could also end their lives if their attackers found them here again. But Sylvie would never stop.

And neither would he.

It wasn't enough that they had the letter her mother had written. It wasn't enough that someone had tried to kill her and they could identify the assailants if they were ever caught. Convincing the authorities to take action would take too long. They needed the thumb drive in their hands, though that hadn't done her mother much good.

Awestruck at the golden sunrise shimmering off the clouds and splaying across the water, Will allowed himself to soak up the peace he always felt at seeing it—and as wonderful as it was here on the boat and open water, it was even more majestic from the air on an early-morning flight.

They were almost to the island, and the channel, where it had started. Will stopped the boat and let it drift while he soaked up the moment. Since he'd flown them to Mountain Cove, he'd let her drive the boat a few hours, and she'd made good time even driving slower to compensate for boating at night. But he hadn't been able to sleep more than a couple of hours and had soon relieved her at the helm. She'd fallen asleep and he'd let her rest a little longer.

He wanted to be sure they were completely alone before they made the dive of their lives.

Then he sensed Sylvie's light-footed approach. When she stood silently next to him, he suspected she wasn't contemplating her next words this time, but instead basked in the glory of dawn, as well.

After everything they had been through together— facing death head-on—Will couldn't help himself. He didn't fight it this time, or berate himself, but did what was only natural and slid his arm around her waist.

Sylvie leaned into him as though there was something more between them. Will knew there couldn't be. He sensed that he and Sylvie were in agreement on that. Then what was going on? Was she as confused as he was?

He couldn't deny there was more between them, more than a physical connection, and there was definitely chemistry. As he held her close, watching the sunrise, Will thought Sylvie could be the one to help him forget the past.

But no, that was wrong. Will didn't want to forget the past. Keeping the past, carrying it around with him, was just the protection he needed. That way, he would never again get hurt.

Except equally as painful was the thought of extricating himself from his involvement with Sylvie. He didn't want to do that, either, but the next few hours would be all or nothing for them both.

Bile rose in his throat so that he could no longer ignore the fear he'd tried to push down.

Sylvie stiffened and inched away. "Listen, Will. You don't need to dive with me, okay? I'm an instructor, a master diver, so I do this all the time. And I've been on search and rescue recoveries."

Will heard what she did not say about finding the victims of a downed plane. Did he really want to see his mother that way—after two months underwater? He shoved those thoughts aside. "I'm going, Sylvie. I'll admit, it's been a while, but it's like riding a bike. And—" Will reached up and brushed a strand of her hair back "—I trust you to lead the way. I'm not letting you go alone."

"But someone needs to watch the boat to make sure that the same thing doesn't happen again."

"If Diverman shows up on his boat, I don't want you down there alone. We do this together. If it comes to that, we'll escape together. You need someone to watch your back down there where it matters most."

Will eyed the horizon, hoping the backup he'd called for would come in time. He hadn't wanted to alert Sylvie to his actions because knowing her, she'd lose Will and attempt to go it alone, believing she was protecting him and any others from getting hurt.

While securing their diving equipment and boat, even though it was during odd hours of the night, Will had texted both David Warren and Chief Winters, informing them of their actions, and that they had no time to delay.

He couldn't live with himself if something happened to her and no one knew where they were, if no help came in time to save her. Maybe help wouldn't be necessary. There were no guarantees this dive would lead them to the plane or the thumb drive, and he could be calling in friends for nothing. But there were no guarantees Will's backup would show up in time to help, if needed, either.

"We should get going. I'll circle the island and make sure we're well alone before we dive." Will steered the boat around the island, watching in the distance for other boats. For the enemy. He'd considered taking a float-plane here. It would have been faster, but cumbersome to get into the dry suits, and they needed the boat to warm up after diving in the cold water. Needed a warm shower. It wasn't practical or safe to stay long in these cold waters, even with the proper gear.

"You never told me what happened to you. Why you no longer dive. You said your father died?"

He took his time to answer, steering toward the island, scanning the horizon. Sylvie stood next to him, peering through binoculars. For just a second he squeezed his eyes shut, and that was all it took. Visions of his father slammed him.

"Will?"

"I'm getting to it."

He shook his head and focused. He had to stay on task here.

"Okay, I'm sorry I asked. If you don't want to talk about it, maybe now isn't the time."

"I'm good." Will punched it, speeding around the island. Searching the area for any suspicious activity.

Someone waiting for them. Like Sylvie, he sensed they were in a race against the clock.

"My father loved to fly and brought Mom out here from Montana to build a bush pilot business. He also loved to climb and dive, and he served as a volunteer search and rescue diver, too." Like Sylvie. His father had been a lot like Sylvie. He didn't look at her, though, just watched the water as he spoke. "He was on a recovery dive. A sunken vessel and…there were bodies to recover."

Will wasn't sure this was the time to talk about it, after all.

"He was only forty-five when he died. He was on a recovery dive that was supposed to be a bounce dive. Two hundred feet."

"Deep and cold." Sylvie nodded her understanding.

"Did the martini effect, nitrogen narcosis, get to him? Scramble his brain like he was drunk? Don't know. But at that many atmospheres down, it's easy to see how it could happen. Even experienced as he was, he somehow got trapped in the sunken vessel, and the other divers couldn't find him at first. You can't see your hand, barely a flashlight, in front of your face at that depth. When they found him it was too late. What I can't figure is how someone could be down there in the deep, just to help others and end up dying, too. It doesn't make sense. I never wanted to get in the water again. My only use for it is to land my seaplane."

"I'm so sorry," she said. "Sometimes we can do everything right and people still die."

He didn't want to think about those words with what they were about to face. "We need to talk about this."

"You mean, what it will be like if we actually find

the plane? I've been on recoveries, Will, but I admit, the thought of finding my mother twists my insides. When I determined to find the plane, I hadn't any intention of getting closer, only to note the location and report it to the authorities. But then Diverman showed up and changed my game plans. Are you going to be able to handle this?"

"Are you?" he asked. "We're going in for one thing only. The thumb drive that will bring justice for our mothers and end the threat on your life. Our lives. Let's agree that we won't look at the bodies. We'll get the drive and get out."

"And get as far away as we can from this place. I don't want to face off with Diverman or his accomplice again. The next time I see him, I want him and Rifleman to be in a lineup."

Sylvie directed him to where she'd anchored before. They would start there in their search. She checked their tanks and equipment while Will secured the boat. She then gave him a quick review to refresh his skills.

Where was their backup? If anything happened to Sylvie, they would never forgive Will. Not that that would matter. He would likely be dead already because he would give his life to make sure that Sylvie lived. After they layered and geared up to look like aliens, they hung over the port gunwale, ready to drop backward into the water.

This was the only reason he would ever dive again.

He had to make sure that Sylvie lived.

Despite her experience, Sylvie had never been more nervous in her life. She readied the mask, holding it over her head, and eyed Will, searching for any sign of fear in his warm eyes. Any reason at all to object to him coming along. He'd already donned his mask and watched her.

"Ready?" she asked.

"As I'll ever be." He winked then thrust the regulator into his mouth before rolling back into the cold water.

Once she joined him, she watched him for signs of panic then gave him a thumbs-up. He reciprocated. From here on out, they'd have to communicate with hand signals. She dove beneath the surface and flutter-kicked. The water was only about twenty feet deep here but would get deeper. She was aware of the currents and underwater topography in the area.

Will was next to her, and it felt good and right. Side by side they headed toward the place where she'd seen the glint of metal, what could have been the lost plane. *Or part of it.* Sylvie's heart jumped. She didn't like to think about what they might find. She'd been on enough tragic recoveries. Some couldn't stomach it.

Visibility was between thirty and forty feet. She would have preferred eighty but not the colder waters of winter that would provide it. Following the same path she'd taken the first time, she pushed them north from the island, searching for the remnants of that shipwreck turned artificial reef. It was just beyond that reef where she'd seen the glint.

The reef came into view. She lingered there for a moment so she and Will could take in the abundance of sea creatures, starfish and anemones. Will pointed at the giant tube worms. Sylvie wished this could have been a joy dive with Will, exploring the sea life for the simple pleasure of it. She doubted she could ever get Will to join her for something like that. It cost him to come with her as it was.

Their relationship had been forged out of necessity and a common goal. Should she even call it a relationship? Why was she thinking about a long-term future with Will? She shook off the thoughts and surged ahead, but then slowed and turned to check on him. She couldn't forget he hadn't been diving in too many years. Common sense, along with her years as an instructor, warned her he shouldn't be in the water with her. But technically, she could offer no reason, even though there was a great abyss between certified and prepared. He was certified, and that was that.

She had to stop thinking about him and focus on the area she thought she'd spotted part of a plane.

And there it was...the wing of a small plane. Sylvie almost gasped at the sight.

Breathe. Steady and even.

Will's eyes grew wide. Did he recognize the wing? Could this be part of the plane that went down?

He swam closer to examine it. When he glanced back at her, his features were grim behind the mask. He gave a subtle nod. Sylvie took that to mean that this could be the wing from his mother's plane. So it had broken apart on impact? Or...had there been an explosion? Was that what caused the crash?

Sylvie couldn't stand to think of that possibility, or of what they might find.

Of what they wouldn't find.

The wing was here, but the plane could be much farther, and could be spread in pieces. She would look for a scatter pattern. If the fuselage wasn't intact, that meant they might never find the bodies.

Or the thumb drive.

Her heart rate accelerated. Maybe she wasn't the right

one for this task, but she and Will were the only ones. She swam forward and floated next to the sheer wall of a deep crevasse. More sea anemones clung to the wall, and down much deeper, eighty feet or so, Sylvie guessed the plane might rest. It could be spread out, or have tumbled a few hundred more feet from the wing.

She thought she might get sick. Throw up. Now wasn't the time to think of her mother's terror. Sylvie couldn't afford to lose it. She couldn't let herself crumple or let racking sobs take over. She steeled herself, imagining this was just another recovery dive. But she'd only thought she had nerves of steel, as Will had said.

She had no choice but to see this through. She glanced at her dive watch, the computer relaying time and temperature, complete with a tissue-loading graph, to reassure her they had time to search and time enough to ascend. Then she signaled to Will.

They were going deeper.

Sylvie guessed at the trajectory and swam toward where the remainder of the plane could rest. Why was the plane here, so far off track, when it had been headed to Mountain Cove?

Sylvie turned to make sure Will followed her and spotted him about ten feet away. Her heart palpitated at the distance between them. They had to stick together. He turned to look at her and then pointed. She glanced to where he gestured, but couldn't see what had drawn his attention. Sylvie swam toward him, planning to close the distance, but he swam ahead of her, leading her on.

Something told her that he'd found the downed plane. *God, I'm not ready for this. Help me!*

Will paused and turned back to face her, features pale behind the mask. There was something behind his brown eyes now that was far from warm. Sylvie never wanted to see that look in his eyes again. She closed the distance. Could just make out a small craft cresting on the edge of an even deeper crevasse. The fuselage was intact, but slightly twisted.

I wasn't prepared to see this.

Will grabbed her. Had she been swimming away? He gripped her and tried to convey what he could not say through his gaze. In his eyes she saw understanding and compassion, and that he shared her horror at the situation—but she also saw his conviction that they had to move forward. Their mothers would never get justice if they didn't find the proof inside the plane.

Sylvie had thought she was stronger than this, and though she'd coached Will to breathe through it when they found what they were looking for, he was the steady one.

But they had a reason to be here. And now it was time to get the evidence that would put her stepfather away—the missing piece to tie him to her mother's murder and attempts on Sylvie's life. The pain stabbed at her now like never before.

Could she do this?

Will left her and swam toward the fuselage. He would do it if she couldn't. She followed him. They would do this together. Now they had discovered the plane, they would come back, of course, with an actual dive team and the proper authorities to recover the bodies. Today was just about retrieving one thing.

She was messing with a crime scene, but underwater crime scenes were the most difficult to comb through. If they didn't retrieve the thumb drive now, it would fall into the wrong hands.

The downed craft was eighty feet deep, resting on the precipice of a much deeper sea canyon. Had the plane rocked forward and fallen farther, she and Will would have a much different kind of dive on their hands.

Sylvie wanted—no, needed—to take deep breaths to calm herself, but she couldn't afford that. Decompression sickness was one thing, but a quick glance at her watch told her that they would soon need to head back up. They would likely need to dive again to complete their task.

When they approached the fuselage, Will was the one to swim to the passenger's side of the plane and search. Sylvie had experience, but Will was the one to take charge, and she let him. In fact, she couldn't look. She averted her gaze, looking at the fuselage of the plane, still in one twisted piece, except for jagged edges where the wing had ripped away. What had happened? A small-enough bomb to simply rip off the wing?

Will had wedged himself deeper, searching for the thumb drive. Her mother claimed to have had it on her when she left—the drive the reason she had fled. Sylvie watched intently, aware that the plane might not be stable against the precipice. Was Will paying attention, too? She needed to warn him and swam closer.

From inside the plane he gestured wildly at her.

Will's leg was caught in twisted metal. Caught and bleeding.

EIGHTEEN

Will held it in his gloved hands—the thumb drive that had cost his mother's life. That had cost Sylvie's mother's life. The price had been too high. With the pain shooting through his leg that was somehow snagged on a sheet of twisted metal, the price might still climb higher.

If he couldn't get free before his tank ran out of oxygen, Sylvie could buddy breathe with him, but eventually she would run out of air, too. The terrified look in her eyes didn't help. He wouldn't have thought it—she being a master diver. That showed him the true danger of the situation they were in. If he couldn't get free, she would blame herself for this for the rest of her life.

He tugged and pulled on his leg, but the pain only intensified, and nothing he did helped to get him free.

Sylvie cautioned him. She signaled that too much moving could jar the plane from the precipice. Will brandished his knife. He had to live. If not for himself then for Sylvie's sake, and Snake's sake, and for his mother's sake, to make whoever had killed her pay for what they had done.

He glanced at Sylvie. She quickly masked the look of no hope on her face, but he'd seen it all the same. He thrust the thumb drive at her. That was what she needed more than she needed him. She could finish this for both of them. He glanced at the knife, recalling the story of the man who'd cut off his own arm to escape being stuck between boulders.

Could Will do that? When he looked back at Sylvie she shook her head, terror in her eyes. He could bleed out before they could get to the surface. Attract sharks. And they would soon be out of oxygen.

Out of time.

She reached for him. He pushed her away. How did he get her to leave him behind? Would it be too horrific for her if he pulled off his regulator and let himself drown? Then she couldn't save him and would have the time to save herself.

He shoved the images of his father's underwater death from his mind.

God, I don't want to die! Help me have the courage to live!

He didn't want to die like this! Nor did he want to put Sylvie through this. It was too much, far too much, for her to handle, even someone as strong as Sylvie.

Then he remembered. How could he have forgotten? His mother always carried a crowbar in the plane. He bent and tried to shift, and pain shot through his leg. He pointed to the back, signaling in hopes Sylvie would understand what he needed.

She nodded.

While Sylvie maneuvered into the back of the cockpit, Will kept perfectly still. The last thing he needed was to cause the plane to shift and fall deeper into the ocean, taking them both with it.

Help could not arrive soon enough. Will wondered

what was keeping his search and rescue friends. They couldn't know just how at stake Will's life was at the moment.

He steadied his breathing, despite the precarious situation. Even though it was becoming increasingly clear he was about to die. *God, please save Sylvie. Please get her out of here!*

Will had been selfish to encourage her to look for—

Sylvie held the duffel bag. His mother's bag of tools and other necessities in case she found herself stuck somewhere. Will took the bag and tried to open it but the zipper caught. Sylvie whipped her knife around and sliced it open. Will pulled out what he'd needed—a crowbar. They needed leverage.

But more than that, Will would have to use his knife and make an incision to free the piercing metal from his leg, before the leverage would work. His vision blurred. He blinked a few times and then made the cut.

The pain was unbearable. He shut his eyes. Stifled a scream. He thought he would pass out. At least the cold seeping in would bring numbing relief.

Dizziness swept through him. He refocused his efforts. Together, he and Sylvie worked to pry him free, but even free, he wasn't sure he could swim to the surface with a bum leg.

His leg shifted, and Will pushed himself away from the craft. Sylvie's concerned eyes beamed. She dragged him farther from the plane, blood quickly coloring the water, faster than before.

Will didn't have time to worry about sharks—another kind of danger drew his attention first. They'd been sidetracked, their attention on freeing him, and hadn't noticed a different kind of predator waiting to take a bite of them. At first he thought it was the help they'd needed, but then he saw the glint of a knife and the hostile eyes.

She had the thumb drive in her grip—it could be dried out and the data recovered—but all she really cared about was that Will was free. What did the thumb drive matter, what did any of it matter, if Will died down here? Died while trying to help her? Suddenly, finding justice for their mothers didn't seem so important. Though they needed this evidence to be free from those trying to kill them, her priorities quickly shifted with this new urgency. Will's life was on the line.

All that mattered was getting him to the surface.

She signaled that they should head up now, and she would assist him to the surface.

Except the look on his face told her something was terribly wrong—something more than his injury. Will tried to pull Sylvie with him to the far side of the plane. They needed to ascend. He was losing his focus.

Oh, God, please don't let him die. Will forced her around.

Two divers had approached, and one drew ominously near. Behind the mask Sylvie recognized the eyes.

Ashley?

Diverman floated a few feet away. Was Rifleman, the man from the ferry, manning their boat?

Shock had her gasping for breath. Ashley and Diverman. Of course. They were working for her stepfather. She'd been such an idiot to trust Ashley.

Will urged her to swim away with him, but no way was he going to be able to outswim these two with an injured leg. Ashley reached forward and tried to snag the thumb drive from Sylvie's fingers. She'd forgotten she even held it there. Sylvie yanked her hand out of reach.

Ashley would have to fight for it.

She thrust a knife at Sylvie, who grabbed her wrist and held it tightly. The thumb drive in one hand, and Ashley's wrist in the other, she couldn't grab her diver's knife. In her peripheral vision, she saw Will fighting with Diverman, and holding his own, even with his serious injury, but he wouldn't last long. Sylvie and Will had just enough oxygen left to swim to the surface, cutting their decompression stops short. She needed to end this and now!

When Ashley eased back on the knife to thrust it yet again, Sylvie twisted her wrist back. Ashley reached for Sylvie's regulator hose, but it was too late. She'd dropped her knife and it sank. Ashley and Sylvie locked grips, then, neither able to get free without risk.

She was breathing too hard and fast, using up her oxygen.

Dizziness took hold. *Oh, no! Please, God, help me! Help Will!*

She would never make it to the surface. That was Ashley's plan. Keep her here, hold her down, until she died. In her peripheral vision, she could see that Will was no longer swimming. He floated lifeless in the water. But so did Diverman.

Had he killed for her, like he said he would?

Fury exploded inside Sylvie. Adrenaline surged and she shoved free from Ashley. Swiped at the woman's regulator, her mask, anything to be free so she could save Will. But Diverman roused and swam toward her. She couldn't take them both.

Her heart would split in two if she left Will behind, and yet she had no choices. None whatsoever.

She turned and thrust away from Ashley to make

a swim for it. Ashley reached for Sylvie, grabbing her fin and then her leg. She sliced at Ashley with her own knife. Terror filled Sylvie. She couldn't die like this. Then the truth would never come out for any of them.

Ashley ripped the thumb drive from Sylvie's fingers then released her. She and Diverman swam away. Sylvie made for Will. She had to haul him to the surface, take her chances with DCS again. There was no time to worry about stopping. And that was when she saw what had sent Ashley and Diverman away without killing her first.

Divers. More divers were in the water. Obviously they weren't there to help Ashley and her accomplice. The next thing Sylvie knew, one of the divers was with her, sharing his regulator.

Cade Warren, her half brother. Will must have told him about their plan. She'd warned him against that, but now she was grateful.

Other divers surrounded Will and took him away from her. Tears slid down her cheeks and pooled in her mask, but they weren't tears of joy, even though she was grateful the divers had shown up here.

She wouldn't have survived even to get to this point if it hadn't been for Will. He'd saved her too many times, and now he might pay for that with his life. She wasn't sure Will would make it. *Please, God...*

He might already be gone.

Moments later Sylvie found herself on another boat. David Warren and Heidi Callahan helped her remove her gear. She pressed into Heidi's shoulder, cognizant of her half sister's growing belly, and sobbed. She'd thought she was so strong that she could take on the world, all by herself. Take on her stepfather, Damon Masters, an international magnate.

She'd been so wrong.

Helicopter rotors drew her attention, and she watched it heading away.

She slumped and leaned away from Heidi. "Will…"

"He's fortunate Isaiah met us here in the SAR helicopter. They'll get him to the hospital."

Sylvie shook her head, confused. What kind of help had Will requested? He couldn't have known they would need it.

Heidi must have read the question in her eyes. "Isaiah was already in the air, returning from a call-out that didn't require it. He didn't want me to come today since I'm pregnant, but I wasn't going to stay behind. So he did what any overprotective husband would do. He did a flyby." Heidi flattened her lips. "My point is that could save Will's life."

He was already dead, wasn't he? Heidi must have seen the doubt in her eyes and gripped her hands. "Believe, Sylvie. You have to believe. Have some faith. We all made it here in time. Before it was too late."

When Heidi released Sylvie's hands she opened her palms, free from the gloves. "The thumb drive. Ashley took the thumb drive. The whole reason for everything."

"It's all right. You can tell the police everything. We need to get you to the hospital, too. Looks like you have a nasty cut on your arm. You could need the hyperbaric chamber, too."

Sylvie hadn't noticed before, but Ashley had caught her with the knife.

"Let's get you below deck."

"Will and I borrowed a boat from one of his friends." She glanced over.

"We got it, Sylvie." Heidi smiled. "This is what we do."

Sylvie decided to let someone else take control. She trusted her search-and-rescue half siblings. And she had trusted Will.

Still trusted him. *God, please be with him.*

Sylvie sat on the cushioned sofa below deck, praying for Will. Letting Heidi offer her hot chocolate and comfort her. But her heart and mind refused to be comforted.

Too late, she realized the letter she'd thought had been from her mother Ashley had generated on her own computer. Made it sound like the words her mother would have said. Ashley must have copied her mother's real letter and twisted it to suit her purpose. Addressed it as though her mother had meant to mail it.

It had been a ruse to send Sylvie back to her search for the plane and to find the thumb drive.

All that so that Ashley could have the thumb drive, and dispose of Sylvie and Will at the same time.

Her stepfather and Ashley were working with Diverman and his accomplice, that much was clear. But why had they initially tried to kill Sylvie when she was searching for the plane, if they had wanted her to find it and the thumb drive?

Sylvie pushed back another tear. She didn't care about any of it. The police could figure all of that out. All she cared about was Will. His warm brown eyes and his thick dark hair. His sense of humor. The sacrifices he'd made for her. He had to live.

Without Sylvie, of course. She had caused him far too much trouble and heartache. She would see that Will was alive and well, and then she would disappear from his life.

NINETEEN

Sylvie leaned against the hospital wall outside Will's room, nursing a tepid cup of coffee. He hadn't wanted to dive. But he'd done it for her. Would the guilt ever leave her? Could she ever let go and move on? They'd both been desperate to solve what happened to their mothers. The price had been too high.

If I lose Will...

No. She couldn't think like that. She had to hang on to hope like Heidi said. Sylvie couldn't lose Will. He'd sacrificed everything for her.

At least it hadn't been for nothing. The Alaska State Troopers had apprehended Ashley at the Juneau airport, confiscating the thumb drive containing incriminating evidence, thanks to Chief Winters. Once he'd heard the story he was quick to act, calling in the "state boys," as he'd termed them.

The state police hadn't wanted to share the status of their investigation with Sylvie, although they'd taken her statement, but Chief Winters had kept her informed. She'd been wrong about so much. Misled. Her stomach soured.

The information on the thumb drive turned out to be

trade secrets that Ashley had stolen from Damon Masters's company in order to sell to the highest bidder. Apparently, she already had a buyer, a company competitor, for millions. With that money, she could live her dreams.

Masters Marine Corporation's R&D had been developing a new eco-ship in order to solve fuel-efficiency problems in the shipping industry. That kind of technology would mean everything to a shipping company. A secret worth millions—money Ashley had been able to leverage to get the hired muscle she needed to take out Sylvie's mother, and try to kill Sylvie, as well.

She peered into Will's room to see if the nurse had finished. Sylvie wouldn't leave his side until he woke up from his induced coma, except for when the nurses sent her away.

Pressing her back against the cold wall, the smell of antiseptic accosting her nose, Sylvie squeezed her eyes shut. Damon hadn't been involved in her mother's death, after all. Shame filled her that she'd believed he would have been. When her mother had taken the information from Ashley and realized what she'd found, she was afraid for her life. She'd already been followed and nearly killed. She had to leave and find a safe haven.

When Ashley learned Regina was planning to leave and that she had the thumb drive, she hired a mercenary to take Regina out. He engineered the plane crash, timing it over waters in no-man's land in southeast Alaska. Unfortunately, Ashley was concerned that Regina had shared her secret with Sylvie. Ashley learned through a contact at the diving school that Sylvie was still searching for the plane. That was when her mercenary accomplice rigged trackers on her scuba gear and boat. As soon as she got near where they suspected the plane

Sarah Varland lives in Alaska with her husband, John, their two boys and their dogs. Her passion for books comes from her mom; her love for suspense comes from her dad, who has spent a career in law enforcement. When she's not writing, she's often found dog mushing, hiking, reading, kayaking, drinking coffee or enjoying other Alaskan adventures with her family.

Books by Sarah Varland

Love Inspired Suspense

Visit the Author Profile page
at Harlequin.com for more titles.

MOUNTAIN REFUGE

Sarah Varland

Which hope we have as an anchor of the soul,
both sure and stedfast.
—*Hebrews* 6:19

To Elizabeth, my editor. I often think that the books should have both of our names on them for how much of what you do impacts the story for the better. I love working with you, look forward to your comments and smile when I read an edited section we added to the book and can't remember if I wrote the addition or if you did. I had no idea when I started writing how much polish an amazing editor like you brings to a manuscript. Thank you for every single book.

ONE

Summer Dawson was alone on a mountain when she heard the first out-of-place sound, felt the first inklings that something might be wrong, that danger might be close.

She'd been running uphill, relishing the burning in her legs and lungs that reminded her that she was alive, when something rustling in the bushes made her pause and listen.

Summer had stilled immediately and stood now, listening to the sounds she'd grown up with. The Alaskan mountain was full of life, even at ten o'clock at night as daylight was starting to fade. She should have started this run hours earlier, and usually did. Her busy schedule working at the lodge didn't leave a lot of time for training, but mountain running was important to her, her outlet, her dream she didn't like to talk about.

A dream she'd mostly given up on.

But still, she ran the mountains because it was what she'd always done.

Today's run, like every Tuesday, was supposed to be up Hope Mountain, across Lupine Pass, then down Cook Mountain, where her sister, Kate, would be waiting for her. From there, they'd drive back to Summer's car at the Hope Mountain Trailhead. Neither would talk about why Summer trained so hard when she didn't compete anymore, not even at nearby Mount Marathon, but they did the same routine every week. Like clockwork.

Until now. A shiver ran through her, followed by goose bumps down her bare arms. She untied the jacket she always wore around her waist, put it on and hoped it was just the cold and the later-than-usual night that had her spooked. Much as she tried though, Summer couldn't deny that something about the rustle in the bushes had her on edge. Her hand went to the bear spray attached to the belt she always wore when she ran. The Kenai Peninsula was known for its large brown bears. Summer had seen more than one in her time in the woods but never too close. So far she'd escaped any encounters like that.

Hesitantly she moved forward again slowly, not wanting to run lest she awaken a bear's predatory instinct if one did have her in its line of vision.

Then she heard nothing. Just the normal sounds. She exhaled, picked up her pace slightly and removed her hand from the bear spray.

And then something had her, from behind, hands on her arms, rough, pulling, jerking her off the trail. She heard a faint jingle, like car keys on a key chain maybe. That was the sound she'd heard earlier—that's why she'd been spooked. She opened her mouth and screamed, but the deep humorless laughter behind her reminded her how futile it was. This wasn't a well-used trail except on weekends. No one would hear her screams.

"There's no use fighting. You're going to die today."

Summer tensed her arms, tried to wrestle out of his grip, but he was too strong, even as he released her with one arm and then threw the other one all the way across her to pull her up against him, his hand heavy, her heart thudding in her chest.

Dying wasn't an option. Not for Summer. Not when for the last three years she felt like she'd barely lived. She'd gone through the motions, fulfilled obligations, even climbed mountains…

But she hadn't really lived. She wasn't ready yet, wasn't done.

No. Dying was *not* an option. She stilled slightly, hoping she could lull him into complacency, somehow trick him into loosening his grip so she could escape. Instead he held her against him even tighter, drew a knife with the other hand—he was left-handed, she should remember that—and ran it slowly up her arm. There was nothing remarkable about the knife except that it was large, four or five inches. Shiny. Sharp against her skin as he pressed just hard enough to leave the smallest of scratches.

"This is how it begins."

Something in the words sickened her, terrified her. *Please, God.* She didn't remember the last time she'd prayed. For now that was all she could muster.

Noise in the bushes startled them both. She felt her captor shift and assumed he was looking at the noise. She moved her head like she was too, but lowered her chin in the process. Took a breath and slammed her head back as hard as she could.

He yelled in pain, and when he loosened his grip slightly, she rammed an elbow into his ribs.

And then she was free.

Summer didn't stop to look back to see if he was pursuing—she just started running. She was free, she was alive and she had another chance to live like it.

She wasn't going to mess this up.

Clay Hitchcock pulled into the parking lot at the Moose Haven Lodge, hoping his fresh start wouldn't turn out to be a disaster. He was already later than he'd meant to be. A glance at the dash reminded him of that. It was 11:00 p.m. If Tyler hadn't assured him any time before midnight was fine he'd feel awful. As it was, Clay just felt tired. He jerked the key from the ignition, exhaled and got out.

Tyler Dawson, the friend who had gotten him this job, ran from the lodge. "I need your help."

"What's wrong?"

"My sister should have been back from a hike an hour ago."

"And she's not?" Cop senses died hard apparently, because Clay's instincts heightened, ready for action as if he was back in his old life.

"No. We're spreading out. If I give you directions, can you drive around a certain area?"

"Of course." Clay might be new here, but he did most of his growing up in the swamps and woods of coastal Georgia. Back roads were somewhere he felt comfortable.

"Here."

Tyler handed him a ripped strip of paper, like they'd written out a list of places to search and divided them up. Not bad for civilians running an informal search. Speaking of which… "You've called the police, right?"

"Yes. But we're a small town with a small department.

There are only three Moose Haven officers and one of them is out on maternity leave. So that leaves two."

Clay winced, knowing from his own police experience that the chances of both even being able to join the search were slim.

"They're both searching because one of them is my brother."

Clay whistled low. "Are you going out too?" He hadn't seen any other cars in the lot when he'd pulled up and had wondered if the lodge was empty this late at night.

"My truck's around back. Call me if you see anything and I'll let everyone else know."

Clay nodded, climbed back into his truck and drove away.

The woods alongside the roads he drove looked nothing like the tall Georgia pines he was used to investigating among, but the situation was familiar to him. He'd been involved in a search or two during his time at the Treasure Point Police Department, but even though he'd only been officially without a badge for two months now, it felt like a lifetime ago.

Unless Clay let himself actually remember it, hang on to that part of his life. And then it felt like yesterday. But he didn't want that. Couldn't take that.

He pulled out of the parking lot and looked at the note Tyler had given him. Howard's Landing Road was the first road, followed by a list of other locations and directions from place to place. He pulled the first road up on his phone's map setting and pressed the gas.

He realized as he drove that he hadn't asked which sister was missing. Tyler had two. Kate and Summer, if he remembered their names correctly from hearing

Tyler mention them in the past. Who was lost? What had happened?

God, we could use some help.

The words came easily. People had let him down in his lifetime, more in the last few months than usual, but God never had. More now than ever, Clay clung to that faith. Having walked away from everything else consistent in his life, God was all he had.

And this job, thanks to Tyler. Which wasn't off to the best start. What had happened to whichever Dawson sister was missing?

He continued praying silently as he drove, even as years of law enforcement thoughts crowded his mind, pushed out any hope of peace he had been clinging to. Odds weren't good that she was unharmed.

Clay hoped, whichever sister it was, she could take care of herself.

And hoped even more that God would take care of her.

Summer Dawson's feet pounded the dirt beneath them as she rounded another corner in the thick spruce forest, desperately struggling to stay ahead of whoever was behind her, whoever this man was who wanted her dead. She could still hear his footfalls, the rocks in the trail scattering behind her, and knew he wasn't far behind.

If only she knew how long she'd be running. She was in good shape, leading hikes at her family's lodge for so many years had seen to that, not to mention her training regimen—but she'd already been out for several hours. Fatigue wouldn't take long to set in, and Summer didn't know where she was—she'd had to divert from the path she knew after she'd rounded one of the corners and *he* had been there waiting.

Summer hadn't had time to react, hadn't had time to assess the situation or use any of the self-defense training or survival skills she possessed. In the moment when she'd needed all of that most, all she'd been able to do was scream. Finally she'd hit him hard enough to be able to run.

But first he'd been able to talk to her, say things she wouldn't soon forget. First, he'd been able to run a knife up her arm and promise her that death wouldn't come quickly.

Summer wondered if, when she stopped, when she'd gotten away and didn't have to run anymore, if she'd feel the cold blade against her skin like it was still there. Somehow she suspected she would.

Determination renewed, she pushed herself harder. She was less than ten miles from her family's lodge, she was fairly certain about that much. Summer didn't recognize the trail she was on right now, but it had to connect eventually to one she was familiar with, didn't it?

As she ran, Summer went over her would-be killer's description in her mind to make sure the details were cemented in her memory and to distract her from the burning in her lungs. He wore a mask. Black Carhartt stocking cap. She hadn't noticed much more than that, his features—the ones she'd been able to see—weren't etched into her mind the way the glimmering silver of the knife was.

Were it not for the noise in the bushes distracting him, Summer would probably be dead right now, bleeding out on the floor of the forest where she'd so often come to feel alive again. The irony wasn't lost on her. No, it cut deep inside, the pain so strong she almost couldn't bear it.

She'd felt safe here. And now that had been stolen from her.

Just like life had stolen so many things from her over the past three years.

She couldn't think about any of that right now, all she could afford to focus on was running, the fall of her feet, pushing harder, faster, as her lungs screamed for air. She silently chastised them. Better to be burning and in pain than dead.

Please, God… She'd prayed more tonight than she had since the night three years ago when everything had changed.

Summer didn't even know what she was praying for at this point. But she knew she needed all the help she could get.

She heard a twig snap behind her. Legs screaming, lungs burning, she sped up even more, one last sprint, that's all she had in her.

The woods grew lighter. Was that…?

There was a dirt road in front of her. A beautiful road that hopefully led to town. And people.

Still running, she whipped her phone out and used her voice-to-text feature to send a message to her siblings. Help. She wasn't willing to chance it by taking the time to say anything else, but she needed help. One of her brothers was a police officer in Moose Haven— she didn't know if they could GPS track her or anything, but it might be the only chance she had.

She emerged from the woods and ran into the road.

And almost ran straight into the path of a red pickup truck not fifty yards away, driving straight toward her.

Summer froze when she saw it, took only a second to make up her mind and then ran toward it, waving her arms. This couldn't be her attacker—he wouldn't have had time to get a truck to come after her, not when she'd heard his footsteps behind her only minutes before. It could be a getaway car, driven by another criminal, but it was a measured risk on Summer's part—it was more likely the driver was someone who could help her. Besides, she couldn't outrun a pickup, and if the driver of it wanted her dead, he'd just run her over while she sprinted down the road. Better to take a chance, maybe get out alive. Still, her heart pounded a crazy rhythm in her chest. How had her night gone from enjoying her usual route to this—running for her life? The driver stopped when she reached him, and she threw the door open.

"Drive."

Amazingly, he didn't ask questions. He just floored it down the road, eating up the gravel and throwing up dust.

TWO

Clay's world felt like it had gone from zero to sixty in less than ten seconds. He didn't know why he was so surprised he'd found Tyler's sister—at least he was pretty sure that was who he had found—because he'd prayed for that very thing. Still, seeing her dart into the road, clearly running from something, and jumping into his truck like she trusted him to protect her, it was overwhelming.

"Are you Summer Dawson?" he asked as he drove. He glanced down at his search directions and planned a quick route back to the lodge.

He caught her frown out of the corner of his eye. "Why?" she asked.

"Your brother has people out looking for you and I'm supposed to call if I find you."

"Which brother?"

"Tyler." Clearly he'd overestimated the amount of trust she'd have in a stranger. She needed to get out of her situation badly enough to jump in the truck, but now that she was momentarily safe, she was trying to keep herself that way by being guarded. Clay understood, but needed a way to convince her he wasn't a threat.

"My phone is on the dashboard. You can call Tyler from it if you want—you'll see that I have his number. He'll also confirm who I am if you ask him to. I'm Clay Hitchcock and I'm guiding at the lodge this summer."

She reached for the phone and pressed the screen a few times. Calling Tyler, he assumed.

"It's Summer. I'm safe and I'm with Clay, your friend?"

He didn't miss how that last part was a question. When he'd found out she was missing, he'd assumed that in this remote area of Alaska, she'd had a bad encounter with a wild animal or had issues with the terrain. The darker possibilities of meeting a human who wanted to cause her harm had crossed his mind, but he hadn't thought they deserved a great deal of consideration up here in this small, picturesque Alaska town and had written them off as paranoia. Now he wasn't sure. She was too upset, too skittish and hesitant to trust to have been running from an animal.

He stole a quick look at her and thought her frown had eased slightly. Good. With that tension on her side out of the way, he could focus on getting whatever information he could out of her about her encounter. He knew law enforcement would want to talk to her as soon as they got to the lodge, but it wasn't uncommon for the edge of a person's memory to fade the longer they were out of a traumatic situation. Maybe talking about it now would help cement some of the details in her memory.

"I'm okay for now, Tyler. I'll be okay, alright?"

Not a very convincing voice she was using, and Clay didn't blame her. Whatever happened had clearly been extremely traumatic for her to get in the car with a stranger when she was so shaken up.

"Alright, bye." She finished the conversation and set the phone down and looked back at him.

Clay kept his eyes on the road, though he could feel hers on him. After so many years in law enforcement, he was more used to being the one doing the assessing than the one being measured. Her stare disconcerted him.

"What happened out there, Summer? Can you go over it for me?"

"Who *are* you?"

"I told you, my name is Clay Hitchcock, and I'm your brother's friend."

"I mean, who are you and why are you asking me questions like that?"

"I'm just someone who wants to help." That *was* the truth now. He may have the heart of a cop, the mind of a cop, but he was a civilian now. His choice, yes, but it was still taking some getting used to.

Her eyes narrowed but she took his answer. Not, Clay noticed, because *he* had done anything to convince her that he was trustworthy. No, the only reason she was willing to entertain trusting him at all was the fact that her brother liked him.

He made a mental note about her character—family was important.

Not that he necessarily needed to make notes about Summer Dawson's character. After tonight they might only see each other in passing. Clay didn't remember what she did at the lodge, but with as many warnings as Tyler had given him not to think about dating one of his sisters, especially Summer, Clay felt it was safe to assume he wouldn't be assigned to any task that would lead them to cross paths often. But his old habit of analyzing people, observing things about them, died hard. He might not have a badge, but he was still a cop inside.

Maybe this was what the chief had tried to warn him about when he urged Clay to consider what he was doing by leaving the force in Treasure Point. But Clay hadn't listened, couldn't have. He'd needed to get out of there.

Out of that whole line of work.

He stole a glance at Summer. Much as he wanted to drive her back to the lodge and accept the no-trespassing sign she'd clearly placed in front of the details about whatever had just happened, he couldn't. Despite himself.

Clay let out a breath. "How do I get to the Moose Haven Police Department?"

"What?" The edges of her tone were sharp from fear or surprise, it was hard to say which—the two were often so intertwined.

"You're running from something," he explained, keeping his voice calm like he usually did when he was talking to a victim. "I'm assuming if it were an animal you wouldn't be so jumpy now that you're in a car and safe. I'd like to know what happened, but I don't need to. However, if I'm right about why you're running, the police do need to know."

Why hadn't Summer paid more attention when Tyler had talked about who he was hiring for work this season?

As this man, Clay, looked at her, she got the impression he knew her somehow better than he should. From Tyler? Or was he just that talented at reading people?

Summer didn't know, but she wasn't accustomed to such perceptive scrutiny, and didn't like it. She made herself not break his gaze though, saying without saying anything that she wasn't intimidated by him. Because she wasn't. He may be seeing her at her worst right now, but Clay needed to know she was no damsel in distress, no pushover.

Still, he had a point about going to the police. "Fine," she relented. "Turn left."

He did so. Then said "thank you" so quietly she thought maybe she'd imagined it. Now it was her turn to study him. Strong, solidly built, definitely attractive. And yet, he didn't seem pushy. Seemed steady, calm.

Actually he reminded her in some ways of her older brother Noah. He was the police chief of Moose Haven now, and at thirty was the youngest person to ever hold that role.

Clay had the same kind of bearing.

"You're a cop, aren't you?"

Clay glanced over, surprise on his face. She'd phrased it as a question but her tone had shown her certainty. He didn't confirm or deny her suspicions. Summer kept going.

"What are you doing in Moose Haven, really?" she asked without waiting for him to answer. His silence was confirmation enough. Summer shivered. Had he been fired from some police department, was that why he'd needed a new job? She'd heard stories about dirty cops, obviously, though she preferred to think they were the exception rather than the rule. Still, Clay's appearance right after she'd been attacked did feel a little coincidental…

Her brothers would have confidently called it "God's provision." Such phrases hadn't slipped off Summer's own tongue comfortably for years.

"I'm working at the lodge, I told you."

"But you're not like the usual workers. You're different." The words slipped out before she could analyze them, decide if they could be read into at all. Summer left them hanging there, and didn't know what to make of it when Clay didn't comment.

They pulled into the parking lot of the small Moose Haven Police Department without any more conversation between them. Summer exited the car as fast as she could and headed toward the double doors at the front of the station.

Not until she heard a car door slam behind her and then footsteps catching up did it occur to her that Clay might be coming inside.

She mustered up the strongest, most take-charge voice she could find. "Listen, thanks for the ride, but I'm good. I can take it from here."

Was that a slight smile? "I'm sure you can," he agreed as he reached for one of the front doors and held it open for her. Summer frowned a bit before entering the building ahead of him. "But they're going to want to talk to me too."

"Why?"

"Because like I told you in the car, I suspect you're running from some*one*, not some*thing*. In that case, this is a crime or a potential crime and they're going to want to know where I was, how I found you, if I noticed anything. It's standard procedure."

It might have been, but Summer feeling like this certainly wasn't. She was already shaken up from the whole ordeal and now she just felt embarrassed by the way she'd treated Clay suspiciously, even after Tyler had managed to mostly convince her that he was one of the good guys.

"Fine." She didn't have anything else to say and ignored the tugs inside her heart urging her to apologize to Clay. She'd deal with those impulses later, but for now she wanted to stay focused on reporting what happened. It had been too long since she'd felt ready to move on with her life after what had happened in the past. Tonight she felt ready and she didn't want this to slow her down.

He followed her into the building.

"Summer."

Noah saw her before she saw him and swept her into a tight hug. Tyler was always the more demonstrative of her two brothers, so having Noah act this way surprised her. She hugged him back and tried not to shudder under the impact of realizing how deeply Noah had been worried. Her family had been her rock through all her troubles—she hated the thought of making them scared for her again.

"Come into my office." He looked in Clay's direction. "You too. Clay Hitchcock?"

Clay nodded and Noah gave him an approving smile. Any fears Summer had about him being on the wrong side of the law dissipated. To get past one of her brothers was difficult enough, but to get past both would be nearly impossible. Clay must be who he said he was.

Which left her really no reason to dislike him other than that she was still shaken up by him seeing her in such a vulnerable state—a state that had made her treat him rudely. It wasn't his fault she'd been attacked, wasn't his fault she'd learned several years ago that vulnerability with men was dangerous and to be avoided at all costs.

They went into Noah's office and sat down in the uncomfortable wooden framed chairs in front of Noah's desk. Noah went behind the desk, looking very officer-like and Summer felt a burst of pride in her brother. At least she knew he would do everything to find whomever had tried to attack her. The man who'd attacked her had really picked the wrong family to mess with.

"Why don't you tell me what happened?"

Summer did so, remembering all the details, which surprised her and the men also, judging by the looks on their faces. She even remembered to tell them that her attacker was left-handed.

"Not something that necessarily helps figure out who did it but it could help you narrow down a suspect list," Clay said so quietly Summer almost didn't hear. She was more convinced than ever that this was a job he was used to doing and surprised herself by hoping she'd get a chance to talk to him about it later. It didn't have anything to do with him, really, or how attractive he was in his quiet way. She was curious. That was all.

She swallowed hard.

"It'll be okay, Summer."

Noah thankfully mistook her expression for worry about the case, which it should have been, not angst over how tangled up her emotions felt from being rescued by this man, whether she wanted to be the type that needed rescuing or not.

"I hope so." She hoped *everything* would be okay.

"What did you notice?" Noah turned his attention to Clay, and Summer let herself relax a little. She hadn't meant to close her eyes, but when she heard the words *safe house* and her eyes popped open she realized she must have been nodding off. Her adrenaline was crashing, no doubt.

"What?"

"I think we need to take you to a safe house." Noah's words were firm and Summer widened her eyes even further, then started shaking her head.

"You can't be serious."

"Someone is after you."

"Someone *was* after me," she corrected. "I got away. That's the end of it…isn't it?"

"Why would she need a safe house?" Clay asked Noah. It didn't seem like he thought it was necessary, either. Good, maybe her brother was overreacting. Although, was it Summer's imagination or did she see something in Noah's expression? Something that implied a bigger issue he wasn't telling her?

"I have reason to believe it would be a good idea." Noah stood his ground.

Summer shivered. "Why don't you tell me what that reason is?"

Noah shook his head. "Summer, listen, you'd go away for just a few weeks, okay? We will do our best to get this solved…"

A few weeks of isolation during her favorite season, missing mountain running, her hikes with the tourists, time with her family… For what? Yeah, this man was dangerous—she definitely knew that. The police department would need to catch him before he harmed anyone else. But this had been a crime of opportunity. As long as she didn't make herself an easy target, there was no reason to believe this man would come after her again… Was there?

Not to mention, the thought of leaving town and going somewhere by herself made her seriously uneasy. She shivered at the memory of how alone and vulnerable she'd been when she'd run from her would-be killer. All she wanted right now was to go home and surround herself in comfort, familiarity and her siblings' love until she felt safe again. The idea of leaving her support network behind felt chilling and wrong.

"I'm not going to a safe house, Noah. You're going to have to figure something else out."

A few beats of silence passed.

"Let me see what else I can work out," Noah said slowly. "Summer, would you mind stepping outside with Officer Lee?"

She looked at her brother, looked at Clay and frowned a little, then looked back at Noah.

Then she nodded, stepped outside of the room with the other officer and shut the door. And hoped she might find an unlikely ally in Clay, that he'd be able to convince Noah to drop the safe house idea. Anything had to be better than that.

"You want me to do what?" Clay said on the off chance he might have heard wrong.

Noah repeated himself. "I'm going to have Tyler assign you to do everything Summer does at the lodge so you can follow her around, serve as a bodyguard and keep her safe."

Clay scrambled for words, managing to say, "You don't even know me." Had he really moved four thousand miles away from the only home he'd ever known for a fresh start only to be pulled back into the job he'd left behind?

"I know you're a good man. You come highly recommended by your friends in Georgia and by the police chief of the department where you used to work. We do a pretty extensive background check for people who work at the lodge. Alaska's a good place for people who are running from something, and summer employment especially can attract those types. I like to know who's working for my family. So I know a lot about you. And I know you're more than qualified for the job I want you to do."

Clay exhaled.

Noah kept his gaze on him steady. The man didn't seem easily phased, or easily dissuaded—a good quality in law enforcement. Something they had in common, at least according to people Clay had worked with before who had said the same thing about him.

"I want to shoot straight with you," Noah continued. "I'm not completely comfortable with turning this protection detail over to you. Nothing against you, but she's my sister and I don't want to trust anyone but myself to keep her safe. But I can't devote all my time to that and still do my job. And if I'm not doing my job, then the Moose Haven PD suffers and this guy might be able to keep operating longer with one less agency searching for him."

"But why me? Surely you've got other resources."

"Limited. You know how it goes in a small town. There's no proof that there's an ongoing threat against her and I only have a few officers. State troopers don't have a lot of manpower to spare down here, either— state cutbacks."

It had been months since anyone had counted on Clay for anything. Sixty days, almost exactly, since he'd officially worked his last shift in a police department. He met Noah's eyes, noting that the other man's look was serious, heavy with expectation. And Clay knew he was going to have to tell him no.

"Don't you think it's likely that this was a onetime thing—just Summer being in the wrong place at the wrong time? Our guy might have no idea who Summer is or where to find her even if he wanted to attack again. And protective details weren't what I signed up for. I came to help Tyler around the lodge." But the excuse sounded weak even to his ears. Clay winced at his own words.

Noah took them in stride. "Tyler won't mind. He wants Summer safe too. And…it may not be a onetime thing."

"What do you mean?" He heard something in the other man's tone. There was more to this story than overprotective brother syndrome.

"Anchorage Police Department has had a serial killer around the city for the last month and a half or so. Summer fits the age range, the general description—female, between ages twenty-five and early thirties, fit. I'm not entirely sure this isn't related to that."

"You think she was deliberately targeted by a serial killer—that he knew where to find her."

Noah grimaced. "It had barely crossed my mind as a possibility down here in Moose Haven until today. I knew about it, of course—it's been in the news and I try to keep track. But he hadn't left the Anchorage area, to our knowledge."

"What makes you think he has now?"

"Just the general similarities…gut instinct mostly, I guess."

"So are the troopers going to come investigate?" Clay had researched a bit about the local law enforcement agencies before he'd moved to Alaska, because even though he knew leaving the job behind with his old life was the best course of action, he couldn't quite give up the idea of returning to it one day.

"No. Not enough similarities for them."

"From what Summer told you, it sounds like a similar MO though?"

"Yes. I can show you the files for details, though it's not pretty."

"What's missing?"

"He usually kills in pairs. Not together necessarily, but two women in a short time span. Every time, it's been that way." Noah stood, paced toward the small window in his office, then returned to face Clay. "Listen, like I told the trooper I spoke to on the phone a few minutes ago, I just have a bad feeling about this."

"Better safe than sorry," Clay said without thinking, without realizing that he was essentially agreeing with Noah that Summer needed protection. Was all but offering to do it.

"How many women have been killed?"

"Six."

"Any survivors?"

"Not until Summer."

Six women dead. Clay would not let Summer be number seven. He exhaled. Nodded firmly.

"I'll do it."

THREE

The fire in the fireplace in the front room of the lodge danced and crackled, the only sound in the quiet. Summer walked toward it, enjoying the warmth. It might be summer, but nighttime in Alaska always carried a chill. It was past one in the morning now, and the sky was darkening into the twilight that would last for another two or three hours until the sun fully rose again. Summer shivered. From the darkness? From the cold? She didn't know, but she was more chilled than usual today, with the events of earlier on her mind.

She'd hoped telling the police about it would soften the details of the attack in her memory, but so far it hadn't worked. If anything, saying everything out loud had pushed the memories deeper into her psyche, on some track that repeated over and over, replaying like a bad movie.

She wasn't eager to go to sleep tonight. Summer felt the chances of reliving the attack in her dreams was too great a risk to take. She'd rather be tired.

She moved to the couch and picked up her sketchbook and a few pencils.

"You draw?"

She didn't turn as Clay's footsteps came closer. Emotions danced around inside her mind as she worked to settle on which one was strongest. Embarrassment, yes, that was it. Not only had she thrown herself into his path like some sort of damsel in distress, a role Summer wasn't used to playing and refused to play, but she'd been standoffish and prickly, something that also wasn't like her. Even Kate had said something to her about it earlier and Kate wasn't the warmest of people when you didn't know her.

She probably couldn't put off the necessary apology any longer, as it appeared Clay wasn't going away.

"I do." She set the pencils in her lap and shifted her weight a little so she'd be face-to-face with Clay, who stood near the couch, just on the edge of the room. "Are you going to sit?"

"Didn't know if you wanted company."

"Does what I want matter at this point?"

"You're still here at the lodge instead of in that safe house your brother picked out, aren't you?" His voice gave away what he thought about that.

Hadn't Clay backed her up earlier on the fact that a safe house wasn't necessary? His tone now seemed to indicate something had changed. What had that conversation between him and her brother been about?

"For now. And look, I'm sorry that messes up what you thought you'd be doing." Noah had informed her that Clay would basically be her bodyguard for the foreseeable future. She knew it wasn't Clay's fault, that he was just doing this because her brothers had asked him to, but the resentment was hard to repress. "It's not what I was expecting, either—I don't want my life arranged for me." She'd spent too much time and energy crafting five-year plans to have them yanked away because of an attack that could have just been random. So far there was no proof anyone would come after her a second time. Summer was hoping, even thinking of *praying*, that it was a onetime thing.

"I don't mind."

Such a quiet, calm answer. Summer didn't know what to do with that.

She exhaled. "Look, I'm sorry. About now and about earlier. You're not seeing my best side at the moment."

"Situations like this don't tend to bring those out in people."

"You've seen them before."

He didn't answer immediately. Just walked around the coffee table to the other end of the couch where she sat and took a seat. "I have."

"Tyler trusts you. That makes sense, you're his friend. But Noah trusts you too. You didn't answer me before, but I was right with my guess, wasn't I? You're law enforcement, aren't you?"

"No."

"But you were." His reaction to the question had made her even more sure, but it was more than that. It was the way he'd reacted when she'd first jumped in his truck—not overly riled but instantly understanding the seriousness of the situation. It was the way he'd listened as she told her story, the way he didn't seem overly excited by anything but at the same time seemed like he never fully relaxed, was always aware of their surroundings and ready to do his part to neutralize any threat.

"I was."

Summer liked that about him, the way he didn't give more answer than he had to at first but didn't attempt to dance around a direct question, either. A straight question deserved a straight answer. It seemed Clay agreed. A mark in his favor.

"I don't suppose you'd tell me…"

"Not at the moment."

The tone of his voice didn't change a bit, his expression didn't flinch. But the subject was clearly closed. Interesting. She was curious, not because she necessarily doubted his ability to protect her, although maybe there was a little of that. But she also just wanted to know.

"What do you think about the guy who's after me?" Somehow Summer felt that if she was quiet, he'd be the one asking the questions and she wanted to avoid that for now. As long as she was asking the questions, she was the one in control.

"We don't know enough yet to make any kind of guesses." He took a sip from the mug she hadn't noticed him carrying in with him. Coffee, she'd guess. Her siblings liked the stuff. Summer preferred tea—had gotten hooked on it one summer she'd spent in Europe mountain running and climbing.

"What do we know?"

"I'm not part of the investigation, Summer. I'm just looking out for you."

"Surely they've talked to you about why that's necessary."

"They have."

She let those words hang in the air for a minute while she considered them. "But you aren't telling me."

"Because right now, all we have are theories. They won't help you. They'll just drive you crazy thinking about the possibilities. I will tell you everything I know the second I think that's what is best for you."

Summer felt her shoulders tighten, the first hint of a frown on her face. He'd met her hours earlier. Who was he to decide what was best for her? She opened her mouth, ready to let him have it. Before she could say anything to him, she heard something. A doorknob being rattled? But everyone was inside already. They weren't waiting for anyone.

She stopped and sat up straight. "What was that?"

Clay was already on his feet, reaching out for her hand, and she took it, the fight she'd been meaning to pick just seconds before mostly forgotten. The door-knob wasn't making noise anymore, but in the seconds that had followed the initial rattling, there'd been a loud clatter, a small crash like one of the small tables on the porch had been knocked over.

Someone was outside.

"Go after him!" Summer urged.

"I can't. I have to stay with you." Clay had his phone out. "Noah, I think there's an intruder on the deck. Okay. Yes. That's what I thought."

He hung up. "This way." He pulled her toward the staircase that led to the upstairs guest rooms and some of the family's bedrooms. Two of those were upstairs—Summer's and Kate's—and Noah's and Tyler's were in another hallway off the main floor.

"You have to go after him," she protested even as she followed him. "He found me, he knows where I am. He's come after me twice now and it's just going to keep happening unless we face it and do something about it."

Clay whirled to face her. "This is what needs to be done right now, Summer. You need to be kept safe and you need to stop questioning the people trying to make that happen."

She didn't say anything else. Just continued up the stairs and entered her own room when he motioned her inside. It was more of a suite than a room, and the door opened into an area with a small couch, a coffee table and a drawing desk. Off that was the bedroom and bathroom.

She stopped just inside the door. "What now?"

"Sit down and wait."

Summer did it, fighting frustration. And maybe…

Was that fear?

Out of all her siblings, Summer considered herself one of the most fearless. Noah and Tyler weren't overly afraid by any means, but they didn't seek out danger the way she and Kate always had. Noah becoming the police chief had actually surprised the rest of them, but he'd explained that he'd rather face danger every day if it meant he was doing something to protect the rest of the town from it. Kate was an adventurer like Summer, but she acknowledged danger, didn't mind staring it in the face. Summer? Summer didn't usually notice danger. Her favorite place in the world was up on top of a ridgeline, running on it as her heart pounded, adrenaline rushing through her body, and dancing over rocks at what always felt like the tippy-top of the world.

There was no room for fear.

So this wasn't a feeling she was used to. Then again, she also wasn't used to losing her sense of control. Sure, there was a point in the run downhill when you had to lose a bit of your control and hope you didn't end up hitting the small, loose rocks of the scree too many times and getting too scraped up. But even then, it was a voluntary surrender of control, for the sake of the race, the run, the exhilaration.

This was control that someone was trying to take from her. Summer balked at that.

"I'm not going to keep running. I hope he knows that. I hope he knows—"

"Shh." Clay had moved to the window and was looking out, watching what was going on outside.

"What's going on?"

"Noah and Tyler are both out there. A trooper car just pulled up and a woman got out."

"Erynn. She works with Noah sometimes." Her brother's opposite in so many ways. Watching the two of them interact was a favorite amusement for most of the people who knew them. "No sign of anyone...who shouldn't be here?" It was two in the morning but even as far south as Moose Haven, there would still be workable daylight—sort of a dark twilight—at this time of night in early summer.

"Not that I can see. They're coming inside now. We'll wait here. Noah knows where to find us."

"He sent you up here?" In the moment she hadn't even thought to wonder how he knew exactly where her room was.

Clay nodded. "He thought it was the most secure place for us to get to. And he's right. It'd be almost impossible for someone to get in here undetected."

"Almost?"

"Can't promise anything with 100 percent certainty," he said with a shrug, like he was used to people taking his control away. But then again, Summer guessed he was. She doubted there was ever a "normal" day for someone in law enforcement. Noah hadn't had to deal with as much since Moose Haven was usually a relatively quiet town—hunting violations and speeding tickets were usually the craziest things her brother dealt with, as far as Summer knew. Until this. Until today.

Someone knocked on the door. "It's me." Noah's voice.

Clay unlocked it and Noah came in, followed by Tyler and Kate.

"He was here."

Summer had never heard Noah's voice like this. Hard. Angry.

"How do you know?" Clay asked.

Noah glanced at Summer. Shook his head slightly, like doing so would make her not aware of the fact that he was trying to communicate without her noticing.

"I can handle it, Noah."

"You don't need to know," Noah insisted, Tyler and even Kate nodding. She'd have to give her sister a hard time later. The two of them had always stuck together as kids whenever their brothers turned bossy or over-protective. Boys against girls and all that.

"I think she does," Clay said.

Summer swung her gaze to her unlikely ally, eye-brows raised, sure her surprise must be showing on her face.

"You've read the reports," Noah said to Clay as if she wasn't even there. She decided to let it go for now and just listen.

"I have. And I think it's unfair to keep so much from her when it's her life that's in danger. We're asking a lot of her to do what people say without understanding the situation, especially people like me who she doesn't know or have any reason to trust."

More than the usual amount of pause dragged out. Clay stood firm, Summer noticed, his posture giving no indication that he was backing down. She'd never thought she'd see someone willing to stand up to both her brothers, but here Clay was taking them on, plus Kate.

It was…nice.

"Alright." Noah looked to Summer. "You want to know?"

She wanted to go to sleep, wake up and realize it had all been a dream. With that not being an option… "Yes, I want to know."

"He was here."

"Who is *he*? You keep talking about him like he's someone else. Someone…specific. Do you have a suspect?"

"Not a name."

"But…?"

"I have reason to believe it may be the serial killer who's been killing women in Anchorage."

Summer's mind couldn't process, wouldn't wrap around what her brother had just said. "You think…?"

"The MO is incredibly similar."

"Surely if that were true I'd need more security than just Clay, right? No offense, Clay, it's just that I've seen the news articles about that killer. People haven't stood a chance against him." She waited for their answers.

No one said anything.

Until Clay finally spoke. "The problem is," he began, and for the first time Summer admitted to herself that the slow Southern accent calmed her, maybe just a little bit. It was easy to listen to him talk when she wasn't feeling her independence threatened with everything he said. "The MO doesn't fit perfectly. So we're waiting to see if this is just our suspicion or if it's founded."

"*Our* suspicion?" Noah asked Clay. Summer wasn't sure what to make of that. Had Clay disagreed at first?

Clay nodded. "I don't feel good about this."

Noah's face seemed to indicate that he agreed. "We'll investigate more outside tomorrow. For tonight I'll stay up and keep watch."

"I don't think I can sleep," Summer said.

"You can and you need to." Tyler pulled her into a hug. "Take care of yourself."

Summer hugged him back. It was possible she had the best brothers in the world. "I'll try." She offered a small smile.

"Good night." Kate smiled at her, but didn't offer a hug. She wasn't the huggiest of people, even with those she loved, so Summer didn't mind.

She smiled back. "Good night."

And then her siblings dispersed, leaving only her and Clay.

She turned to face him, not sure what to say. At first, she'd disliked him because she'd been embarrassed. Then it had been convenient to ignore him because she hadn't wanted his presence infringing on her independence, one of the things Summer held the most dear these days.

Now…

Summer wasn't sure. But she owed him a thank-you for convincing her siblings to see reason and to keep her in the loop.

"Thanks for getting him to talk to me," she offered softly, sighing after she did so. "I'm not the youngest, Kate is. But for whatever reason if someone needs extra care, they always assume it's me."

"Siblings are well-meaning but I hear they can be smothering."

"You have siblings?"

Clay shook his head. "I've got a friend who's about as close as you can get, but no, not really. Must have been nice growing up with friends around all the time."

Summer couldn't argue with that.

"Listen, they are right though—you need to sleep."

"I can't sleep up here." So far from everyone else, with no easy escape route. At least downstairs had multiple routes to the outside. Here in her room it was the door or the window. She felt trapped and exposed at the same time.

"It's the safest place for you, Summer. Like I said earlier, it's all tucked back here so that you're almost impossible to get to."

She wouldn't sleep a wink. But if he was going to push the issue, she'd sit up and read all night.

"Alright," Summer said without further fight.

Clay moved toward the door. "I'll be right outside in the hall." Then he turned toward her, his eyes focused and thoughtful. "You aren't planning to even try to sleep, are you?"

"Not even a little."

He laughed. A real, actual laugh. "May as well head downstairs, then. Maybe you'll nod off on the couch."

Summer followed him down the stairs, his laughter echoing in her mind, almost pushing away the niggling fears that reminded her that someone wanted her dead.

Almost.

But not quite.

Clay didn't know what had gotten into him earlier, snapping at Summer when she'd tried to tell him to go after the guy. He could count on one hand the number of times in his adult life he'd lost his temper. He had his own struggles, wouldn't say he was 100 percent the man he wanted to be, but temper wasn't usually one of his issues. It disconcerted him that fear for Summer's safety, combined with him being upset over her persistent stubbornness, had made him lose it like that.

He looked over at her stretched out across the couch, eyes closed. Clay had tried to convince her that her room was actually safer, tucked away and on the second floor, but she hadn't listened, just like she hadn't listened to her brother when he'd brought up the idea of the safe house earlier.

She was stubborn. On one hand, the stubborn ones usually survived when they were attacked, something Summer had already proved true in her first and hopefully only encounter with the attacker. On the other, the stubborn ones were bad about taking precautions and following advice—something Summer had also proven. She clearly wasn't going to listen to anyone, even when it would be wise, if it went against what she thought.

Clay exhaled.

This wasn't what he'd wanted from his fresh start in Alaska. He'd known Tyler's brother was in law enforcement, but he hadn't expected to have any part in it himself. Not that he blamed them for asking for his help. It was the logical choice, Clay just wasn't sure he was ready for it, wasn't sure he trusted himself to have the instincts he used to have, before he'd started to doubt himself.

But he owed it to his friend to try to keep his sister safe.

And doing that, he was seeing now, also probably meant he couldn't keep his distance, not even emotionally. The Dawson family needed as many people as they could get on their side convincing Summer to listen to whatever recommendations law enforcement made—and he wouldn't be able to do that unless they were something resembling friends.

He glanced at her again while she slept.

It wasn't that being Summer's friend would be unpleasant. He admired her strength, her spunk, was intrigued by her and thought she was beautiful. Maybe those things were the problem. He had to think of her as a *friend* only, nothing more, because it was all she could possibly be. He wasn't staying in Alaska long. He was friends with her brother. Reasons to keep his caring on a friend level and not allow it to go any further ran through his mind like facts on a ticker board.

The biggest one was that he wasn't an emotional kind of guy. He kept emotions out of his work life and he'd been a good cop, the possible exception being that last case that even his chief insisted he couldn't have seen coming. Besides that, he'd always done a good job keeping a cool head, staying logical and by the book. Letting himself get any closer to Summer might not allow him to detach the way he needed to in order to keep his focus sharp, keep his senses on alert.

Something he desperately needed to do. Because tonight he felt in his own gut the sinking feeling Noah had seemed to feel in his. Something about this ongoing menace toward Summer felt weightier, more heavy with evil than a random attack. Clay was almost sure Summer *was* the target of a serial killer. One who had been successful six times so far. Who would feel he'd been robbed of his seventh victim and would likely keep coming back until he could kill her too.

And it would be up to Clay to stop him.

FOUR

"Clay, you need to see this."

Tyler's voice.

Clay blinked his eyes open, exhaustion impossible to deny after the small amount of sleep he'd managed the night before. At least it had been more than anticipated—he'd planned to stay awake all night, but Tyler had come in around three thirty in the morning and told him he'd be awake doing lodge business and promised to wake him if anything happened. Clay had argued at first, but when Tyler insisted that Clay wouldn't do them any good exhausted, he finally gave in.

He sat up and glanced at his watch. It was 6:03 a.m. He slid his feet back into his boots, which sat beside the couch he'd slept on. Easy access. He wanted to know he could be ready at a moment's notice. He glanced at the other couch in the room, where Summer had fallen asleep last night, though he'd known she wouldn't be there. Kate had come down and finally convinced her to go up to her room somewhere around 3:00.

"What is it?" Clay was up and following Tyler in seconds, as Tyler walked toward the front door. Clay's eyes went to the stairs. "Is Summer okay?" He needed to know.

"She's fine. Sleeping, thankfully. She doesn't know about this yet and I'm not sure she needs to."

Clay understood Summer's siblings were only trying to protect her, but he disagreed with their methods. He didn't plan to keep anything from her permanently, at least not as it related to the investigation, though he supposed he could see some value in carefully choosing the timing for revealing information to her. There were things about himself he might keep from her, but only because that *was* truly for her own good. It was in both of their interests that he keep his distance from her, be her friend on only the most basic level. Acquaintance, really. An acquaintance tasked with keeping her safe. And nothing more.

"Did we miss something last night?"

"I'm not sure. But look."

Tyler pointed up at the front of the lodge. At first, Clay didn't see anything, just the wide log beams and siding that made up the lodge. He looked toward Summer's window.

There.

The window itself was outlined in red. Spray paint, Clay assumed, from the tint and the lack of drip pattern on the logs. Underneath the window, above the slant of the house's roof, were the words, YOU'LL BE EVEN MORE BEAUTIFUL WHEN YOU SLEEP IN DEATH.

"What…?" Clay clenched his fists and fought the childish desire to kick at the gravel rocks at his feet.

"I know." The anger in Tyler's voice reminded Clay he wasn't alone in his feelings, and that of the group of people worried for Summer's safety, he'd known Summer for the shortest amount of time. If he cared this much about keeping her alive, her family must be stressed beyond all reason.

"And you checked on her this morning?"

"Before and after I saw this, just to be sure. Yes, she's fine."

Clay exhaled. That reassurance did a little to calm him, at least. He pictured Summer as she'd been last night on the couch, eyes closed. Her face had stayed tense though, as if she wasn't able to relax, not even in sleep. Was that only because of the threat against her? he wondered. Or did it have to do with something else?

He didn't know her well enough to ask. Never would, he reminded himself.

"This isn't right." Clay walked down the parking lot a little, parallel to the lodge, looking at the painted words. "He was just trying to kill her and now he's leaving notes?" He shook his head, pulled his phone out of his pocket and called Noah. He didn't see the man's squad car in the parking lot so he assumed he'd already gone to work, probably hoping there'd been a break in the case or that looking at the notes with fresh eyes would help him *make* a break.

"Noah, someone was at the lodge last night after we were outside investigating, sometime after 2:30. Did you see his handiwork painted on the wall?"

"No. It was light when I got up but I was focused on making sure the perimeter was secure before I left, not looking at the whole place. What happened?"

Clay read the message to him.

Noah seemed to consider it. "As far as we know the serial killer in Anchorage hasn't left notes, either before *or* after the victims' deaths, so at least that's good news."

"You don't think it's him anymore?"

Noah let out a breath. "I may have been hasty to assume it was. I don't know yet. I want security around her just as tight as though he is the threat though. I'll be back to process the scene. Give me about thirty minutes. We'll talk more then. There are things I'd rather not say over the phone."

"Alright, see you then." Clay hung up the phone, turned his attention back to the message, looked over at Tyler who was still staring at the wall too, then focused back up at the chilling words.

"We figure out why he did this, we might figure out more about him," Clay thought aloud, considering the message, the placement of it, the logistics of leaving it. "He had to climb up there," he observed. "You keep a ladder near here?"

Tyler nodded. "Around the side of the lodge."

Clay headed in the direction the other man had indicated. Tyler started to follow but Clay stopped him. "You stay there. Don't let your sister's window out of your sight."

"Why shouldn't he let my window out of his sight?"

Clay jumped at Summer's voice in front of him. She'd come from around the side of the lodge, down a stone path that Clay guessed led to the back door.

"How much did you hear?"

Summer raised her eyebrows. "So I was right. You wouldn't have let me out here for some reason."

Tyler had mentioned checking on her. At that time, had he told her to stay in her room? It seemed likely. But even Clay knew that telling this woman to stay put would just make her curious about what she wasn't supposed to see. Tyler should have known it would make her come right outside.

"I didn't say that. But you're supposed to stay where you're put so we can try to keep you safe."

"Stay where I'm put?" Clay wouldn't have said her eyebrows could get any higher, but apparently that would have been wrong. Her shoulders squared, her chin lifted.

Frustration at the morning built inside Clay, but he took a breath to keep his temper in check. Most of the frustration he was feeling was aimed at Summer's attacker and Summer didn't deserve the brunt of that, even if she did seem determined to make his life harder by making her life more dangerous. Somehow though, he was beginning to understand her family's tendency toward being overprotective. Summer was so strong, brave. So independent. And maybe…maybe Clay just didn't want her to have to be all those things all the time if she didn't want to be. Because while it was clear she didn't want to be coddled, somewhere in her blue eyes he'd caught the smallest hint of vulnerability that made him think part of her *did* want protection, wanted to lean on someone, but didn't feel she should. It made him curious about her, made him want to know her more.

Something he needed to ignore, *would* ignore if he had any sense. For both of their sakes.

Her eyes went to the window and grew wide. "Why? Why would anyone do that?"

Clay admired how quickly she'd asked the question that had come to his mind. Motive was one of the key elements in solving any crime, and in a crime that could be related to a serial killer—he wasn't ruling that out yet, even if Noah sounded uncertain—it would be one of the hardest things to figure out. But once they had, understanding motive could be key to unmasking who was behind all of this.

"I don't know. It's something we're going to try to figure out today."

Was it his imagination, or did she edge closer to him? Not that he blamed her. She'd withstood more than the average person could take, pressure-wise, in the last several hours. Everybody had a breaking point. While it didn't look like they'd found Summer's yet, Clay knew they had to be careful.

She leaned closer to him and he searched for words to reassure her. "Stop looking at me like that," she whispered, her eyes meeting his. She held his gaze for a long span of seconds, then backed away.

And he'd thought she needed encouragement.

This woman wasn't going to stop surprising him with her strength, was she?

"Here's what we're going to do," Clay stated. "I'm going to sit here until Noah comes. It's unlikely he'll return to the scene, at least right now, but I'm not going to risk the evidence being compromised."

"You think the guy who did this could have left something behind that could help us ID him?"

Clay didn't want to give her too much hope, but then again, wasn't hope one of the things that made Christians different from people who didn't believe? He had to remember that. "It's possible. I can't promise anything."

Summer looked at him…funny. "No one can, Clay. No guarantees in life, I get that."

Once again, she'd surprised him.

"Anyone hungry?"

Tyler's abrupt question was out of place, but Clay recognized it as an attempt to break up the private conversation between himself and Summer. He stepped back, almost without realizing what he was doing.

"I'll go get some breakfast," Summer volunteered. Did she understand what Tyler was doing too and was going along with it, or was she just eager to eat? "I'll bring it out and we can picnic outside. Make the best of things, right?" She gave a small smile that seemed like a peace offering. She was still feisty this morning, stronger than almost any woman Clay had ever met, but she seemed softer around the edges somehow, at least with him. Like she'd determined maybe they should tolerate each other as long as they were going to be in such close proximity for the time being.

Toleration was fine, as long as it stayed professional. The more he learned about her, the more he needed reminders not to get too close.

He was leaving Alaska at the end of the summer. Tyler knew that, had been fine with it. Whether that had factored into his warnings to leave his sisters alone, Clay wasn't sure. But he'd made no secret of the fact that this wasn't a permanent trip. Of course, he had no idea where he was headed from there. Georgia still didn't seem right. It had changed in too many ways and he…hadn't.

Maybe Arizona. He'd never seen the Southwest and had always wanted to see the Grand Canyon.

But staying in Alaska wasn't likely. There was nothing for him here, except for a job that would only last over the course of the season. And anyway, Clay probably wasn't the settling-down type. It would be better to stay on his toes, keep moving, than have life come crashing down again in any way similar to what it was like when his parents died.

"You'd better not," he finally answered Summer. "I need you to stick close to me."

"I'm starving," she stated flatly.

"I'll bring breakfast out," Tyler offered, having walked back close enough to hear them. He looked at Clay. "Since you have to keep an eye on the scene."

He saw the warning in his friend's eyes. Message received. Clay nodded.

Tyler studied him for another second, then glanced at Summer. He shook his head slightly and walked away.

Great. Now Tyler was seeing things that weren't there.

Clay looked back at the writing on the house, thought about the case and tried to puzzle out why someone was after Summer in the first place. He knew there was no guarantee it was the Anchorage serial killer. In fact, he hoped for the sake of Summer's safety that it wasn't, because the guy was creepy good at what he did. Clay had spent some time searching online last night while he watched Summer sleep and kept an ear open for any suspicious activity.

He'd killed six women in the span of two months. Always two at a time, not necessarily together although once he'd done that, but within about four hours of each other. There was nothing too obvious that tied the pairs of victims together besides their basic demographic. They were women, all in their twenties and early thirties. Slim, athletic. All blonde.

Summer fit the profile. But Clay understood Noah's hope that she hadn't caught the serial killer's eye.

Besides, Summer was the only victim, or attempted victim that they knew of this time. While it was possible the killer would have moved locations and started targeting women on the Kenai after largely sticking with women in the Anchorage area, it wasn't likely he'd also change his MO enough to stop killing them two at a time.

So if they weren't dealing with a serial killer, then the attack against her must have had some other motive. Come to think of it, even if they *were* dealing with the serial killer, there were still questions about motive that needed to be answered. Why here? Why Summer? What about her had caught this killer's eye? To figure that out, he needed to know more about Summer.

"So tell me about yourself."

Summer's eyebrows raised. She laughed a little. "What?"

Clay realized he'd said nothing aloud for the past few minutes. No wonder Summer was confused. But the more he thought about the situation, the more he realized the opportunity they had. There were few leads on the killer because none of his targets had survived... until now. While the files for the other victims had been examined carefully for connections, the authorities were still at a loss to explain how the killer found his victims, and why he chose to attack.

Maybe having a survivor could help uncover answers.

"Say the guy after you is the serial killer."

"Um, I'd rather not."

"I mean, if he is. Assume for now that he is until we get another lead. It's all we have to work with and we should be as careful as if it were for sure true."

"Okay, I'm following."

"If it is the serial killer, then finding links between you and the other women...the ones he did, uh..."

"You don't have to sugarcoat it for me, Clay."

Hearing her say his name did weird things to his insides. He wanted to roll his eyes at himself. Please. Was he a fifth-grade boy with a crush or an adult man who knew when things were and were not a good idea?

"The women he killed have things in common. That's how serial killers work—they have a pattern, a type if you will, and they're after them for a certain reason. Sometimes it's because they remind the killer of someone in their past they were obsessed with for one reason or another. Sometimes the victims have something else in common the killer wants to make a statement against. Sometimes it's just people who the killer happened to have access to, because of where he lived, or what he or they did professionally. There are all kinds of options. I think because of the physical similarities in the women who have been killed—and you also—there's a good chance that's the link between the women. But in case there's more to it than that, I think finding out more about you and more about them might be a good way to figure out who's behind this."

"In that case…" Summer began.

"What?" he asked.

She hesitated. Studying him, weighing him, like she was trying to decide to what degree he was on her side.

"If that's the case, then maybe I could talk to some of the victims' families? See if there's anything else I have in common with the other women who were attacked?"

Clay's heart fell to his stomach. She was asking to get involved in the case in a more proactive way. The urge to take charge and actively fight against this guy was something he understood, but had hoped wouldn't happen for her. For one thing, if Summer insisted on being more involved, Clay would have to be too, something he would rather avoid. He'd made the choice to leave that life behind.

Besides that, he did want Summer safe and he knew that the chances of being able to keep her safe diminished if she insisted on taking an active role.

It was with that in mind that he said his next words. "I'm not so sure that's a good idea."

"You're not going to start sounding like my siblings are you?"

Maybe he was.

"Explain why you don't think it's a good idea." She said the words like she meant them, like she really cared about his thoughts.

Summer was trying to see Clay's point of view just like she was trying to see her siblings'. Really, she was. And it wasn't that she was brave or ignorant of the danger she was currently facing, but she'd never been one to sit still and wait for life to happen. She was the one who ran up mountains, across ridgelines.

She'd been accused more than once of looking for trouble, and while she disagreed with that assessment, she didn't go out of her way to avoid risk. It wasn't her style.

Life was too short to be lived half-heartedly. Summer had always believed that and still did now, despite the fact that she'd shifted her priorities in the last couple of years, more toward family and away from some of the selfish dreams she'd had when she was younger.

"Summer, the safest thing for you is to lay low while we figure out who attacked you. Proactively going and talking to other victims' families isn't that."

"Right, I can see that, but if I'm helping solve the case faster, isn't it for the best?"

Tires crunched the gravel in the driveway. Noah parked and walked over to them. Summer's stomach growled. Tyler sure was taking his time with breakfast.

"Glad you're here." Clay stuck out his hand and Noah shook it. Something about the scene made Summer smile. Her brother liked Clay, something that couldn't be said for most men.

Not that it mattered to Summer. She'd tried romance before, and it had cost far too much. She'd almost lost her family, and she wasn't going to risk that again. No matter how great a man seemed at the beginning, there was no telling with her judgment.

"I'm going to go see what's taking Tyler so long with breakfast."

"You shouldn't be alone," Clay insisted. Summer looked to Noah.

Noah shrugged. "We'll both be right out here so it's probably alright. Don't be long, okay?"

Summer jogged easily to the stairs of the deck and ran up and inside. She found Tyler in the kitchen, icing some cinnamon rolls.

"Oh yum, where did those come from?"

"They were in the freezer. I warmed up a couple. Sorry it took so long."

He set down the icing bag and looked at her a little funny.

"What is it?"

"You seem to mind Clay a lot less today."

Was it her imagination or was Tyler not as thrilled by that as Summer would have guessed?

"I guess I felt like I was kind of a jerk to him yesterday. I'm trying to make up for it."

"Just don't try too hard."

"Why?"

"Because you two wouldn't be good for each other."

The absurdity was so great Summer just laughed. "Tyler, someone is trying to kill me. The last, and I do mean the very, very last thing I am thinking about is getting into a relationship with someone."

"Clay's not the kind of guy to do anything half-heartedly." There he went, the caution in his voice still strong. "If he falls for you, he'll fall all the way, Summer. I don't want you to hurt him and I don't want him to hurt you."

This conversation was giving her a headache. "I thought I should be nicer today. That's all."

"I just wanted to make sure—"

"Listen, message received, Tyler. I don't flirt with every male I come into contact with, okay? I was just trying to be friendly."

She took the plate of cinnamon rolls he handed her, though she doubted she'd eat more than a bite or two—her appetite was suddenly not as large as it had been a few minutes ago.

"Summer, I didn't mean—"

But she'd already left the house, wishing she could step away from the thoughts he'd put in her head just as easily. The truth was that Clay Hitchcock was attractive, sure. She'd noticed yesterday in the truck when he'd rescued her. She wasn't blind. But today she'd truly only been trying to make peace for the sake of making the next few weeks more tolerable. She knew better than her brother did how much she needed to avoid a relationship for now. Or the next few years. Or forever.

Still, it hurt to know that no matter how much she'd changed, how much she'd said she was sorry for hurting them, for not considering the reach of her choices, her family didn't truly believe she'd changed.

Her mistakes might not require her to wear a literal scarlet letter like Hester Prynne had in the book she'd been forced to read in high school, but in this small town and this family, they may as well. There was no escaping what had happened. She'd forever be the sister who had pushed her family away and run off with a man who didn't deserve her love, trust or innocence.

Years later and she'd asked forgiveness from everyone she'd hurt. God included, most of all. In return, she'd gotten an outpouring of love and acceptance. But that couldn't actually erase what had happened, or the damage it left behind.

No one seemed to be able to let it go and really put it in the past.

If she were honest…?

Herself included.

Holding the plate of cinnamon rolls, she hurried down the stairs from the front deck. "Breakfast."

Clay frowned. Summer knew he was too perceptive to have missed the shift in her attitude in the last ten minutes. Whatever, it wasn't something she could deal with discussing right now. He'd have to stay curious about what had come over her.

Noah and Clay each took a cinnamon roll. Summer took the one that was left over and nibbled at the edges of it. Moose Haven Lodge's cinnamon rolls were practically famous, so she couldn't resist them, no matter what kind of mood she was in.

"Did you find anything?" she asked her brother.

Noah shook his head. "Nothing Clay hadn't already thought of or found just by looking at it."

"Because there wasn't anything to find?"

"Because Clay's that good at this job." Noah eyed him. "After the summer, if you stay in Moose Haven I'd like to talk to you about a job. The city is increasing our budget for next year and adding you to the force would be money well spent."

"I appreciate you saying so."

He didn't respond any further to the suggestion. Interesting, at least to Summer. Was he not planning to stay in town? It wasn't uncommon for people to come up to Alaska to work only during the summers, but it still surprised her a bit anyway. Or maybe it had more to do with the offer of the job in particular?

"What we did learn is that both of us agree on the 'why' you were asking about earlier," Clay offered.

"And what did you decide?"

Noah spoke up. "It's odd for someone to try to kill you and then de-escalate, essentially, to trying to scare you. With that in mind, the only logical motive is that he wanted to unnerve you, keep you off balance, basically scare you as a tactic to feel like he still has you under control."

"Why would he do that? Just because he's mentally unstable?"

"It's not that simple," Clay replied. "We can't guess anything about his mental state besides the fact that he has a disregard for human life. Some serial killers are mentally unstable for sure. And some are people who seem to have all their faculties and then just…snap."

"Did you get a lot of serial killers where you're from?" Summer couldn't help the snarky comment as she hadn't really wanted to hear any of Clay's opinions. She trusted her brother.

"We got more crime than you might expect." Something in his face had changed, hardened, and Summer knew she'd crossed some kind of line—she hadn't expected her words to affect him to the degree they had.

"Besides," Clay continued, "the FBI-led academies I've been to, the conferences I've learned at, all of which have taught me plenty, thanks."

It appeared two of them could play the "let's be short with each other now" game.

Summer exhaled. Why was she doing this? Just because of a little goading by her brother? She should know better.

"I'm sorry."

Noah looked at her oddly and she shook her head slightly. Better to drop it and try to be normal around Clay, at least to the best of her ability.

"So that's why you think he's doing this?" Summer tried to redirect the conversation.

Clay looked to Noah to answer, apparently sensing that Summer was taking him more seriously. She felt bad about that. The truth was that she trusted Clay's opinion a great deal and didn't want to.

"That's the working theory."

"And do you think it's the serial killer or not?"

"No."

"Yes."

The two men answered at the same time. Noah's answer was more reassuring...

But Summer felt somewhere inside that Clay's was probably right.

"What do *you* think?" The question came from Clay.

Summer had to take a minute to compose herself before she reacted to his question. Had her expression given away that she agreed with him or had he just really wondered what she thought?

"I think it's him." She exhaled as she voiced the words she'd hoped to keep inside. Something about saying them out loud made the threat seem more real.

"Why?"

Now she knew he was interested in what she thought. With that in mind, Summer considered her answer carefully.

"Just the way it felt when he had me, with the knife..." she began. Images flashed in her mind and she squeezed her eyes shut tight for a second. Gut instinct said to push the images away, to try to forget about them, but Summer made herself focus on them instead, hopeful that some detail would stand out that she hadn't noticed before. Anything that would help them make progress in this case. Because if someone was after her, she wasn't going to sit around and hide. She was going to do something about it.

"I've got my team working on it and I've also alerted the troopers." Noah's words were meant for reassurance, but they could only do so much. Nothing changed the fact that someone was after her.

"Thanks."

"I'll keep you posted on what I learn today, alright? Thanks for telling me as much as you did yesterday. I've got some calls in, and a forensic artist in Anchorage is doing a full body sketch today based on the description you gave me."

"I didn't notice much." At least, Summer wouldn't have expected it would be enough to help.

"You'd be surprised what those guys can do with just a little bit of information," Noah said. "It doesn't always give an exact picture, but often it's close enough that someone recognizes them."

"Let us know," Clay said.

Noah nodded. "I'm going to climb up there, process the message for evidence and then head back to work. What are your plans?"

"I'd hoped to take the tourists who arrived last night on a hike," Summer said.

"No."

"Noah, this is my job."

"And no job is worth your life."

Summer knew that but also didn't think Noah understood how important her job at the family's lodge was to her.

Or why. But that was understandable. She tried not to talk about the *why*, tried not to think about it.

"I understand you want to keep me safe. Believe me, I want that too, but I can't stop everything because of some what-ifs."

"Someone has already grabbed you and then tracked you down to threaten you. I hardly think anything we are considering in any arena is as far-fetched as a what-if at this point. It's just what is, Summer. Someone wants you dead."

"I know. And they're going to want me dead whether I'm doing my job or not."

FIVE

Clay watched Summer plead her case with her brother with a little bit of amusement and a lot of observation about both of them that he was mentally filing away. He respected Noah so far—he seemed like a decent guy. And Summer... Clay couldn't get a handle on her. One minute she was friendly. Then next she acted like she couldn't stand his presence.

In either mood, she remained stubborn though, and he couldn't help but admire the trait. Because the stubborn ones tended to be the ones who had the fight to stay alive when it came down to it.

And anyway, he saw something desperate in her eyes, something that told him she'd be better off in the woods, climbing mountains, than trapped inside. He took only a second to decide the extra work it would bring him was worth it, and that the benefits to what she was asking outweighed the risks.

"I think we should let her hike." He winced a little internally at his phrasing. She wasn't going to like the idea that she needed his permission to *let* her hike.

"See, Clay agrees with me." She passed right over it in appreciation for having someone on her side, apparently.

"What's your plan for keeping her safe?"

"I'll be with her, obviously. We'll take my car in case someone is watching hers and hasn't taken note of mine yet, and we'll choose less popular hikes where people aren't going to see her in case the killer is working with a partner."

"Do you think he is?"

"No, I don't. But we need to be as aware as possible. Not cautious in a way that keeps you locked in the lodge till this is figured out, but very aware."

She nodded.

"What do you think?" He directed the question to Noah. Though Clay took his assignment to protect Summer seriously, he knew that Noah's position as her brother, and police chief, meant that he might have stronger opinions and he certainly had the right to them. Clay was just summer help, just a friend, not someone who mattered much in the grand scheme of Summer's life. Even if keeping her safe felt more personal than any job he'd taken before.

"If you're comfortable with it, we'll try it for now."

"Thank you, thank you, thank you." Summer threw her arms around her brother and grinned. She looked back at Clay. "I'll be on my guard. I don't want to make your job any more difficult than it already is."

"Fine. Work it out and call me as soon as you're back at the lodge," Noah said.

Summer nodded.

"We'd better get back inside for now. The fewer people out here in the parking lot, the less chance that one of the guests' attention will be drawn to the vandalism." Clay didn't want to point out the possible implications for their business when Summer's life was so much more important, but the welfare of the lodge seemed important to Summer.

"Right. Thank you." Surprise was in her eyes as she turned to him.

Clay offered a small smile. "So what was wrong earlier?"

"When?"

He studied her face. Shook his head. "Never mind." Whatever the reason for her odd behavior, it seemed to be over now and Clay was only overly curious when it benefitted a case. Otherwise he believed in letting people have their privacy. Their secrets.

He wasn't much of a secret keeper himself. Or he hadn't been, until recently. Now there were parts of himself he didn't have any desire to share with anyone else—thoughts that haunted him when he tried to fall asleep at night.

"Where are you planning to hike today?"

"Bear Creek Falls."

Clay raised his eyebrows. "Bear Creek? Really?"

"Yes, bears. As in those creatures in the woods up here. Why?" The smile that tugged at the edges of her lips showed a hint of amusement. Clay knew he was what Alaskans would occasionally refer to as a cheechako—basically a newbie, unfamiliar with the area—but he'd done a little research on the dangers he could expect to face before coming to Alaska.

"You carry bear spray when you lead these hikes, right?"

Summer rolled her eyes. "I'm from Moose Haven, Alaska, Clay. I carry a .44."

He laughed, something he hadn't been doing enough of lately. "Noted."

"Although I carry spray too. It works out better for everyone if you can deter a bear from attacking with the spray."

Clay nodded. He had both lines of defense Summer had mentioned also, and had planned to wear one on either side of his belt. Better safe than sorry. While the killer after Summer posed a bigger threat, it would be foolish to ignore the wildlife threat on the Kenai Peninsula.

"And this place is not somewhere you regularly hike, correct?" he confirmed as they headed into the lodge. Summer was walking toward the living room.

"That's right. It's been years since I've been there at all." She frowned a little. "I wish I could use my usual places. I have my list of hike routes carefully thought out and edited to include what I think will challenge tourists just enough but still provide a payoff in views or something else. Anything not on that list, there's a reason why it's not ideal for tourists."

"That matters less than keeping you safe."

"True. But I don't think you understand how much my family's lodge means to me."

"Why is that?"

She shifted in her seat. Clay waited, observing the tell and knowing she was either planning to lie—something that didn't seem like her—or avoid telling him the whole truth.

"It's my family's lodge. Why wouldn't I care about it?"

"It just seems to mean even more to you than that."

"Let's focus on the hike, okay?" She opened a drawer in the small end table beside the couch and pulled out a map.

"I should probably get a couple of those while I'm up here so I can learn my way around."

"You'll figure it out quickly enough, at least where roads are concerned. There aren't that many of them. It might take a little longer to get the trails down. Even I don't know where all of those go, which is why I was in trouble the other day."

"What happened that you ended up somewhere you didn't realize where you were?" Clay asked, realizing he didn't think he'd heard that part of the story.

"I had to run from him when I had the chance. He was standing between me and one route I knew, and another route would have meant backtracking down a wide-open trail that would have made it easy for him to follow. I figured the smaller, less used trail was my best bet because I grew up hiking these mountains, dodging trees, running over roots."

"You took a risk and it paid off."

"A calculated one, but yes."

He nodded. "Impressive," he told her truthfully. He wasn't sure Summer understood how remarkable her whole handling of that situation had been.

She shrugged. "I did what I had to do. I still keep replaying it in my mind. First, in case there are any details I missed that might help and, second, because I wonder what I could have done differently. Could I have avoided it? Should I have reacted in a different way than I did? Things like that." Summer exhaled, her shoulders dropping as she did so.

"You did a good job. Trust me. Now show me where we're going today."

She set the map on her lap, paused and shook her head. "Actually, come with me."

She stood and walked to the stairs, and Clay followed her to the second floor and into her room. "What's up?"

"I just had a bad feeling. I'm probably just jumpy from talking about the attack, but I didn't want to risk being overheard by anyone. If we are supposed to keep the location a secret until we're heading on the hike, to minimize the chances my attacker can find me, that includes keeping it from *everybody* who isn't family. Or you. Or Erynn."

"You don't think there's a connection between your attacker and one of the guests, do you?" The idea had crossed Clay's mind but he'd written it off fairly quickly. If one of the guests wanted Summer dead there would have been plenty of opportunity to attack her closer to the lodge. Following her up the steep mountain trail would have been unnecessary.

"I don't know. I just don't want to take chances."

"Just calculated risks, right?" Clay smiled a little. Whether she acknowledged it or not, Summer was a risk taker. She just had her own unique ideas about what constituted a risk and what didn't.

"So have a seat." She motioned to the two chairs on one wall of the room. Clay sat, Summer taking the seat next to him. She unfolded the map again. "We're here." She set her finger down. Clay nodded, doing his best to memorize the general topography around the lodge, looking for landmarks. "And we're going here."

"Is it a pretty steep hike?"

"Not as steep as the trail I was on yesterday."

"Yeah, but you were on your way up a mountain."

"That's where I prefer to be."

Summer stopped, almost cutting herself off in the middle of the last word. She gazed up at him, her face giving nothing away, but looking like she was studying him, waiting to see if he'd caught something.

"What is it?"

She shook her head. "Nothing."

"I'd already figured out the mountains are home for you, Summer. It's not a secret."

She flinched a little at the word *secret* unless Clay was mistaken.

"So what will you tell people about the hike, as far as difficulty level? I'm guessing you're planning to advertise it in some way so people will know what they're getting into, right?"

Summer exhaled, the tension lines in her face easing. One of these days Clay's curiosity was going to get the best of him—she'd react to something he said, and he wouldn't be able to let it go—but for now it seemed like the right thing to do. Even if Summer was becoming more and more intriguing to him.

"I'll probably call it moderate. A young kid who's a good hiker could do it. I have a friend in Anchorage whose son climbed one of the peaks up here—they call it Little O'Malley—when he was four."

"I'd probably try that one if a four-year-old could do it." Clay laughed.

"I didn't say it was easy. I said a good hiker could handle it. Hiking is less about age or agility and more about your mental state, and how badly you want to be on top of that mountain."

"You think so, huh?"

She nodded, and Clay could tell that once again they were dangerously close to an area of Summer's life that meant enough to her that she guarded it from other people. So there was something about the mountains that was crucially important to her. Interesting.

"What time should we leave on the hike?" she interjected as Clay reminded himself not to push her for answers about things like this, that intrigued him but didn't have anything to do with the case.

"When do you usually schedule them?"

"Sometimes morning, sometimes afternoon. It's just after eight now. We could easily post a 10:30 departure time and take lunch with us, or we could eat here and hike afterward."

"Let's do that, then."

"Thanks for doing this, Clay."

He nodded, smiled back at her and tried not to second-guess everything as she stood up to get ready for the day. He only hoped he was doing the right thing, and not taking risks that would put her in greater danger.

SIX

Hours later, Summer walked along the path to the start of the trail, trying to project the confidence she usually felt. She wasn't sure she was fooling anyone with her attempts not to be scared out of her mind by the fact that someone was after her, but she sure was trying.

Not that she wanted to deceive anyone, but she didn't want to be babied. And most of all, she didn't want anyone blaming her, in any way more than they already legitimately could, for the failure of Moose Haven Lodge.

Summer had no idea why Clay didn't understand how much the lodge meant to her. He had no idea of the circumstances of her past few years, true. So he didn't know that if it weren't for her, the lodge would be sitting pretty, bringing in more than enough money to support all of them. But she'd left right when they needed her most and now things were tight. Most of that weight was on Tyler's shoulders, but Summer didn't want him to have to shoulder that alone.

Besides, whether Clay understood or not, it was her family's lodge and family mattered, so it was her responsibility too. Did Clay not understand that? Maybe not.

She didn't know enough about him. Didn't know if he

even *had* a family. She shuddered at the very thought of being alone in the world. She didn't know what she'd do without her family. They had never let her down…even if she hadn't been able to return the favor.

Pushing the past from her mind, something she felt like she spent too large a portion of every day doing, Summer stared down at her favorite hiking boots. They were covered in dirt, now not just from enjoyable adventures in the woods, not just a visible symbol of how she loved to push herself, but also from running for her life.

Summer wasn't sure how she felt about that. It seemed wrong, somehow. Another thing her mystery attacker had tainted. Nothing about this situation seemed right though. Right down to the fact that as protective as Noah was, her brother didn't have the time to invest in keeping her safe one-on-one, not if he was going to make any headway in solving the case and making something like a protective detail unnecessary.

So she had a stranger keeping her safe.

That was something she needed to get over sooner rather than later. The way she'd behaved toward Clay wasn't something she was proud of and it needed to change.

Summer took a deep breath at the trailhead as she eyed the woods. "'Lovely, dark and deep,'" she muttered under her breath, reminded of a poem she'd studied in high school.

"Robert Frost, right?"

She jumped, not having realized Clay was right behind her. She nodded. "I think so. You read a lot of poetry?" She wouldn't be surprised if he said yes. There was more to him than she would have assumed.

"Not since high school English—I think that's when I read that poem."

She laughed. "Me too."

"It must be required across the country or something."

Summer nodded, having forgotten in the seconds of kinship there that they came from different ends of the country, different worlds if you thought about it. This corner of Alaska was familiar to her, where she was raised—the mountains that were her home. She'd looked Clay up online and learned that he was from South Georgia, near the beach. They couldn't be more opposite if they tried.

"You nervous about going back in the woods?"

The perception she'd noted as being part of his character seemed to be coming out even stronger now. But she didn't see a need to answer. He could take that however he wanted to.

"Alright," she said, raising her voice to be heard by the small crowd, "if everyone will meet me here by the trailhead I need to go over some rules."

She went through her spiel the way she did before every single hike she led—some tourists underestimated the terrain or Alaska itself, and she liked to make sure they understood the risks as well as how to minimize them before they started. Among other things, she reminded them of how to act during a bear encounter and to make sure they stayed with a hiking partner.

"Does this mean you're my hiking partner?" Clay drawled softly as she walked by.

Summer whirled and caught the smile in his eyes. This playfulness was a new side of him. She smiled back for a split second, welcoming the more lighthearted interaction, before realizing she really couldn't afford to let her guard down. For the sake of her safety and her heart. "I guess you don't have much choice right now, do you?"

Not waiting for a reply, Summer started down the trail. Of course, a quick glance over her shoulder not many seconds later, which she told herself was to check on the hikers she was leading, confirmed that he'd caught up and was directly behind her. From the little she knew about him, she was certain he wasn't going to let her go far from him. He took keeping her safe seriously, something she appreciated.

"On the right in just a few more minutes you'll get your first glimpse of the falls," she called back to the group. "We won't reach the base of the falls for another two miles because of the way the trail twists and turns through the forest."

Some appreciative murmurs behind her from the tourists confirmed to Summer that she'd made a good decision for this hike. Of course, it wasn't long after that that she remembered why it wasn't one of her favorite trails—the mud could get slick on some of the uphill sections.

She made it up one particularly steep section and then turned to the group. They seemed to be doing okay so far. She saw more smiles than frowns—so far this hike was a win. She felt her shoulders relax a little as she prepared to deliver her next fun fact about this trail. That was something that made her hikes more enjoyable than people just wandering through the woods by themselves. She was able to offer tourists her expertise about the area and help them recognize some of the unique elements they were seeing.

"I'm sure you're noticing the mud helping you break your hiking boots in." Summer kept her voice light. "For those of you who don't already know, both Moose Haven and the nearby town of Seward are in the farthest north rain forest. I know when you think *rain forest* you probably don't picture spruce trees but it's true."

"Explains the mud," Clay muttered under his breath. Summer glanced at him, catching his smile. He did have a nice smile. More than nice.

They kept hiking.

"Just about another mile to the falls."

Most of the people had stopped talking by now. This was the most intense part of the hike. Thankfully the wind had shifted, bringing some of the cool moist air from the falls their way. Summer brushed her hair from her face as she hiked, noting in amusement how the hairs by her forehead had curled up in the forest's humidity.

A quarter mile from the falls, Clay's demeanor changed. He moved closer to her, keeping in step with her perfectly, walking beside her now, not behind her like he had been earlier.

"What is it?" Summer didn't think anything the man did was without intention.

"I'm not sure yet."

Cryptic, but she was working, she didn't have time to crack his evasive-man code right now.

"Alright, up ahead you'll see Bear Creek Falls." Summer glanced at Clay, who was looking elsewhere, back in the direction they'd come maybe. What did he see back there? She intended to find out, once she'd gotten the tourists settled.

"Please finish making your way to the falls, take some pictures and enjoy—" she glanced at her watch "—forty-five minutes on your own before meeting back here." She motioned to a large spruce tree with a rock underneath it. "Remember, this is the Alaskan wilderness, so be cautious. Yes, there are trails and if it weren't safe in this area, then I wouldn't have brought you here, but you still need to stay alert and pay attention to your surroundings. Make notes of landmarks if you want to wander at all and keep an eye on the clock. I've given the lodge our approximate return time so someone will be coming to check on us if we aren't back when we should be."

Summer stayed still while the group wandered toward the falls, making their way at a leisurely pace down the trail.

When the last tourist had passed her, she turned to Clay. "What is it?"

"I told you I'm not sure yet."

"But you suspect something."

His face was serious, his eyes giving away nothing. He was 100 percent in police officer mode, Summer knew.

"You found something, didn't you? We have some time. Take me with you and let's see what it is."

He shook his head. "I'm not sure you want to be there."

"So what, you're going to take me back down to the lodge, find someone to cover bodyguard duty and come back up here? It would take hours—whatever you thought you saw could be long gone. Plus, you don't know the trail. And anyway, I thought keeping me safe was your job."

Summer was right about one thing. His primary job was keeping her safe. Not just from physical danger, but from anything that would add to her nightmares.

The smell of decaying flesh wasn't something you easily forgot once you'd smelled it, and Clay had before. He'd caught the first whiff on this trail about five minutes back from where they were right now and hadn't decided how he was going to go investigate.

He didn't want Summer to see what he suspected he would find. But he knew that there was no way to stop her from coming with him. And she was right that it made more sense not to wait until later. The faster they confirmed his suspicions, the faster they could notify the authorities and get a proper investigation started. He started walking back along the trail, and Summer followed him.

"Remind me how far this trail is from where you were attacked."

Summer shrugged. "It depends. It would take probably about four hours following the twists and turns on the trail from where we are now, give or a take a little time, unless someone took the ridgeline." She motioned upward. Clay wasn't sure where they were on this mountain.

"How close are we to the top?"

"Not quite two-thirds of the way up. This is the last of the tree line. Another quarter mile or so and it's clear mountain."

"Have you done the ridgeline, then?" Clay suspected he knew the answer but wanted to hear it from Summer.

She nodded. "Yes."

"Were you planning to do it the other night?"

She exhaled. "No."

"No?"

She shook her head.

"Is it possible that someone could have attacked you

over on Hope Mountain and then come over here by the ridgeline, or vice versa?"

"Sure, but I don't know why it would matter."

Clay picked up his pace and Summer followed. "What is that smell?"

It was getting stronger the closer they backtracked to where Clay had first smelled it. The wind had shifted again, which apparently was causing Summer to notice it too.

"We'll see in a minute," he said with no hint of amusement in his voice.

Clay paused and motioned to the left. "Is there a trail that will get us that way?"

"Besides the ridgeline?"

Her voice still had a hint of teasing—she must not recognize the smell.

"I need a trail that goes that way, Summer."

She seemed to finally recognize that he didn't have any room for humor at the moment.

She studied the direction he'd pointed and seemed to finally find a way that would work. "Game trail. This way."

She stepped in front of him but Clay caught her arm. Summer paused, then looked at his hand on her arm.

Clay released it immediately, breaking the touch. She'd been attacked just hours before, what had he been thinking?

He hadn't been thinking at all—he'd been reacting on instinct. And he'd learned the hard way that his instincts couldn't always be trusted.

"I'm so sorry."

"It was fine, actually." She was still studying her arm, where his hand had been. She looked up slowly, met his eyes and held her gaze there. "It wasn't the same at all, the way you touched me. I could tell your intention was to keep me safe."

She exhaled. Relieved to know her attack hadn't scarred her more than it could have, maybe? Clay knew she was fortunate to have escaped more mental trauma. Some people weren't so fortunate.

"I need to go first." Clay focused back on the task at hand.

"Why?"

"Summer." He didn't seem to have more words than that, couldn't find any in his mind. They hiked in silence for a minute. Then Summer spoke up again.

"Why won't you tell me what we're looking for?" Summer coughed. "And what *is* that smell?" She looked around.

And saw it a split second before Clay did, if the way she stilled was to be believed. She inhaled sharply, but didn't look away. Neither did Clay, because that was what he'd been searching for.

The source of the smell. Fifteen or twenty yards away.

Female. Midtwenties.

Blonde.

This was a match for the serial killer's MO after all, which meant the case had turned from bad to worse. Their worst nightmare for keeping Summer safe seemed to be coming true.

Clay had called the Moose Haven Police Department to report the discovery of the body as soon as he saw it. Summer, seeing they were going to have to wait there for a while until law enforcement showed up to secure the scene, called Kate, who agreed to hike up to Bear

Creek Falls to meet the group and lead them back to the lodge. The group of tourists wasn't going to be told about the body, though if it ended up in the paper they'd make the connection eventually. For now, it was better they not know.

Now they were waiting, one of the worst parts when something like this happened. In the movies, once a body was discovered or a crime was committed, everything sped up, but real life didn't work that way. The Moose Haven PD was sending officers but it would take them a while to arrive at the scene and then it would have to be processed, with a methodicalness that wouldn't allow them to rush at all, needing to see if there were any clues the killer had left behind.

"Do you know who the victim could be?" He hated to ask but needed to. The police would want to know and it helped him think through the implications of finding a body in the woods also. Besides, it gave him a reason to try to keep Summer looking at him, rather than at the body lying there on the forest floor not too far from them.

Not that either of them could forget it was there.

Summer started to shake her head and then paused. "Possibly. Someone mentioned this morning on a hiking page I follow online that a friend was missing. It didn't jump out at me because that's fairly common up here. When someone goes missing it's rarely foul play, at least among missing persons cases I've heard of."

"Tell me about the person who was missing. Do you remember anything specific about her?"

"Basically what you can see." She winced. "Just that she was around my age... That she was an avid hiker and adventurer. She did some hiking videos telling people about the hikes she liked to do. Those are online somewhere."

Clay's heartbeat quickened. "Did she post ahead of time what hikes she'd be talking about next?" That could have given their killer a way to find her. He'd been wondering how the man had managed to track two women on mountains next to each other at the same time unless he'd known where they both were going to be ahead of time. They'd already established that Summer's routine was set enough he'd probably been able to know exactly where she'd be, but this woman's death and the circumstances around it were still a mystery.

Clay's gut said that once they cracked the mystery, the answers would bring them a step closer to whoever was after Summer.

But that hadn't happened yet, he reminded himself. He needed that investigative team to hurry up and get here.

"I think she did, yes," Summer answered his question, nodding slowly like she'd realized why he'd asked it and was putting the pieces together for herself.

"And someone could hike that ridgeline."

"Only someone experienced. It's not a ridgeline I could see a novice doing with any success."

He pressed for more details. "How experienced?"

"Intermediate."

"Okay." So it wouldn't narrow their suspect list solely to expert mountain climbers, but at least it gave them a direction to look in.

Movement down the trail caught his attention. His hand immediately went to his side, the familiar bulk of his service handgun there and ready if he needed it. Thankfully he spotted Noah and a female state trooper officer coming up the trail. He moved his hand off his weapon and called to them.

Noah's face registered the exact moment he smelled the distinct odor of decay. He felt for the police chief. Clay had kept himself and Summer there not only because the body needed to be kept under supervision until the law enforcement could come to process it, but also because he'd learned in his years of police work that the best course of action was to stay at the scene and let your nose get used to the smell. It was better than getting fresh air and coming back in, a mistake rookie cops often made. It usually didn't take them long to learn though.

"Tell me how you found her." Noah's voice was all business, the strain of the day already evident in his tone, and Clay knew it was only going to get worse.

"The smell first. Then I came this way to investigate."

"Did it occur to you that you were marching my sister into a crime scene?" Noah practically growled the words.

"Noah. Calm down. He did what needed to be done." The trooper stuck her hand out to Clay. "Trooper Erynn Cooper."

"Trooper... Cooper?"

She rolled her eyes. "Yeah, never heard that before. Clever."

Clay smiled. "Sorry, ma'am."

"Ma'am?" Now her brows were raised. The woman had a really expressive face. "Where are you from, because it's sure not here."

"Georgia."

"The South. That makes sense."

"Could we save the introductions for later?"

Erynn rolled her eyes and gave Clay a sympathetic smile. "He's really not always such a bear."

Clay looked between the two of them. "Do the troopers work with Moose Haven police often?"

Erynn nodded as Noah shook his head.

Summer sighed. "They have to cooperate because Moose Haven is in such an isolated area of the Kenai Peninsula. Because of that our police force is small and sometimes needs backup." She nodded to Erynn. "And sometimes the troopers need Moose Haven PD's help with particular cases because they technically have jurisdiction and the troopers don't like to supersede that when they don't need to." She nodded at Noah. "Did I balance that well between the two of you so we can give up the fighting for now?"

Noah glared.

"So." Erynn moved closer to the body. "I think this is our missing person from Kenai. The hiking blogger—Melissa Mitchell."

Noah stepped closer to see as well, and then looked back at Clay. Clay knew what the other man was about to ask. It was time for Summer to get out of there. Pretty soon reality was going to hit, the knowledge that she could have ended up just like that, how close she'd come to being a body in the woods.

It roiled Clay's stomach, and without thinking he reached out his left hand. Somehow he just needed physical contact with her right now as they made their way through the growing dimness of this thick area of forest. It was still early enough for plenty of daylight but the clouds had darkened, another heavy rain promising to be released soon in the future.

If she was surprised at his gesture, she didn't show it. Just accepted his offered hand. It took him off guard how much smaller her hand was than his. So feminine and soft. He guessed he hadn't spent much time thinking about what her hands were like, but for someone who was so tough and independent, she was also so fragile.

Clay couldn't let anything happen to her.

"Let's go," he said to her.

"You don't have to ask me again."

SEVEN

Summer couldn't quite get comfortable anywhere at the lodge, not after what they'd found that afternoon. Clay had been quieter than usual since they'd returned and the several attempts at conversation she'd made had been unsuccessful.

She'd finally given up and sat down with a sketch-book and some charcoal pencils. Her family teased her about how rarely she sat still, so this old hobby wasn't one she had much time for anymore, but she did enjoy it when she got the chance.

"You're very good." Clay sat down beside her on the couch, leaning over slightly, she guessed to see what she was working on.

"Thanks." She tilted the pad toward him. "Bear Creek Falls. I wanted to remember what the falls themselves look like, remind myself right now that I like that trail, it's a good spot in the woods and it's not the mountain's fault that…" She couldn't make herself finish.

Everything that had happened was settling into her mind, and she knew it was changing the way she viewed the world. Darkening it. Even the lodge that had been her home since she could remember wasn't the same.

That was why she hadn't been able to get comfortable. Somehow everything had changed for Summer since the body had been discovered.

Because it wasn't *a body*. It was a woman who'd been living, moving, warm flesh and blood like she was right now.

And the person who wanted Summer dead might be the same person who'd taken that other life.

It could have been her.

It almost *was* her.

"I see why you'd want to draw it. Got any others in that book?"

She didn't know how much to show him. Was he humoring her, or was he really curious? Then again, did it really matter? He was offering them both something to distract them from the case and the overwhelming feeling that when Noah got home any minute, the news he brought with him might crush her beyond what she could bear.

"A few." She kept her voice calm and handed the book to him. It might be easier if she just let him look rather than be involved in showing him.

He took the sketchbook, started at the beginning, something she admired about him. Any artist's work, in Summer's opinion, should be viewed not only as individual pieces but as a series, because that's how people were—a series of things that happened to them, ways they'd changed, different characteristics...

"These are amazing, Summer."

It only took him a minute or two to flip through them all slowly. She thought she might be up to sketch number eight in this book. Not much compared to the hundred or so pages waiting to be filled. But it had been a long time since she'd slowed down, or *been* slowed down enough to pick the hobby up again.

"Thank you." She never knew what else to say when someone complimented something she enjoyed that came so easily to her.

"It's easy to see that you love the mountains. How long have you been hiking seriously?"

"Hiking? Since I was a kid." She could ignore his "seriously," right? Maybe he hadn't meant it the way she would have naturally interpreted it.

"Not just hiking in general, but like you do now. You hike like an athlete, like it's something you've trained for."

Were *all* cops this observant?

"Since I was seventeen." The words tumbled out before she could question them, and now she couldn't call them back. Summer didn't know how to interpret her current emotions. She was scared, tense, but somehow felt less guarded around Clay than she had. Because of what had happened today, what they'd been through together so far?

She wasn't sure.

The front door of the lodge opened before Clay could ask any follow-up questions, something for which she was thankful since she wasn't sure she was ready for those yet.

"Clay? Summer?"

It was Noah.

"In here," Summer called.

She heard Noah's heavy footsteps approach and studied him as he entered. He looked like he'd aged a couple of years today, and his eyes had growing dark circles underneath them. Had he slept since all this had begun? Summer wasn't sure.

"What did you find out?" she asked before she could stop herself, before she could consider she might not want to know.

"I've got to head back to the station. I'm just here to grab food and check in with you to make sure you're fine."

"She's okay," Clay said. "I'm not letting her out of my sight for longer than it takes to use the bathroom."

"Keep it that way." Noah's voice was nearly vibrating with tension.

"So it's him."

"Him? You found a guy?"

Neither man answered. She understood, gradually. "Ohh. You didn't find anyone. But now you think it's the…serial killer." The last two words she had to force from her mouth, and even as she did she could hardly bring herself to believe this was her real life. That the words *serial killer* had any place in her vocabulary.

Noah exhaled. "I'm almost positive."

"Because we know now that there was a second victim—like his usual pattern?"

Noah hesitated, then nodded. Summer narrowed her eyes. Her brother wasn't lying, but he wasn't telling the whole truth, either.

"What other reason do you have?"

Noah looked at Clay. Neither one of them said anything.

"You've got to stop keeping things from me. It's not making me any safer." Surely they'd respond to that line of argument, since it was such a high priority for both of them.

"Fine." Noah took a breath. "A forensic artist in Anchorage was able to generate a sketch of the suspect based on the description you gave us." He reached into the backpack he'd set on the floor and motioned for them to follow him to the back kitchen, where the family had a private eating area.

They did so. Summer took her seat, trying not to get her hopes up that the sketch was accurate and detailed enough to be useful. She'd have drawn it herself but she didn't draw people, the nuances of facial structure and expression had always eluded her, and though he'd had a mask covering all but his eyes, she'd still feared she wouldn't get it right if she did it herself. But as an artist she knew what an almost impossible proposition it was to draw something based on someone else's description.

Noah set the manila envelope down on the table and opened it.

And there he was, staring at her behind the mask he'd worn. Everything, down to the expression in his eyes, was right. Summer shivered.

"That's him."

Noah nodded. "It also matches the only possible description we had of the serial killer. One of the women who ended up dead, Holly Wilcox, was seen with a man a few hours before her death, walking on one of the multiuse trails in Anchorage. A bicyclist remembered him and gave a description that was, unfortunately, too vague for the artist to work with, as talented as he is. But when I asked him if what he'd drawn for you fit that other man, he thought it did."

"Interesting that she was seen with him and no one noticed a struggle or anything," Clay mused.

"She knew him, then," Summer said. "Right?"

"Possibly."

"And you think he's the man who's killed those other women and is after me." Her mind was refusing to wrap all the way around this new bit of news. Maybe the human mind wasn't made to absorb so much in such a short period of time, because try as she might Summer couldn't quite get herself to acknowledge that this was her reality.

"What else?" she asked, even though she wasn't sure what else she could handle.

The two men looked at each other again, but right before Summer was ready to let her frustration explode again, Clay took her by the arm. "We'll be back," he said to Noah, leading her back farther into the private part of the house and stopping in a hallway where he stood across from her, facing her.

"You've got to stop asking to be told more than you need to know."

"I'm the victim...attempted victim, whatever the correct terminology is." She shoved back a piece of her hair that had fallen in front of her eyes and lifted her chin a little, doing everything she knew how to do to project confidence and certainty, hoping to convince Clay that she was strong enough to handle this.

Clay only shook his head.

"Do you know anything about cases like this, Summer? Do you even have a clue what Noah is dealing with?"

"I don't," she admitted. It was as far from her comfort zone as anything could be. But it *was* happening to her, and Summer was not the kind of woman to back down from a threat, or hide from it. Much as some people might prefer to live with their heads in the sand, that wasn't Summer.

"Everything we saw today was just a glimpse. Do you realize that? There's so much more that will go into the investigation. Autopsies. Analyzing time of death, exact cause of death, whether there was any other trauma… I don't want you to hear those details. And neither does Noah. But even if he did, I'd fight him on this."

"Why? Why do you care so much?"

"Because you're the kind of person who shouldn't have to deal with this."

"I'm not some fragile Southern belle, Clay. I'm an Alaskan woman who has dealt with life and death more than you could probably guess and has faced down both, when they seemed equally scary, and barely flinched."

A slight hint of a smile crossed his face. "First, if you think Southern belles are fragile, you haven't met one. I should introduce you to some of my friends. Second, I'm sorry you've had to do that. I have no doubt you did it well and bravely, but I'm the one in charge of protecting you right now and if I can protect your heart and your mind as well as protect your physical life, I'm going to."

Summer swallowed hard. Her heart was pounding, higher in her throat than it should be from the intensity of this entire conversation. Much as she was worried about her physical life and her mind, it was her heart that had her on shaky ground right now. It was time to stop denying she felt any attraction for Clay Hitchcock. Her only course of action now was to remind herself of all the reasons why it didn't matter, why it would never work.

Because the man had a passion and a caring that wove together into an almost irresistible combination, and Summer couldn't pretend any longer that wasn't true.

But she would protect her heart. She had to. Because she knew what happened when she let her heart get involved—she lost sight of everything but the object of her affection, and last time she'd done that her family had suffered.

She felt the rhythm of her heart beating, enjoyed for just one more second the weight of Clay's hand on her hand and then pulled hers away.

"Keeping me entirely safe is not a job anyone is asking you to do Clay. And it may not be a job you can do."

They rejoined Noah and heard one more update. The crime lab in Anchorage had analyzed the fibers found on Summer's clothes and on the tree branches where the struggle had taken place. They were fleece, and the composition matched the Anchorage Outdoor Gear's store brand. As people from all walks of life shopped there, it still didn't give them much to go on.

Clay would ask Noah what else he had when Summer went to bed tonight. She may not want the kind of sheltering he was trying to give her, but that wasn't going to stop him for now, not when Noah agreed she didn't need to know all the details.

The truth was that this guy was vicious. From a quick conversation when Summer had gone to the bathroom, Clay had learned that the killer was worse than anyone either he or Noah had ever dealt with. The only plus side to anything they'd learned about him today was that with as bold as he was, the risks he took were going to lead law enforcement to catch up to him eventually.

All that troubled him was whether or not that would occur before anything worse happened to Summer.

Time moved slowly. Summer spent some time updating Kate on what had happened. After they all ate a late dinner, Clay suggested a card game to Summer to help pass the time, but the look she gave him more than answered his question about whether or not she was interested in that. Finally he gave up on trying to entertain her and just sat quietly, his mind going over and over the details of the case they knew already and wondering how they'd fill in the ones they didn't. There had to be something more proactive they could do than sit in the lodge, but Clay hadn't figured out what that could be yet.

He glanced at Summer, something telling him he should ask her, but he couldn't quite convince himself to willingly put her through the stress of thinking through the case in deeper detail.

She caught him staring and met his gaze. "What?"

He shook his head. Maybe tomorrow he'd talk to her about it. But he just wasn't sure enough yet that it was a good idea.

"I'm going to bed." She stood. Clay glanced at the clock. Not long past ten but it had been a long day.

"Sleep well." He stood too and started to follow her.

"You don't need to follow me."

He let her walk upstairs alone, but when he heard the door to her room shut, he headed up too and sat down in a chair he'd positioned earlier in the hallway outside her door. He and Noah still hadn't figured out quite what to do about nighttime. Someone needed to be watching Summer at all times, but if the two of them didn't get sleep they wouldn't be any good at providing daytime protection in the long run. Clay had mentioned Tyler as an option, but Noah didn't want his brother adding anything to his plate since he was the one keeping the lodge going while the rest of them focused their energies on this. Clay suspected Noah probably hadn't slept more than three or four hours since all this had started. The man wore a double weight—he was her brother and the police chief. Clay didn't have that pressure…

Instead the pressure he felt came from inside. He cared about Summer not because of anything he *was* to her. He was her friend, and barely that. But he still cared. He chose not to examine the reasons why.

EIGHT

Summer lay in bed staring at the ceiling for what felt like hours, turning one way, then another. A serial killer was after her. She was being protected by a man who threatened the security of the walls she'd been building around her heart for years. Her brother had morphed from his lighthearted self into 100 percent police chief mode. Stress had always made Noah more driven, but Summer never would have guessed the intensity a threat against one of his siblings would bring out.

For the first time, Summer felt like she understood a little more why her siblings had reacted about Christopher the way they had. She'd always seen herself as sort of the extra sibling. Noah was saving the world; Tyler had always wanted to save the lodge; Kate was strong enough to never need saving by anyone but God.

And then there was Summer. The dreamer. The one who made mistakes and needed to be rescued.

She was tired of playing that part. She was going to help with this case, was going to be the one to solve it even, maybe. She was determined, and had already thought of some ideas for how she could contribute to the investigation—she just needed to get Clay on her side. She'd seen in his eyes though his dislike of being on the sidelines, so she should be able to convince him.

She exhaled, exhaustion finally creeping toward her, sleep begging her to close her eyes. She gave in, nodded off slowly and surrendered to unconsciousness.

Her eyes stayed closed when a hand gently stroked her cheek the first time. The second time she blinked her eyes open, confusion muddling with tiredness in her mind. She should be the only one in her room…

As her eyes focused on the black mask in front of her, the man leaning over her bed inches from her face, she almost couldn't breathe. Her nightmare there, in her room. While she slept.

She hadn't even opened her mouth to scream before he put a gloved hand over it. The gloves weren't rough, a detail her mind somehow noticed. They weren't soft, either. They were…squishy. Almost like neoprene?

Summer took note of the detail, even though she didn't know what difference it made. She wasn't trained for what to notice in situations like this and wasn't sure she'd make it out of it anyway.

No, that was no way to think. She refused to keep thinking like a victim, refused to be one. She'd spent too many years of her life living that way, as a self-inflicted victim of her own bad choices. She wasn't going to be anyone's victim now.

She bit down hard on the hand over her mouth, causing the intruder to cry out.

Rather than release her though, he gripped her arm with his other hand even tighter. Summer shivered, not just from his touch, and her eyes went to the window. Open.

At least she'd figured out how he'd gotten in the room.

The handle of her door moved.

Another intruder? The serial killer worked alone, didn't he? Or could the person at her door be help? She fought a wave of dizziness after thinking of the man holding her as not just "her attacker" but "the serial killer." She had been pinned down, and was now being hauled to the window by the hands of a man who had brutally murdered seven women.

"Are you okay in there?" Clay's voice. *He* was the one at the door. She could have cried, if she could get herself to feel anything but terror in the deepest core of her being. All the other emotions seemed dormant. Yet his voice still reminded her to struggle, to make it as difficult as possible for the man trying to haul her away.

"Stop fighting me. This is for your own good." Her captor moved her toward the window another step.

"I'm coming in, so if you aren't decent, now would be a good time to grab a robe or something." Clay's voice was low and serious, heavy with fear that mirrored exactly how she felt. Had he heard the man when she bit him?

"Summer. Now. We have to leave before they stop us." The killer was insistent.

And he knew her name. Summer shivered. It was something that made sense, but it eliminated any possibility that this could be random. And it might mean something to the investigators that he knew it, called her by it. Summer didn't know, didn't know much of anything anymore.

She swallowed hard, tears finally finding their way to her eyes and threatening to spill over. She blinked them back. No, she wouldn't give him the satisfaction of seeing her as anything even approaching weak.

She shook her head and pulled against him. The pressure on her arm increased as he squeezed her. She fought back, twisted away, but he held tight.

The door slammed open.

"Freeze!" Clay yelled.

Summer fell to the ground instantly as the man released her. She took a deep breath. It was almost over.

But her attacker was through the window before Clay had even made it past the bed.

There was a shuffling in the hallway. Before Summer could look up from where she'd crumpled on the floor, Clay addressed him.

"Noah, he's running."

Then more footsteps as her brother took off, presumably out of the house to chase whoever was responsible. It wasn't over yet. And if he could get this close and they still couldn't catch him… A small sob escaped.

Clay bent down, sat on the floor beside her. "Are you okay?"

He asked it slowly, somehow the sound of his low voice putting her more at ease. She shook her head. Paused, then nodded. "I'm okay. Scared. But not injured. Not broken."

She looked up from the floor, where she'd been staring, processing, trying to get ahold of herself now that adrenaline had faded and her hands had started shaking a bit.

"I can't believe I just sat out there in the hallway while he was in here. That he got to you on my watch…" Clay shook his head, then took a deep breath that was long enough for Summer to tell he was having a hard time getting ahold of his emotions too. "I'm sorry, Summer."

Hearing his voice say her name erased some of the

tension in her shoulders. He was helping the whole experience lose its power, being here with her like this. She
reached a hand over to him, knowing he wouldn't mis-
interpret it as a romantic gesture, but just as her needing
reassurance that someone was there. That she was okay.

He took her hand. Slowly ran his thumb across it and
tightened his grip ever so slightly.

"You did the best you could," she offered, wanting
him to stop blaming himself.

"No. And I need to let you help."

Leaving her hand in the warmth of his, she looked
up at him. "What?"

"Sitting around waiting for him to attack is crazy. We
have to do something."

He was so closely echoing her own thoughts from
earlier. Summer nodded. "I have an idea."

Before she could tell him, Noah burst back into the
room.

"Did you get him?"

"He's gone." Noah shook his head. "Vanished completely, as if he knew of some hidden trail even though
I've lived here on this property my whole life. I looked
for tracks and I've got Kate out there now, with one of
my officers, looking in case I missed anything."

Summer respected the fact that her brother wasn't embarrassed to admit that Kate was the better tracker of the
two of them. She was one of the best trackers in all of
Alaska, which was saying something. Summer couldn't
read signs like she could, but she could find her way
around in the woods with ease, which was why her being
disoriented after the attack and not recognizing where
she was had cut so deep and disconcerted her so much.

"He can't just have disappeared."

Noah shook his head. "I'll stay with Summer if you want to investigate."

Summer watched the two of them stare each other down. There seemed to be something going on that she wasn't aware of, some sort of unspoken conversation happening between the two of them.

Feeling frustrated that she was once again being left out of the loop, she tried to think of a way she could help. "Listen, I can go check myself if you want."

"You won't be leaving the house until it's time for you to go to a safe house, which is as soon as I get a place cleared and set up." Noah's voice didn't leave any room for argument.

Didn't faze Summer.

"I'm not going to a safe house."

"We'll talk about it later."

She shook her head. "No. Not unless you can be absolutely certain I'd be any safer there." Besides, even if running and hiding did appeal to some cowardly place inside her, not only did Summer refuse to give in to that, she also needed to be here at the lodge. Her hikes were usually some of the best-rated amenities the lodge offered. It wasn't so much that she did anything that was so different from anyone they could have hired to lead the hikes, but rather because she was something of a minor celebrity in athletic circles. If people were fascinated by her mountain running credentials and the brief note in her bio about the time she'd spent in Europe running with some of the world's elite on some of the most stunning peaks on the globe, then that was fine with her—as long as it brought more business to the lodge. It meant she was finally doing something for her family, contributing.

Atoning.

"I'm not leaving." Her voice was just as firm.

Noah exhaled. "Fine. I'll leave it for the moment. For now, get dressed." He looked at Clay. "Someone else will cover your assigned tasks at the lodge for both of you today. You need to go to Anchorage to talk to some of the officers who have been working this case. I've communicated to them everything you've told me, but maybe a face-to-face will help and they'll uncover something that will point us to our target. We need a break in this case. This guy is too good."

Clay was nodding. "I'd been thinking we should go up there."

Summer's heartbeat quickened. She'd been planning a trip to Alaska's largest city also, but for slightly different case-related reasons. "Alright, when do we leave?"

Noah raised his eyebrows. Surprised by her easy acquiescence? She wasn't sure. But she didn't flinch, didn't lower her shoulders.

"As soon as you're ready," Clay answered.

She glanced at the clock. It was 3:52 a.m. She wasn't going back to sleep. "Give me five minutes."

"We might need to stay in Anchorage through tomorrow." Summer waited till they were well down the Seward Highway headed toward Anchorage before she started sharing the pieces of her plan with Clay. They were out of cell phone signal range right now, so she knew he couldn't call Noah to get his thoughts on it, a detail that may or may not have factored into her decision to broach the subject right now.

"Why is that?" Clay looked over at her, only briefly as he put his eyes right back on the road, but it was long enough for her to wonder about the thoughts behind what she saw in his eyes. He'd weathered the situation well, showing up in town right as everything in her family went crazy and jumping right in to help. She remembered Tyler talking about him from college but hadn't realized they were that close—close enough for Clay to put himself in danger to protect Tyler's family.

Or maybe Clay was just like that. That wouldn't surprise her. He seemed like the kind of classic Southern boy who would pull his friends' trucks out of ditches in the middle of the night, no questions asked, like the kind you heard about in songs. Until now she hadn't been sure they actually existed. Alaskans had their own code of honor, committed to taking care of their own, but it still wasn't the same as whatever she saw in Clay.

She wondered how much of it had to do with his faith. She'd seen him reading his Bible on more than one occasion when they'd been sitting in the lodge. Really reading, like he was paying attention too, not just holding it and staring into the distance like she'd done the last few times she'd tried it.

Before she'd acknowledged that maybe, possibly, it was too late for her.

She shrugged the uncomfortable thoughts away before they could settle too deeply in her mind. "Because I have a plan."

"Go on."

His voice was cautious. Hesitant, but not necessarily filled with any kind of opposition. Not yet anyway.

"After we talk to the police, I want to talk to some of the victims' families."

"The police will have handled that, Summer. And I'm not sure they'll give us access to that—though it's likely something Noah can get ahold of if he feels like he should."

"Hear me out."

Another glance. Some crazy part of her wanted to reach out her hand, hold his again like she had in the early hours of this morning and see if the same electricity shot through her, the heart-shaking, unsettling but so-very-welcome kind.

Welcome?

No. That kind of heat was dangerous. Lack of sleep and extremely close proximity to Clay were just getting to her, that was all. People had all kinds of weird emotions when they were stuck with someone in these kinds of emotional, tense situations.

She shook her head, focusing on what she'd been saying. "I just need to talk to them myself and ask some questions I don't think the police would have asked."

"The police are good at what they do. And they won't release any additional information on the victims or their families. I'm sorry, I'm trying to hear you out, Summer, but none of this sounds like anything I can help you with."

"I've got a list of names and addresses," she said before he could say anything else.

"How?"

Summer shrugged. "I read the news articles, did some digging online, as much as I could."

Clay didn't say anything for a minute. Summer looked out the window as they started gaining elevation, moving into Turnagain Pass, the last bit of isolated highway before they started edging closer toward the limits of the Municipality of Anchorage.

"Why?"

"Think about it, Clay. I'm being targeted. I must have something in common with these women, or he wouldn't have gone after all of us. I'm one of them, but...not."

"And you won't be if I have anything to say about it."

He practically growled the words, but in a protective way. She almost smiled, but Summer had more to say, so she kept going. "Are you going to listen to the rest?"

"I'm sorry, go ahead."

"Thank you. I think it's more than just a physical description connection. There must at the very least be some way he knew all of us, or had seen all of us... something that drew us to his attention. Right? Surely he didn't just drive down to the Moose Haven area of all places and stalk the first two people he met who looked like the other women he'd killed?" Summer wasn't sure, she could be reaching there, but she knew if she was Clay would tell her. To be honest, she wasn't sure if her speculation had her on the right track or not, but sitting around waiting for someone to try to kill her again wasn't working for her. She had to do something, be involved somehow, and this was the best way she could think of. Besides, it made sense to her, that maybe this could help them make progress. If there was even a chance, it was worth it to her to try.

"It's a reasonable question to be asking."

"So if he knew all of us, maybe I'll be able to figure out a connection if I can talk personally to the families."

"They may not let you, you know."

"The police?"

"No, the families. This is painful for them. They may not want to revisit it, especially with a woman who at least vaguely resembles the person they lost."

"That I understand." Summer hesitated. "But if it

would save someone's life? Or maybe more important for them, if it would bring a killer to justice?" Her heart was beating faster now, but for once in the last few days, it wasn't because of fear but anticipation. Somehow she thought this would work.

He reached over, squeezed her hand and let it go before she even knew what was happening.

Blinking, she moved her hand to her lap when he released it—which was almost as soon as he'd touched it, it was that fast—and looked over at him.

Clay smiled. "I think we've got a shot at finding something we can use today. It's a good idea, it really is. I just don't want you to get your hopes up."

She understood that. That was the dangerous thing about hope—when it didn't come through for you, it was almost worse than if you'd never had any in the first place.

Her hand still tingling from Clay's touch, she angled her body a little more toward the window and looked out at the scenery as they drove, ticking off reasons in her head why she shouldn't let herself care that he'd touched her hand.

She was being stalked by a killer. He was only staying for the summer.

And most important, she'd made mistakes and he seemed like the poster child for a Christian nice guy.

Yes, sometimes hope wasn't worth the pain it caused.

NINE

Summer had gone quiet after sharing her plan with him, and while Clay knew his mental energy would be better spent thinking about the case, he couldn't stop thinking about how she was acting.

Was it his fault, because of that quick hand squeeze?

He wasn't the best with women, wasn't one of those guys who charmed his way into a date often. He wouldn't say he couldn't, he'd just rarely tried to be flirtatious because it seemed dishonest to him—if he wanted to get to know a woman better, he'd be straightforward.

Not that he'd been trying to do that with Summer. Nothing like that had been on his mind. Only a strong admiration for how quick thinking she was, and the desire to show her he was on her side. That he cared.

All it had done was push her away.

It took all Clay's focus to keep driving and not pull over and go for a walk in the woods. Or a run, that would be better. He missed the routine he'd had to keep himself in shape back when he was a police officer. He could easily maintain the same habits now but driving across the country had thrown that schedule off some. He needed to get back into the swing of that. He glanced at Summer. He considered bringing up to her now the idea of them running together—to get him back into shape and to let her get out of the house while still being protected—but from the way she leaned away from him to the way her arms were folded, everything about her said "no trespassing."

Instead he just drove, through the vastness of the Kenai Peninsula, up into Turnagain Pass, then around Turnagain Arm as they approached Anchorage from the south side.

Summer broke the silence. "When we get to the police department, they won't separate us, will they? I mean, we're not suspects so it's not like TV. Right?"

Clay's shoulders relaxed a little at a conversation he could easily handle. "Not at all. They just want to share information, really. They may treat you a bit like—"

"Like a victim?" Her tone made no secret of her hatred for that word. It wasn't something anyone wanted to be, a *victim*, but something about how strongly Summer rebelled against the designation made him wonder if there was more to it in her case, some aspect of her life that he didn't know about. Which wouldn't be difficult as he hadn't known her for a full week yet, though in some ways it felt like he had known her for years.

"Right."

"But you'll be there."

"Yes. I'll make sure they understand we have to stay together. Your brother wouldn't want us separated."

"Just my brother?"

Something about the way she asked it caught his attention—she was not speaking in a coy way at all, her tone was just honest. Like she wanted to know what he thought of her, if he cared. How much of this was a job and how much was because he didn't want to see her hurt.

Clay didn't know. He was afraid to let himself think through any of the possible answers.

"I don't want it, either, Summer. I can keep you safer when I'm with you." He took a deep breath, determined to make up the ground he'd lost with the hand-holding incident. "It's my job." He added the last three words knowing full well he cared more than he would about some random person he felt obliged to protect, which was all Summer had been to him before he had started to get to know her.

"It is. You're right."

She grew quiet again and Clay didn't mind it as much as they entered Anchorage and traffic started to get thicker. They'd hit right about at the morning rush hour, or so it seemed. He wasn't sure how long rush hour lasted there, he only knew that compared to Treasure Point and Moose Haven, the traffic was thick. He got off the highway when they were well into town and, following the directions he'd gotten from the internet, arrived at the Anchorage Police Department.

"Has Anchorage been working on tracking this guy, or would it be better to talk to the troopers?" Summer asked with a frown after Clay pulled into a parking place in front of the building.

"We'll talk to both. They have both worked on the cases here in town."

"So they don't mind sharing information with each other, things like that?"

Clay laughed. "Don't believe everything you see on TV. Most law enforcement departments are perfectly happy to have more manpower working on a case. Gets through evidence faster, prevents some backlogging."

She nodded, but didn't say anything more.

They entered through the front doors and Clay told the receptionist who they were there to see. The detective Noah had told him to ask for came through a security door only a few minutes later. He held it open and motioned for them to enter.

"Clay Hitchcock? Summer Dawson? I'm George Walters. Thank you for coming. We've been hoping to talk to you, but it didn't sound initially like you'd be able to make the trip up from the Kenai. Did your drive go well?"

"No traffic, roads were great," Summer confirmed. "It's nice that the snow is melted now."

"It is. It's tricky getting up here in the winter."

Clay hadn't considered that, but when he thought about it, he realized the Seward Highway, which they'd just taken, was the only road between the whole Kenai Peninsula—not just Moose Haven but also five to ten other medium-sized towns, he'd guess from the maps he'd looked at—and Anchorage.

"If you'll both come to my office." He stopped at a doorway and motioned them inside. Clay stopped to let Summer go first and she did so, and then he followed.

"Thank you again for meeting with us," Clay said as he sat. "We had another incident last night and wanted to make sure everyone working on this case had as many details as possible."

"Chief Dawson told me some of it this morning, though not specifics. I wanted to get those from Miss Dawson firsthand. I appreciate you both making the trip—anything that could help us make some progress."

Walters ran a hand across his forehead as he shook his head. "I don't like knowing this guy is out there somewhere. I don't feel like any of the women in our city are really safe—or apparently the entire area." He looked at Summer.

She didn't say anything but Clay thought she looked a little nervous. He decided he'd better talk first. She could answer questions once Walters asked some.

"Do you guys happen to have any idea why he might have moved onto women on the Kenai?"

Walters seemed to weigh his words. "I understand you're former law enforcement, Clay. So you'll understand why I can't answer that question fully. Here's what I know. We're working with a profiler at the FBI to try to figure out his motives, try to decipher if his MO might change. The move to another location surprised the guys at the FBI and us too, but there are possible explanations."

Clay nodded. He could respect if the other man didn't feel like he could say more since he wasn't technically an officer anymore. He knew everything Walters did tell him today was a favor.

"Speaking of that subject though, could I ask you a few questions, Miss Dawson?"

"You can call me Summer." She sat up a little straighter, leaned forward a little, Clay noticed.

"Alright. Summer, do you have any idea who might want to attack you?"

The man didn't pull punches; Clay liked that.

She shook her head, as Clay had already known she would.

"I have no idea. I'm working on…compiling a list of suspicions I have."

"Of people the killer could be?" The detective raised his eyebrows. "I didn't realize you were being so pro-active."

Summer laughed it off, which Clay appreciated. He didn't feel the other man needed to know the effort Summer, and he by extension, planned to go to find a link between her and the other victims. Since it wouldn't impede the official investigation and might yield useful clues, some things were just better left unsaid.

"I'm working on figuring out possible ways the killer might have met me. Things like that. I thought that might help?"

"It might. It's worth a try as long as you're staying out of danger." He looked at Clay. "Do you have her in a safe house?"

He shook his head. "The situation in Moose Haven currently makes more sense if we don't. I know you've talked to her brother Chief Noah Dawson, and he'll change her protection plan if it seems our current plan isn't sufficient."

"She has someone with her 24/7 though. Right?"

Clay nodded. "Yes, sir."

"Good." The other man looked relieved, Clay noted. He was glad that the Anchorage police were taking the threat as seriously as they were, liked that someone else had Summer's back, even if it was from a distance.

"Can you tell me in your own words what happened last night?" he asked Summer.

Summer did so and Clay listened, impressed at the way she was able to share everything with so much confidence, apparently unaffected. He knew better than to believe she was as nonchalant as she seemed. He knew how much the idea of someone being after her shook her. But he appreciated how she was able to deliver information in a detached sort of way.

When she'd finished giving her answer, the detective nodded and then slowly stood. "I'm going to pass this information on to the rest of the team. I can't tell you how much I appreciate you coming up. I know it's a long drive."

"We have other things to do in Anchorage anyway," Summer said with a smile. Clay tried not to react but wished she hadn't shared that particular tidbit.

Thankfully the detective didn't ask questions, he just saw them out politely and then they were climbing back into Clay's car.

"That went well, right?" Summer asked when they were both buckled in.

"It did." Though it hadn't been quite as informative as he had hoped. For the first time since he'd left Georgia, Clay honestly wished he had his badge back. He'd love to know what was going on in the police department right now, what leads were going to be pursued with the new information they'd been provided. He had guesses, of course, based on how he would handle it, but that wasn't the same thing as knowing.

He was surprised by how much his civilian status stung.

He glanced over at Summer. Was it endangering her, being protected by someone who didn't have the full power of the law behind him? It was better than nothing for sure, but he'd have to talk with Noah. The other man had floated the idea of Clay being sworn in as a Moose Haven reserve officer once, but Clay had brushed him off.

Maybe it was time to accept that offer. Anything that would keep Summer safer.

Summer gave Clay the address of the first house she wanted to visit. That of the first victim's parents. Not every victim had relatives living in the state, so it worked out well for Summer that the first one had. She wanted to start at the beginning, talk to people who knew the victims while following the order of their disappearances just in case that was somehow significant.

The farther into the neighborhood they drove the heavier the pit in Summer's stomach grew. She reached for the thermos of tea she'd brought and took a sip. Lukewarm. She winced. She'd known when she came up with this idea that it would be difficult, tracing the killer's movements from one grieving family to another. Especially when her own emotions seemed to be waging a war between thankfulness that she was alive, that her family wasn't one on the list, and at the same time feeling guilty. Why her? Why was she alive when these other women were dead?

Classic survivor's guilt, Summer knew and was able to acknowledge. But it didn't change the weight that seemed to sit on her, that made it a little harder to breathe. And also drove her to answer the whispered question from somewhere inside herself. *It doesn't matter why. You're alive. What are you going to do about it?*

What was she going to do?

"Which way here?" Clay asked.

Summer smiled at the irony of his timing. "Turn left," she said after looking down at the directions she'd pulled up on her phone.

Working at the lodge was the right thing to do, she

told herself as they approached the first house. There had to be a way to make it feel more like her passion. She already knew it was worth doing because it made her family happy and family was important, that was a lesson she should have learned long ago.

She wasn't going to make that mistake again.

"This one?" Clay nodded toward a blue two-story house.

"Yes." He pulled into the driveway.

She didn't move, didn't unbuckle. She suddenly couldn't. Summer swallowed hard, tried to remind herself of all the reasons this was a good idea. Maybe their only chance.

"Ready?" Clay asked, his voice gentle and not pressuring. She smiled a little even as she still fought to keep herself from spiraling into panic.

"I'm not sure."

"Nervous?"

"I don't know what I am. Too many emotions to name, I guess."

He nodded. "I understand."

"You do?"

"It's hard to face someone who's been through this kind of tragedy, much less to ask them questions. Your part in this case, the fact that you're not just someone investigating, that's got to make it harder."

She nodded.

He started to reach his hand over, then seemed to remember earlier and pulled it back.

Summer took his, accepted the squeeze he gave once she had and gave him a small smile. "I can use all the encouragement I can get right now."

"I think what you're doing is smart."

"You're coming with me, right?" The thought of facing the family without Clay hadn't occurred to her.

"Yes," he answered before she could worry any longer. She exhaled, let go of his hand and opened the car door. "I'm ready as I'll get."

She crossed the driveway and followed the sidewalk up to the small front deck of the house. Without hesitating, because she suspected if she hesitated she'd get back into the car and ask Clay to drive straight back to Moose Haven, she knocked on the door.

Waited.

The door opened slightly and a woman she'd guess to be in her midfifties looked at both of them. "Yes?" Summer detected a slight European accent, something that was common in Anchorage and other parts of Alaska. In this woman's voice, it sounded almost musical.

"Mrs. Hunt?"

"Yes?"

She opened the door slightly farther after they mentioned her name. Summer realized she shouldn't waste time before explaining who they were. The woman's life had just been changed by violence. She was probably going to be slightly suspicious of anyone she didn't know.

"I'm Summer Dawson. I wanted to ask you some questions about your daughter." The words spilled out before she could decide if that was the best way to approach saying who she was.

"Jenna?"

"Yes." Summer nodded.

"The police have been here. You're not the police."

"No. I'm not. I'm..." She weighed her options, then

decided to take a chance with full honesty. "Police think the same man tried to kill me."

Her eyes and the door both widened. "Come in. And your friend?"

"Clay. He's a former police officer who's my full-time protection at the moment."

The older woman nodded and moved aside.

Summer walked inside the house.

"Please, have a seat." She motioned to a couch and Summer sat. Clay sat beside her. She was grateful for the fire in the fireplace, since she'd started to shiver slightly. While she wasn't convinced it was from the weather, since it wasn't cold or rainy outside, the heat might help anyway.

Mrs. Hunt sat across from them. "Why don't you tell me why someone who isn't a police officer needs to ask me questions."

Summer weighed her words. She hadn't counted on how difficult it would be to talk to people who had been so personally affected by the man who was after her. Here she was, doing what she'd planned, taking charge and getting involved, and right now all she could do was sit there.

"I just… I need to see if I can find any answers to explain why this is happening. Maybe help find the man responsible."

The other woman studied her. "You seem, Summer, like the kind of person who has her own grief. You're careful in how you talk to me. I can tell that."

Avoiding Clay's eyes, Summer shrugged. The woman could read people, Summer would give her that. But she wasn't there to talk about past griefs. She wasn't even there to make the woman feel better about her own, though if she somehow could she'd certainly be happy to know she had done so. She was there for answers.

Mrs. Hunt shifted in her seat, leaned forward and rested her elbows on her legs in a graceful gesture. "Tell me about yourself first."

"Um…" Summer fumbled for words. This wasn't how this was supposed to go. She had her questions, on another page of her notebook, written down, ready to show how she could help in this investigation rather than being the one person everyone else was protecting. Not that she minded being kept alive—she appreciated that part. But she was tired of being treated with kid gloves. Again.

If only it was the first time people had seen her as a victim. At least this time she wasn't to blame. That first time, she'd been a victim of her own life choices.

"Please." The older woman smiled and Summer sighed.

"I'm twenty-eight. I live in Moose Haven, with my family. We run a lodge." She glanced at Clay, noticing how carefully he seemed to be listening. Did he want to know more about her? Summer knew it was silly to wonder. It wasn't as though anything could come of any possible interest. But she still wanted to know—did he have any interest in her? Or did he just see her like so many other people did at the moment, as someone to protect?

She turned her attention back to Mrs. Hunt. "I love Alaska. It seemed like your daughter did too from her Facebook profile."

Mrs. Hunt nodded. "She was a fan of yours, you know."

"Of mine?" Summer shook her head. "I haven't done anything in years."

"But you were a mountain runner back in the day,

weren't you? Jenna followed your career. You weren't too far apart in age and she was amazed at all you accomplished, starting with those records you broke back in high school."

Once again, the tables were uncomfortably turned. Summer had researched this victim and her family but it had never dawned on her they would know details about her life.

"I was. Yes."

"You still are."

"Why do you say that?" Why was this woman insisting on talking about Summer?

"I think it's a gift God gave you. You can't just ignore it. It's still part of who you are."

Summer didn't know what to say.

Mrs. Hunt smiled slightly. "I just felt like I was supposed to tell you that. Now, let me tell you about my Jenna."

For the next ten minutes she shared information about her daughter. Summer didn't think that all of it was relevant to the investigation, though she supposed there was a chance it could prove useful later. But a lot of what she said did pique her interest. She and Jenna had been in a lot of the same circles, even though they had never met. She ran 5Ks, hiked almost every weekend, rain or shine, and many of her favorite hikes were Summer's favorites too. She wrote a note to herself in her notebook to follow up on that possible lead. Did they both hike those mountains consistently enough that someone could have targeted them both because of it? And did the other victims share their love for those hikes?

If anything, this visit was leaving her with more questions than answers, but at least Summer felt like they were making progress. They were on the right track.

"I appreciate you talking to us today," Summer said as she finally stood. "It was extremely helpful."

"I hope something helps you find who is behind this." Mrs. Hunt shuddered. "I don't know if I'll ever feel like the world is a safe, good place again, but him not roaming the streets would go a long way toward that."

"I understand." Summer smiled sympathetically. And she did.

Clay stood also and walked to the door before Summer, to check for threats outside, she assumed. He stepped out before she did and walked down the steps of the front deck, not far but close enough to give her a tiny bit of privacy with the woman she'd felt an unexpected connection with.

"Dear." Mrs. Hunt laid a hand on Summer's arm as Summer started to step through the front door. "Could you do something for me?"

"If it's within my capabilities, of course. I really appreciate the information you gave me today."

Mrs. Hunt didn't say anything for a minute. Summer started to prompt her for an answer, since Clay was still walking toward the car in the driveway and she felt she needed to hurry.

But then the older woman met her eyes. When she did speak, her voice was slow, gentle, firm. "My daughter... she's with Jesus now. She knew Him. But her time here is finished. Yours isn't, Summer."

Summer's eyes stung as tears started to gather at the edges.

"Here is what I'd like you to do for me. For Jenna." Now Mrs. Hunt's eyes were watering. She didn't break her gaze though, kept her eyes straight on Summer's and Summer couldn't look away. "I want you to *live*, dear. Really, truly live without regrets. Fully. Freely."

There was no need to ask what she meant, to think about how her life would change if she did that. Summer already knew. Instead, she nodded. She owed it to the woman and the daughter she'd lost.

To herself. To the tiny unborn baby daughter *she* had lost three years ago.

"I promise."

TEN

Summer had been quiet since they'd left the Hunts' house. Clay had driven her to several more places after that, but so far no one had answered the door. He didn't know if they were just not responding to people they didn't know or if they'd left town until the man behind the death of their loved ones had been caught. Either would make sense.

Someone finally answered at the fourth house they drove to.

It was the sister of one of the victims. "Who are you?" was the first thing she said when Summer knocked on the door.

"I'm trying to learn about your sister."

The door shut most of the way.

"The same man who killed her is trying to kill me."

Even Clay caught his breath at Summer's words, at the reality of them and the way they didn't pull any punches. The woman at the door blinked, opened it wider. "Come in."

The conversation that followed was much like the one with Mrs. Hunt, in Clay's opinion. They didn't learn anything new, just what they knew already. The woman said that her sister, Amanda, had lived with her, but had been on a camping trip in Chugach State Park, the mountains behind Anchorage, when she'd disappeared, and then her body had been found a few days later.

"Did she hike often?" Summer asked with a frown.

"Every weekend and at least two days a week after work in the summer. She loved all outdoorsy kinds of things." A small smile escaped the woman's face. "She'd just started to learn stand-up paddleboarding. Amanda was just always outside." The smile disappeared. "Are the police any closer to discovering who did this?"

"Aren't they keeping in touch with you with updates?"

"They are," she admitted. "But there haven't been any lately. I've been wondering if they're even still working on this or if they've given up."

The frustration in her tone was evident, and Clay guessed that the kind of helplessness she was feeling must be grating.

"They'll let you know," Clay told her with confidence.

"But you must not trust them to do their jobs, either, if you're out trying to get clues or other information."

Summer looked at Clay. Both of them seemed to be thinking. Summer was the first to shake her head slowly. "No, I do trust them. But I can't sit by and be nothing more than a victim. I can't be helpless. I've got to do something."

"So this is for you."

Summer nodded. "It's for me."

It was another glimpse into the kind of person she was, and Clay admired her more for it. To say that she trusted the police—and to mean it, Clay could tell she did—but to also know herself well enough to know when she needed to do something… Summer was thoughtful, self-aware and brave. And beautiful, not that he was supposed to be noticing that.

If they weren't in the middle of this case, he might be close to admitting that she intrigued him more than the sister of a friend really should. Might be close to admitting that in normal circumstances, he'd have asked her on a date by now, tried to figure out if she felt the same fascination with him that he did with her.

"Thanks for your time," Summer said and they walked back to the car. "Gorgeous view," she commented before they climbed in.

They'd driven up to an area of Anchorage that Summer had told him on the way there was called The Hillside. "There are tons of hillsides here. What about those houses, are those on The Hillside?" He'd pointed to a cluster of large, nice homes on a hillside up against the mountains.

She shook her head. "Stuckagain Heights."

"But they're on a hillside," he'd teased, and it was one of the lightest moments they'd had in days. They'd needed the levity, both of them. Human beings were only meant to sustain the intensity they'd been running at for short periods of time. They were both dangerously close to running out of steam.

Now, as Clay maneuvered the car carefully back down the mountainside, he kept his eyes on the road rather than take in the view.

"Clay."

Summer's voice was tense, short, and he chanced a quick look in her direction before returning his eyes to the road. "What's wrong?" He couldn't see any obvious answers. She seemed fine.

"The car behind us. He keeps getting closer."

"Is it a man behind the wheel? Can you see him?" There was still the possibility that the car behind them was an innocent bad driver.

But if it wasn't, at least Clay wanted to know if they could identify him.

"I can't really tell, but I think it's a man."

"You can't tell?"

"His windshield is tinted, I think? Or maybe it's the way the sun is hitting. But no, I can't see anything clearly distinguishing. I'm sorry. Do you think it's him?"

"I don't know." He glanced in the rearview mirror. Summer was right, Clay couldn't see anything, either, except the fact that someone was in the driver's seat. "Could be?" He took a left on the next road that would lead them to town, twisting around a hairpin turn.

Did the car edge closer?

Clay hit the gas, accelerating a little.

"What are you doing?"

"I'm not going to keep going slow and risk him hitting us here."

He twisted around the curve, looked down the road that lay head of them. After this stretch of road there was only one more spot where losing control of the car would be truly disastrous.

He came up to that danger spot, tightened his grip on the wheel and glanced in the rearview.

The car was accelerating. And Clay had nowhere to go. He didn't dare risk speeding up here lest he send them careening over the mountainside without any help from whomever was tailing them.

"Hang on, Summer!"

The car behind them hit them, lurched them forward, and Clay fought to maintain control as their car slid right, toward the guardrail, barely clipping it. The mountainside dropped off there, and Clay knew if they hit the rail too hard, he wouldn't be able to keep their car on the road.

He jerked the wheel hard left, hitting the car that had been behind them as it sped up and disappeared down the road that led down the hillside. He tried to catch a glimpse of the license plate, but all he noticed was that it was an Alaska tag, one of the gold ones with blue numbers, which he couldn't read because it was covered in mud. That didn't narrow it down much.

The threat gone, Clay slowed their car to a stop, pulling as close to the side of the road as he dared. Exhaled.

Looked at Summer. She was crying.

"Are you okay?"

"I'm just ready for this to be over. I don't understand how someone could want another human being dead, especially not the way this guy does." She let out a shuddering breath and Clay wanted to hold her hand, maybe pull her to him, tell her it would be okay.

But he couldn't. He hadn't earned the right. And anyway, he couldn't stay here on the side of the road. They needed to report a crime—and they needed to move away from this location, in case the killer was still watching them.

But even if they'd had all the time in the world, and he'd had every right to comfort her, he wouldn't have been able to tell Summer that everything would be okay.

Because Clay didn't know if it would be or not.

He drove straight to the police department, not just because the attack needed to be reported, but also because he knew if their attacker decided to follow them again, he almost certainly wouldn't follow them to the police department. Clay might not be able to control the madman who was after Summer, nor was he really able to minimize the danger to her nearly as much as he'd like to, but he could give her a few minutes of safety at the police department, a few minutes to catch her breath.

And then they'd have to face reality again.

They were met once more by Detective Walters and Clay gave him a quick rundown of what had happened. He motioned for them to follow him to his office again and they both did so. This time another officer appeared and asked if Summer wanted coffee or tea. She asked for tea and when the officer brought it back, Summer held it tightly, like the warmth of the drink in her hand was comforting her.

Clay had turned down the refreshments. He couldn't drink anything at a time like this, couldn't relax in the slightest when the threat level had risen once again. How many more times could Summer weather an attack like that? Statistically speaking, how many close calls could they have before they didn't escape alive?

Clay didn't want to think about it. Instead he made himself think through what needed to be done, starting with other people who could be in danger.

He looked up at the officer. "Can you send a car over to check on Amanda Holbrook's sister? We were followed from her house."

The officer nodded and left to arrange it. Clay waited with Summer, who was quiet, eyes wide. She took a long sip of tea and then put the cup in front of her again, holding it in both hands and staring straight ahead.

"What?" It didn't seem right to ask what was wrong when the answer to that question was unfortunately more obvious than he'd like it to be. But it seemed like something more was bothering her than just the attack itself.

"I can't believe we might have put her in danger." She shook her head.

"No, we didn't, you didn't. No one did except the deranged man who is behind this." Clay had more he wanted to say, but he kept it short, knowing from experience that direct messages were the best for this situation. She was still too shaken for more detailed explanations.

Fortunately they soon learned that Amanda Holbrook was safe. APD promised they'd ramp up patrols in her neighborhood also and communicate with her on an even more regular basis given how doubtful she'd been.

As for Summer, they offered her a safe house in Anchorage, but she refused, as he'd known she would. Clay didn't know if she didn't fully grasp the severity of the danger or if she just didn't want to live that way no matter what. But he understood.

"Be careful." One of the officers told him as he left the building with Summer.

"I will be."

I'm running out of time to solve this, God. We all are, I can feel it. Clay prayed as they walked to the car, which was still mechanically sound, just a little dented from their hair-raising ordeal. *Help us figure this out before anyone else ends up hurt, or dead.*

He looked over at Summer. Much as he might want to deny it, it wasn't just professionalism that made him pray that prayer with her in mind specifically.

His heart couldn't handle losing her.

Summer closed her eyes in the car, letting Anchorage disappear in the rearview mirror without her paying attention. She felt the curves of the road as the car swung around the Seward Highway between the mountain cliffs and Turnagain Arm. She'd had friends in Anchorage back when she was a competitive mountain runner, and had made the drive many times to visit them and to train on some of the nearby mountains—O'Malley, Wolverine, Ptarmigan and the like.

Now this drive that was so familiar, which should have been relaxing, was another source of tension for her. She hadn't put any of it into words for Clay, but the knowledge that there were two hours of no-man's-land ahead of them scared her—nothing but the road, with no houses, no stores and no cell phone reception.

There, she'd said it. She was scared of something.

Scared that the man who wanted her dead would succeed. Scared of how much she was getting used to Clay's presence. Scared of the fact that one way or another, this arrangement with him as her bodyguard couldn't last forever, and then what was she going to do? Tell him that despite the fact that she didn't deserve a man like him, she was starting to…

What? Fall in love with him?

She shook the thoughts away. Surely it was too soon for that, even for someone like her who felt so deeply, gave her heart away so freely. Summer would have laughed aloud at the ridiculousness of the situation, except she wanted Clay to think she was asleep. She didn't trust herself to have a normal conversation right then. The sky was dimming as the clouds moved in and it grew closer to midnight. Even though the sun wouldn't disappear completely, there was something about the end of the day that made her relaxed and vulnerable. Made her want to answer Clay's unspoken questions about why she'd stopped competitive mountain running. About her past.

And that couldn't happen.

It just couldn't.

She shifted in her seat slightly so she'd have a view out of the window. The water was calm today. She'd seen it before when the rain was falling and it churned in slate gray that looked more like some kind of molten lava than water. Angry. Thick.

Today it was calm, the exact opposite of how her heart felt.

She turned her thoughts somewhere productive, wondering once again who could be after her. Even though she'd been attacked in Moose Haven, it seemed more likely the culprit was someone from Anchorage since his first victims had been from there. What had made him come to Moose Haven? Had he come specifically to target her, or had he found her after he arrived? Which had come first? Knowing that would give them somewhere to start.

The problem with trying to put together any kind of suspect list was that there was no knowing how the serial killer's mind worked—what connection he saw between the women he made into his victims. Summer didn't know if this particular killer was targeting people he knew well—she hoped it wasn't that one; she only knew a few people in Anchorage, and she couldn't picture any of them being behind this.

If he was someone who killed people he'd only seen in passing, then the possibilities were limitless. It could be someone she'd passed at Costco in Anchorage, someone who got gas at a gas station where all of the victims and Summer had been before.

Another impossibility to think through.

The third option was the one that intrigued Summer. If the killer was killing acquaintances…that was something she needed to think through. What acquaintances did she have who might have run across the other women as well? She'd been preparing a list to share with law enforcement if they were interested in it, though so far it was limited to mountain running friends and the barista at her favorite coffee shop, who she very much doubted had a mean bone in his body. Not to mention, the body type didn't match her attacker at all. Summer could probably bench-press the barista—he was tall and thin and the essence of a hipster right to the thick glasses that sat on the end of his nose.

Yeah, it wasn't him.

She kept thinking. If this option was right though, it had to be someone. She went to the post office often. Anchorage Outdoor Gear. A local knife shop that carried her favorite kind of custom knives, which she carried with her on hikes when she took tourists, because they were so useful to have in the woods.

The last one caught her attention the most. She tapped out a quick text to Noah, hoping it would send when they came back into service. For now they were entering the longest dead zone of the trip. Summer shuddered. The word *dead* wasn't her favorite lately.

She looked over at Clay, who had kept quiet, giving her space to think. She almost said something but then she closed her eyes again and pretended to sleep.

It was probably better for both of them if she kept pretending. Not just to sleep—but not to care about this intriguing man next to her who fascinated her more than she wanted to admit.

ELEVEN

Clay gripped the steering wheel as he took the hill up into Turnagain Pass. They'd been back on the Kenai Peninsula for less than half an hour, and still had well over an hour to go before they made it back to Moose Haven. Clay wished he could teleport them there—his nerves were shot after the day they'd had.

He turned the CD up—neither the radio nor streamed music on his phone worked there, he'd discovered the first time he'd driven through the massive dead zone extended from the start of the Kenai all the way to Moose Pass, the tiny town just before the turnoff to Moose Haven.

Five or ten minutes after Turnagain Pass—he hadn't been keeping track of time but it hadn't been long—he spotted upcoming construction, dropping his speed as the signs dictated. He didn't remember it being there this morning, but he'd heard orange construction cones bloomed in Alaska like the state flower in the summer so it shouldn't be surprising.

He took advantage of the break from driving fast to look around. The scenery was some of the most gorgeous he'd ever seen, vast wilderness covered by spruce trees.

On the right side of the road was a creek, with a hill behind it that gradually climbed toward the mountains.

Gorgeous. But also desolate.

Clay shivered as he looked around. He saw no other vehicles on the road. He looked at the construction cones, narrowed his eyes.

It could be legitimate construction. But if so, he was going to have to make some apologies to whoever caught him doing this.

He hit the gas, unable to shake the unease he felt slowing down in this isolated area.

The first *bang* told him he was too late. The front left tire blew. The shooter was on Clay's side of the car, hidden somewhere in the woods.

Summer's head snapped up. "What was that?"

Another shot.

"We've got to ditch the car. Summer, when I stop, open your door, jump out and run into the woods. I'm right behind you." Clay had spent a lot of time in the woods hunting deer and knew more about long-range rifle shots than most people, law enforcement or not. The shooter wasn't particularly close—which was good because it gave them a better chance to escape from him personally, but bad because if he was this accurate a shot from far away, they were in a huge amount of danger.

Clay hit the breaks.

"Run?"

"Now! Run!"

Clay searched the woods to his left for anything that would give away the shooter's location—maybe a reflection of the scope in the sun, anything. He saw nothing but heard Summer's door.

She was out and he needed to be with her.

He opened his door, ran for the back of the car. One more shot—this one took out the back tire. Clay heard it explode just as he made it past, running for the other side of the car and sprinting off the road, into the thick woods.

"Summer?" he shouted, hating to give away her position but knowing that whoever was shooting at them already knew they were together, and that it was worth the risk to get back to where she was so he could protect her.

"Right here!"

Ahead of him, slightly to the right. He dodged a spruce branch, rounded that tree and saw a game trail. "Game trail?"

"I saw it. To your left. Don't take it, it's the first thing he'll check."

She was right but he wouldn't have realized she'd know that.

"How'd you know?"

"My sister, Kate. She's the best tracker. She's taught me a few things. I figured some of it could come in handy if we use it backward. I've already made a couple false trail starts."

She might be the most amazing woman he'd ever met.

"Is he following us?" she asked, not slowing down as she ran. Clay ran too but struggled to keep up—Summer's strides were that effortless. Then again, she did this often for fun, didn't she?

He resolved again to make running part of his daily routine. Assuming they both lived through this to have a daily routine again.

"No way of knowing."

Clay glanced backward though, just in case. This time

he caught the sun reflecting off something that looked to be about seven hundred yards away.

Clay guessed he'd made the shot from about five hundred yards, somewhere up there on that mountainside. A shot not every accomplished marksman could make when they were shooting at a moving target the size of his tires.

The big question was, was he moving? Clay still couldn't tell but knew he had to assume the answer was yes—which meant they couldn't stop or they'd risk being targeted again. He kept running.

Turned around again. Nothing.

"Clay?" Summer's voice was desperate. She'd stopped running.

"Keep going. I'll catch up to you." He needed to know.

Long seconds stretched into almost a minute before he caught another flash.

Fifty yards closer.

He was coming for them.

Clay sprinted up the hill, following Summer's footsteps.

She exhaled. Blew out a breath. "We can't just keep sprinting. We have to be smarter."

"Where are we?" Clay hated that he was reliant on someone else's knowledge, but he just didn't have the backcountry familiarity that Summer did.

All the sudden he was struck by how much he needed her. Here this whole time he'd been thinking of himself as her rescuer, her protector, but she'd brought him back into law enforcement, given him daily purpose again when he'd been struggling and now was half the reason they weren't in more danger than they already were.

Summer Dawson was not just another woman to protect.

"We should be crossing a creek soon."

"You can tell that?"

She smiled. "I've studied maps. I've hiked fairly near here. Not precisely here," she warned. "So I don't know exactly what we're getting into, but I may know enough that we have a chance."

"Okay, which creek?"

Summer shook her head. "I'm not sure, especially since I was asleep, so I'm not positive of our exact location. Either Silvertip Creek or Six Mile Creek. If we follow Six Mile we'll end up at a rest stop, near the Hope Cutoff."

Clay remembered that road, one that led to the small town of Hope. "So we have options for contacting civilization if we can get to either of those locations."

"It'll be a long hike. But yes. The rest stop has an emergency phone."

"I hear the creek."

It was wide enough to give Clay some pause, especially as it ran cold and fast like most creeks in Alaska. A slip in one of those could be deadly.

"Let's go." Clay broke his hesitation and stepped in. Summer followed.

"He's coming, isn't he?"

"Why?"

"You've gotten faster."

"Maybe I just wanted to keep up with you."

"Nah. You're running like it matters." Summer made her way across the creek with the calm aplomb of an Alaskan woman who'd done this many times before. Clay was still dealing with the shock the cold water was to his legs but continued on.

Then they were out.

"Up?" Summer asked.

The landscape in front of them rose dramatically to a lower mountain ridge that connected to a bigger mountain that loomed in front of them.

"Yes. Let's go."

They ran without talking anymore, both of them sweating at this point even in the mild temperatures.

"I really hope we don't startle a bear. We should be making noise."

"It's a risk we have to take. I'd rather meet a bear than whoever's at the other end of that gun."

Summer turned and met his eyes before she kept running. "I don't want to meet either."

Summer ran like she was in the World Mountain Running Championships and victory was on the line. But there was so much more at stake than that here. The adrenaline coursing through her, it was all wrong. Running had never been a method of escape for her, she'd never run *from* anything. Always *to* something. Like her dreams.

Then again, hadn't she been running from her past for years? Running from the memories of when her dream career almost came true?

She stopped when she noticed something in the trees. The light was changing, getting brighter. She turned to Clay, who was keeping pace well, even if he did seem winded.

"We're almost out of the tree line. We need to head one direction or another along the edge of it or we'll be back in plain sight again."

"We need to stay out of his sight, that's what's most important right now."

"That's what I figured. So left or right?"

She waited for him to decide. Left took them toward Moose Haven; right took them back toward Anchorage. Neither place was close enough to walk to. On one hand, she guessed the killer might expect them to head toward the Hope Cutoff on the left, but then again it was impossible to know for sure what he'd be expecting. It wasn't worth making a bad choice just to try to throw him off.

She looked left, thought about Silvertip Creek and Six Mile Creek. They widened toward the Hope Cutoff, near the Canyon Creek rest stop, and the land around the creek became steeper.

Summer glanced at Clay. Should she offer her opinion, treat him like they were some kind of team, them against a serial killer? Or wait and let him do the protecting?

"What do you think?" He turned to her.

Summer smiled. She should have known he'd ask for her input. Clay Hitchcock may have drifted into Moose Haven like so many loners who came to Alaska to work short-term jobs, but he wasn't the same as they were. He was a team player, something she assumed had served him well in law enforcement.

"We need to go left, toward the cutoff."

"Left it is, then. Keep going."

Summer kept moving, careful not to trip on the roots that tangled on the forest floor. Her muscles were handling the climb fine, but her heart rate was pounding—mostly, she assumed, from the certainty that their lives were in danger.

"Where are we headed, specifically?" Clay asked after a minute.

"Do you want to keep going until we can't run anymore? Or take shelter somewhere?"

"I think we're better off taking shelter to rest after we've gone a decent distance. The town of Hope is within range of us technically but I don't know if there's a way for us to pick our way there on trails."

"I'm not sure, either. I know we are headed that way but I don't know how realistic it is to make it all the way to Hope." Summer winced. "There's bound to be a trail near the creek, at least a game trail, but that's not very sheltered and I'm hesitant to stick next to a creek when it's summer."

"Bears?"

She nodded. "And of course neither of us has bear spray."

"I've got my weapon." He patted his side.

"What is that, a .45?" She raised her eyebrows. "So if we need something noisy to try to scare the bear away we're set, but I'm afraid it's not going to help with much more than that."

"Okay, so we'll take the route you mentioned. We'll go as far as we can, take a rest and then decide where we should hike out."

"You think he'll track us for long?"

"I have no idea. I do know that as well as you know these woods we have a fighting chance. I'm not sure we would without you."

Summer loved the way he smiled at her just then, like she mattered, like she was important. "Thanks, Clay."

And just that fast, the moment was over. He nodded to the left, where they'd planned to go. "Let's go, okay. He's probably still back there."

Summer was careful not to leave much of a trace as

she picked her way through the spruce trees, between them, sometimes doubling back to mess up the trail, and showing Clay how to do the same, but never straying too far because time was still important and she couldn't afford to waste too much of it on deception when they didn't even know if the man who was after them was a capable tracker.

They'd been running for well over a mile in difficult terrain, Summer would guess more like two or three, when Clay finally said they should stop.

"I think we've lost him." He glanced at his watch. "And it's getting later. I would be surprised if he searched all night."

"So we stop, then?" She shivered. As it got closer to nighttime, the daylight didn't change much, but the temperature started to drop even in the early evening, hours before.

"We stop. I'm going to build a fire to warm us up some."

"But the smoke?"

"We'll be careful. I'm not going to let it get very big so the smoke shouldn't be visible." He didn't say anything more, but somehow Summer got the idea that the reason he wasn't concerned about the smoke might be a little disconcerting to know.

"You think if he's going to find us he'll do that whether there's smoke or not."

He met her eyes and nodded slowly. "You'd make an excellent police officer, do you know that?"

She laughed. "Not my kind of danger. But thanks."

They hiked in silence for another few miles before they came to where Six Mile Creek made a large canyon lined with huge masses of rock. They were on the far side. Whether their shooter would expect that was still unknown. They had chosen to cross immediately, but there was a slight chance, Summer assumed, that he might wonder if they'd just stayed close to the road and followed it along the perimeter of the woods rather than cross the creek at all. He almost certainly wouldn't guess they'd crossed here because the rapids where the canyon walls enclosed the creek were some of the best in Alaska.

"We should stop here." Summer turned to Clay. "It's the location with the best options for places we can sort of tuck back into, and the noise of the creek will cover the noise we make moving around."

"You know best here."

They stopped running and Clay gathered what they needed to make a small fire. They would need to warm up, especially if they needed to run again.

Once he'd gotten the fire started, Clay turned to Summer. She almost looked away, but something in his expression made her meet his eyes. Wait for whatever he had to say.

"What did you mean earlier about 'your kind of danger'?"

"What?" Summer only vaguely remembered what he was talking about.

"When I said you'd make a good cop."

"Oh." She nodded once, remembering now. The words had slipped out and she wasn't sure now, in retrospect, that she'd meant to reveal so much of herself.

She considered brushing him off, dodging the question. Then again, what was the worst that could happen? Usually she'd say looks of judgment. But while Clay was a man whose character made him seem almost too good to be true, she suspected he wasn't the kind to judge other people harshly. He didn't seem critical.

"I guess I meant…" She shrugged and laughed a little. "Exactly what I said. It's not my kind of danger."

"So you have a kind?"

"I'm pretty sure you've figured out by now the whole mountain running thing isn't just a hobby for me. Or if you haven't figured it out, you've looked up my background online."

"I don't look up other people unless it's someone I'm investigating."

Summer hadn't seen that one coming. "Why not?"

"It's not fair to them. The internet is changing how relationships work. Have you realized that? Once upon a time you got to know someone little by little, with what they chose to reveal to you at each step, and now you can go on their Facebook, see their hobbies, interests, favorite music, learn about that time they went to Peru on a mission trip and got lost in the jungle, all of that is right there, from the start."

She settled back against the fallen log she'd been using as a backrest and thought for a minute before responding. Finally, she nodded. "You're right. I hadn't thought of that." She winced a little. "I looked you up a little. Just enough to see you were an officer and see what happened in what looks like your last case."

Clay nodded, like he'd been prepared for that, although she did notice his shoulders went back a little, and Summer could almost sense an invisible wall between them that hadn't been there five minutes ago. What Clay had said about the internet and friendships made even more sense now. Like her, it seemed that he had things in his past that he didn't want to share online with the whole world. She could respect that. She'd taken his chance to talk about that in real time, as their friendship grew.

Odd she'd never thought about that before.

"I'm sorry." She blew out a breath. "I do see what you mean now."

He shrugged. "It is what it is. Technology changes things. So tell me about you and mountain running. I'd figured out it had to be more than a casual interest."

"How?"

Clay laughed as he worked on the fire, placing more medium weight logs on it. "Today was the giveaway. You spent forty-five dollars on a T-shirt."

"Hey, that was the clearance price too, and totally worth it. It's not just a T-shirt. It's an Arc'teryx that's moisture wicking and technical so that it—" His expression looked remarkably like Kate's anytime Summer tried to talk about clothes, outdoor gear or not. She laughed too. "Okay, fine, so the gear gives me away."

"And your dedication," he continued. "Not to mention the way your face looks when you're running up a mountain."

She tilted her head to the side, unsure what he meant. So she sat, listening to the creek and the small crackle of the fire and waited for him to explain.

"You look like you're somewhere else, almost. It looks a lot like worship."

Summer was already shaking her head. "Worship?"

"Thanking God. Praising."

"I know what it is. I'm just curious why you think I would."

"Your brother's faith is one of the reasons we became friends in the first place. Two guys at a state school—we stuck out a little bit wanting to follow Jesus. I've talked enough with Noah to know he shares that faith. I don't know much about Kate, she's pretty busy and keeps things to herself but I've seen her Bible in the lodge in your family's area and it moves around, like she takes it different places to read."

The man really did take "observant" to a whole new level.

"And you're telling me that with three siblings who know Jesus, you honestly don't?"

Heartbeats passed. "That's not what I said, either." Summer forced the words out slowly.

They sat by the fire in silence. She didn't offer any more information. Clay didn't ask any questions.

Her shoulders fell. She wasn't giving up on escaping from this man who wanted her dead. Not by a long shot. But his silent, unknown, possible presence made everything feel heavier, made her consider everything more deeply. What if he did succeed, did manage to kill her? Was she happy with her life now?

If she died now, could she honestly say she'd been living for the last three years?

TWELVE

Clay knew he'd misstepped, at least where Summer was concerned. What he didn't know was how, exactly. He'd assumed up until now that Summer might be in one of those seasons of life where she was busy and her times with God were inconsistent, but it appeared she intentionally avoided God.

As a police officer, Clay had seen more than his share of how life could break people. He'd seen people who had let tragedy push them to vices. Drugs. Alcohol. It wouldn't surprise him if Summer used mountain running to escape in the same way. What he didn't know was how to convince her that he understood, that he didn't think worse of her because she wasn't living in her faith right now. He was sad for her. But it didn't change his opinion of her.

"What did my brother tell you about me?"

"What do you mean?" Clay asked in an attempt to stall for time, to give himself a minute to figure out how to react to her question. This was the kind of conversation he hadn't anticipated ever having with Summer. They were friends. Bodyguard and woman in danger. It wasn't that the topic was anything too intimate, but it was certainly personal, more personal a conversation than he'd have guessed they would be having.

How long was he going to have to tell himself those things until he finally and truly believed it?

He met her glacier-blue eyes, swallowing hard at the knot in his throat that had nothing to do with this particular conversation and everything to do with the draw he felt toward her.

Summer took a breath and continued, "I was under the impression somehow, when we first met, that he'd told you about me."

"Just that you were his sister and to stay away from you."

"That's what I thought."

Her voice had hardened. Interesting. Why?

Clay shook his head, not sure what he was reassuring her about, but wanting to anyway. "I don't think he meant anything bad by it."

Her laugh was hard, cold. "Sure he didn't. I get it, okay, Clay? You're this great guy. You've got real faith. Guys like you deserve women who believe as strongly as you do."

"There you go again, talking about yourself like you don't know Jesus when you haven't answered my question yet about whether or not you do. Are you a Christian, Summer?"

He wasn't usually so blunt, didn't usually feel it was the best approach, but Summer was pushing him toward it. Maybe she was pushing to see if he'd give up on her? He wasn't sure but he could tell she was going for some kind of reaction. He didn't know if it was best to give it to her or not, but the woman touched such a raw place inside him, ignited his emotions to such a degree that he didn't want to measure what he said, didn't want to keep his distance anymore and keep his feelings uninvolved.

Honestly he wanted to kiss away every frown line on her face that said she didn't think she was good enough. Good enough for *whom*? She was the kind of woman who was so hopelessly out of his league he had hardly allowed himself to consider her.

"I asked Jesus to save me when I was seven," she said softly. "Told him I knew I was a sinner. That I believed His death on the cross was for me too. And I did, Clay." She sniffed. He didn't know if she was crying or if the smoke was bothering her. So Clay didn't do anything, just waited.

But after a long moment of silence, he finally prompted her, "And?"

She smiled wryly. "My faith may be a bit…lapsed at the moment, but I know that's all that's required. What do you mean, 'and'?"

"Something happened to take the childlike faith of a seven-year-old and dampen it, push it aside."

Summer let out a breath. "Even if you had looked me up I guess you wouldn't know this part."

"I told you I didn't. I don't know anything about you that you haven't told me. Besides that your brother wanted you to be off-limits—but, Summer, I think that was because he doesn't think I'm good enough for you."

She was already shaking her head. "No, he just knows…" Her cheeks flamed. "He knows how easy it is for me when my heart gets involved to forget everything else."

Clay's chest was tight, it was getting harder to breathe. Something about the heartbreak coming off Summer was affecting him. Was this what it felt like to be really truly close to a person? He'd had a few solid friends in high school, guys from his town who he was still pretty close to today. But there was an added element here, and it was not just attraction.

He stoked the fire a little more. Looked at Summer. Her face was a mixture of so many expressions. Even though he hadn't pressured her to share anything, he felt like he should step back, give her a chance to see if she wanted to continue this story. He had a feeling it wasn't one she told often.

"I'm going to take a quick walk around."

"Without me?"

"I'll be within sight at all times," he promised. "I just want to check the perimeter, basically make sure I don't see any signs that someone's hiding."

She blinked. "Okay."

He nodded. Walked away. Whatever happened between them or didn't, Clay never wanted her to feel anything resembling pressure. This story was a piece of Summer. If she wanted to share it, it was a piece he'd accept, whatever it held. But Clay needed to know she'd thought through what they were doing, the way they were quickly crossing the line into a relationship that wasn't in any way superficial anymore, was barely resembling professional at this point, though it was still completely appropriate.

Clay's check of the woods around them didn't yield anything, which was reassuring but also concerning. Was it too quiet? Or was he just jumpy? Clay still had no way of knowing whether the shooter would come after them again tonight. On one hand, it was logical to assume their shooter had a plan of attack—a reason why he had chosen to strand them in this desolate place. On the other, he might have assumed animals or exposure would ensure they didn't make it out of the woods alive, even if he didn't personally follow them far.

Only time would tell. And Clay was a patient man. He could wait.

He just wished for Summer's sake that he could reassure her.

Instead he sat back down near her and the fire, and glanced over at her.

Her emotions weren't written as plainly on her face anymore, the familiar mask had come back over it. He expected that was the end of that.

"I ran off with another mountain runner."

The words had no preamble, nothing to soften the blow.

"He wasn't a Christian, and my parents and especially my siblings made it clear how they felt about me giving up on what I'd been taught, leaving with him, living with him…" Her voice trailed off and Clay heard what she left unsaid. He had no idea what to say. There didn't seem to be anything he could say to encourage her, and he could feel that she wasn't done—she was just giving it to him in parts the best she knew how.

"They warned me." She blew out a breath. "They told me nicely, harshly, any way they thought I'd listen, all of them taking turns playing good cop and bad cop, really." Summer shook her head. "I put them through so much and I didn't even know it at the time." She shrugged as a tear, only one, ran down the edge of her cheek. "I didn't think about it."

"People usually don't."

"Anyway. I pushed them away enough that they finally left me alone. And I was happy. I thought *we* were happy. And then…"

Clay's stomach rolled. He thought he could feel what was coming next.

"I got pregnant. But…"

She didn't pause long enough for the words to sink into Clay's mind before she kept going. He fought to stay focused, keep his mind from spinning, asking questions he didn't know if he should ask aloud or leave unsaid. *God help her tell me what You want her to share.* He finally managed to form the words to a prayer in his mind. It was all he could think to do.

"I lost the baby. Miscarried at thirteen weeks."

He didn't know much about babies but did some quick math. Three months? And the whole pregnancy was only supposed to last nine? He thought he recalled that the risk of losing a baby usually happened in the first trimester. She'd been a third of the way there, out of the woods…

"He had a new girlfriend by the time I got out of the hospital." Her emotions had shuttered again, her eyes revealed nothing in the darkening light. "I couldn't run for a couple of months due to complications. By the time I was physically ready to get back to it, my family needed me. I owed them an apology that was more than just words. The lodge was in trouble so I came back, hoping the tiny bit of fame I had leftover would be enough to give the hikes we offer at Moose Haven Lodge an edge over some of our competition, especially the bigger chain resorts. If I'd helped out the summer they'd asked me to, rather than leaving with Christopher, the lodge might never have been in trouble to begin with…" Her voice trailed off.

Another exhale. "And that's why he wanted you to stay away from me. I'm not the kind of woman you deserve."

"What makes you so sure? You've been through more than most people your age dream about and you've come out stronger. Don't you see that? You aren't broken."

"I am, Clay." She shook her head. "I am."

He hesitated. "Fine. But if you are, it's just so God can put you back together. Stronger. Even more beautiful." He lifted her chin, softly, slightly.

He looked at her face but she wouldn't meet his eyes, kept hers on the ground. He didn't move his hand, didn't look away. Finally her eyes lifted to meet his, filling his heart with something stronger than he'd ever felt, some kind of pull, attraction that Clay had to fight with all his might to resist covering her lips with his. He wanted to kiss away the pain she'd shared, kiss away her insecurities, but it wouldn't be fair to her, to either of them. Not right now. It wasn't the right time or place. For either of them. Especially in light of all Summer had just shared. He was starting to care about her, much more than she realized, Clay was pretty sure. But she was vulnerable right now and he wouldn't take advantage of that.

"I'm just not that woman, Clay. I don't know if I can be."

Her words fell in the quiet like weights. He could almost feel the pull of them inside his own chest, sinking any kind of hope of convincing her otherwise.

And he had to sit there, not do anything physical to convince her that she was wrong. His arms felt empty with how much he wanted to pull her close, just hold her. Tight. Maybe forever.

A gunshot broke through the air.

Clay was instantly on alert but couldn't place where it came from—except that it was close.

He finally located the spot where dirt had flown up. Just behind and to the left of Summer.

She looked up at him, eyes wide. Glanced at her leg.

And the red soaking her khaki hiking pants just below her knee.

Summer's breath came faster as she tried to process what had happened. Shot. She'd been shot.

"We have to run. Go as fast as you can. I'll find you but I need you safe." Clay's voice, so soft only moments before, supportive, understanding, was firm. He left no room for argument even though she knew he'd seen the blood spreading on her leg.

It didn't burn much, not the way she'd always heard about gunshots hurting. She didn't know if real life was that different from fiction or if she'd only been grazed.

Summer stood, hoping the second was true. She had to hold on to hope, it was all she had.

Hope. How long had it been since she'd used that word, really held on to it and believed it did any good at all?

She pushed her past out of her mind, something she was well practiced in, and did what she always did, but this time with the urgency that her life depended on it. Summer ran.

She heard footsteps behind her, hoped they were Clay's and assumed since she hadn't been shot yet that they were.

More gunshots. The big, louder kind. The man after them was still using a rifle, her experiences hunting caribou had taught her the distinct difference in the sound.

Then small caliber shots from right behind her. She glanced back. It was Clay, shooting at a dark shadow of a person maybe thirty yards away—pretty good range for a handgun.

His second shot connected with something. She heard a voice cry out.

"Go!" Clay yelled at her. "He's down, at least for now."

He was right behind her, and Summer somehow ran faster than she ever had, down the edges of the creek, toward the Hope Cutoff, careful not to slip on the rocks near the creek. *Please don't let there be bears out to-night, God.*

The second prayer that had slipped out since this ordeal had begun just three days ago.

She kept running, the dim twilight of the middle of the Alaskan night giving her just enough light to see by.

"Where do you want to cross?" They'd have to cross in order to reach the road, and at this point there was no more stopping. They'd have to find someone, someplace to make a call and have backup sent. It was all-or-nothing time.

Her heart pounded as she waited for Clay's answer, and Summer kept running.

"Whenever you think it's best."

There wasn't anywhere that was a great option. Alaska rivers and creeks ran cold and fast, and a misstep could cost a healthy adult his or her life. It had happened before, people slipping on the round, smooth rocks, then falling into the cold water and being swept away.

Even if they ever found their way out, hypothermia was quick to set in and was unforgiving.

Still, she and Clay didn't have a choice. Every chance of help they had was on the other side of Six Mile Creek.

Summer kept running until the topography changed and the solid rock cliffs gradually diminished in size and then faded entirely, giving way to land that was almost flat, leading straight down to the water.

Now or never.

Taking a deep breath and steeling herself against the cold, Summer stepped into the water. It was colder than earlier. Of course, they'd crossed at such a narrow spot earlier that they hadn't had to stay in the water too long, and the fact that the sun had been fully up in the sky had given them enough warmth to make up for the cold on their feet.

Dry, clean socks. If they made it out of this, that was what Summer wanted, even more than she wanted someone to check on her leg. That was the one advantage to the cold water. It reached high enough to numb the wound.

The water was calmer there than it had been upstream in the rapids, much calmer. Summer was pleasantly surprised at how little they had to fight with the water to hurry across it. Still, she didn't dare risk slipping by running across, but instead chose her steps carefully.

Two more and she'd be out. She glanced back to make sure Clay was making it. Her eyes widened and she realized her mistake as her foot slipped under her.

Clay caught her by the elbow and held his footing firm as Summer's stabilized. Her heartbeat pounded in her ears, a reminder of how close she'd come to falling, an accident that could have cost her everything.

"Thank you."

"Of course."

Summer took one more step in the water, then stepped out onto the shore, feeling somehow like that last brief "thank you" had been about more than just rescuing her from her fall. She was thankful to him for everything. For listening. For his protection.

For seeing her. And still…not leaving.

"Run to the highway."

Summer had been planning on it but was glad they were both on the same page. "Got it." She took a deep breath, fatigue starting to creep up on the edges of the rush of adrenaline that had overtaken her when the shot had rung out.

Running through the grass should have been easier than running down the mountain, but it wasn't what she trained for, so without the extreme adrenaline she found herself tiring out.

"Keep going, Summer. You've got this."

She pushed herself. Her leg throbbed. The more she thought about it, it had to be just a graze or she knew she couldn't run on it, but that didn't mean it didn't hurt. She'd never even been *grazed* by a bullet before.

She saw headlights in the predawn fog. The highway was close, just through a small patch of spruce trees. They kept running, and then she stopped just short of the clearing on the side of the road, still in the cover of the woods. "Do we just go out there and hope no one shoots at us?" The moon had come out from behind a cloud and was providing more light—not the best timing but not something they could change, either.

"Yes. He should still be behind us in the woods."

"But what if he's not?"

"I can't promise you anything, Summer. But he's not everywhere. And I don't think it's likely he's going to be driving by anytime soon. He has to make it down the mountain with whatever wounds he has. And we can't afford to spend too much time waiting. When we get to a phone we need to report all of this to the troopers so they can try to catch him and also give him any kind of medical assistance he needs."

She looked at him, eyes wide.

"They teach us to shoot to eliminate the threat," Clay said softly. "You don't do that, you end up with dead officers. But we also are taught to do everything we can to save a life. Even the life of someone who doesn't deserve it."

The man was a cop to his core, had he realized that yet? Summer felt a pang in her chest. When he realized it, would he leave Moose Haven, head back to his little Georgia town and the police force he'd left behind? No matter how she felt about him—something she hadn't had time to decide anyway—she didn't think she could leave to go with him. She couldn't abandon her family, or the lodge when they needed her there.

She wouldn't let history repeat itself.

THIRTEEN

Clay could hear the fear in Summer's voice, something he'd heard in it so rarely that it surprised him, though he knew it shouldn't have. She had every right to fear after what she'd been through.

So he grabbed her hand, squeezed it and smiled. "We're going to make it, Summer." And then he pulled her out of the darkness of the woods, knowing the safety they felt there was an illusion. Staying in the shadows would only endanger them.

And Clay knew it. Which was why he made his feet move even though he understood Summer's hesitations, felt them too.

The highway was mostly empty at this time of night. He glanced down at his watch, unable to tell from the deep blue of the sky how much time they had until it was good and daylight again. The deep blue was deceiving, not really darkness but not light, either. Alaskan midnight sun confused him.

It was 3:17 a.m.

The headlights continued approaching from the south. Clay hadn't been counting on anyone headed up from the Kenai at this time of night, although he guessed getting an early start to Anchorage would make sense for some people. He hoped it was that and not people who were up to no good. Even if they could get a driver to stop for them, there was no guarantee that the man or woman could be trusted—that was the risk they had to take if they had any hope of getting back to the lodge safely.

"I'm going to flag them down." Clay released Summer's hand, then clicked on the flashlight he'd had in his pocket, a small penlight that gave off enough lumens that it should be able to catch a driver's attention. He only prayed it didn't catch the attention of the man who was after them.

The car slowed slightly. Clay kept waving his arms and the light.

They moved to the side of the road, then slowed to a stop.

Clay approached with caution. "Stay behind me," he said to Summer in a quiet voice as he moved forward. The driver of the car had only lowered the window slightly and he didn't blame them. He must look odd out there in the middle of the night, no car in sight, waving.

"Can you help us, please? There's a man after us and we need a ride to Moose Haven. Or to Hope if that's all you're willing to do." Moose Haven was another hour and a half, Clay guessed. Hope should only be about fifteen or twenty minutes away.

"Who are you?"

Clay could only see part of the driver's face but it looked to be a woman in her forties. Not their shooter. Summer had identified him as a man. He was thankful for that.

"Ma'am, I know it sounds odd. But we're from Moose Haven. You can call the police chief there, Noah Dawson, and he'll tell you. I'm Clay, I work at Moose Haven Lodge and this is Summer Dawson."

The woman's face brightened. "Summer Dawson? You were a mountain runner?"

Summer nodded.

"My daughter started running cross-country because of you."

Clay heard locks on the car click and held his breath. Was she giving them a ride?

"Jump in." She nodded toward the back seat, then looked around. "But hurry, would you? If someone is after you I'd rather them not see us. I promised my husband I'd be careful on this drive. I don't think he was expecting anything other than the usual dangers and I wouldn't hear the end of it if I got shot."

"Thank you. Thank you so much," Summer said. Clay opened the back door and let her slide in first, then followed her. The woman pulled an impressive 180 in the middle of the road, since there was no traffic coming in either direction, and hit the gas.

"I'm going to call the police as soon as we have a signal," Clay told Summer.

"Shouldn't be long. Moose Pass is about thirty minutes away."

Clay had guessed longer than that. Then again, when he checked the speedometer over the driver's shoulder it said seventy-five. Not exactly what he'd consider a careful night speed, but then again, it might be best for all of them in these odd circumstances.

They rode in silence. Adrenaline was crashing in Clay, tiredness making his mind fuzzy. He knew he needed to stay focused long enough to get them safely home and talk to the police officers on the case, and he knew he would do it, but he was also looking forward to sleeping later, something he'd arrange with Noah so another officer could watch the lodge at that time. There was no way either he or Summer could hold up without one.

Just as they came into Moose Pass, the first town they reached and the last before Moose Haven, Clay's phone showed that he had service. He called the troopers first, gave the location he'd shot at the suspect and a brief explanation of what had happened. Then he called Noah.

"Clay? Is everything okay?" Noah answered his cell immediately.

"Mostly. We were shot at on the highway. Summer's got a graze on her leg and we'll need someone to look at it. We flagged down a woman, who is giving us a ride."

"Where is she bringing you?"

"Ma'am? Would you mind driving us all the way to Moose Haven Lodge or should I ask someone to meet us?" Clay asked the driver, whose name he realized he still hadn't gotten.

"I'm driving you to the lodge." She looked back over her shoulder at Summer. "My daughter really looks up to you. I couldn't face her knowing I hadn't done what I could to keep you safe. I read in the paper about the attack the other day."

Clay hadn't considered it being in the papers, but of course, especially in the small-town-feeling Kenai Peninsula, it would be widely reported.

"Thank you." Summer's voice was soft. Clay glanced at her, wondering if the words about the woman's daughter looking up to her had affected her. Unfortunately he couldn't talk about it with her right then.

He went back to his conversation with Noah. "She says she'll take us to the lodge."

"Great. I've been calling you for hours. We expected you just a few hours after dinner."

"I know. Like I said, we were ambushed on the highway and shot at."

"Just the one guy?"

"Yes, but he's got the skills of someone who's an experienced hunter or maybe former military."

Noah muttered under his breath.

"We're okay."

"Not okay enough."

Clay agreed, but he wasn't the kind of guy to get upset at circumstances he couldn't change. They were alive. Now it was time to move on.

His personal past, that last case, flashed in his mind. Was he following his own advice with that one?

No time to think about it now.

"I'm going to let you go." Noah's voice was gruff with emotion. Clay couldn't imagine being on the other end of tonight, knowing they were hours late, knowing literally anything could have happened to them.

"Alright. We'll see you soon."

"I hope so."

Clay pocketed his phone. Then remembered the man he'd shot. He dialed 9-1-1, figuring the troopers might be closer than the officers in Moose Haven.

He filled them in on the situation and the trooper he spoke to promised they'd send an officer and an ambulance to the scene.

"I'd send more than one officer," Clay advised, fearing they might be underestimating the man they were dealing with. "I don't know if he has some kind of formal training, but while I wouldn't go right to 'sniper,' he's an awfully good shot at long range."

The trooper thanked him for the information and Clay hung up. They were well through Moose Pass now, not far from Moose Haven.

As they turned off the Seward Highway, Clay noticed the deep blue of the sky had turned to a medium, vivid blue he couldn't describe but that he knew meant dawn and daylight wouldn't be far behind. He'd never been so thankful for Alaska's odd sunlight hours—somehow he just needed to see daylight right then.

The miles passed quickly as they approached the lodge. "Thank you again for the ride," Clay said as the woman pulled into the front of the lodge. Two trooper cars were waiting, as was Noah's Moose Haven cruiser and one other.

The driver whistled. "Backup is waiting, huh?"

"Yes, ma'am."

"You keep saying 'ma'am.' Where are you from? Not here." She turned to Clay.

"Georgia."

She smiled. "I guessed the South somewhere from that accent. My husband and I are originally from Athens."

"Go Dawgs." Clay smiled as he mentioned what was arguably the state's favorite football team, headquartered at the University of Georgia in Athens.

"Go Dawgs," she agreed. "You keep this woman safe, okay?"

"I'll do the best I can," Clay promised and they climbed out.

She drove away and they walked toward the entrance to the lodge. They were met by a swarm of law enforcement, a paramedic and Summer's family, all of them surrounding them, engulfing them.

Tyler grabbed Summer as soon as he saw her, hugged her tight the way Clay wished he had a right to.

"I'll be okay. Really," she said with a sniff.

Clay believed it was true. About all of it. The woman was strong, maybe the strongest he'd ever met. And certainly much stronger or braver than she knew.

If they could keep her safe for just a while longer. This guy was bound to mess up eventually, leave some evidence they could use. For all Clay knew, he might have left some already back where he'd shot at them along the highway and the creek. He'd have to have Summer give the troopers her best estimate of exactly where they'd been when the shooting had taken place. Maybe this would be the key to closing the case—and Summer not needing his protection anymore.

"I know you must be exhausted," Erynn Cooper said to Summer.

"I am." Summer's eyes were dry and it was getting harder to keep her eyelids open. At least the troopers had let an EMT see to her leg wound first. As she'd suspected it was only a graze, though a bit of a nasty one. She'd gotten worse gashes falling down scree slopes on mountains before though, so she knew she could handle it. Summer yawned. She supposed she should just be thankful that she'd had the burst of energy that enabled her to run so much that night without any rest.

"But I've got to talk to you now and get some answers while things are still fresh in your mind." Her voice was apologetic.

"Just ask her the questions, Erynn. Don't waste her time," Noah snapped as he walked up.

"Noah."

"I'm sorry." He looked at Summer, then at Erynn. "Sorry, Erynn."

"I get it, she's your sister. But you've got to keep it together if you're going to help her at all. Not to mention if you want to be part of this investigation with how close you are to it."

Summer looked at her brother, who'd raised his eyebrows. "I'm the police chief of a town who's had a murder and an attempted murder in the last week. I'm staying on this case."

"She's your sister. Do you really have the right to ignore that connection and how it might be affecting you?"

"It's a small town. We're all connected somehow. It wouldn't make sense for me not to be on it. And I don't technically report to you, I'd like to remind you."

Summer looked back at Erynn, exhausted but still awake enough to be slightly amused by the familiar tension and banter between her brother and the other law enforcement officer.

"Let's focus on your sister and not jurisdiction, alright? I'm sorry I said anything." She looked back at Summer. "Can you tell me what happened yesterday in your own words, starting from the beginning?"

"I can. You know about the break-in here…"

"It was more than that. It was attempted kidnapping," Noah interjected.

Summer shuddered.

"We all know, Noah." Erynn spoke softly, her eyes never leaving Summer. "Keep going."

Summer knew her brother was getting testy because

he was so concerned, and appreciated Erynn ignoring his displays of crankiness. She also appreciated Erynn's quiet voice. Her head was starting to hurt a little. Lack of sleep and dehydration, she guessed.

With that in mind, she reached for the water bottle Clay had brought her before he'd been taken in another direction to give his statement. Summer wished they hadn't been split up, but she supposed she understood why they'd all want to talk to the two of them separately, see if their stories had any differences or if they'd both noticed the same details.

She took a long drink and then looked up. "Clay and I went to Anchorage because…" She hesitated. Neither of them was technically supposed to be investigating so she wasn't sure how to phrase what their intentions had been without giving that away. Noah had been the one to suggest they talk to APD, but Summer still feared if she phrased it wrong they'd know she'd been investigating. "We felt like the case had reached a dead end and hoped talking to the officers at APD might help, since they've been working the case longer." There, that was vague but true.

Erynn nodded.

"They had nothing and then we were run off the road while we were driving in Anchorage. We didn't feel safe staying in town so we headed back to Moose Haven. We'd been driving awhile outside Turnagain Pass—"

"Can you guess how far?"

"I'm not sure. We'd crossed Silvertip Creek but hadn't reached the Canyon Creek rest area yet. That's the best I can tell you." Even when they'd gotten into the car earlier, it had taken Summer about twenty minutes to focus and realize she should have been paying attention when they passed landmarks to give herself a better idea of exactly where they'd been. Thankfully if someone drove her back, she believed she should be able to pinpoint their location fairly accurately. Mountain trails tended to imprint themselves on her memory.

"That's pretty good. That's the area troopers went to just now after they got Clay's call."

Summer thought again about how he'd been genuinely concerned for the well-being of the man who'd been after them. Something about that messed with her mind. What a weird balance a man in his line of work—former line of work, technically—had to maintain, between justice and mercy. Summer wasn't sure she could keep both of them in mind like that so well.

"We'd slowed down, I think. I was asleep, but when I woke up we were almost stopped, so I assume Clay had slowed. There were construction cones, I do remember that, so maybe that was some kind of setup."

"Extremely likely, I'd say based on gut instinct, but we should know more when the team out there is finished investigating."

"The man shot at us, at the tires, I think, and then Clay told me to get out and run, so I did."

"And you ran for how long?"

"I have no idea. Miles? Hours?" She shook her head. "It's hard to think about either when you know someone behind you has a gun and wants you dead. Maybe Clay will know. I do know we stopped eventually, near a large canyon wall-type area of Six Mile Creek. Clay thought we should rest a bit, I think he'd planned on at least me getting some sleep, though that didn't happen. He was hoping to reach either the Hope Cutoff or the

Seward Highway, whichever made more sense to get to, to get help."

"And you did, right?"

Summer shrugged. "Basically. But while we were stopped the shooter caught up with us and shot at us." She motioned to her leg. "That's when I was grazed, not when he shot at us on the highway." Frowning, she looked at Noah. "Where is the car anyway?"

"Troopers are going to retrieve it and take it to the state crime lab in Anchorage for processing. It's possible the killer could have done something to it while you were in the woods, and you know we don't have the capability to check for threats the way the state lab does."

"What do you mean? You've looked at it before," she reminded Noah.

"We've checked for signs of mechanical tampering, bombs. We looked for tracking devices once." Noah shook his head. "But I don't like how it seems like this guy always appears to know where you are. Either he has a source on the inside or he's tracking you somehow."

Summer understood. And shivered.

"Those are all the questions I have for now," Erynn said and looked at Noah. "Did you have any to add?"

"You covered it well." He looked at Summer. "I did get your text about the knife shop in Anchorage. Did you send that before you were run off the road?"

"Yes." She nodded. "A little while before. I'm not sure how long, but I didn't figure it would send until we were almost home. I just didn't want to forget to ask you."

"Well, I got it. And good thinking, but I called APD and they actually already checked out that guy. The knife shop was on their radar because of the weapon the killer has used. It may be from that shop, based on some evidence I can't tell you about, so they already checked him out and they don't believe it's him."

Summer didn't know whether she should feel relief or not. On one hand, she was glad it wasn't that particular acquaintance, but on the other hand, her attempts to come up with a suspect list hadn't been very helpful.

And she was exhausted. Inside and out.

"Can I go sleep now?" Summer asked Noah, feeling like she was on the edge of falling apart emotionally, something she didn't want Clay to see. He'd seen her at her most vulnerable already, earlier when they were talking, and she needed to maintain just a little distance.

He nodded. "Yes. I'm going to stay close. I'll probably just sit in one of those chairs in your room once you fall asleep."

She wanted to ask if that was necessary, but knew that it was. Besides, after what had happened the last time she'd fallen asleep in her room, she didn't think she'd be able to rest peacefully without having someone there with her. So without arguing, she stood and walked to the stairs, then up to her room where she laid down in her dirty clothes and fell asleep within seconds.

FOURTEEN

When Clay woke from his nap the sun was high in the sky, not that that told him much about what time it was. He reached for his phone, which sat on the bedside table. Just past 2:00 p.m.

He threw back the covers, stretched and counted. Better than six hours of sleep, which was like gold in an investigation like this. Noah would have understood how much he was helping Clay by letting him take a break this long.

Clay took a quick shower and changed into clean clothes, then hurried down the stairs, wondering if Summer had slept, if she was awake yet.

She wasn't downstairs in the family's living room, so he headed out into the main great room of the lodge.

"How are you doing?" Tyler asked from behind the desk, coming around to look Clay over. "You look pretty good. No injuries that I can see. Why'd you let my sister get shot?"

"You know I'd have taken the bullet for her if I'd been given the choice." Clay said the words and meant them, realizing too late that the tone of his voice would probably convince Tyler all too well how much he meant them.

Sure enough, his friend studied him. "I asked for one thing."

Clay shook his head, ran a hand through his hair. "It wasn't on purpose, okay?"

"But you are falling for her."

Was he? Maybe. Yes. No. Clay just needed to keep them both alive long enough to find out. "I care. A lot." It was what he knew was true, so it was what he told Tyler. He didn't want to hide anything from his friend.

"She's been through a lot."

"I know."

"No, you don't know this part. There was a guy—"

"I know all of it."

Tyler looked at him.

Clay nodded.

"All of it?"

"Yes. I'm sure."

"Don't break her heart, Clay. That's all I ever wanted, was to keep her heart from getting broken. You're here for the summer and then what?"

"I'd planned to leave."

It was the worst time for him to catch sight of Summer coming down the main stairs, but there she was. Clay didn't know how much she'd heard. The last part without context sounded pretty bad. But he didn't know if he was ready for her to understand how much he felt for her. How dangerously close to crazy about her he was.

"You're leaving?" she asked quietly as she approached where the two of them stood.

Clay looked over at Tyler.

"Not right now," Tyler said. "I just meant he'd only asked for a job for the summer."

Clay watched Summer's defenses go up again and

wished he could do something about that, but having that conversation in front of her brother wasn't something she'd appreciate, he was sure.

"I've got to get back to work," Tyler said to Clay. "We'll talk more later?"

"Sure." He'd have agreed to almost anything to have Tyler leave so he could get Summer alone to explain. "How did you sleep?" he asked her.

"Pretty good. I woke up around half an hour ago and just laid there being thankful I wasn't in the woods anymore." She smiled a little. "Dry socks never felt so good, either," she added, holding up one wool sock–clad foot.

"I'm sure. I wanted to talk to you about today. Mind if we sit somewhere?"

"Let's go back to the family room." Summer led the way and they each took a seat on the sofa. She only sat two feet from him but it felt farther, with the way her arms were crossed defensively, shutting him out.

"I know you walked in on a weird part of the conversation I was having with Tyler." Clay had never been one to beat around the bush.

"You're leaving. I get it."

"Not now. And I don't know if I want to. Anymore."

She looked at him, then shook her head. "You've got to be a police officer again, Clay. You're too good at this to run from it forever."

"Who says I'm running?"

"Aren't you?" She met his gaze, level, looking more confident than she ever had. Because of how her story had drawn them even closer together?

Clay still wanted to talk more about that. The shooter had chosen the worst time to come after them, not that there ever would have been a good time.

"About the conversation we had…"

"Is it okay if I don't want to talk about it right now?" Her voice softened, making the words not sound harsh or demanding.

Clay could do nothing but agree. "Of course. The case? Can we talk about that?"

Unless it was his imagination, she relaxed a bit, leaning back against the sofa cushions. She grabbed a throw pillow from beside her and brought it into her lap to hold. "Sure. If there's any chance it will make this nightmare end sooner, I'm all for it."

Clay was too. He'd miss being with Summer every day but her safety wasn't worth extending his time with her.

"I was thinking about the man who is after you."

"Me too." Summer shuddered. "Almost every time I close my eyes."

"I'm trying to figure out who it could be. I think we should make a list."

"I don't exactly have a list of enemies, Clay." Summer shook her head.

"I know you don't. But someone is after you, and chances are good you've met them."

"Why do you think so?" Summer asked but immediately shook her head. "No, of course they'd have to know me. Unless he was just waiting on the trail for anyone, but if so it's entirely too coincidental that I share so many similarities with the other victims."

"Let's talk about them more."

"I wrote everything down in a notebook." Summer's eyes widened and she paled. "It was in the car."

Problems with that ran through Clay's mind in a line, one after another. They didn't have her notes, problem one. The *killer* might have their notes, problem two. The police might find their notes and know they'd been investigating. Problem three.

"I didn't write everything down. I tried to keep it pretty bare-bones just in case."

"Good thinking on your part," Clay said aloud, wanting to calm her down some as he could see her eyes widening. "Why don't we not worry about that right now. The police will bring our belongings back once they've processed them for evidence, and then we'll know if there's any fallout from the notebook."

She nodded. "Okay. I can do that. Not worrying. Much."

"Good. Now, what do we remember?"

"All the women were outdoorsy. That's the first thing that comes to my mind."

"If we assume that's the critical factor connecting the victims, where could he have met you?"

Summer held up a finger. "Hold on just a minute…"

She stood and walked toward the door. Clay followed her. He thought he heard her sigh and he understood—having personal security was restrictive to be sure. But it was necessary still and Clay wasn't going to take any chances.

She walked to the front desk and said something to Tyler. Clay wasn't close enough to hear—he thought she'd appreciate the slightest bit of space.

Tyler opened a closet that was to the side of the front desk, behind it. What were they up to?

He reached in and pulled out a whiteboard, and handed it to Summer. She smiled and turned back to Clay. A bag of dry-erase markers was taped to it. Smart. They could brainstorm and then erase the evidence so they wouldn't have a second notebook situation, some-thing Clay appreciated. Even though he'd told Summer not to worry, he was still slightly concerned about the fact that the investigating they'd been doing might be made public.

They returned to the living room.

"Okay." Summer opened a marker and set the board in front of them, leaning it against the coffee table. "Places he could have met any of us."

"Hiking. That's the first and probably most obvious."

Summer nodded. "I agree. It's also the hardest to prove or to track down. It's not like most trails have any kind of log system and it would be almost impossible to get witnesses or really anything to back this one up."

"That doesn't mean it isn't a possibility."

"You're right, I suppose." She wrote it down. "What else?"

"Races? Have you run anything lately? Some 5Ks? Outdoorsy people are often the ones who do those too and I know Anchorage has a lot."

She shrugged. "I've done a couple this year. Could be." She wrote it down.

"What about a store for your equipment?"

"It's possible. I get most of my stuff at Anchorage Outdoor Gear, where we were, but I've gotten shoes at Mountain Central before." She wrote down the names of both stores.

"What else?"

"Trailheads?" she suggested.

"What do you mean?"

"What if he isn't a hiker but he fishes or something and that was how we crossed paths?" She shrugged.

"It's a stretch. It's basically the same as hiking, so I just thought I'd toss it out there."

"Go ahead and write it down," Clay suggested, and Summer seemed to agree. She nodded and set the marker down on the coffee table.

"Hiking. Races. Stores. Trailheads," he read aloud.

"There's no way to make a list from those things. There's no way to know who hiked somewhere at a certain time or shopped somewhere when I was there." She shook her head.

"Technically in a store like Anchorage Outdoor Gear we might be able to access online copies of receipts if we needed to prove you were there on the same day as someone else, but I see your point. We might be able to use it to prove a connection when we have a suspect in custody, but it won't help us narrow down a list."

"So we're at another dead end for now though." Summer didn't sugarcoat things, did she? While he wished he could soften the blow of what she'd already realized, Clay appreciated that about her.

"At the moment. But I think we're close."

"Why do you think so?"

He shifted his weight to face her and waited until he was sure he had her attention. "I think he is afraid you can identify him."

She stood. Paced. "Why do you think that?"

He stayed seated on the couch but watched her carefully, tensing every time she walked in front of a window. That might be an overreaction on his part—no one else involved in the investigation would agree with his tension there...but then again, no one else had seen how well the guy after them could shoot.

"He's changed how he's coming after you. That's unexpected. I think you have him rattled."

"But you saw the sketch APD did. He wore a mask, Clay, I don't know who he is."

"So maybe it's his voice that he thinks you could identify. But he wouldn't go to this much trouble to kill you if you hadn't become a threat."

"Isn't that the very definition of a serial killer? Someone who tries to kill other people?"

"Sure, but think about it. He killed those other women with a knife, the same way he initially tried to kill you."

She nodded slowly. "Okay. But he's not doing that anymore. And you think that's significant?"

"I'm sure it is. Serial killers fit a profile, they play by their own set of rules. Even though they obviously have extreme issues, what they do makes sense to them. They tend to follow patterns even more so than other criminals. He has broken his. It must be for a reason."

"I did notice things had escalated. Tracking me down to my home, almost being run off the road, being shot at multiple different times..."

"It's not about his usual motives anymore. Now he just wants you dead."

"Wow, don't beat around the bush at all, Clay."

"You can take it."

"What makes you so sure?"

"Because you're the strongest woman I know."

Summer didn't know how to react, not to Clay's words or his nearness. Sometime in the span of a few minutes he'd ended up shifting over to where she sat on the couch and now she was leaning in his direction. Eight more inches and she could kiss him.

Six.

Four. She held there, met his eyes and swallowed hard as she tried to decide what she wanted, what he wanted, what she was doing.

Clay lowered his chin, just slightly. But enough for Summer to tell that her unspoken "kiss me" invitation might be getting an answer.

She jerked backward. "We should go down to the station and tell Noah what we came up with."

Clay hadn't moved, hadn't backed up or apologized for his part in the almost kiss. Not that she wanted him to. Not that she wanted him to acknowledge it, either.

Summer stood, brushed her hair, which had fallen in her face as she'd leaned toward Clay, behind her ear and straightened her shoulders. "We'll drive your truck, then, right? Since my car is…"

"Yes."

She hurried outside, even more flustered by the calmness in Clay's voice. Did nothing rattle him?

Maybe not, and not that many things rattled her. But the way she still felt drawn to Clay, the way he still seemed like he might share those feelings even after she'd told him all she had…

Neither of them said much on the way into town, but much to Summer's surprise the silence wasn't awkward. Just full. Like there was so much to say and neither of them wanted to say it. Summer knew they'd eventually have to finish the conversation she'd started in the woods if there was ever going to be anything between them. Not that Clay had said there was, and besides, wasn't he leaving?

Summer walked with Clay into the building and took a deep breath. Reliving this over and over was getting a little easier, but that didn't mean it was objectively easy. The fact was she couldn't stop looking over her shoulder to see if anyone was watching, if anyone was waiting to attack. Because this was actually her real life. Where someone wanted her dead.

"Summer. Clay." Noah was walking past the door as soon as they walked in and immediately turned to face them. "Did you come to talk to me? I was just on the phone with the troopers and was about to call you. They recovered Summer's car. No indication it's been messed with since you left it."

She breathed a sigh of relief. Maybe that meant they didn't have to process the car's contents and no one would notice the notebook?

Noah frowned. "They wanted me to ask you why you have so much information about the case in a notebook?"

Summer looked at Clay. They both looked back at Noah but neither said anything.

"We'd better go to my office."

They followed him there. Summer ran her hand over her forehead, trying to do anything to ease the tension that had developed when Noah said they had the notebook. How did they explain that?

"Don't be mad, Noah," Summer said as soon as he'd shut the door behind them, before either she or Clay had even had the chance to sit down.

"I don't know what exactly I'd be mad about. I just don't understand why the two of you seem to be conducting some kind of unofficial investigation."

There wasn't much worse than getting caught doing something you weren't supposed to be doing. Especially by Noah. Because when he wasn't working, wasn't worried about a serial killer terrorizing his town, he was laid-back and funny. But the sense of humor all but disappeared under the pressure of the job.

"I'll explain," Clay started. Summer was more than willing to let him do so. She leaned back a little in the chair.

"We're not interfering," he continued, "and we haven't done anything illegal or unethical."

"Not telling me what you were up to dances close to both of those."

"Maybe it does. But it's not either one and I stand by that." Clay's shoulders were straight, his posture not defiant but confident. Summer cracked a tiny smile. Her brother was a difficult man to stand up to but Clay was doing an admirable job.

"Why don't you describe exactly what you *have* done, if you don't mind."

Summer held her breath. Waited.

"We sorted through some ideas we both had, and compiled them in the notebook."

"I wrote them down. That was my fault." Summer wasn't proud of it, but she knew that first of all, it was true, and second of all, Noah was much less likely to be upset with her than Clay, and for some reason, she didn't want him to have any reason to dislike Clay.

"What else?" Noah kept going.

Clay looked at Summer. She winced. This was where he was going to be the least happy with them.

"We talked to some people with…connections to the case and asked them some questions."

"You conducted unauthorized interviews?" Noah's eyes widened. He pressed a hand on his forehead, closing his eyes. Summer half wondered if he was counting to ten to calm himself down.

"Again—" Clay's voice was still steady "—we didn't do anything unethical. Unadvisable, maybe. But we just talked to them. Summer is the one who has the most in common with the other victims and we thought she might be able to find a connection that law enforcement officers might overlook."

"I don't know what to say to either of you right now." Noah looked between the two of them. "You." He focused on Summer. "You need to take your safety more seriously. And leave the investigating to the people who are in charge. And you." He fixed his glare on Clay, and Summer thought it was harsher than the one she'd gotten. "You should have known better."

"Than what? There's a serial killer still terrorizing south central, no law enforcement agency I've talked to is making progress and it's not anyone's fault because I've seen how hard people are working. I thought I might have found a way to make some progress."

"Involving my sister in an investigation you're supposed to be protecting her from?"

"I'm supposed to be protecting her from the killer. Not from a knowledge of the very real danger she's facing."

"I'd prefer she was protected from both."

Summer threw her hands up. "Stop, both of you. Please."

Both men looked at her. Though neither had been out of line and Clay had kept his usual calm tone, Summer couldn't take it anymore. "Aren't we all on the same team?"

"Technically I'm on a team with my officers here and the troopers, and my team is trying to keep you safe." He directed the words at Summer.

"Okay, then," she began, growing more frustrated with her brother by the moment. "Doesn't that mean Clay is on your team?"

Her brother looked at the other man—and then his shoulders sagged a bit as the ire seemed to drain out of him. "Yes. He's keeping you safe, doing what I ask. Yes, he is. You're right, Summer." He studied Clay for another moment, then stuck out his hand. "I apologize. That was unprofessional of me."

Clay shook it. "I understand. I care about your sister too."

Noah nodded, taking the words at their true face value rather than reading into them like she suspected she would do in whatever few quiet moments she had for the rest of the day.

"The troopers will be bringing the car into town sometime tomorrow if all goes according to plan. They took it to Anchorage and the lab needs time to examine it."

Tomorrow? Summer wasn't counting on it. That seemed like an unrealistically fast turnaround and besides, plans didn't seem to mean much these days, not with the high stakes her life had turned into.

"Thanks." She smiled.

"I'd like to look at that notebook when we get it back, with your permission, Summer."

She knew he didn't have to ask and so she nodded. "Sure. I don't know what we have that could help, but if there's anything…"

"Actually I think we should tell him what we'd come here to talk to him about," Clay broke in.

"I'm all ears."

"I told Summer that I was thinking, sort of rolling

things around in my head about this case and realizing that the killer's MO has changed substantially."

"Not hard to notice."

"No, but I think it lets us make a few assumptions or at least gives us some conjectures and possibilities to investigate."

"Such as?"

"I think the killer believes Summer can identify him."

Noah's brows rose. "If that's true, then you realize security will need to be tighter."

Clay nodded and Summer frowned. They hadn't talked about this. What did he mean by that? More officers, or were they going to push the safe house issue? She couldn't imagine being stuck somewhere isolated without the freedom to hike and explore the mountains around her.

"We can talk about that in a minute. But as for the why, think about his MO. He's a serial killer, he does things with a purpose, deranged though it may be."

"I'm still following."

"And he isn't trying to kill Summer in his usual way anymore. He's realized he's probably not going to get that chance. But rather than give up on her entirely, he's fixated on her."

"Could just be some weird psychological obsession."

"I would agree if he kept trying to attack her with the knife that was used in the other murders. That's personal to him."

Summer felt like she was going to be sick, remembering the glint of the blade. Instead she drew a deep breath and focused on the patterns in the carpet while Clay kept talking.

"But you're saying that now his methods of attack are so impersonal you don't think his motives are the same."

Clay nodded. "Exactly. Now he just wants to eliminate her. He's acting like he views her as a threat."

Summer looked up from the carpet long enough to chime in. "But I don't know who he is, I really don't." She shook her head. "I've thought through almost everyone I know who hikes, random people I've seen often on the trail who might fit the build, on Facebook groups. I've got nothing."

Noah blew out a breath, slowly. "Okay. If that's true, and I think you have a good reason for believing that it is, how does this change our investigation? Where should we be looking differently?"

"I'm not sure it gives us any clues in that direction but it does give us some ideas about how he might continue to operate," Clay offered.

"How?"

"He's going to hit hard and he's not going to stop until either he is captured or Summer is dead. Because at this point, he believes he has nothing to lose."

FIFTEEN

Past one in the morning and Clay couldn't sleep. The sky outside had finally darkened to something that resembled nighttime, but still he couldn't shut off his thoughts. His body was exhausted despite the rest he'd gotten earlier in the day, but his mind refused to follow suit.

He turned over again. Glanced at the clock one more time only to find less than one minute had passed. Noah was on watch now, since Clay had agreed to take the first sleeping shift. They were switching at two.

An hour to sleep.

He turned over again and closed his eyes. They snapped open and he threw back the covers. Gas. He smelled gas.

He grabbed his jacket on the way out of the door of his room, thankful he'd slept in all his clothes.

Noah met him in the hallway. "I smell gas downstairs."

"I just smelled it too. Where's Summer?"

"Her room. I'll get her." Noah threw the door open and ran inside. Clay waited in the hall but was ready to take Summer's hand as soon as she came out. Noah hurried ahead of the two of them. "Get Summer outside!"

"What if it's a trap?"

"It's a risk we have to take." The other man's expression was grim. Clay ducked back into his room, grabbed his handgun from the bedside table drawer and tucked it into the side of his waistband, then took Summer's hand again.

He and Summer ran outside, the cold wrapping like an unwelcome blanket around them. He felt Summer shiver and wished he'd taken the time to grab his jacket so he could offer it to her.

Tyler and Kate both ran out only a minute later. Kate was carrying an extra jacket. "I wasn't sure you'd have gotten yours," she said to Summer as she handed her one.

Summer smiled, something that surprised Clay a little. "That's my always-prepared sister."

"How are you smiling?" Kate shook her head, looked at Clay. "Does she not get it?"

"Get what?" Summer asked.

Clay didn't know. She didn't seem nearly scared enough to understand the full range of danger they could be facing even now.

Worst-case scenario now that they were outside and presumably safe was that the gas smell was some kind of trap to get them outside so the killer could pick Summer off. It wasn't a scenario Clay wanted to consider but it had the potential to be the very one they were facing, so he made sure he stayed on alert, looking in multiple directions. There was enough light to make out shapes, a dim sort of twilight, but so far nothing looked out of place to him.

"You don't get that this is really bad!" Kate frowned, her frustration obviously overcoming her vocabulary in Clay's opinion because *bad* didn't begin to cover it.

"I haven't exactly thought a guy after me was good. Ever."

"No, but you're not taking it seriously. I heard Noah talking last night, again, about how you'd be better off in a safe house." Kate threw her hands up. "What else needs to happen to convince you to listen to him? He's not just your brother, he's the chief of police here and if I were you I'd do what he says."

"I don't want to leave you guys, leave the lodge with no one to lead the hikes."

"Someone's trying to kill you and you're worried about leading hikes?" Kate didn't bother to hide her disbelief.

"I don't want to hurt the lodge."

"We don't want *you* hurt. That's what matters most." Kate glanced back at the building. "But if you don't want to hurt the lodge, consider what happened tonight. That's certainly not helping it."

Summer's smile fell from her face, her shoulders slouched as the reality of the danger sunk in. Clay wished Kate had been more careful with her words— Summer already carried so much guilt. But gentle or not, she was right.

Summer looked at Clay. Then back at Kate. "Alright. I'll do it."

Kate nodded once. "Tell Noah when he gets out here."

No one said anything after that. Kate had killed any kind of optimism Summer had been showing. While Clay wished he could see her smile again, he knew that right now she needed the reminder of the seriousness of the situation.

If they'd been trapped inside, if the gas had kept leaking, they could have succumbed to carbon monoxide poisoning. It was also possible that whoever caused the leak had intended to set off an explosion.

That scenario was probably the deadliest. Thankfully it hadn't happened.

But it could have.

The building alarm went off. Clay wondered if the CO detectors hadn't detected a problem until then or if Noah had had to set them off manually.

It didn't take long for the guests who were staying at the lodge to start filing out, most in what looked like pajamas and bathrobes. All of them looking understandably upset.

Clay hated to admit it but the safe house was looking like the best option to him too. Not just for Summer's safety, although that was his top priority, but for the safety of those around her, like Kate had pointed out. If the worst had happened tonight, the death toll would have been extreme, and would have included far too many innocent people who had no involvement in this case at all. This wasn't something they could handle in the same way they'd been trying to. It was time to admit they needed another plan. There, standing in the darkness, he felt like he'd failed somehow. Yes, Summer was still alive, for which he was thankful, but he hadn't been able to handle keeping her safe on his own. He hadn't been able to eliminate the threat completely.

He hated when it felt like the bad guys were winning. He knew that, thanks to God and His plan, evil never won in the end. Ever. But sometimes on earth that wasn't how it felt. And it grated against his sense of justice, against all the reasons he'd become a cop after high school in the first place.

I don't know how to handle this, God. Help.

Noah stepped out of the building. Shook his head.

And Clay knew it was good that Summer had decided about the safe house on her own because at least she'd feel better about it that way.

Because he was pretty sure Noah was no longer giving her a choice in the matter. And Clay didn't blame him. Whoever was after her wasn't stopping. And her life was growing more dangerous every day.

When the Moose Haven Fire Department finally left, having declared the building safe, Summer was still standing in the parking lot, staring at the lodge. A light rain had started to fall as dawn broke across the sky, but she didn't care. Let the rain fall.

She had to leave.

Summer wished tears would come, anything to give her some way to work through the overwhelming wave of emotions crashing against her right now, but none did. She just stared ahead, aware that Clay was close by talking to some other police officers, that her siblings were nearby. And yet, she'd never felt more alone in her life.

She'd fought for her chance to lead the hikes at this lodge, and she'd checked as recently as last week—occupancy at the lodge was up since she'd started doing them. Summer didn't know why people seemed to care so much about whether or not she was there. She was a has-been mountain runner, but that one season she'd spent in Europe, even placing in some races, had helped her make just enough of a name for herself that it appeared she really was good for business.

And now she had to leave. Because rather than helping her family's lodge recover from economic setbacks, her presence was hurting it. Of course that was the secondary reason she was leaving—hers and everyone else's safety being the first priority. Still, she felt the sting. For the first time since the man had grabbed her in the woods, Summer let a dark thought flicker through her mind.

Was this all punishment for the way she'd lived a few years ago? For the choices she'd made?

She let the thought linger. Considered it.

"Summer?"

She blinked. She'd almost forgotten she wasn't alone because it felt very much like she was. She looked at Clay.

"It's me, you and Noah. And we need to leave as soon as possible."

Summer nodded, looked back at the lodge and wished one more time for tears that didn't come. "I'll go pack."

Not long after, Summer had her turquoise backpack strapped to her back and was dressed for hiking. After feeling so overwhelmed earlier, she felt strangely calm now that they were about to drive to the trailhead for their family's cabin, the location they'd decided made the most sense as a safe house. She had failed in how she wanted to help her family, for now. But that didn't mean this was the end. Once the danger was over and she was able to come back, she would do better, try harder, somehow make the lodge work and make up to her family for how she hadn't been there for them in the past.

The ride to the trailhead was quiet. Neither of the men seemed like they were in a talkative mood and Summer definitely wasn't, so no one spoke. There was no need to talk as they began hiking, either. Summer and Noah both knew where they were going and Clay just followed close behind.

How much longer was this going to last? Summer wondered as she pushed her pace faster, not from any sense of danger but because she needed to feel her muscles burn, needed to feel alive. She'd always loved the way hiking focused her, making her feel like if she could conquer this hike she could conquer anything. But today, the hike wasn't enough to clear her mind. How much longer would she have to live like this, with someone after her?

She kept putting one foot in front of the other. The next right step, the next right thing, just like the pastor of the church in town her family attended had told her to do when she returned to town and wanted to know how to make things right with God, with her family.

The next right thing with her family had been to stay at the lodge, devote herself to helping it succeed. At least, that had been the plan.

The next right thing with God?

Summer had never stopped long enough to figure out what it was. Only knew it was there, hovering just out of her reach and feeling like if she just tried hard enough, focused hard enough, she'd know. Whether or not it would be something she'd be willing to do, she wasn't sure. But right now she didn't even know what it was.

Thinking in that direction made her feel unsettled, a feeling she'd had quite enough of lately, so she turned her thoughts to Clay.

He'd said nothing about her past, about the conversation they'd shared. Of course when had he had the chance? They'd been too busy reacting to events they couldn't control.

Summer flinched when she thought that. Was that what her life had been the last three years? Just a chain of reactions to events because she knew she wasn't ultimately in charge of her life and so she felt perpetually like she was spinning out of control?

Oddly enough, except on ridgelines.

Summer exhaled, managed to stop thinking so much, stop analyzing as she continued to hike through the trees. They broke through the tree line after about forty-five minutes of hard hiking, and then they were on the edge of the mountain, taking the trail that led straight up to the ridge, which they'd travel for another half a mile before reaching their family's cabin.

It was the best possible place for a safe house because they could see the trail to it clearly over a considerable distance. Anyone coming would be obvious because the cabin sat at the end of a ridge. To approach it from any other direction, avoiding the path, would take climbing skills that few people had.

When Summer was up on the ridge her thoughts drifted back again, pounding in her heart to the rhythm of her quickened heartbeat.

Up here, what Jenna Hunt's mom had asked for felt easy. Up here, she could feel alive, even now. The irony got to her, but she couldn't explain it. How could someone who wanted control so desperately possibly feel the best up here, at the mercy of nature?

Because the ridgeline was a visible reminder that she wasn't in control. That life wasn't about that, wasn't about risk management.

It was about…life.

Abundant life.

Summer stopped, there in the trail. Looked up at Noah, but he didn't turn around. Turned back to Clay, but he just frowned like he was worried about her. "You okay?" he asked after she'd been staring at him for a minute.

Abundant life. Where had that idea, which felt almost like a correction to her thoughts, come from?

She looked out over the landscape of the Kenai Peninsula beneath them, breathing deep as she surveyed the green of the trees in the valley below, the ethereal blue-green of the river below and then Seal Bay off in the distance, and the town of Moose Haven.

Then her eyes looked out farther, to the next mountain range. Ridges, valleys, endless nothing, and Summer felt like she always did on a ridgeline. So very small.

You are so big, God. So much more powerful than I am.

The admission was the first prayer she'd prayed in years that hadn't been asking for something, the first attempt at conversation she'd made with her Creator since she'd walked away from what she'd believed.

Summer started walking again. She didn't want the men to have to wait for her, and she knew they must both be on edge with them so exposed at the moment, outside of the relative safety of the cabin's walls.

But as she walked, she kept praying.

Did You remind me about that, about abundant life? Because I know You're right. Life isn't the point, not even living it to the fullest, though I think that's better than not. But You want us to live to the fullest not just for those we've lost but for You. As a way to thank You for this world, for the ridgelines, for the valleys, for all of it.

Tears stung in her eyes. For innocence lost. A baby whose tiny feet had melted Summer's heart, though they would never walk on earth. For the family she'd gotten back but had held at arm's length.

For her relationship with Jesus. Which she'd pushed away or ignored for so long that it felt like a natural re-action. Much more natural than this looking around, praying, praising.

"Do you want to be made well?"

Summer recognized the quote, from somewhere in the New Testament. Jesus had asked that of a woman when He'd walked the earth.

Was He asking her that now? Or was her mind just recalling Scriptures it had known in the past?

Either way, Summer nodded, felt her chest tighten a little and then release, her shoulders feeling lighter than they had in years.

"Yes," she whispered to God as she looked out over the mountains He had created. And still created her. "Yes I do."

SIXTEEN

The cabin was the perfect safe house. Clay had seen as soon as they'd begun their approach down the ridgeline why Noah had been so sure they had the best possible location in mind. Egress would be almost impossible without detection.

He and Noah had talked while Summer was packing, working out logistics. Noah had a SAT phone with him, since regular cell phones wouldn't get service this far from a tower, and he'd call the Moose Haven PD to keep in touch with the other officer there to see if any progress was being made. They both voiced the hope that maybe tampering with the gas lines at the lodge would be where the guy would mess up, that maybe he'd made some kind of mistake that would result in him finally getting caught.

But neither of them was counting on that, and they'd made plans for who would take which watch, what to do in case of several contingencies. Clay felt they were as well prepared as they could be. Having at least one more officer would have been ideal, but there just wasn't the manpower to spare. Even two men were more than was practical, but this was Summer and no one was taking chances with her safety.

Ten feet from the cabin Noah stopped hiking and turned back. "Stay with Clay," he told Summer.

She did so and Noah went inside to clear the building, though they had no reason to believe the killer would have been able to anticipate them coming up here.

Clay's only concern was the fact that this cabin wasn't a secret. Noah insisted it wasn't extremely well-known, but the fact was that *someone* might know, and Clay didn't want their location to somehow make it to the attention of the man who wanted Summer dead.

He had the uncomfortable feeling that he might be wrestling with some trust issues. But it was a valid question his heart couldn't stop asking—Why was God letting Summer be stalked by this man? Why wasn't He helping the police find his identity so they could eliminate the threat by putting him behind bars where he belonged?

Clay had seen enough evil in police work that he'd already worked through questions about injustice, about why God let bad things happen to good people. But it didn't stop a few persistent, unanswerable questions from popping up now and then. Clay asked them when they came though, knowing that ignoring them wouldn't help and wouldn't strengthen his relationship with God the way the hard stuff did, much as he didn't like going through it at the time.

"Are you doing okay?" Clay asked Summer quietly. He'd prayed for her, especially on the hike up this morning. The things she'd been through… He understood more after hearing part of her story why she struggled with faith the way she did, even though he knew God hadn't abandoned her.

"I'm okay."

"Seriously?" Clay wanted the real answer, not to just be brushed aside. Besides, if she wanted to back off a little from their growing friendship, she'd picked an impossible time to do it. The three of them were going to be stuck in a relatively small cabin indefinitely.

"All clear."

Not that Noah being with them would give Clay and Summer much time to talk privately.

Clay followed Summer to the cabin. The front was a wide deck that looked out over the landscape below. There were four steps up to the deck. The front door was off the deck—Clay hoped there was a back door because while having only one entrance and exit meant less places to protect, it could be bad if they needed to escape in a hurry.

He leaned back around the side of the house. The windows were wide enough to serve as exits if there were an emergency, something Clay was hoping to avoid.

He stole another glance at Summer. Despite her initial protests, she looked more relaxed here at the safe house than she'd looked in Moose Haven for a while.

Clay felt relaxed up here too, like it was easier to see clearly on the top of the world.

For the first time since he'd left Treasure Point, he could think through that situation, analyze what he'd done wrong—the mistakes that had shaken his faith in himself as an officer of the law. And he came up with…

Nothing. Well, almost nothing. He should have listened to Kelsey, his cousin, when, months ago, someone had been trying to kill her and she'd had suspicions that someone in their police department was the would-be killer. That had been his only mistake. And while it was a big one, nothing else had indicated who the traitor was. There had been no clues. Thankfully, Kelsey was okay, and didn't blame Clay for not believing her gut instinct.

The man who had tried to kill her bore all the blame, she'd told Clay. Clay hadn't done anything, which was what grated him so badly. He hadn't done anything. But still, the situation itself, his cousin being in danger…

It hadn't been Clay's fault.

Somehow a weight lifted, he felt even lighter. Then looked up at the sky.

Did You allow those things to happen so I'd end up here? Do You sometimes allow something we view as bad because of the fact that You are working all things for our good?

The questions he asked God didn't have immediate audible answers. But something that felt a lot like peace edged over his heart.

He looked back at Summer. Tried to exhale some of his worries about her safety.

You're taking care of her too, in this situation, right, God?

Yes. God was in control, had His good purposes in mind. Clay just had to learn to let his trust rest firmly on Him.

Summer took a sip of coffee and winced. She hated coffee, but mornings in the cabin were cold if no one had kept a fire going overnight, which none of them had because the weather hadn't been forecasted to be especially cold.

Well, the weather hadn't gotten the memo. All of her

was cold, down to her toes. She shivered, then took another sip of the nasty brown liquid some people apparently liked. Noah watched her with amusement. Clay was still sleeping since he'd taken the first watch last night.

She was about a third of the way through the coffee when Clay walked out. "Is that coffee?" He raised his eyebrows. "I thought you only drank tea?"

Summer sputtered a little, having attempted another sip. "I'm freezing."

Clay smiled and shook his head, then reached into his backpack and pulled out a box of Irish breakfast tea. "I'm sorry I wasn't up sooner. Want to trade?"

Before she could stop him he'd started heating the water. She watched as he steeped the tea for her, finding something spellbinding in the fact that the same hands that were prepared to defend her from any threat were now gently making her tea. It seemed so domestic and such a contradiction but also so *Clay* that she just smiled.

She took the tea from him, handed off the coffee and sat in the silence, feeling for half a second like she could imagine a future like this. Her and Clay as…something. Friends? More? They would have to see, but she wanted him in her life.

Wanted a life like this. With some peace. Rest.

Summer glanced out the window. They were on top of a ridgeline. That summarized her desires for life well, didn't it? Rest on a ridgeline.

"I've got to call Moose Haven in a minute so I may step out onto the deck," Noah said to Clay, glancing at Summer as he did so.

So much for her few minutes of peace. Everything about the investigation slammed back into her mind, creating dark corners and shadows and worry where a few minutes ago there had been quiet and calm.

If Noah was concerned about her trying to overhear his conversation, he didn't need to be. Summer was done with interfering. She'd tried to get involved, tried to help with the investigation and do some good, and it hadn't helped. If anything, it had hurt. They were no closer to finding him than she'd been before she stepped out of her comfort zone and tried to do something that made her feel less like a victim.

So maybe it was time to sit back and acknowledge that she was out of her depth here.

Clay looked over at her. She could tell he wanted to say something. Amazing how well you could learn how to read someone else's facial expressions when you were with them almost constantly.

Noah went outside, shutting the door carefully behind him.

"Are you okay?"

Summer looked at Clay. "I'm not sure."

"Why?"

"I…" Her mind felt like it was spinning. She'd felt so good only a few minutes before but right now the weight of her situation was pressing on her and she couldn't handle it. Was this what a panic attack felt like? Summer struggled to shake it off, but nothing helped. She looked down at her hands. They were shaking.

She shrugged.

"Hey." He set his coffee mug down, reached out for her hands and took them both. "This will be over soon."

She didn't know if she didn't believe the words or if she was worried it was true, that it would be over soon in a way that would mean the killer had succeeded in—

"I'm not going to let him get to you."

Clay's words were quiet.

Summer nodded. Looked out the window as she replayed the conversation she'd had with Mrs. Hunt. *Really, truly live without regrets.*

The desire to do that wrestled with the unexpected fear that had found her two nights ago at the lodge when there had been the gas leak. For some reason it was that incident that had gotten her attention, more than any other attempt the killer had made on her life. Maybe because it hadn't just been her in danger. It had been innocent people.

"So what's the plan?" Summer asked after taking a long sip of tea to steady herself. It seemed to work at least a little.

"We wait." Clay's face sobered.

"For him to come try…"

Clay shook his head. "No. It's a safe house. There's no sort of plan to use you for bait, Summer. We don't anticipate this place being compromised at all. We're just waiting for a break on the case."

"How can anyone get that if he doesn't try anything else?"

"They're still working on the previous crime scenes. It's not as fast as the movies make it seem—there are other crimes to investigate, other work that has to be done, and most of it is manual, done by actual people."

Summer sighed. She didn't like seeming high maintenance but it seemed like there had to be a way for things to go faster. Waiting had never been a strong suit of hers.

Noah walked back in then, the SAT phone in his hand.

"Any news?" She hated how eager her voice sounded.

He shook his head. "Nothing. I'm afraid we're going

to be up here for a while, so I'm going to go get some firewood."

"I'm in favor of that. I'm not drinking coffee again tomorrow."

"I'll be back soon." He looked at Clay. "Take care of my sister. I shouldn't be more than an hour."

And then Noah was gone again.

Summer looked over at Clay, feeling his eyes on her. "What?"

"You won't have to drink coffee ever again if I can help it." He smiled.

"I didn't say thank you…for bringing the tea." She blushed a little, suddenly self-conscious of the nice thing he'd done for her, and the fact that they were alone.

And that he knew her deepest, darkest secrets and still seemed to care…

"Summer, something you said when we were running near Six Mile Creek…"

Her body stiffened. She looked down, then felt Clay's hand on her right shoulder. Felt a soft squeeze, brotherly almost.

But when she looked up at him and met his eyes. There was nothing brotherly in the gentle expression he was giving her.

"You are that kind of woman. You're the kind who goes through hard things and comes out stronger. You still have your childhood faith, I can tell by the way you talk about what happened. If you didn't believe in God, still have a relationship with Him even if it's messed up right now, you wouldn't care so much. You are stronger than you realize, and you can be more than you imagine. It's up to you."

He exhaled. "That's all I wanted to say. I just didn't

get a chance the other day and it has bothered me ever since to think of you wandering around with such a low opinion of yourself. Seeing yourself that way."

She laughed, but it was without humor. "I do see myself that way. Every single time I look in the mirror."

"I'll never see you that way."

Their faces drew closer. Summer didn't know who moved first. All she knew was that he was close enough now that she could see the stubble on his jaw, the roughness contrasting with the smoothness of his lips, which were close enough for hers to brush over.

Summer closed her eyes and let her lips find his. And let him convince her with his kiss.

SEVENTEEN

So the timing could have been better, since they were in a safe house and everything in Summer's life was so uncertain. Clay still wanted to be careful, and he didn't want it to seem like he was taking advantage of her vulnerability, even a little, but she'd kissed him first. He'd just finished it.

And then he'd pulled away, like the gentleman his mama had raised him to be.

"Clay…"

He smiled, brushed a hand along the edge of her jawline, so softly it felt like he'd barely touched it. "I care about you, Summer. A lot. Enough to tell you that I'm not going to complicate your life more than it is now by making promises or plans. But when this is over…"

She nodded. Smiled just enough that Clay had hope that, even though she wasn't vocalizing it right now, maybe she felt the same way he did.

He stood and walked to one of the windows, feeling like he should give her a little space, though it was hard in a cabin this small. He glanced at his watch. Forty-five minutes since Noah had left. He'd said he'd return within an hour. Clay didn't think Summer had noticed how much time had passed yet, so he left the subject alone. She didn't need to add any worries about her brother to the ones he could already see she was carrying.

Although something had seemed to lessen that weight a little since the hike yesterday. She seemed different somehow, her face a little lighter. But she was still carrying a burden on her shoulders. Her past? The killer? Clay didn't know which. But he wished he could fix it for her.

Instead he prayed, knowing God could handle whatever it was. And then he made her another cup of tea because it was always nice to do something tangible too.

She took the tea with a smile, then it flickered away into a frown. "How long has Noah been gone? It seems like it's been a while."

Clay hesitated before answering. He looked at his watch again. "Just short of an hour."

"You've got to go look for him."

"He's not late yet."

"He said within an hour," she argued. "He wouldn't have said that if he didn't mean it."

Clay shook his head. "He may have misestimated. He'd have had to hike back down to the tree line for firewood and that may have taken longer than he expected it to."

Her expression made it clear she wasn't comforted. "And he may have walked into some kind of trap."

Clay looked out the window. The sky was a cloudless blue. After taking so long to get to the Kenai, the summer weather seemed to be showing off for them. The early morning chill was probably gone too. There was no visible reason it should have taken Noah longer than he'd planned.

But Clay wasn't leaving Summer. That wasn't even

an option. And taking her with him back down the exposed ridgeline wasn't a good idea in his opinion, either.

"You've got to find him, Clay." Summer had come up behind him and he turned to face her, already shaking his head.

"I can't, Summer. You're my first priority."

She didn't argue but her expression made her thoughts clear. Another stretch of time passed. Noah was now half an hour later than he should have been.

"We've got to do something," she muttered, looking at Clay with such a wide-eyed look of desperation that he nodded.

"I'll use the SAT phone and call the Moose Haven Police. Maybe they can send someone up just to double-check." It would extend the circle of people who knew where they were, which was something they'd taken great care to avoid, but it was the best option he had.

"Thank you." Summer's voice was quiet.

Clay made the call, gave them the location where Noah should be and also called Tyler at the lodge to let him know. It didn't seem fair for him to be kept in the dark.

"Thanks, man." Tyler's voice was genuinely appreciative.

"You'd do the same for me," Clay said.

"I would. You take care of my sister, okay?"

"I'm not planning to let anything happen to her."

"I mean… I mean more than that." Tyler sighed. "I'm trying to tell you if you want to pursue her, if you really do know everything that happened and you feel like you can treat her like she deserves, you have my blessing for what it's worth."

Clay smiled. Maybe a little late considering that kiss,

but he appreciated knowing his friend wouldn't have a problem knowing he'd fallen in love with his sister. He'd truly only been trying to protect her. "Thanks, Tyler."

He hung up the phone and filled Summer in on everything except what Tyler had said about the two of them. It wasn't the time for that.

He noticed her looking out the window while he talked and finally asked her what she was looking at.

"It's so sunny…and yet, did you notice it getting hazier out there?" She sniffed the air. "And I smell smoke."

Clay shook his head. "I don't smell anything."

She leaned closer to the window, then turned and walked to another one. "I'm sure, Clay. That's where it's coming from, the smoke. Look."

He followed her and looked where she motioned. There was smoke, billowing from somewhere just behind the cabin. Maybe from the cabin itself.

Options seemed limited at that point. He ran through them, discarding them as he went. Bringing Summer with him to check out the fire was a bad option. Leaving Summer alone in the cabin was a bad option. Both of them staying in the cabin was a bad option.

If this wasn't an accident, wasn't a patch of dry grass that had sparked somehow…

The chances of it being a natural, accidental fire seemed slim. Lightning was rare enough in this part of Alaska, and when you added in the fact that the sky still had hardly a cloud, nothing that would indicate lightning…

If the killer wasn't out there, Clay had no idea what had happened.

But if it was the killer, then he had them. Checkmate.

Clay couldn't let the two of them burn to death up there, knowing they hadn't even tried to fight.

"Okay, Summer, listen to me."

"This is really bad isn't it?"

She had paled and Clay grabbed both her upper arms, gently but with enough firmness to get her attention. "I need you to look at me. I need you to stay focused and I need you to be the amazing, tough mountain runner you always have been and conquer whatever this situation is becoming."

"Is he out there?"

"I honestly don't know."

"But you're going to go see."

He nodded as he removed his weapon from his holster. "I'm going to leave this with you."

"You can't go out there knowing there may be a killer with nothing to fight with, Clay."

"I can't leave you without anything, either."

"You have to. I've got bear spray, but you have one chance at eliminating the threat before it gets to me and that's the goal here, right? I think that is the best option."

Clay nodded. He couldn't argue with the facts she'd presented and all things considered it was probably the best choice of two less-than-perfect ones.

"Stay in here. And stay safe." He took one long look at her, wishing he could kiss her again but knowing that there wasn't time. The smoke was growing thicker. And the threat was growing.

He shut the door and walked onto the deck. The smoke smell in the air was thicker out there. He walked down the steps, awareness heightened, ready to respond to any threat he saw with his .45 out and ready to fire. He kept it angled down slightly at the ground as he ran around the side of the cabin. Nothing there, but yes, the cabin was on fire. Ironically it looked like it had started on the outside of the chimney on the back of the cabin. Clay moved his feet slowly, picking his steps with care as there wasn't much room between the back of the cabin and the cliff off the back of the ridge.

He looked at the fire. Too much to handle with the water they'd brought to drink, but he could try. Maybe use some dirt too…

If all else failed, he'd get Summer and they'd head down the mountain as soon as possible. He'd run anywhere on the planet if he needed to, or hole up anywhere he could find if it would keep Summer safe. Either way.

He just needed her to be okay.

Clay turned to go back inside and alert Summer that possible threat or not, they were going to have to evacuate. But he hadn't moved from where he stood before he saw something out of the corner of his eye. Someone.

And before he could react, something hard hit the side of his head.

Clay was taking too long. There was no way around it and Summer was facing the truth. Noah was gone. Clay was gone. It was extremely likely that she was next.

Summer paced the cabin, walked by another window and looked out. She didn't see any signs that someone other than the three of them had been up there. Even the smoke could still possibly be an accident. Or, well, it could have been if both men hadn't disappeared.

At this point, Summer had very little hope that this wasn't a very intentional setup.

She needed a plan, that much she knew, but she had no idea how to go about coming up with one. Fight back.

That was the best plan she had. Why had she insisted Clay take that gun? She hadn't heard it go off, so he hadn't used it.

Summer had bear spray, but it sprayed in such a wide arc that she knew it would get in her eyes too, especially inside a room like this where it lacked the open air to disperse and she'd also be at the mercy of the super-powered mace.

She looked around for something else she could use as a weapon. Anything else.

And the door creaked open. Her shoulders sagged with relief as she closed her eyes and let out a breath of relief. One of them was back.

But they didn't say anything, and even though only seconds had passed, she would have expected Noah to immediately explain where he'd been and Clay to tell her where the smoke was coming from.

Summer opened her eyes.

The man in the doorway was backlit by the sun, but after she blinked a few times she figured out how the form was familiar and identified the only vaguely familiar face. "Wait…"

"Hello, Summer."

"I know you." She squinted, still trying to place him. "You work at Anchorage Outdoor Gear. Ryan, right?"

He only stood and smiled as he gave a nod at his name, not moving an inch.

"But why are you here? You're not…you're not…"

But as he continued standing silently, that smile sending chills up Summer's spine, she realized that yes, he was.

As an employee of one of the best outdoor stores in Alaska, he'd had access to all of the women. They were outdoorsy types; they'd almost certainly all shopped at his store. And the reason she knew his name wasn't just because of his name tag, he was also part of a Facebook group for hikers.

Summer swallowed hard. She hadn't thought to look, but she was sure now that if she got online and looked at the members, every one of the victims would be on the list. Many people posted photos of their favorite hikes, shared trail conditions.

Whether he'd chosen his victims on that Facebook group or at the store, it made sense.

It was him.

"You're the killer."

EIGHTEEN

Clay had the worst headache of his life, but it was the least of his worries. He hadn't gotten a look at the guy who'd hit him, but he was at least Clay's size, maybe bigger, and in good shape. Summer wouldn't stand a chance in a hand-to-hand fight.

The side of his head where he'd been hit throbbed. He'd blacked out for a second or two, and then he'd opened his eyes but stayed still as the guy walked away from him. Clay had known that headache or no, he wasn't fast enough to get past the man and get back inside to Summer first. So he'd have to let this man make it into the cabin and get distracted by Summer. It was the only chance Clay would have for taking him out. He was counting on the fact that this was the serial killer, and that since he had Summer alone he planned to take his time, like his usual MO, and not just immediately eliminate her.

It was a risk, but it was one Clay had to take for Summer's own good.

Now he crept along the side of the cabin, listening. He heard Summer's stunned voice as she realized the identity of the killer. She was quiet for a few seconds after that, and Clay wondered if she was figuring out how it had all worked, how the man had met her and the other victims. It was clear she knew him and he thought he'd heard her say something about an outdoor store.

He took a quick glance in the window he was crouching under. Summer was standing at the rear of the living area of the cabin, her back to a wall. The man was at the door, barely inside.

As far as Clay could tell, he didn't have a firearm on him, but he wasn't willing to bet their lives on that. If Clay chose the wrong time to attack him and this man did have a gun, everything would escalate too quickly for him to keep the situation under any sort of control.

At least he had a gun he could use if he needed it, though he couldn't in good conscience take the guy out when he was just standing there. But if it was clear he was trying to kill Summer, and Clay could get a shot…

He felt his hip for his weapon. Closed his eyes tight and rubbed his head.

The holster was empty.

The killer must have taken it when Clay blacked out. Had it been longer than a second or two? But if it had, why had it taken so long for the other man to walk away from him? And why hadn't he shot Clay?

He knew he might not get answers to those questions even if the guy ended up in police custody. Sometimes there were no answers.

Knowing the killer had Clay's weapon changed the plan. Now he had to wait for just the right moment. He'd only have one chance.

And if he picked the wrong time, they'd all end up dead.

"You're on that hiking Facebook group, aren't you?" She was surprised at how the question came without hesitation. Her voice wasn't even shaking. It was like Summer was watching herself from somewhere outside her body. Shouldn't she be too scared to speak?

She didn't know. All she knew was that she was terrified, sure, but she was also mad. How dare this man steal the lives of those other women? How dare he try to steal hers, both by trying to kill her and by making her too scared to do the things she loved and enjoyed?

Really live.

That was what she wanted to do. Really live. And she was sick of this man getting in the way of that. Tired of the lack of justice.

"I'm surprised you figured that out." The look of admiration he turned on her had an element of creepiness that did make goose bumps run down her arms, but she kept staring him down. Summer had no idea where this bolder version of herself had come from, but she felt more like the Summer she'd been before she'd run away with Christopher. Before…everything.

But it wasn't just that. She felt like a stronger, braver version of that woman.

Is that because of You, God?

She didn't have time to wait for an answer to her quick prayer. She took a deep breath and stared at him. "So you watched people's conversations to learn where they would be and found places to lie in wait for them." She didn't bother to hide her disgust and his expression twisted slightly. It bothered him that she was disgusted. Interesting.

She'd stopped posting her favorite hikes on that site last year, stopped posting anything other than the occasional unlabeled picture after Noah found out and told her that it wasn't safe to give complete strangers so much information. He'd said it wasn't just because she was a woman who often hiked alone, but also that her name recognition played into it.

She'd agreed and stopped posting.

But it had apparently been too late. She'd already said too much.

"So that's how you knew where I'd hike." She restated it, piecing the other elements they'd wondered about together in her mind as they came to her. "How did you know exactly where I'd be the other times? When you tried to run us off the road, when you shot at us…"

He laughed. "GPS tracking really has come a long way."

Of course. The Anchorage Police Department still had her car, but as far as Summer knew they hadn't been able to process it yet. She was sure they'd find the tracker, but knew that it wasn't suprising that Moose Haven hadn't been able to. They simply didn't have the resources to scan for trackers electronically and the new ones were so tiny and so easy to hide that it wasn't something they'd have been able to readily identify even in a thorough search.

"How did you find this place?"

He shook his head. "Small towns talk. It wasn't too hard to find out your family owned more property than just the lodge."

She wanted to ask him about his background, to see if he had spent time in the military or hunting, the way Clay had suggested, to become such a good shot. But she didn't know if it was better to keep him talking or to start trying to figure out exactly how she was going to get out of this alive.

Because she *had* to get out alive. The edges of her

eyes stung and she blinked, refusing to show any sign of weakness. She hated feeling like prey. Animals in the wild chose the weak ones, the ones with wounds to attack. Any sign of weakness attracted predators.

While she didn't for a second believe that this human predator had chosen his victims with any kind of logic— none of the women had done anything to deserve his fixation, his desire to see them dead—she still refused to give him the satisfaction of seeing her afraid.

Even if the thought of dying, of not seeing Clay again, made her throat tighten until she could barely breathe. She wanted to look into his eyes again, see him smile. Tell him that if she was going to live her life to the fullest, really live, then she wanted him in it. Tell him she loved him. Hoped that maybe she'd hear the words back.

Where *was* he? Understanding hit her hard. There was a good chance he was dead. Though she hadn't heard gunshots, there were many ways to kill someone, and if Clay was alive he wouldn't let her face this man alone.

God, help him please. Don't let him die. Or me.

She turned her attention back to the killer. Frowned a little as a thought crossed her mind.

He was wounded somewhere, wasn't he? Summer knew Clay had hit him with one of his shots only a few days before, which meant Summer had that on her side. If she could figure out where it was.

"You're going to die today, Summer Dawson." He moved toward her slowly, catlike in the way he prowled along the edge of the room toward her rather than walk straight in her direction. She shivered, not liking the feeling that she was being toyed with.

Of all the ways he'd tried to kill her, this one, this up close and personal slow death, was her least favorite.

And Summer wasn't going out like this.

She took a deep breath. Watched him. His right shoulder. Was it her, or was he holding that oddly, like he was more conscious of it? Could that be where he was wounded?

She waited as he walked toward her, prayed he'd continue circling her rather than stop in front of her. She glanced down at her foot quickly, then back up at him, calculating exactly where she'd need to kick to hit him the hardest.

He shifted his weight to the left, exposing his shoulder perfectly.

Summer kicked fast and hard. He yelled.

Seconds passed in a blur, flashes of activity catching Summer's attention. The man's screams, him clutching his arm. Footsteps, coming from somewhere.

Then Ryan was on her, grabbing her arms, rage evident as he channeled all his strength into fighting her. Summer tried to fight back but he was enormous compared to her. For an instant she felt like she understood what had gone through the heads of the women who had ended up dead at Ryan's hands. Fighting was useless. Futile.

But no, it was the only choice she had. She struggled, punched him in the nose, kneed him like she'd seen Sandra Bullock do in a movie once.

He shoved her hard against a wall, and then advanced toward her. Summer stood tall, readying herself for whatever blow was coming next but knowing she couldn't take many more. She could already taste blood on her lip.

The front door slammed open.

Clay was there. Within seconds he was inside, taking

Summer's place and drawing Ryan's attention to himself. The two men were fighting and Summer backed away, experiencing the first small taste of freedom and glimmer of hope she'd felt since Ryan had burst into the cabin. She watched the men fight, wondered how she could help Clay. He was hurt. He had a long, deep gash on the side of his head. She winced—he'd been hit by something. A rock? That could explain why he hadn't come back when he should have and why she hadn't heard anything.

Smoke billowed through the open front door, and when Summer looked back she realized the back wall of the cabin had flames growing, from the base of the wall near the fireplace.

Ryan had set the cabin on fire?

Ryan.

She turned her attention back to him, found Ryan and Clay still fighting. Ryan had an inch or so on Clay, but Clay hit hard. It hadn't taken him long to discover the spot where Ryan was wounded, either, and Summer could see he was focusing his hits on Ryan's right side.

Summer ran to the front door and pushed the door shut since more smoke seemed to be coming from outside than from the fire inside. She didn't want them to die of smoke inhalation before they had a chance to end this. She knew they didn't have long before the entire cabin was in flames but she didn't know how long. It was fire-treated wood but it wouldn't withstand direct fire for long. Seconds? Minutes? She wasn't sure.

She hurried back to where the fighting was taking place, did her best to stay out of the way. Maybe she should run? But no, what if Clay needed her later?

He was starting to seem unsteady on his feet, she noticed, but she couldn't tell why. From what she could see, Clay seemed to be getting in the best hits.

But still, he stumbled backward. Summer rushed toward him, not sure how much help she'd be but determined to try.

The door slammed open again and relief almost overwhelmed Summer as she caught a glimpse of her brother Noah, still alive after all. Summer looked back at the killer, watched as Ryan's attention went to the door. Ignoring the throbbing in her foot, she landed one more hard kick against his shoulder. As she did so Clay seemed to gain just a little more strength and no sooner had she kicked Ryan than Clay landed one last punch, directly on the side of the man's head.

He fell to the ground, unconscious.

Everything stilled. Summer took a breath, listened to her heart pounding and looked around the cabin. "We've got to get out of here."

The back wall was engulfed now, flames dancing and advancing toward them.

"Noah," Clay called to the other man. "Summer, get out."

She wanted to argue but Clay's tone made it clear that wouldn't go over well. She went to the deck, which was as far as she dared go in case they needed her help, and waited, holding her breath almost from fear, for them to come out.

We're alive, God. You did it. You saved us.

She swallowed hard. God wasn't finished with her, wasn't ignoring her because she'd made mistakes. Wasn't punishing her.

Forgive me, Lord.

Just when she was about to run back inside to make

sure her brother and Clay both got out, they came through the door, dragging Ryan behind them. They'd handcuffed his hands together.

Noah nodded behind him. "The SAT phone. It's on the counter."

Clay ducked back inside. Summer didn't think she took another breath until he emerged.

There he was safe. Both of them safe.

He tossed the phone to Noah. "Call the troopers. We need to get this guy off the mountain."

NINETEEN

The troopers had managed to get a helicopter close enough to get Ryan loaded into it. He was on his way to Spring Creek Correctional Center in Seward.

He wasn't going to take any more innocent lives.

Clay finally took a deep breath when that man was gone from the mountain, out of their lives. Summer would have to testify, more than likely both of them would, but that wouldn't be for months or years to come. For now, it was over, and for today that was enough.

The remains of the cabin were burning down behind them. Emergency personnel had decided the best course of action was to let it burn, since it was surrounded by rocks that wouldn't be able to spread the fire. Unfortunately saving the cabin itself would have required too much resource-wise, and the cost and risk would be higher than it was worth, especially since the scene would be compromised anyway from a crime scene perspective.

Clay had detected a note of relief on Summer's face when that decision had been made.

"I'd rather our family rebuild anyway. Start over."

The words had seemed to carry a double meaning for

her that Clay suspected had something to do with how she felt she'd let them down. Did that mean she wasn't holding the past over her head anymore?

He wasn't sure. But he walked over to her now, to where she stood a safe distance back watching the flames finish the work Ryan had started. The sky overhead was still blue and cloudless, the air warm. It was a gorgeous summer day.

A day for new beginnings.

Clay took Summer's hand in his. "Are you okay?"

She turned to him, glacier-blue eyes clear. "I'm better than okay." She sniffed as she wiped what he thought might have been the remains of a tear from the corner of her eye.

"Want to take a walk down the ridgeline or did you want to stay here?"

"A walk would be good, I think."

Hand in hand, they walked back toward the trail where they'd come up. Had that just been yesterday? The last twenty-four hours had seemed like days, moving slowly and quickly all at the same time, so packed full of changing and near-death experiences.

Clay reminded himself to take a deep breath. It was over, the danger, the case. And hopefully, he and Summer were just beginning.

"I noticed this spot yesterday, when we hiked up here." He looked at Summer. "I thought it was the most beautiful place in the world."

She smiled up at him. His heart caught.

"And I think you're the most beautiful woman I've ever seen." Clay was surprised at how easily the words came. They were true. He felt them with everything in him. "And if everything that happened to me in Treasure Point had to happen for me to get here, to meet you, it was worth it."

Summer squeezed his hand, and somehow it meant more than sentences full of words ever could have. She understood.

"I know…" Clay cleared his throat, tried to breathe around the tightness in his chest. It wasn't every day he asked a woman to marry him and he wanted to do this right. He'd already messed up by not having a ring ready, but he'd learned from the last week that life was short. Some risks were worth it, and loving Summer, asking her this question today, here on the mountain where they'd both been given a fresh start, it was worth everything despite not being perfect.

Because she was. Perfect for him. He hoped he could be half the man she deserved. And if she said yes to his question, he'd spend the rest of his life making sure he was.

"I know we haven't known each other for long. And I know everything has been crazy. But I also know I love you, Summer."

"I love you too."

The words, said quietly but with certainty, relaxed the tightness in his chest. He tightened his grip on her hand. She squeezed back and he turned to face her, lifted a hand and stroked her cheek. "I want to spend the rest of my life loving you."

Her eyes widened. Hopefully in a good way. Clay kept talking. "I want to marry you, Summer Dawson, and live up here with you, having adventure upon adventure, watching you run up mountains and along ridgelines. Would you be my wife? Will you marry me?"

She laughed, full hearted, her eyes shimmering with so much hope Clay felt it too.

He brushed a tear from her face. A happy tear, the only kind he ever intended to be the cause of for the rest of their lives.

"Yes, Clay. I would love to marry you."

He wrapped her in his arms, squeezed her in a tight hug and then released her just far enough back that he could tip his head down and claim her lips in a kiss.

Their happily-ever-after was just beginning. And Clay couldn't wait to see what their future held.

* * * * *

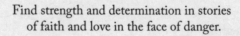

A groan echoed in Ariel Potter's ears. Was someone
hurt? She needed to help them.

She heard another moan and decided she was the
source of the noise. The world seemed to spin. What was
happening?

Somewhere in her mind, she realized she was being
turned over onto a hard surface. Dull pain pounded the
back of her head.

"Miss? Miss?"

A hand on her shoulder brought Ariel out of the foggy
state engulfing her. Opening her eyelids proved to be a
struggle. Snow fell from the sky. Then a hand shielded
her face from the elements.

Her gaze passed across broad shoulders to a very
handsome face beneath a helmet. Dark hair peeked out
from the edge of the helmet and a pair of goggles hung
from his neck. Who was this man?

The pull of sleep was hard to resist. She closed her eyes.

"Stay with me," the man murmured.

His voice coaxed her to do as he instructed, and she forced her eyes open.

Where was she?

Awareness of aches and pains screamed throughout her body, bringing the world into sharp focus. She was flat on her back and her head throbbed.

Ariel started to raise a hand to touch her head, but something was holding her arm down. She tried to sit up, and when she discovered she couldn't, she lifted her head to see why. Straps had been placed across her shoulders, her torso, hips and knees to keep her in place on a rescue basket.

"Hey, now, I need you to concentrate on staying awake."

That deep, rich voice brought her focus back to the moment. Memory flooded her on a wave of terror. The horror of rolling down the side of the cliff, hitting her head, landing in a bramble bush and the fear of moving that would take her plummeting to the bottom of the mountain. She must have gone in and out of consciousness before being rescued. She gasped with realization. "Someone pushed me!"

Don't miss
Alaskan Rescue *by Terri Reed,*
available wherever Love Inspired Suspense
books and ebooks are sold.

LoveInspired.com

LISEXP0321